EX
LIBRIS

Romance
Treasury

THE ROMANCE TREASURY ASSOCIATION

NEW YORK · TORONTO · LONDON

These stories were originally published as follows:

A MAN OF KENT
Copyright © 1973 by Isobel Chace
First published by Mills & Boon Limited in 1973

THE RED PLAINS OF JOUNIMA
Copyright © 1974 by Dorothy Cork
First published by Mills & Boon Limited in 1974

GARDEN OF THE SUN
Copyright © 1972 by Janice Gray
First published by Mills & Boon Limited in 1972

ROMANCE TREASURY is published by
The Romance Treasury Association, Stratford, Ontario, Canada

Dust Jacket Art by David Craig
Story Illustrations by David Craig
Printed by Alger Press, Oshawa, Ontario and
bound by T. H. Best Printing Co. Ltd., Don Mills, Ontario

ISBN 0-373-04039-3

Printed in Canada A039

CONTENTS

A MAN OF KENT

A Man of Kent

Isobel Chace

"I won't have you sacrificing your career for me," Sarah's ailing father protested, but Sarah knew he couldn't manage on his own.

Since her stepmother had no intention of giving up her career on the stage to accompany him, Sarah dropped her own promising acting career to move to Kent with her father.

Not that she really minded—especially after she met Robert Chaddox, their attractive and fascinating landlord. She found country life more appealing than she'd expected.

But Robert had a low opinion of theater people. Despite their growing love for each other he couldn't rid himself of his inborn distrust of them. Would his prejudice wreck their chance for happiness?

CHAPTER ONE

SARAH BLANEY almost ran along the pavement. She scarcely noticed that the trees were now in full leaf and that the traffic was as unbearable as it can be when an important match is being played at Lords. If she had been listening, she could have heard the sound of the ball striking the bat and the soporific applause that floated through the heavy afternoon air. But Sarah was not listening. She skipped in and out between the cars, came at last to the door of her mother's house and took the steps that led up to the front door two at a time. She was successful, sublimely successful! Above all, she had arrived! And she couldn't wait to tell her parents all about it.

Waiting impatiently for someone to let her in, she kept her finger on the bell in a way that she knew would irritate her stepmother into answering it. It did. Her stepmother, sleepy-eyed and frowning, pulled the door open and, seeing her, very nearly shut it again.

"Madge!" Sarah exclaimed. "I got it! I actually got it! I had to come and tell you about it!"

"Got what?" her stepmother asked, yawning.

"The part!"

"Do I know about it?"

Sarah surveyed her stepmother with amusement. "Of course you know all about it. I phoned you yesterday to remind you. I asked you what Alec Farne was like as a producer. Now I can tell you! He's fabulous! And I've got the part!"

"Oh," said her stepmother. "Oh, lord!"

Sarah's smile faded. "Aren't you pleased?"

"Delighted, darling—in a way. Quite a nice little triumph for you. It's a pity you won't be able to follow it up."

"What on earth are you talking about?"

"Darling, I'm sure I mentioned it to you—"

"Mentioned what?"

"Sarah, I can't bear it when you look cross like that. It makes you look so terribly *plain*, god knows, you're no beauty at the best of times! So unfair, I've always thought, seeing that you did have a nice-looking mother, and your father was quite a heart-throb before. . . ." She broke off, her eyes glinting with unshed tears. "I *know* I told you!" she declared.

Sarah sighed, her joy dissipated. She should have known. It had always been the same for as long as she could remember. Every time she had come home bursting with some piece of good news, there had always been something more important to discuss, or another success of her stepmother's that was so much greater than her own.

"I'll make some tea," Sarah said. "Then you can tell me about it."

"How sweet you are!" her stepmother breathed. "But of course I did tell you, only you've forgotten, you naughty thing. Such a pity, now that you've caught Alec Farne's eye. Oh well, it can't be helped! You'll have to keep in touch somehow, by seeing him every now and then. That shouldn't be beyond you?"

Sarah didn't answer. She walked through the hall, pausing briefly beneath the portrait her father had once painted of her and wondered what she could have been so amused about at the time. He had caught her smiling, and as always, her face had reflected her amusement like a shaft of light. She had no particular beauty to recommend her, no outstanding feature. Even her hair was quite ordinary, cut short and worn in a cap, with a fringe in front, rather reminiscent of an acorn. But for an actress, she thought, that was quite an advantage, and anyway, the gorgeous Madge Dryden would have hated to have had competition from her stepdaughter. Life was quite difficult enough without that!

She made the tea and took it into her stepmother's private sanctuary, a room she referred to as her study but that her husband more accurately called her boudoir. Madge Dryden was already posed on the chaise longue, idly turning the pages of a magazine.

"Well, Madge?" Sarah said.

"Now, Sarah, there's no need to look at me so accusingly! Your father hasn't been at all well."

"I know," Sarah said simply.

Madge moved restively. "I suppose you've kept up your lunch dates with him?"

"Of course."

"I've never understood why you can't come here to see him. *I* don't stop you!"

"Of course you don't! But when I come here, I come to see you. Poor dad doesn't get much to say when the distaff side of the family gets its tongue wagging. We do rather overwhelm him!"

"You mean that I do!" her stepmother said dryly. "Well, I don't apologize for that! A man should hold his own, if he's a man at all!"

"I think he does," Sarah said gently.

Madge Dryden pulled herself together with an effort. "You're right as usual, darling. Don't pay any attention to me, but I have to admit this whole business has annoyed me. It wasn't *my* fault that Daniel couldn't do the sets for my present show! It wasn't my decision! But I'm sure he blames me for it. I always get the blame for everything in the family! Sometimes I wonder what you'd do without me. You'd have to find someone else to blame."

Sarah preferred not to think about it. "Dad has always done your sets," she remarked.

Madge sniffed. "He thinks they've had a lot to do with my success."

"They have," Sarah said.

Madge looked decidedly cross. "Just because you think legitimate theater is the only way to succeed, you underrate my efforts! Well, let me tell you it isn't! I have to be able to act just as much as you do for your kind of parts, and I have to be able to sing and dance *as well*!"

Sarah looked amused. "And you excel at all three!"

"Well, yes, I do." Madge preened, half-smiling. "I wish he had done the sets for this show," she went on, sounding anxious. "It's a bad show and the sets are terrible! I don't wish to sound in the least bit conceited, but if Madge Dryden weren't in it, it wouldn't have a prayer of succeeding!"

"Why didn't dad do the sets?"

"You wouldn't appreciate it if I told you. Daniel Blaney has a reputation for being awkward about things. We couldn't afford perfectionism this time around."

"I think dad was hurt about it," Sarah suggested.

Madge shrugged. "He shouldn't blow these things up in his mind. It's very tiresome for me! And now we have all this business about his asthma."

Sarah sighed. "It's worse, isn't it?"

"That's what I've been telling you!" At any other time Madge's irritable expression would have made Sarah smile, but for once she felt annoyed with her charmingly selfish stepmother. She had been worried about her father for some time. "Sarah, in spite of the way he fusses about his health, it seems he's really quite ill. I had a word with the doctor and he advises that Daniel get out of London and away from the pressures of work for a while. He has to live quietly in the country, somewhere where there are no fumes and nobody to irritate him."

"Oh, Madge, I am sorry! You'll hate that!"

"I?"

"Are...aren't you going with him?"

"Darling, what on earth would I do in the country?"

Sarah was at a loss. "But he can't go on his own," she objected reasonably.

"I knew you'd see it that way," her stepmother said with satisfaction. "As you say, someone has to go with him, and even if I would be of any use to him, I can't possibly leave the show at the moment. It *depends* on me! No, dear, you will have to go with him!"

Sarah's hands trembled, spilling her tea into the saucer. "I can't!" she said abruptly. "I can't give up my part either. It means everything to me! It's the West End, Madge! I can't say I won't take the part."

"You haven't started rehearsals," Madge retorted. "I admit that it's a bit of a problem to have to face Alec Farne *and* keep him sweet for future occasions, but we can think about that in a minute. Your father and I have never asked anything of you before, dear, and I think you owe us this one little favor."

Sarah swallowed. "Dad is always miserable apart from you," she murmured.

Madge smiled, looking quite, quite lovely. "It was his idea that you go with him. I wouldn't have dreamed of asking you if there had only been myself and my little affairs to consider, darling, but Daniel said at once that he wanted to have you with him for a while. We haven't seen much of you since you grew up."

Sarah wondered how her stepmother managed to look both noble and sacrificing at the same time as she relentlessly pressed home her advantage.

"I had to be myself, Madge! If I hadn't found a room

of my own, I'd have been Madge Dryden's shadow all my life!"

Madge considered her stepdaughter for a moment. "Darling, you don't look in the least like me!" she said, not without truth, for Sarah had taken after her own mother and had her cast of features. "But whatever your reasons were, your father felt it very much, and now I think you should make it up to him. It isn't asking very much. If Alec Farne thinks you're good enough for a West End part, so will someone else. It will only mean a *delay* in your plans. You don't have the welfare of the whole cast, to say nothing of my own reputation in the theater, on your shoulders. No, Sarah, it's all arranged and I won't hear another word from you about it. Daniel is so happy that you're going to be with him and I won't have his pleasure spoiled! I forget now where he said he was going, but he'll tell you all about it. He's in his room because I simply can't bear to watch him struggling for breath—it might cause my voice to be strained in sympathy with him! It's a good thing you're not as sensitive as I am and won't mind half as much!"

Sarah bit back an angry retort. "I'll go and see dad now," she said tonelessly.

Madge smiled graciously. "I knew you'd see things my way!" she exclaimed.

Sarah gave her a quizzical look. "I only hope I'll sound as convincing when I tell Alec Farne!" she sighed.

"Nonsense!" her stepmother rallied her. "Confess, darling, you have that young man on a string!"

Sarah blushed helplessly. "I scarcely know him," she breathed. "He looked decidedly formidable from the other side of the footlights. I don't relish telling him that I'm turning down the part after all. He hasn't any reason to pull his punches as far as I'm concerned!"

"If he sees you looking frightened and vulnerable it will appeal to his gallantry," Madge gurgled happily. "I'll have a word with him too, if you like?" Sarah muttered something quite unintelligible and fled before her stepmother could make any more uncongenial sugestions. She paused for an instant in the hall to collect herself, determined to show her father a more cheerful face. Whatever happened, she would not have him knowing she was reluctant to go with him. Indeed, at any other time she would have fallen over herself for the opportunity to spend some time with him alone, but not at this particular moment. The first plum of her career lay before her, waiting to fall into her eager hands. She had spent more than four years working toward this part, and now it was to be snatched away from her. It was difficult not to blame her stepmother for doing it to her.

Her father was seated in a chair by the window of his room. He looked up when she knocked at the open door, his face creasing into its familiar smile.

"I thought I heard your voice, my love. I suppose Madge has told you all my news?"

Sarah nodded. "I'm sorry, daddy," she said.

Daniel Blaney coughed spasmodically, his distaste for his own weakness written clearly on his face. "I'm sorry too. Did you get the part?"

Sarah smiled at him. "How did you hear about that?"

"You hinted at it last time I saw you. I may be a has-been, but I do still have some friends in the theater and I see them from time to time. Did you get it?"

"In a way," Sarah compromised. "I'm thinking of turning it down after all. I don't think I'm ready—"

"Because of me?"

Sarah's eyes met her father's. "Yes, because of you. I didn't know it was so bad. You should have told me."

"I won't have you sacrificing your career for me."

Sarah grinned at him. "How melodramatic you make it sound! I'm not mad about this part and I am mad about my father. I can't wait to have you all to myself in the country. Where in the country? Madge didn't know."

"Madge doesn't want to know," Daniel said with unaccustomed sharpness. He began to cough again, gasping for breath. "This show was never any good for her, but she won't listen to me any longer. Seems to think I'm sulking because they wouldn't use my sets. I was a bit touchy at the time, till I saw that the whole production was out of gear and wasn't going to be any good for anyone. Sarah, are you sure you want to come with me? I could hire myself a nurse."

"You'll do nothing of the kind!"

Her father's eyes grew warmer. "I think it might be fun. I've always wanted to live in Kent. This is a little village near Canterbury called Chaddoxbourne. Never heard of it before, but then we've always lived in London, so it's not so surprising, is it? Anyway, I heard that there was a converted oast house for rent and I arranged for someone to go down and have a look at it. It has a small garden and an orchard, which seems only right in the Garden of England, and enough rooms for all of us. I've taken it for three months, with an option to stay there for the whole year. I've always wanted to see the inside of an oast house."

"Aren't they used for drying hops?"

"I don't know if they still are, but certainly they used to be. I particularly like their shape. They're as fascinating as windmills to me."

Sarah's smile flashed across her face. "I'm looking forward to it too," she averred. "I seldom get you all to myself!"

"And what about your career?"

She made a face at him. "What about it? I daresay the play will flop in a matter of weeks and then I'd be 'resting' anyway. What nicer place to go to than an oast house in Kent?"

"You almost convince me," her father said. "Almost, and I'm grateful. But I don't have to tell you that, do I?"

Sarah kissed him lightly on the brow. "You can be convinced," she told him. "You see, I happen to love you very much!"

"You don't say!" he coughed. "With a face like yours, you can't help but wear your heart on your sleeve. I suppose there's still no news on the romantic front?"

She shook her head, laughing. "I haven't the time," she said.

HER HANDS were shaking when she dialed the number that Alec Farne's secretary had given her. Her picture of the man did nothing to encourage her that he would be sympathetic to her reasons for turning down the part. She imagined him as she had seen him across the footlights, crouched in a seat, his hand shading his eyes as he listened to something his secretary was saying to him. And then the sudden burst of rage that had followed, while she had stood trembling on the stage, the floodlights lighting up her face, waiting to begin.

"Miss Blaney," he had said, "I will be with you in a minute."

And she had stood there and waited.

She waited now for someone to answer the telephone. A man's voice muttered something quite incomprehensible followed by an irritable "Yes?"

"This... is Sarah Blaney."

"Oh yes, Sarah. What is it?"

"Mr. Farne?"

"Get on with it, Sarah."

"I can't take the part," Sarah burst out. "I'm terribly sorry, but my father isn't well and I have to look after him."

"What? I didn't hear what you said. Sorry, Sarah."

"Mr. Farne, I can't take the part."

"Rubbish. Where are you?" He took down her address as she dictated it. "Funny," he said, "I thought your family lived in St John's Wood?"

"They do," she whispered.

"But you don't?"

"No."

"Very wise. Okay, Sarah, I'll be around in about an hour to take you out to dinner. You can tell me all about this hang-up of yours then. Only don't pull the devoted daughter with me, honey. I know too much about your stepmother for that! Devotion to the boards comes first, last and all the way!"

Sarah choked. "I'm not my stepmother, Mr. Farne."

He laughed. "You're telling me! She's a real beauty, is she not? Never mind, love, we'll turn you into something too. You don't have to have cold feet about it. Alec will look after you."

Sarah made an angry sound. "I do not have cold feet."

"Sounds like it to me. Be seeing you!"

Sarah replaced the receiver with a shake of her head. It had been every bit as difficult as she had thought it would be and she was no further ahead. She felt that he was taking her out to dinner under false pretenses. It was useless to convince herself that he would have taken the trouble with her if he hadn't thought he could talk her around, and he would only be angrier when he found he couldn't.

Sarah changed into a long black skirt and brushed her neat cap of hair until it was shining. She never wore much makeup, but to give herself courage she put on some eye-shadow and gave her white face some artificial color. It was ridiculous to think that she might be afraid of Alec Farne. He was young and madly successful, but he couldn't eat her.

She was ready far too early and prowled about her room, looking for something to do before her nervousness ate up any confidence she might have had. When the door bell went she almost fell down the three flights of stairs to answer it, arriving breathless at the old-fashioned, heavy front door that was decorated by a glass peacock in striking colors.

"How long have you had a room here?" Alec Farne demanded as she opened the door to him.

"Nearly a year," she answered.

"Not very comfortable," he murmured.

She smiled. "Not very, but I've known worse."

Alec Farne gave her an interested look. "You're not at all like your mother," he said.

"No, I'm Penny Plain and she's Twopence Colored! In any case, she's my stepmother, not my mother."

"Twopence Colored sounds like her," he admitted. "Your stepmother, is she? Did you get your expressive face from your own mother?"

Sarah sighed. She wished he would forget all about her parentage. "I'm said to be more like her than my father," she explained. "That's why I can't—"

"We'll talk about that later on, my dear. Those auditions were some of the worst I ever remember. If you think I'm going through that again, I'm not!"

Sarah chuckled. Her fright had departed like magic, for she simply coudn't be in awe of Alec Farne. He was far too like a petulant boy for that.

"I think you enjoy it," she accused him. "I was terrified of you, you looked so fierce and furious!"

"Of me? Oh yes, I remember now, I was in rather a bad temper. The girl I had first wanted for the part had lost her voice. Still, her loss was your gain!"

"It would be if I could accept the part, but my father really is very ill, and someone has to look after him."

"Your stepmother?"

She gave him an expressive look. "My stepmother has...commitments," she said gently.

"So have you!"

He led her over to a nearly new car and opened the door for her, tucking her skirt in after her. The car slid into the busy traffic and Sarah thought how nice it was to be driven for a change instead of struggling with buses and the subway system.

"Will you settle for Chinese food?"

"Sounds lovely," she agreed.

Apparently he didn't like to talk while he drove the car. She made a halfhearted effort to make conversation, but seeing his frown she desisted, quite happy to retreat into her own thoughts. When he pulled up and reached across her to open the door, she was surprised to find that they had arrived.

"You get out here," he ordered. "I'll park the car and come back."

Obediently, she waited on the pavement for him to take her into the restaurant. It was a typical June evening, and although it was late, the streets were still crowded with people out for the evening or just reluctant to go home. The trees were green, if dusty and wilted in the heat from several days of scorching sunshine. Sarah became aware of a man watching her and colored slightly, putting a hand up to pat her hair back into position.

"Know him?" Alec Farne asked in her ear.

"No," she said and blushed again.

"He'd like to know you!"

"I don't think so, not really. Look," she added with obvious relief, "the woman he was waiting for is getting out of that taxi."

"So she is!" Alec Farne sounded amused. "How old are you, Sarah Blaney?"

"Twenty-one," she answered without hesitation. Her eyes filled with laughter. "Three years in rep. Is that what you want to know?"

"Strangely, it wasn't. I want to know about you, not the actress that you hope to be."

"How horrid you are!" she exclaimed. "I like to think that I already am an actress!"

"You've yet to prove it to me," he said. "An actress has the theater in her blood, my dear. The Show Must Go On and all that! She doesn't throw in the towel just because her father is ill."

He held open the door of the restaurant for her, his eyes already looking for the waiter to show them to their table. Sarah waited until they were seated and then she looked at him gravely.

"Do you really expect me to put your play before my father's health?" she asked him.

"I do."

"I think that's inhuman!"

"Then in my book you're not an actress."

She hesitated as the hurt of that verdict struck deep within her. "As simple as that?" she asked at length.

"'Fraid so, my dear. This is your moment of truth. Are you going to be Florence Nightingale or follow in the footsteps of your admirable stepmother?"

She was silent for a very long time. Alec Farne made no effort to help her. Rather, he ignored her, busying himself by ordering their food and inquiring whether she thought wine really went with Chinese food, or if she would prefer to have jasmine tea. But in the end she had to answer him.

"I'm taking my father down to Chaddoxbourne, in Kent," she told him. "His asthma has become much worse in the last few days and I'd never forgive myself if anything happened to him."

"All right," Alec Farne drawled. "If that's the way you want it, I have nothing more to say. Did you say Chaddoxbourne?"

Sarah nodded unhappily.

"Funny, that. I was at school with a fellow called Chaddox who came from Kent. He used to boast that he was descended from the Saxon kings of old. Probably was! He was a standoffish fellow, with very little time for the likes of me. I don't envy you if you're going to live anywhere near him. He'll freeze you to the bone!"

Sarah blinked thoughtfully. "Why would he? I don't suppose he'll even notice me, even if he's still there."

"Probably not," Alec agreed with unflattering promptness. "Heavens, it's a waste! If anyone cried out for greasepaint and somebody else's skin to get into, it's you! Why can't that stepmother of yours take your father into the country?"

With a grimace, Sarah forced a laugh. "Because she's a real actress?" she suggested.

"Gracious, you quaint, old-fashioned thing!" Alex teased her. "Well, perhaps she is as much of an actress as Nell Gwynn was in her day!"

Sarah's ready smile faded. "I don't think I quite understand," she said with dignity.

"No? Oh, your stepmother has her place, my love. She's a good trouper and she knows the kind of thing that suits her rather mediocre talent, which makes her appear much better than she really is. But when it comes to acting, she doesn't hold a candle to you, and if you don't know that yet, you don't know anything about it at all." He glanced up, his eager eyes holding hers. "Look, have you ever seen your stepmother in anything different from her usual song-and-dance romantic story?"

Reluctantly, Sarah shook her head. Alec Farne favored her with a crooked smile. "Exactly. It breaks my heart to see you getting away from me, but there you are! There's always something wrong. With you, it's your temperament!"

Sarah licked her lips, unwilling to argue further with

him. "Tell me more about Chaddoxbourne," she pleaded with him.

"I don't know a thing about it," he insisted. "Oh, yes I do, now I come to think about it. At least I can remember Robert Chaddox. His stepmother was on the stage too—a pretty piece of no acting talent at all but enough talent in other directions to be a great deal more successful than she deserved. Robert didn't like her! Naturally. I don't remember Robert liking anyone, though, certainly not any of the guys I hung around with. Later on, I heard his father had died and that he'd inherited the estate of Chaddoxbourne and very little money to run it on. It's more than likely that he'll be your landlord, but I don't advise you to allow him any closer than that! You need someone with a discerning eye who can see that other you that's bursting for recognition!"

"What a terrible thought!" she laughed.

"But astute? I'm not the best young producer-cum-director around for nothing!"

Sarah chuckled. "Astute and very conceited."

"Why not? Someone has to appreciate me!"

On the way home in the car Sarah thought about what Alec had told her about Robert Chaddox. She wondered if he were really descended from the ancient Saxon kings of Kent, not that she knew anything about them, but it sounded a romantic kind of background to have.

She left the car as soon as it came to a stop outside the house where she had her room, but she was not quick enough. Alec Farne held out his hand for her key, laughing at her nervousness.

"Aren't you going to thank me nicely for your dinner?"

"I don't—"

"Well, I do!" He reached out for her and kissed her without fuss. "Was that so bad?"

"N-no," she admitted.

He slapped her lightly on the rear. "You'd better make the best of your opportunities, my dear. There won't be any in Chaddoxbourne, not if Robert Chaddox is a sample of the local talent! You won't get any kisses from him!"

Sarah ran up the stairs, listening for him to shut the door. At least, she thought, Chaddoxbourne had something to recommend it if she didn't have to suffer any more embraces like that one. She had liked Alec Farne until that moment, but she had not liked his kiss. In fact she had disliked it very much indeed.

CHAPTER TWO

MADGE DRYDEN took another turn about the room, looking distraught.

"Darling, you don't understand how difficult it is for me! He always made it his life's work to make me happy. And now this!"

"Well, you could come too."

Real tears formed and fell down Madge's cheeks. "Of all the people I know, I thought you would understand!" she said tragically.

"I do," Sarah assured her.

"You're becoming very hard," her stepmother informed her. "I never would have thought it of you when you were a little girl and absolutely devoted to me!"

"I'm pretty devoted now," Sarah sighed. "I must be, or I wouldn't be burying myself in the country."

"That," Madge said with dignity, "is because of your devotion to your father. I was speaking of how fond you used to be of me."

Sarah tried to smile, failed, and settled for looking amused instead. "Isn't it rather difficult to quantify such things?"

Madge took another turn about the room, now angry as well as tragic. She looked for all the world like a ruffled hen, squawking her displeasure at the world. "I don't believe you love me at all!" she claimed.

Becoming irritated in her turn, Sarah merely looked sulky. "Is this why you asked me to come today?" she asked.

Controlling herself with an effort, Madge sat down on the sofa and stared silently at her stepdaughter. "You don't have an ounce of feeling!" she burst out indignantly. "I'm so unhappy. I thought we were a family."

"I'm sorry, Madge."

"Sorry! You're not a bit sorry or you would think about how I feel at the prospect of being all alone week after week." The tears began to fall thick and fast. "I'll have to be brave, that's all." Madge sighed heavily. "With all this worry around him, your father is no better either. I'll be glad when we have everything settled and we all get a bit of peace. I'll have asthma myself if I have to watch him wheezing away much longer!"

Sarah hesitated to interrupt her stepmother's thoughts, but there had to be some reason why she had been so peremptorily sent for that morning. It had been highly inconvenient to drop everything she had been doing and make the rather difficult journey from Fulham to St. John's Wood. She had been having lunch with a friend and had had some difficulty in putting her off. She was also tired, though what from she couldn't imagine, since she hadn't had to turn up to rehearsals or auditions, or anything!

"Sarah, there's nothing to keep you in London now, is there?"

"Not a thing." Sarah managed to erase the bitterness she was feeling from her voice and thought that her technique was improving now that she wasn't going to have to make use of it.

"Good. You'll have to go down to Chaddoxbourne and get the house ready. I'm bringing Daniel down next Sunday."

"Oh," said Sarah.

"I'll bring him down in the car—"

"Is that wise?" Sarah interrupted. "I mean, I don't think he should be driving, do you?"

"Sarah, mind your own business. I've been married to Daniel for a good many years and if I don't know what's best for him by now, I never will! Your task is to get the house ready and make everything comfortable for us by Sunday. Daniel will need a room to himself, of course, so that means three bedrooms. Nobody seems to know if we've hired bedding along with the house, or what. I thought you could go down tomorrow."

"Tomorrow?" Sarah was jerked out of her own thoughts with a bang. "But I can't! I haven't given up my room yet!"

Madge shrugged. "It won't take you more than an hour to pack your things. Those things that you don't need you can leave in your old room here—if you can find room for them in there. I don't believe you've ever thrown anything away since you were a schoolgirl!"

"I'd forgotten all about leaving my stuff here," Sarah admitted. "I think it's mostly books."

"Very likely. You'd better bring your other things over tonight and then you can start early tomorrow."

"But I haven't sorted anything."

"You can do all that later. You won't have long to get the house organized as it is. You realize that it's Thursday tomorrow, don't you?"

"I hadn't thought," Sarah admitted.

"Daniel says on Thursday everything closes in Canterbury, but I expect you'll find some way around that if you put your mind to it. How will you go, dear? In your car? I suppose it is still going?"

"Yes, it's still going."

"I can't think how you afford to run a car," her stepmother complained. "It was ridiculous of Edith to give it to you!"

Sarah remembered her godmother with affection. "She didn't exactly give it to me," she reminded Madge. "She died and left me enough money to buy the car, and a little over to run it too. Aunt Edith probably thought I'd spend it on clothes."

"In her salon!" Madge crowed. "She would!"

Sarah said nothing. Edith Hyams had been an unlikely choice of godmother in many ways, but she had been a great friend of her mother's and had remained as a link with the parent Sarah couldn't even remember. She had been worldly, amusing and had disliked Madge as much as she had liked the first Mrs. Blaney. Sarah quite frankly had adored her.

"I'd better go, if I really have to go to Canterbury tomorrow. Is there anything else?"

"What else could there be?"

Her stepmother's pained surprise made Sarah want to laugh.

"I thought there might be," she said. "You could have told me about getting the house ready on the phone."

"I don't like the telephone when it comes to my own family," Madge retorted. "It isn't a comfortable way of speaking to anyone!"

Sarah merely smiled, kissed her stepmother and escaped before Madge decided to ask her to make tea, or do one of the hundred other little jobs that she spread around the people about her. Standing in the doorway, she hesitated. "Madge, you won't let Daddy drive on Sunday, will you?"

"Oh, darling, don't fuss! Anyone would think I wasn't interested in your father's health. I am. Why, I'm going to come down every Sunday morning and stay over until Monday afternoon just to see how you're both getting on. You're not the only one to make sacrifices! Now, off you go, love. I probably won't see you this evening, will I?"

"Probably not," Sarah agreed.

Looking around her room when she got back, Sarah

was suddenly very sorry to be leaving. True, it was an attic room, with high windows she couldn't see out of and fading wallpaper that had flattened her when she had first seen it, but she had grown used to the chubby cupids on the wall just as she had grown used to climbing up and down the three flights of stairs that led up to the room. She had seldom been in her room in the middle of the afternoon, however, and the heat beat down on her mercilessly as the sun crept around the sky sending long sticky fingers in through the paint scaled windows.

Sarah tried to ignore the increasing discomfort of the unaccustomed warmth. She packed her clothes in one suitcase and the few ornaments and books she had gathered during the past few years into another. The room that had been her home for the past few months looked strange and ugly without her personal things to catch her eye. Perhaps she would enjoy living in the country after all, she thought, longing for the clean air and traffic-free spaces. She pictured to herself what the village of Chaddoxbourne would be like, complete, as her father had told her, with medieval bridge and a watermill. Oh well, tomorrow she would see it for herself—and she might even see the mysterious Robert Chaddox who was descended from the Saxon kings, though why she should think of him at such a time, she really couldn't imagine.

In the morning, she said goodbye to her landlady and was a little surprised when that lady kissed her warmly and assured her that she would always be ready to welcome her back when she wanted to return to London.

"You have to be bred to the country to take to its ways," she said dourly. "There's not a thing to do there. You're used to doing as you please and going to movies and things. You'll be back sooner than you think!"

"I do hope so!" Sara responded. "When I come back it will mean that my father's better!"

"Poor man!"

Sarah winced from the sympathy in her landlady's eyes and hurried out to her car, stowing her single suitcase on the back seat. Her landlady came after her, her unsmiling face peering in through the windows of the car.

"You mind yourself in that traffic! Hear it's bad going down to the Channel ports."

"I will," Sarah promised.

"See that you do!"

Sarah drove away with a sinking feeling of failure that she couldn't shake off as she made her way through London, across Vauxhall Bridge and slowly out into what had once been part of Kent but which was now considered part of London.

She went straight on down Shooters Hill to the highway entrance that led eventually to the motorway to Canterbury.

Despite the open windows, it was blazing hot in the little car. Sarah would have liked to have stopped halfway, but the only place on the road was taken over by a convoy of buses and, anyway, seemed to have little to recommend it, so she decided to go on to Canterbury and have lunch there.

To her surprise, it was relatively easy to find somewhere to park in the city. All she had to do was to follow the signs and go into the parking lot. What was more difficult was to find her way around the city after that. Canterbury had been badly bombed in the war and much of it had been rebuilt since, which was sad when she thought of the old hostels that had once lined the streets and the bowfronted shops of a later era. All had now given way to the utility styles of the present century. Here and there a glimpse of the past still remained and was perhaps all the more appreciated because it was less commonplace than it had been before.

On the advice of the parking-lot attendant, Sarah chose a restaurant a little way away from the Cathedral and the main body of tourists that thronged the narrow surrounding streets. She was unaccustomed to going into a restaurant by herself and she braced herself unconsciously as she pushed open the door and went inside.

"I'm afraid we have no free tables just at the moment, madam. Are you on your own? Would you mind sharing?"

Sarah smiled at the pretty girl who had accosted her and shook her head. "If the other person doesn't mind," she murmured as the woman led her toward a minute, spindly table that looked even smaller than it was because of the coiled length of man that was already in possession of it.

"You don't mind sharing, do you, sir?"

The man started, half rose, thought better of it and shook his head silently. Sarah hurried forward before he could change his mind, her eye firmly fixed on the vacant chair on the other side of the table. It was unfortunate that at that moment another customer pushed her chair back from her table, knocking into her, and she in turn ricocheted into her own table, jogging the arm of the man. With wide eyes she watched the red stain of his tomato soup drip slowly down his uncannily white shirt and flowered tie.

"Oh!" she exclaimed.

He glanced up at her, his eyes gray and wintry. Without saying anything at all, he picked the table up bodily and motioned with his head for her to pass by and sit down. She did so hastily, coloring a little.

"I'm terribly sorry," she said.

He nodded, dismissing her apology and reducing her to silence. She watched him as he took out a spotless handkerchief and dabbed at the front of his shirt. Feeling flustered and breathless, she stared in helplessness. It wasn't only that she had made a fool of herself, there was something electric in the long length of man opposite her, in his ice-cold gray eyes and in the wiry way his hair grew. Sarah looked away from him hastily, uncomfortably aware that she was blushing and that he knew that she was.

When she could bear his silence no longer, she leaned forward a little and cleared her throat. "Could you tell me how to get to Chaddoxbourne?" she asked him.

For an instant his eyes met hers. "Chaddoxbourne?"

"Y-yes. It's a village near here."

"Do you have a car?"

She nodded helplessly. "It's in a parking lot. The one by the theater." To her surprise his lips parted in a faint smile. "Well," he drawled, "if you manage to get it out of there still intact, you turn right at the main road, go across the island and on through the lights. Turn left about a mile out of town and then follow your nose."

Sarah blinked, realizing that she hadn't listened to a single word of his instructions. "I drive quite well!" she heard herself say.

The man grunted. "I doubt it, unless you show a better judgment of space and distance on the road."

"I have apologized for jogging your arm," she interposed.

His lips parted into another, rather bleak smile. "So you have."

For an impossible moment, Sarah wished that she was as pretty and vivacious as her stepmother instead of knowing herself to be completely ordinary and never likely to dazzle anyone, certainly not this man in front of her.

"I should apologize all over again," she said aloud. "I didn't listen to your directions. I meant to, but I was looking at your shirt."

"Let's hope all my clients don't do the same."

"I suppose you haven't time to go home to change?"

"To Chaddoxbourne? Hardly!"

She flushed with sudden pleasure. "Do *you* live in Chaddoxbourne too?"

The man gave her a long, level look and her enthusiasm died away, leaving her exposed and vulnerable to his thoughtful gaze.

She made an effort to recover, wondering whatever could be the matter with her. She sat back in her seat, pretending an interest she was far from feeling in the menu in front of her.

"What are you doing in Chaddoxbourne?" the man asked her suddenly.

Sarah started. "It's my father," she explained, immediately confused again. "He isn't very well. He has asthma and has to get out of London. I'm coming to look after him."

"Where's your mother?"

Sarah put the menu down and took a deep breath. "My stepmother couldn't get away just now," she said.

He frowned at her. "And what about you? Haven't you a job to keep you in London, or wherever it is that you come from?"

"Nothing important."

He looked sterner than ever. "Just filling in until you get married?"

"Not exactly," she managed.

He gave her an impatient look. "What is that supposed to mean? If you don't want to talk about yourself, why don't you tell me to mind my own business and be done?"

She took in her breath in an audible gasp. "Oh, I wouldn't do that!"

"Why on earth not?" he demanded, looking amused.

"Well, it's kind of you to be interested. My father is Daniel Blaney," she added inconsequently.

"Kind?" he exploded. "My dear girl, I'm not in the least interested. It so happens that I live in Chaddoxbourne and I thought we might be neighbors and that it might be awkward if I were still glowering at you for spilling soup all over me for the next year or so."

Sarah gulped, chuckled and broke into a wide smile of sympathy. "What a horrible fate!"

She was unaware of how her smile changed her whole face. In repose there was nothing at all remarkable about her face, indeed sometimes she could look thoroughly sulky, but she had only to smile for her whole being to light up, giving her a fleeting beauty that was all the more remarkable for being transient. She became aware now of the faint answering flicker of a smile on the man's face, making her heart lurch in the most uncomfortable way.

"Are you Robert Chaddox?"

It was his turn to be at a disadvantage. His eyes narrowed a fraction as if he was summing her up before finally making up his mind about her.

"Yes, I am," he said briefly.

Sarah extended her hand to him across the table. "Then my father and I are your new tenants. We're going to live in your converted oast house."

He accepted her hand and she was pleased to note that his grip was firm. "I suppose I should have known when you said your father is Daniel Blaney, but somebody else made all the arrangements—his secretary, perhaps?"

"More likely my stepmother's," Sarah answered.

He looked at her sharply. "No, I think it was your stepmother herself—Madge Dryden. I suppose that's why she isn't coming herself?"

Sarah nodded. "She's in the middle of a run."

"The traditions of the theater don't make for an ideal family life," he remarked casually. "But I suppose your father is in the theater too and knew what he was doing."

"Don't you like the theater?"

He shrugged. "I haven't any views either way. I think people in the theater are apt to have a different set of values from the rest of us, that's all."

Sarah lifted her eyes to him. "But you should understand the importance of tradition, if anyone should!"

His eyebrows rose giving him an arrogant look. "Meaning?"

Sarah's eyes fell. She muttered something about his pedigree and his Saxon forebears in an agony of embarrassment, only to discover that he was laughing at her. "You have been doing your homework!" he observed.

"Not really," she stammered. "You were at school with... a friend of mine. He told me about you when I said we were going to live near Canterbury."

"Really?"

"I don't suppose you remember him," Sarah hurried on. "He works in the theater, Alec Farne."

"Oh yes, I remember him," Mr. Chaddox said grimly.

Sarah blushed. "He said you didn't have much in common at school."

"An understatement," Mr. Chaddox grunted. He watched her closely as she ordered a steak from the overworked waitress and then ordered coffee for himself. Needless to say, his coffee came first, long before her steak, and she was still waiting while he stirred sugar into his cup with an abstracted air.

"How ill is your father, Miss Blaney?" he asked her suddenly.

Sarah's worries about her father returned to engulf her. She bit her lip, horribly aware of the stinging tears in her eyes. "I don't know. I think he's pretty bad, but only my stepmother has actually spoken to the doctor, and my father always makes light of everything."

Mr. Chaddox looked severe. "What makes you think you'll be able to nurse him by yourself?"

Sarah looked with frank envy at his coffee and longed for her own meal to appear. "I love him," she said simply.

"That's scarcely a recommendation as a nurse!" He summoned the waitress with a beckoning finger and pointed at the empty space in front of Sarah. The waitress nodded an apology and came flying over with the steak that Sarah had ordered. "If he's really ill, I would have thought he'd have wanted his wife with him!"

"Madge Dryden?" Sarah said weakly.

"I suppose you're accustomed to standing in the wings as your stepmother's understudy?" he grunted.

"Up to a point," Sarah admitted.

"What point?"

Sarah hesitated. She was strongly tempted to do as he had first suggested and tell him to mind his own business, but somehow she was defenseless before him. It was as if he had a right to know.

"Well, she's the star in the family and that counts, but one day I'll be just as famous. Not musical comedy, of course, I haven't much talent for that sort of thing, but as a legit actress. I had just landed my first West End part when this came up."

Mr. Chaddox could barely keep the contempt out of his voice. "With Alec Farne, I suppose?"

Sarah nodded eagerly. "He was furious when I said I couldn't take the part."

"How convenient to know all the right people!"

"Oh, but I didn't know him before!" Sarah protested.

"Didn't you?" His face softened a little. "It's quite something to meet an actress who's prepared to put her family before the play, but perhaps you weren't very sure of your success?"

Sarah lifted her head, looking him straight in the eyes. "I was quite sure, Mr. Chaddox."

"Then you're unique!" he tossed back at her with a

curious bitterness. He rose to his feet, forcing a smile. "I must be going. I hope you find everyting in order at the house and that you find Chaddoxbourne without too much difficulty."

"Thank you," she said.

He nodded briefly and was gone, paying his bill on the way out. Sarah subsided into her chair feeling as though she had just stepped off a scenic railway and had not yet caught her breath. So that was Mr. Robert Chaddox of Chaddoxbourne! If only she had been able to make the same sort of impression on him as he had on her! But it was no use wasting her time in idle regrets for something she could do nothing about. She would never dazzle anyone and she might just as well face up to the fact.

Sarah finished her excellent steak without having tasted a single mouthful of it. She drank her coffee in much the same state. In a way she found she was quite enjoying the effect Mr. Chaddox had had on her. A naturally friendly person, she had known more people of all ages than she might have done in another walk of life, but none had stirred her to more than friendship. Mr. Chaddox was different. She didn't feel in the least bit friendly toward him and he acted on her with all the sympathy of an electric shock! It was astonishing that anyone could have such an effect on her, when no one ever had before. It was a new, strange sensation that needed thinking about, when she had the leisure to think about anything. Nevertheless, Chaddoxbourne had suddenly become a highly desirable place to live and she couldn't wait to get there. She almost danced out of the restaurant, leaving the waitress a tip of quite undeserved proportions, and went in search of her car.

Chaddoxbourne lay to the north east of Canterbury, in a little valley at the bottom of which wound a lazy stream. The medieval stone bridge allowed the traffic to cross only one way at a time, but there was a way through the stream for the impatient who didn't mind taking their cars through nearly a foot of water. On the bend of the river, a little farther up the bank, stood the watermill, now abandoned and sad, though there were signs that someone was fixing it up, probably to turn it into a private home. Behind the mill stood the church, built of golden stone and with a very fine rose window. Over the door was a carving of Christ in Glory and a number of ancient sun clocks carved into the portal that had once told the villagers the times of the masses in the days before the reformation.

Sarah took one look at the village and fell in love with it. To her, it was the perfect English village. She had never imagined it possible. The sun shone on the slow-moving water which glinted with light beneath a line of weeping willows. The houses were old, some of them of the traditional Kentish clapboard, some of them built of red brick grown pink with age. The oast house stood a little apart, its windows gleaming white. Beyond stood the imposing gates of the manor house, its stately Georgian lines just visible beyond the walled garden full of magnificent trees, beeches, ash and cedars. There was even an oak tree so old that it had had to be supported by a framework of wooden scaffolding.

Sarah drove up to the oast house, stopping at the gates closed against her. They swung open easily and she fastened them back, eager to see what the house itself was like. She parked the car in the driveway and hurried up to the front door. A note had been pinned under the knocker. She opened it, hoping to find the key enclosed, but there were only instructions telling her to collect the key up at the manor.

The manor proved to be an even more beautiful house than she had expected. The rampant white horse of Kent stood on either side of pillars that supported the porch over the door. The legend *Invicta*—undefeated

—was cut deep in the flagstone in front of the door. Sarah rang the bell, a little impressed despite herself. If Robert Chaddox lived here, he had something to be proud of indeed.

The door was opened by a young man who greeted her with a cheerful smile.

"Hullo there!" he exclaimed. "Don't tell me, you're the new tenant? I'm Neil Chaddox."

"Sarah Blaney," said Sarah. She thought he looked much younger than his brother, but he was also a much easier character to deal with.

"I was expecting an ancient man," Neil informed her. "I was going to hand over the key and tell him to get lost. But now that I've seen you, I'll do my duty as a gentleman and escort you over to your new home. There is a Mr. Blaney, I suppose?"

Sarah suppressed a smile. "My father," she said.

"Then all is not lost! I suppose your mother will be with you too?"

"On weekends. My stemother's in the theater and can't get away just now."

Neil grinned at her. "My mother was on the stage too. I knew the instant I laid eyes on you that we'd have a lot in common. See how right I was!"

Sarah looked around her as they walked down the drive together. "Have you always lived here?" she asked him impulsively.

"Always. My mother was away a lot, but my father was always here—and Robert, of course. It was bad luck for him to inherit when he did. My parents were killed in a car accident, but unfortunately our father died before my mother and there was double the amount of death taxes. Robert's mother left him quite a bit, but with a place like this anything less than a million is just a drop in the bucket."

"I suppose so," Sarah agreed. She had never had anything to do with property and knew nothing about the expenses of its upkeep, but she could see that someone had to cut these magnificent lawns and keep the roof repaired. "What happened to Robert's mother?"

"She was drowned somewhere or other. I've never known much about it." He gave her an engaging grin. "I came along some time later." he explained.

Sarah smiled. "Naturally."

They both dissolved into laughter. "Yes, naturally," he said. "Come along and see your new home!"

CHAPTER THREE

SARAH'S FATHER had been quite right in thinking that Thursday the stores closed early in Canterbury. Neil suggested Sarah go to either Dover or Folkestone if she had any urgent shopping to do, but Sarah had had enough of driving for one day. She followed Neil into the oast house, not knowing what to expect, and the charm of the building immediately captured her.

"It's fascinating having a room round like that at one end!" she exclaimed.

"If you say so," Neil answered. "Robert took quite an interest in the conversion of this place himself. Yes, it does look good. I'll tell him you think so."

Sarah doubted that the elder Chaddox brother would be interested, but said nothing. She enjoyed Neil's easy-going company and was sorry when he glanced at his watch and said he would have to be going.

"Think you'll be okay on your own?"

She laughed. "I hope so. Every strange noise I hear, I'll tell myself that it's the country for you and hope for the best!"

"You'll probably be right," he answered. "See you around!"

She went to the door and stood there for a moment watching him as he closed the gates and vaulted easily over them into the road that she shared with the manor. She waved a tentative hand and went inside. There was still a great deal to be done to prepare the house for her father and she had yet to discover whether there were any sheets and blankets. It turned out that there was plenty of everything. Her first urge was to put her father in the large circular room above the sitting room, but she knew that he would immediately give it to her stepmother, although she was only to be there for one night each week. The second bedroom had the better view, however, and she was glad of that. It looked over the manor gardens, down to a small lake in the distance and across a small walled orchard that she saw with delight was attached to the oast house. She could approach it through their own tiny, but immaculate, garden.

She could hardly wait to go down to the orchard and see what it consisted of, but she restrained herself long enough to make up the beds and to arrange her own few possessions in the third bedroom, which also, to her delight, looked out across the orchard to the manor. She even imagined that one of the windows she could see might be Robert's room, but then she caught herself with a start, amused by her own foolishness. It was something she coudn't understand, for she had never been concerned, even in idle moments, with romantic thoughts of any man before.

She was glad to have the orchard to think about instead. It was every bit as lovely and romantic as it had appeared from the window upstairs. The trees were very old and probably didn't bear much fruit, but their gnarled, twisted shapes were perfect. Sarah decided in her own mind that there were at least four apple trees, two pear trees, a fig beside the wall, and what she supposed was a cherry tree in one corner. They were enclosed by a high wall of golden stone warm from the sun. Sarah leaned against it, smiling a little, astonished by her mood of complete contentment. It would all be different when the inevitable rain came, she told herself, but even that prospect failed to disturb her pleasure in the trees and the curve of the Kentish ragstone wall. How long she stood there, she didn't know, but it was only slowly that she became aware of voices talking. She recognized them immediately as belonging to the Chaddox brothers.

"I hope none of your customers thought it was blood!" Neil was saying.

"It does look a bit like it."

"A bit!" Neil's laughter was raucous and infectious. "It wouldn't be so funny on anyone else, but on the immaculate Robert Chaddox! I never thought I'd see the day when you'd drop your lunch all down your shirt!"

"It was that ham-fisted new tenant of ours!"

"Miss Blaney? I didn't know you'd met her!"

"She came into the restaurant where I have my lunch and shoved her way into the only vacant seat. That unfortunately happened to be at my table. This was the result!"

Neil laughed again. "Didn't she apologize nicely enough?" he teased.

"She said she was sorry," Robert admitted grudgingly. "Went on to say she was an actress. More like a bull in a china shop! Her mother—or stepmother, apparently—is obviously glad to find her something to do and has sent her down here with her father for a bit. She tried to tell me she was giving up some West End part, but can you imagine her on the stage? She hasn't much to recommend her, has she?"

"She's all right," Neil said without enthusiasm. "Not to be compared with the fantastic Samantha, of course!"

"Everyone falls for her!" Robert agreed. Sarah could tell by his voice that he was smiling. She longed to creep away before she could overhear any more, but then Robert was speaking again and she found herself rooted to the spot. "Don't have too much to do with the Blaneys, Neil. Their kind of life and ours don't mix."

"Back to mother?" the younger brother said sulkily.

"She was a good example of how they carry on," Robert stated. "Our little Blaney may be plain, but she's bitten by the bug and is probably as unreliable as all the rest of them."

"Perhaps that's why," Neil suggested. "With a wig and makeup and somebody else's character, she probably imagines she's lovely when she gets on to a stage."

"Blundering her way across the other characters and treading on their toes? No, I hardly think Sarah Blaney has much to recommend her as an actress. Her stepmother knows all the right people though and probably pulls a string or two."

Neil's laughter came thundering over the wall. "Why do you dislike her so much? I thought her nice enough for a casual acquaintance. Not much to look at, but not ugly either."

"Unremarkable," Robert said, and he sounded angry. "Except when she smiles," he added surprisingly.

So much for any illusions she might have been harboring about Robert Chaddox, Sarah thought ruefully. Well, now she would know better than to think about him at all. So what if she tingled all over when he looked at her. It had probably been no more than a figment of her imagination! Why, if anyone was going to bowl her over, it would have been Alec Farne. He at least looked the part!

Sarah crept along the wall and made a final dash out of the orchard back into her own garden. She was too late. Two pairs of astonished eyes watched her progress with interest, as the two men leaned on the gate that was at right angles to the path she had chosen. She glared at them both, suddenly angry because she felt ridiculous and knew they were laughing at her.

"Eavesdroppers never hear good of themselves!" Neil remarked, his eyes lit with amusement.

"I d-didn't mean to overhear," Sarah stammered. "I was just here!"

"Evidently!" Robert remarked. She thought he might have had the grace to look embarrassed when she thought of what he had said about her, but the gray eyes that met hers gave nothing away.

"And you're wrong! My stepmother doesn't pull strings for me! I stand on my own two feet and I always will!"

"Then what are you doing here?" Robert retorted.

"What do you mean?"

"Not many young actresses would pass up a West End part unless they were sure of picking up where they left off."

"I didn't have any choice!" Sarah said, stung.

Robert had the effrontery to grin at her. "I believe you mind being called a Plain Jane," he teased her.

"Well, I don't! Far from it! Neil was right, as a matter of fact. My undistinguished features are the best stock in trade I have. And if you really want to know, I'm a bloody good actress!" It was seldom that Sarah swore and when she did it didn't trip lightly off her tongue as it did with other people. It embarrassed her quite as much as it surprised her audience and she colored, her anger collapsing into awkwardness.

"I'll take your word for it," Robert said in clipped accents. "I seldom go to the theater myself."

"We go to the Marlow Theater sometimes, in Canterbury," Neil added. "Why don't you get yourself in a play there and we'll both come and cheer you."

"Because you'd more likely boo!" Sarah snapped.

Robert laughed. "You apparently haven't much faith in your spellbinding talents," he pointed out. "Never mind, Sarah, I'm sorry you heard us talking about you. You'll have to smile more often and then perhaps we'll change our opinion of you."

To his surprise, she did smile then, her anger completely forgotten. "I was already feeling prickly because I didn't want to come," she said. "The orchard was like balm to my soul, it's so beautiful and peaceful, and then you spoiled it all."

Robert glanced at her sharply. "I'm sorry for that. It's one of the joys of living in the country that I wouldn't be without myself. There's nowhere to stand and think in London, or if there is, I've never discovered it."

"There are the parks," Sarah told him. "But it isn't the same. May I go into the orchard occasionally or is it forbidden to the oast house tenants?"

"And refresh your spirit? Use it all you like. Nobody else goes there." He stood upright, pushing himself away from the gate with his hands. "We must be going," he added. "I hope you settle in all right, Miss Blaney."

It had been Sarah a minute ago, she thought sadly, touched by the instant of sympathy between them that had revived the feeling of trembling excitement within her again, just as though he had never said that he found her plain.

"Thank you, Mr. Chaddox."

He sketched her a quick salute and was gone, Neil by his side, already talking of some other matter. She could smile like the Cheshire Cat, she told herself, but she would never make any impression on him. And then she found herself wondering who Samantha was and what she was to Robert Chaddox.

The "fantastic Samantha," Neil had said, and she wished with all her heart that someone would find her fantastic, someone with the electric attraction of Robert Chaddox.

SUNDAY CAME almost before Sarah was ready for it. In answer to the steadily tolling bell, she walked across the field, finding her way into the churchyard. The church itself was almost empty of worshippers, but the sound of the organ filled the Victorian-restored interior, delighting her with the familiar, measured tunes of the well-known hymns and psalms of Morning Prayer. When the service was over, she shook hands with the vicar, agreed that it was yet another lovely day and then walked slowly home again. She had thought that Robert might have read the lessons, like the great landowners she had read about in books, but there had been no sign of either him or his brother in the church and she had not liked to ask after them.

She had barely taken off her hat when she heard the scrunch of her stepmother's car in the drive. With a whoop of joy, she rushed out to greet her parents, aware of a peculiar feeling of relief as she saw Madge at the wheel.

"You're earlier than I thought!" she told them, kissing her gray-faced father on the cheek. "This is a perfect place, dad! Did you have a good journey?"

"Terrible!" Madge replied for him. "I thought we'd never get here. I hadn't realized it was quite so far away from London. Daniel says anything nearer is now considered to be commuter country, but there are limits! Nobody, but *nobody*, has ever heard of Chaddoxbourne, or anything like it, even in Canterbury!"

"Only because you asked for a converted oast house, dear," Daniel said fondly. "There is very likely more than one, you know."

"So you kept saying! Well, here we are! Put the kettle on, Sarah, for some tea, will you? I'm parched!"

Sarah cast her father a swift look of concern, but although he looked terribly tired he smiled and winked at her. "That's only the beginning," he told her. "We finally asked the way of a young man who said he's our landlord's brother."

"Neil Chaddox?"

"I wouldn't know, my dear. Madge has asked them both, and somebody called Samantha, to have dinner with us tonight. I hope you have enough food."

Sarah jumped. "Not enough!" she sighed. "I'll have to spin it out somehow, I suppose. At least there are piles of vegetables and fruit in the garden. Doesn't that sound grand?" she added.

"It does indeed."

He leaned heavily on her arm as they went into the house, wheezing painfully all the way. "So you like it here, do you?" he said, lowering himself into a chair.

"Yes, I do. It's rather nice not to have to race everywhere all the time. Of course the sun can't always shine, but it has so far, and everything in the garden, and the orchard too, is lovely!"

"Good girl," said her father, amused.

But Sarah's mind was on the unknown Samantha as she went into the kitchen to make the tea for her stepmother. She looked anxiously at her small stock of food and began to plan the meal for that evening. She could make soup, she thought, from the garden vegetables, and at a pinch, the leg of lamb would serve six, though it wasn't as big as she would have wished, and she could follow that with a gooseberry pudding, also made from fruit from the garden.

Samantha would be beautiful, she knew that, and she would resent her because she was almost sure that Robert Chaddox was in love with her. She sighed deeply. Perhaps if she made up very carefully and was madly witty and smiled a lot she would outshine Samantha's beauty? However, that was only another silly dream and better forgotten. However she did wish that it didn't hurt quite so much to resign herself to the inevitable.

When she went back to the circular sitting room, Madge was busy trying out all the chairs to find the most comfortable for her own use.

"Ah, tea! Sarah, my love, are you going to die of boredom in this dreary hole? What have you done with yourself these past few days? I nearly fainted when I saw how isolated it is here."

Sarah forebore to say that she had spent much of the time dreaming that she had been transformed into an outstanding beauty overnight. "I like it," she said and laughed. "I've spent most of my time in the garden. I never knew it was such a fascinating occupation before. I don't know the names of anything, or which are the weeds, but everyone who passes gives me advice and marvels over my ignorance. One man even offered to keep the lawn mowed for me. I think he means to use the manor's lawnmower, but I'm not inquiring too much into that! When I tried, it took me nearly an hour with the machine I found in the shed, and he does it in about ten minutes flat!"

Her stepmother stared at her in astonishment. "But your hands!" she said faintly.

Sarah glanced down at her neat, well-kept hands and smiled.

"They seem to be tougher than they look. Where's daddy?"

Madge shrugged. "I couldn't bear him wheezing over me any longer. I told him to go upstairs and get into bed. By the way, darling," she paused significantly as Sarah poured her father out a cup of tea and prepared to take it up to him, "I suppose my room is the one above here?"

Sarah nodded abstractedly. "Is daddy all right?"

"I suppose so," her stepmother returned with a touch of irritation. "He would have called out if he wasn't. He's not completely helpless!"

"No, I suppose not," Sarah agreed.

She thought her father looked very tired and drawn when she took him his tea.

"Will it be a nuisance to you to bring my lunch up

here?" he asked her, breathing with a painful intensity. "If I have to get up for dinner—"

"You don't have to!" Sarah exclaimed. She caught sight of the spray that he had half-hidden by his pillow. "Isn't there anything to be done?" Her voice caught in the back of her throat and she swallowed hastily.

"A change of atmosphere," he said slowly. "Don't worry, my dear, I'll pull out of it when we're here on our own for a bit. Madge thinks it's revenge because they wouldn't use my sets in her show. If it is, it's quite unconscious! My conscious mind would have chosen a far less exhausting way of showing my displeasure!"

"Did you mind so much?" Sarah couldn't resist asking.

"No. It seemed remarkably unimportant, as a matter of fact. Perhaps that's why they rejected them. I didn't care enough about the show to produce anything of any value."

"But is it good for Madge?"

His twisted smile made a mockery of her indignant question. "A rather elderly teenager, don't you think?" was all he said.

"I haven't seen the show," Sarah said.

"Take my advice, don't!" he smiled at her.

Madge lay in the sun in the garden that afternoon. Dressed in the barest of bikinis, she still looked better than her stepdaughter would have done in the same garb and she knew it.

"Fetch my book, darling, will you?" she asked Sarah. "I'm too lazy to go upstairs again. Have you got dinner under control? It was quite difficult to persuade Robert Chaddox that it would be quite all right for them all to come. I don't care for him much, I must say. He looked at me as if I were something the cat had dragged in."

"He doesn't go for Thespians," Sarah murmured.

Her stepmother smiled with a self-satisfied air. "Well,

well, we'll have to change that! My book, please, dear. It's the thriller with the lurid cover beside my bed."

Sarah was too busy after that to exchange more than a few words with her stepmother. Cooking was still a relatively new art to her and she fussed over the meal as though her life depended on it. It would be too awful, she kept telling herself, if anything was to go wrong the first time Robert came to the oast house as their guest. Even if she wasn't pretty, she would like him to think that she had all the usual feminine skills that instinct told her he would approve of.

In the end she hardly allowed herself sufficient time to change and she was still upstairs when the doorbell rang. "I'll go!" Madge's voice floated up to her.

Sarah struggled into her dress and at the same time tried to catch what they were saying in the hall below. Her stepmother's voice, clearly produced as always, was warm and distinct.

"Mr. Chaddox! Or may I call you Robert? And this is your brother Neil. I was so afraid I'd get your names wrong and look the perfect dunce that I am. And you must be Samantha!"

Sarah gave way to temptation and, still smoothing down her dress, tiptoed across the landing and peered over the banisters to see the unknown Samantha. All she could see was a cloud of bright red hair and a splash of brilliant yellow of the woman's dress. Sarah went back into her room and took a long look at herself in the mirror. Her own nut-colored hair looked dull beside the fiery locks she had just seen, and her features, with her high cheekbones and mobile expression, only managed to annoy her by their very ordinariness. With a petulant gesture, of a kind that she seldom indulged in, she turned on her heel and went in search of her father.

Daniel Blaney was not yet dressed. Sarah took one look at him and hurried him back into bed.

"Madge won't be pleased," he whispered.

"Nonsense, dad. The whole point of our coming here is that you should get better. I'll bring your dinner up on a tray. Okay?"

He nodded, breathing heavily. "Thank you, my dear."

Sarah fled down the stairs and into the kitchen to check on her last-minute preparations for the meal. Someone had shut the door into the sitting room and she had shut the kitchen door earlier, and so the hall was dark and she didn't see anyone standing there. She ran slap into Robert Chaddox, spilling the jug of water he was holding in his hand.

"Oh dear!" she exclaimed.

"Where's the fire?" he countered at precisely the same moment.

"I didn't see you," she excused herself.

"You didn't look!"

"Well, you shouldn't go around hiding in shadows!" She took a step backward and looked at him more closely. "Did any of the water go on you?"

"No, I heard you coming and took appropriate evasive action!" He shook his head at her. "Is your father coming down?"

Sarah blinked quickly to hide tears that the thought of her father brought, unbidden, to her eyes. "No," she said. "He doesn't feel well enough. Won't you go back to the others? I'll join you in a minute."

But if she had hoped to escape his sharp gray eyes until she had herself under better control, she was doomed to disappointment.

"Are you doing the cooking?" he asked her. "Smells good! I hope such a large invasion of guests hasn't severely strained your resources?"

Sarah glanced at him uncertainly and then she smiled. "Most of it comes out of the garden," she admitted.

"Ah yes," he observed. "I've heard that you spend most of your time digging up the flowers and tending the weeds! If you care to come over to the manor some time I'll show you over our gardens and lend you a few books on the subject."

Sarah's pleasure in the suggestion was so obvious that he chuckled.

"The trouble is," she confided, "that I don't always recognize the flowers from their illustrations. I have a great deal to learn!"

"All the more reason to come over and begin your education!" His gray eyes glinted at her, bringing an unexpected blush to her cheeks. "Have you finished peering into those pots?"

Sarah was glad of the hot steam from the boiling vegetables on her face.

"Yes. I think so."

"Then stop dithering and come into the living room. Samantha is waiting to meet you."

Samantha was everything Sarah had been afraid she would be. She was tall and her hair was truly her crowning glory. Even more unfair, she had a pair of laughing green eyes and an air of enjoying everything that came her way. It was impossible to dislike her but, unfortunately, only too possible to envy everything about her.

"Sarah Blaney?" she exclaimed. "But I've heard of you! I saw you in an Agatha Christie! I was staying with my aunt...." She broke off to put her arm through Robert's to gain his full attention. "I wish I'd known it was you! It would have been fun to come around and dragoon you into having a drink with us, or something!"

"Thank you," Sarah said simply.

Madge glanced across the room at Samantha. "Was she any good?" she asked prettily.

Samantha's smile was equally charming. "I'm not competent to say. She remembered all her lines."

"And tripped over the hero's feet to boot!" Robert interrupted.

"I did not!" Sarah protested.

"You surprise me!"

Sarah gurgled with laughter, peeping up at him through her lashes. "The hero didn't get in my way!"

Samantha frowned. "Is this a private joke?"

"Yes," Madge added. "Tell us all about it. Though I can tell you how good my stepdaughter is as an actress. She was recently offered a part by Alec Farne in his new play. Of course, I won't pretend that it was because she is the Actress of the Year, or anything like that! I think, though Sarah won't admit it, that Alec found her equally taking off stage!"

"Oh, Madge!"

"Well, he did take you out to dinner, dear!"

"When I left the part," Sarah said bitterly. "Largely to give himself the pleasure of telling me that I'd never get anywhere if I didn't put the part of the moment before my family and everything else. He told me I hadn't the temperament to be great."

"True," Madge put in. "Clever Alec! He wouldn't have given you the part, pet, if he hadn't been a bit in love with you. I told you that!"

There was a silence in the room. Sarah clenched her fists by her sides and faced her stepmother. "Why not?"

Madge shrugged, laughing kindly at her. "Darling, you know why not! You may have been all right in a little repertory company, but surely you never thought you'd be a second Sarah Bernhardt?" She laughed again. "You need something extra for that! It's a pity you are your mother's daughter and not mine, darling!"

Sarah lifted her head proudly. "Not that it matters, but Alec Farne had never seen me before I auditioned for him. You should ask him if you don't believe me."

"I will," said Madge. "You must invite him down

here some time and then we can all judge for ourselves!" She smiled. "Or do you think he wouldn't think it worth his while with me here to chaperone you?"

Sarah blenched. "I don't know him well enough to say," she insisted.

Samantha exchanged glances with Robert and anxiously cleared her throat. "I thought Sarah very good," she began. "I remembered her, didn't I?"

Sarah could have wished that she, of all people, didn't feel compelled to be nice to her. With an effort she forced a smile and even laughed. "You haven't got a drink, Mr. Chaddox," she said. "What will you have?"

But Robert ignored her. He was still looking at her stepmother, his admiration for her written clearly on his face.

"I think you underrate your stepdaughter," he said slowly. "Sarah's speaking voice is one of the most attractive I've ever heard. It was the first thing I noticed about her. And that, surely, is a great asset on the stage. Besides," he added, with an apologetic glance at Sarah, "Neil assures me that makeup is everything on the boards. His mother was on the stage."

Sarah's heart warmed within her. "I thought you only noticed the soup!" she told him.

"That too!" he agreed. "But I wasn't half as rude as I might have been if you hadn't sounded so huskily apologetic."

Sarah chuckled. "What an escape! I wish I'd known and I would have sounded sorrier still!"

"Was he mean to you?" Neil asked with interest.

Sarah made a face at him. "What do you think?" Unconsciously she assumed Robert's outraged expression. "If you can manage to get your car out of the parking lot intact," she mimicked him.

Samantha and Neil both doubled up with laughter and even Robert gave her a dry smile that sent her spirits rollicking upward. Only Madge found nothing funny in Sarah's clever imitation of Robert's way of speaking.

"Darling, I come down here to get away from stage talk! Be a dear and see what your father wants to drink, will you?" She watched her stepdaughter leave the room, her eyes narrowing thoughtfully. "And now let's talk about Chaddoxbourne, shall we? It's such a pretty place and I long to get to know it better. Daniel and Sarah are so lucky to be going to be here all the time! If I didn't have to work, but then someone has to pay the bills! And Robert certainly knows how to charge a fair rent!"

"It compares pretty favorably with London prices, Mrs. Blaney," Robert said flatly.

"I'm not complaining!" Madge assured him. "And what's all this about Mrs. Blaney? Nobody *ever* calls me that! You must all call me Madge!"

CHAPTER FOUR

THE SUNNY SPELL showed no sign of abating. Sarah was surprised to find that she had been in Chaddoxbourne for nearly four weeks and had never seen a spot of rain. It was a happy time, the only disturbances being her stepmother's weekend visits. That last weekend her stepmother had been busy in London giving a charity performance and there had been nothing to upset the even tenor of their routine. In fact, Sarah admitted to herself, she didn't have nearly enough to do. Her father was so much better that he was able to potter about the garden and sometimes to go down to the village store to buy their supplies. Apart from the cooking and keeping the place clean, Sarah found herself living a life of complete leisure and knew if it went on for very long she would soon be bored stiff.

She had discovered a woodland trail near the village and as she walked along it, she amused herself by recalling what Robert had told her about it. It must have been a very similar summer to this one when St. Augustine had first set foot on English soil. They said then that the intermittent streams came and went according to the prevailing fortunes of the Christian faith. St. Augustine's first summer had been a very dry one and he had prayed for rain, a spring gushing forth on the spot where he knelt. But Woden and Thunor, the gods of old, who had caused the drought in the first place, were very angry and they dug great caverns under the earth and dried up the diverted waters with their fiery breath. So when Christianity is winning, the waters run, but when the old gods prevail, the waters disappear from the face of the earth.

Woden and Thunor were doing particularly well that year. The riverbed was completely dry. Along its bed Sarah could see various places which were sometimes flooded, and even a mark on the side of a barn where the waters had reached during one particular night of flood. It wasn't very far to the river, but it was a pretty walk and had soon become one of Sarah's favorites. It led past a hops field where the luxuriant bines were already heavy with the golden hops and nearly ripe for picking. Their strong smell scented the surrounding countryside and had caught at Sarah's interest, especially since the house she was living in was a converted oast house.

The local farmer had told her that the bines are perennial, sending up new shoots every year. These grow up a network of strings that are set up anew every year in the spring. The hops have to be coaxed up the strings by hand at first, a process known locally as "twiddling," and then in late August the hops are picked, formerly by vast armies of women and children from the East End of London, but now more often by machine.

The hops, when picked, are packed into "pokes" and taken to the oast houses, where they are spread out on a hair mat that covers the lattice floor of the upper story. The dryer has charge of the oast house, and that complicated process of firing the anthracite fires and adjusting the picturesque white ventilating cowls according to the wind depends on his experience. Once dried the hops are packed again, this time into pockets, and taken away to the breweries.

It was hard to imagine the comfortable home she and her father were enjoying had once been a working oast house. Sarah had never seen one still in use, but she promised herself that she would one day before they, too, were swept away in the wake of more modern processes. Sarah followed the riverbed. The sun made it impossible to see into the depths of the water, but she found by squatting on the bank under a tree she could see quite well and she settled herself down without moving for a few minutes to see if she could see any fish in the river. Her own reflection peered back at her out of the water, rippled and vanished only to reappear again, joined this time by another shape, far taller than herself. She looked around, startled, to see Robert Chaddox smiling down at her.

She stood up hastily, looking at her watch to make sure the time hadn't slipped by without her being aware of it. "Are—aren't you working?" she asked him. She had discovered that as well as owning most of Chaddoxbourne Robert was a solicitor, with a valuable practice in Canterbury.

"Not this afternoon," he answered.

He sat on the bank beside her, easing his back against the trunk of the tree. "It's nice to have nothing to do for a bit," he added.

Sarah looked at him seriously. "It palls, after a while. Even in this beautiful weather I'm beginning to wish that I had something positive to do."

"Your father is looking better. Isn't that enough?"

"It should be," she admitted. "I must be very hard to please!"

"I doubt it. I think I'd feel much the same. Neil is the one in our family who enjoys being idle. He doesn't start work until September and he's reveling in this long, hot summer."

"He's going to teach, isn't he?" Sarah confirmed.

"Heaven help us!"

Sarah laughed. "What about the small boys he teaches?"

"Nothing will help them!"

Sarah laughed again. She eyed Robert covertly for a long moment in silence, wondering at her own pleasure just in having him sit beside her.

"Mr. Chaddox, do you think there's any work in the village I might do?"

His expression changed to one of surprise. "Am I still supposed to be calling you Miss Blaney?"

"Of course not!"

"Then perhaps you could bring yourself to call me Robert?"

Her heart lurched against her ribs. "If you don't mind, I'd like to."

His gray eyes met hers. "You're a funny girl," he remarked. 'Don't you think you have enough to do, looking after your father, without taking on anything else?"

"I thought so for a while," she admitted soberly. "But the truth is that if I go on like this for very much longer I'll be really bored."

"Have you never lived in the country before?"

She shook her head. "I don't think it's that though—I mean, I'd feel exactly the same in London, or anywhere!"

"You're not missing the theater?"

She looked straight at him for the first time, her eyes laughing. "It's terrible of me, but I don't think I am. I'd like to do something ordinary for a bit, something that wouldn't interfere with my father when he doesn't feel well. Do you know of anything like that I might do?"

"If I did I'm not sure I'd tell you about it," he said at last. "I don't approve of people playing at work. It's almost as bad as playing with other people's lives."

"Oh, surely not! Besides, I wouldn't be playing! I really need something to do. I'd do it as well as I possibly could, whatever it was, whether it was paid or not. I do know what work is!"

"In the theater?"

She found that she was angry. She turned away from him and studied the river intently, following a small fish with her eyes as it swam against the rippling current close to the opposite bank. She felt his hand on her shoulder and shrugged away from him, her muscles tensing.

"I'm sorry," Robert said. "How would you like to work as my secretary?"

She was surprised into forgetting her momentary anger. "Don't you have one? Besides, I don't know all the legal terms you use and I don't know shorthand."

"But you can type?"

She nodded. "Enough to make copies of scripts and things like that."

Robert sat up straight, making sure he had her whole attention. "I have an excellent secretary in Canterbury. I was thinking of the Chaddoxbourne estate. At the moment I fit in the work attached to that when I can and hope for the best, but I've been thinking for some time that I ought to arrange things better. It would involve sorting out the tenants' problems, writing piles of letters to the various government departments, sending out receipts for rents, and making the plumber call when anyone springs a leak. Do you think you could do all that?"

"I could try."

"I'd expect you to keep regular hours, except when your father needs you. You won't be able to come and go as you like."

"Of course not," she said simply. "It would be a business arrangment." Her face broke into laughter. "Are you going to make me sign a legal contract?"

"Not until I see if you're going to be of any use," he returned. He lifted an eyebrow at her. "Not quite as meek as you appear at first, are you?"

She blushed, looked at her watch and leaped to her feet. "I must get my father's tea," she said in a breathless voice. "Would you care to join us?" He shook his head, grinning at her. "Robert, it is settled, isn't it? I mean I'd like to have the job."

"Then it's yours."

"Thank you," she said. "Thank you very much." She hesitated an instant, half expecting him to qualify her apointment with some remark about a trial period, but he was silent, his gray eyes looking mockingly up at her.

"Well?"

"N-nothing," she stammered and almost ran along the path to the oast house, her heart hammering within her in the most uncomfortable manner.

Her pace slowed down as soon as she was out of sight of the river. Pleasure in the idea of working for Robert fountained up within her. She would be bound to see a certain amount of him and that alone was enough to set her spirits leaping. It would be good to have something to do again. How pleased her father would be when he knew, for he too knew how frustrating it was to be at a loose end, without the discipline of work to give shape to the days.

But, when she opened the front door of the oasthouse, she could hear his distressed breathing coming from the sitting room and immediately forgot all about everything else.

"Do you have your spray?" she called out to him, hurrying into the room.

Her father was sitting in his favorite chair, his face gray and strained, and it was a moment before she realized that he was not alone. Standing beside the chair with his back to her stood Alec Farne. He turned at her entrance, a smile of welcome on his face.

"Sarah, you're looking very pretty!"

Sarah faced him angrily. "What have you said to upset him?" she demanded. "What are you doing here?"

"Well, I like that! I thought you'd be pleased to see me! I haven't said anything to him. I found the door open and since nobody answered my knock I came in here. He took one look at me and started gasping for breath. I did what I could for him, but... well, I've never seen anyone with asthma before."

"Gave him a fright!" her father panted apologetically.

Sarah tried to still the dart of anxiety that shot through her. Surely no one could go on like this for long, fighting for breath at every gasp.

"You should be in bed, dad," she said.

He attempted a smile. "Yes, Sarah. You'd better make some tea for this young man who's come all this way to see you. I expect he's still hoping to talk you into doing his play."

"Then he'll be unlucky," Sarah retorted lightly. "I've found myself a job here, as a matter of fact. Secretary to the Chaddoxbourne Estate! What do you think of that?"

Her father smiled weakly. "So Robert found you by the river?"

"Secretary!" Alec Farne exclaimed. "Sarah, you can't! I won't allow it! Good heavens, girl, don't you have any idea of how talented you are? You can't waste all that doing secretarial work for some village yokel!"

"Robert is a solicitor," Sarah said carefully.

"That doesn't make you a typist!"

Sarah turned back to her father, controlling her temper with some difficulty. Alec Farne was often referred to as being handsome, but he looked pale and drawn to her when she compared him with the men who lived locally, men like Robert Chaddox, tanned by the sun and fit enough to walk miles without collapsing.

"Not a good typist," she agreed. "But I hope to make an adequate one. Dad, don't you think you'd be better off in bed?"

Daniel Blaney nodded, his labored breathing worse than ever. "Alec will give me a hand upstairs. You make the tea."

She watched them set off, hoping that Alec would ignore her father's objections and lift him bodily up the stairs. The producer was not a particularly strong man, however, and he was panting from the effort when he came back downstairs.

"Your father weighs a ton! What have you been feeding him?" He looked her up and down as she stood by the stove, waiting for the kettle to boil. "You've put on some weight yourself!"

"I have not!" Sarah denied.

"It suits you," Alec smiled. "What makes your father go like that?"

"I don't know," she admitted. "He's been so much better recently. When I went out he was breathing absolutely normally. I can't think what set him off. You didn't say anything, did you?"

"I'll say I did! I told him what I thought of your coming down here to look after him and that he was a selfish old man. Well, what do you expect, Sarah my love? The other girl has two left feet on any stage and can't learn her lines!"

"Oh, Alec, you didn't!"

Alec Farne stared at her moodily. "It's true, isn't it?" He gnawed at his lower lip thoughtfully. "Why did you tell him that you were better off without the part? It would have made you, do you know that?"

Sarah made the tea, pleased to see that her hands were completely steady.

"I think I am better off," she said finally. "It never occurred to me before that I might like to do something else, but I'm enjoying living in the country and being like everyone else. It was odd at first to be at home in the evening instead of working when everyone else was relaxing, but now that I've tried it, I find I prefer it. Even when my father is quite well again, I still may not go back to the theater."

"You must be mad!"

She smiled at him, amused because even as recently as a couple of weeks ago her own reaction would have been exactly the same. "Perhaps it's sanity," she murmured.

"If you ask me, you're putting a brave face on things. Why can't your stepmother take over for a while?"

"Because the theater really is her life. She'd curl up and die if she were away from it for more than a day or so. She wouldn't flourish on good country air and feel absolutely marvelous on a diet of fresh food and early nights!"

Alec Farne shuddered. "Perish the thought!"

Sarah grinned at him, a touch of malice in her eyes. "There you are then! You'll have to make the best of your clumsy halfwit. I imagine she can learn lines as well as anyone else if you were a little nice to her. She's probably scared stiff of you. I was!"

"Never!" he declared. "You never gave me cause to shout at you!"

"If you had, I would have died there and then, I was so nervous!"

He looked surprised. "Really? You're rather a poppet, Sarah. Do you always do battle for every underdog you hear about?"

"No, that's a new development too! I've never had time to do anything except scratch a living for myself before. Now I have time, and you don't know how marvelous it is! I'll enjoy doing this bit of secretarial work, but that's something quite different from the stresses and strains of repertory life. For the first time in my life I have time to be myself, and I'm reveling in every moment of it!"

His look was frankly admiring. "It suits you, love," he said. "When you do come back to the theater you'll knock 'em cold!"

Touched, she blinked rapidly and poured the boiling water into the teapot. "And you're quite resigned that I'm not coming back yet?" she inquired.

"If you say so, Sarah sweet, if you say so. I'm prepared to give you a bit more rope at any rate. Will that do?"

She nodded quickly. "Thank you, Alec."

They had tea in the garden. Sarah took a cup up to her father, sitting on the edge of his bed while he drank it.

"Listen, Sarah," he said. "You won't go on with this job until you've talked it over with Madge, will you? She might not like your going behind her back."

"I've already decided, dad," she said gently.

"Madge won't like it!"

"Perhaps not." She smiled at him. "Don't worry about it anyway. You've been so much better recently. What brought this on?"

Her father shrugged. "How should I know? I suppose I thought young Alec Farne might take you away from me. He wants you in his play, doesn't he?"

"He did," she admitted. "Now he thinks I'm doing a good job of growing up a bit here and he'll keep me in mind later on. That will suit both of us very well!"

"I'm glad." Daniel Blaney coughed and fought again for breath. "I'm enjoying having you with me. It's almost worth feeling worthless most of the time."

Sarah took his cup from him, still smiling. "I'm enjoying it too," she told him. "In fact you'll be heartily sick of me before I'll leave you, so you'd better make up your mind to it! Will you be all right if I take Alec to Canterbury for his train?"

Her father merely nodded and sank back against his pillows. She thought she might have imagined that his breathing was already easier. It was so easy to be over optimistic when he had one of his attacks. And yet, with his eyes shut and his body quite relaxed, he was having less difficulty drawing breath. A little comforted, she tiptoed out of the room and closed the door behind her.

Alec accepted her offer to drive him to Canterbury with enthusiasm. "You can show me the village on the way—what there is of it!"

"There's the church," she said somewhat doubtfully. "And the watermill. Robert says it worked right up to the end of the war, and that all our bread was locally made, instead of coming from Canterbury as it does now."

"'Our' bread?"

Sarah colored. "It's a manner of speaking," she said defensively.

"Very revealing!" he mocked. "But yes, I should like to see your watermill. I suppose it's that weatherboard building beside the river as you turn into the village by the church?"

"Yes." Sarah picked up her car keys and began edging towards the front door. She was not usually inhospitable, but she was suddenly longing for him to go, to leave her in peace with the new life she was discovering for herself. "I'll get the car out."

Alec folded himself into the car beside her, protesting that her car was too small to be of any use to anyone.

"On the contrary," she said sharply. "There's plenty of room for the shopping and it will take three people at a pinch. Besides, it's easy to park and goes miles to the gallon. What more could you desire?"

"Something a little larger than a roller skate!"

Sarah laughed. "I don't see that you have anything to complain about as long as it gets you to Canterbury. Do you want me to open the window? It's still quite hot."

Alec didn't answer. He waited until she slowed down beside the watermill and then he opened his door with determination. "I didn't think any car was too small to kiss a girl in," he commented.

Sarah sat up very straight. "That has its advantages too." She hoped she sounded cool and sophisticated and that Alec wouldn't continue the topic. She didn't want him to kiss her. She didn't want to touch him at all.

Alec looked down at his watch. He was sweating slightly in the hot sun, she noticed with disfavor, and she couldn't help hoping that his train was sooner than he had planned and that there would be no time to dally by the watermill. In this she was unlucky.

"I've been thinking about you, Sarah my love," he began. "You have such a beautifully expressive face! I'm beginning to wonder whether there isn't a great deal of feeling buried deep down beneath that 'touch me not' exterior."

"Rubbish!" said Sarah.

"No hidden fires?"

"Nothing so corny!" Sarah assured him cheerfully. "Do you want to see the watermill?"

"Not particularly. Rustic pursuits are not much in my line. I'd sooner discover how the land lies with you. Any boyfriends who'll be hot on my heels if I make a quick reconnaissance?"

"No boyfriends. But I'd rather you didn't."

"Not very convincing," he murmured. "Come on, show me around this watermill of yours."

"There isn't much to see. Nothing that you can't see from here!" Sarah protested. "What time is your train? We should be going if you don't want to miss it!"

Alec slid his arm behind her shoulders.

"Did you really think you were going to escape so easily? What's a little kiss between friends? Come on, Sarah, relax and enjoy it. You did better than this in London."

"I didn't enjoy it," she told him frankly. It was impossible to tell him that it was because his eyes weren't steely gray, and his touch was nervous instead of firm.

Impossible, too, to admit, even to herself, that it seemed disloyal to be kissing anyone else when she was actually on Robert's land, and her dreams were all of him. "Please don't!" she protested.

But she was too late. He held her very close and kissed her cheek and then her lips. Sarah struggled against a sharp desire to slap him. Instead she flung open the door on her side of the car and slid out, angrily smoothing down her dress and wiping her face on the back of her hand.

You'd better take a taxi to Canterbury!" she said furiously.

Alec sat and watched her, his expression enigmatic. "Okay, Sarah," he said. "You can get back in. I won't touch you again. I haven't the time anyway, as you pointed out, if I don't want to miss my train. Oh, for heaven's sake, woman, don't make such a big thing of it! Anyone would think—"

"I asked you not to!" she exclaimed, very near to tears.

"So do they all! Another time, my pet, and I'll prove to you that you didn't mean it either. Now get in, there's a good girl, and drive me to Canterbury, and we'll say no more about it."

Sarah stared back at him. She couldn't believe that he really thought he had only to persevere to overcome her reluctance to play at love with him. Perhaps he had reason to think so. She was sure that there would be many girls who would be flattered by his attentions, only she was surprised that he was obtuse enough to believe that she was one of them.

Slowly she climbed back into the car, grinding the gears as she flung the car on to the road, her anger getting the better of her driving. It was a good thing that it wasn't far to Canterbury, she thought, as she narrowly missed hitting a truck that was thundering along the road. She took a deep breath and forced herself to concentrate on what she was doing. In a few minutes she felt calmer and more in control of the situation.

In silence they drove through Canterbury to the railway station, and in silence she waited for him to get out of the car.

"Look, Sarah."

"I'm sorry, Alec. I'm not casual about that sort of thing and that's all there is to it. There's your train coming in now."

Alec hesitated, thought better of whatever it was he had been going to say and walked slowly away from her. Sarah grasped the steering wheel so tightly that her knuckles shone white and she realized that she was afraid that he would turn back and say something further, something she couldn't either forget or forgive. She liked Alec, she thought, and she didn't want an open breach between them, especially not over something so trivial as a kiss that meant nothing to him and even less to her.

But he did not come back, and as soon as he was out of sight, she released the clutch and drove carefully back through Canterbury and out along the road to town. As the shops and offices emptied and people took to their cars to get home the roads grew crowded and she was glad to turn off the main road and drive the last little way into the village. She drove slowly along the road until the watermill caught her attention and she found herself going back over the incident with Alec. Why did he want to kiss her? He knew many prettier women than herself, women who would be only too willing to fall into his arms when they knew who he was and what he had to offer. If she had been a different kind of person, she supposed she would have been flattered by his attentions. Why then did she feel only sick at heart and shamed by the embrace?

She looked at the watermill with disfavor, allowing the car to edge on to the wrong side of the road. With a start, she caught herself just in time to avoid hitting Robert, who was walking along the road in the opposite direction. She had a vivid picture of his furious face as he stood in front of her hood, glaring at her, with his hands on his hips and the light of battle in his eye. With a comprehensive gesture, he wrenched open her door and motioned to her to move over into the passenger seat. Too frightened to speak, she watched him set the car in motion again and drive in silence through the open gates, parking it neatly in front of the front door of the oast house.

"I'm sorry," she said at last.

He exploded then, blowing up with a completeness that left her startled and inwardly applauding. Words flowed out of him, berating her, and whoever had taken it upon themselves to instruct her in the art of driving and finally to the maniac who had seen fit to pass her as fit to drive on the public highway.

"I'm sorry," she said again.

"Sorry! You shouldn't be allowed out by yourself! If kissing that fellow can put you in such a dither, you should be a candidate for a nunnery!"

"I *was* angry," she admitted.

His steely gray eyes glinted dangerously. "Indeed? You didn't look particularly angry to me. Was your stepmother right after all? Was that how you got your famous West End part?"

"*No*!"

"Okay, so you were angry. It didn't stop you from getting back into the car and driving him to Canterbury, did it?"

Sarah bit her lip. "I did suggest he get a taxi," she excused herself. "I'm very sorry, Robert."

"Sorry because you nearly hit me?"

"N-not only for that," she said.

She felt him tense beside her, but she was too busy trying to sort out her own emotions to wonder at it. He must have seen Alec kissing her, she thought in dismay, and somehow that was the last straw in a trying afternoon.

"I can't think why he came!" she burst out. "All he did was to upset my father...."

"And you?"

Sarah nodded. He put his hand under her chin and turned her face toward him. She was astonished to see that he was smiling and wondered what could have amused him. She could see nothing funny in anything that had happened.

"I don't kiss casually. I never have! You must believe me!"

"Why?"

She tried to avoid his glance, but there was no escape from the gentle pressure of his fingers on her chin. "I don't particularly *like* him!"

"Perhaps you'll be more free with your kisses with me," he said against her lips. Her whole being leaped to meet him. His touch was ecstasy and with a sob her hands slipped up behind his shoulders and she pulled him closer still. Then, just as suddenly, Robert had pushed her away from him. "I thought so!" he said with contempt. "Don't bother to pretend that you didn't want that!"

Sarah felt herself shaking, but she was too proud to give him the satisfaction of knowing how much he had hurt her.

"I won't!" she declared.

She had no way of reading the expression in his eyes. It was enough that his arms were about her again, pulling her roughly against him, and then she gave herself up to the bliss of his deepening kiss.

CHAPTER FIVE

SARAH SAT in the car for a long time after Robert had left her. So this was what it felt like to be in love! She should have known by the unbearable excitement she had felt whenever he had come near her, but that he could turn her inside out and upside down by merely holding her close and kissing her face and lips, she had not known.

Her cheeks flamed with the memory of how eagerly she had responded to him. And he had not kissed her out of love. She thought with despair of how he had asked her again what Alec Farne meant to her and how once again she had told him nothing, but she wasn't sure that he had believed her, even then. Surely, though, he would know that she had never kissed Alec, or anyone else, *like that*! Even the memory brought a feeling of sheer delight to constrict her breath and send her blood cavorting around her veins. How strange that Robert Chaddox could do this to her, of all the men she knew. Why, in other circumstances, she might not even have liked him!

When she felt more or less normal again, she left the car and went inside, trying to feel her usual self-concern about her father and all the things that she ordinarily felt. It was easy enough to worry about her father. She could count his recent attacks on one hand and each one had come on during one of her stepmother's visits—and now when Alec had come to see them. She was beginning to think that anything that reminded him of the theater was enough to set him off again, and yet surely that was rather an unworthy thought? It was certainly not something she would care to mention to anyone else.

Her father felt well enough to get up for supper. Sarah watched him sitting at the other end of the table, his dressing gown flapping loose around him. He looked quite normal again. His face was more lined than it had been, but otherwise he looked as he had always looked, his puckish, humorous face intent on boning his kipper, with just the same expression that he had when he was working. She wondered if he missed his work and whether he wanted to talk about it. He had never mentioned the theater or anything to do with it since they had come to Chaddoxbourne.

"You are going to consult Madge about this job of yours, aren't you?" he said suddenly.

"I'll tell her about it when she next comes," Sarah compromised.

Her father looked up. "She won't be pleased," he warned.

Sarah didn't think so either, but she determined to put a good face on her fears on that score. "I can't tell her before I start the job. I start tomorrow. Dad, you don't think Robert is making this job for me, do you? I'd hate it if I weren't going to be really useful to him"

Daniel grunted thoughtfully. "Seeing a lot of him, aren't you?" His eyes ran over his daughter's expressive face. "By the way, what did Alec Farne want?"

"He's worried about that play of his."

"Wants you, doesn't he?"

Sarah nodded slowly. "But, do you know, I'm not sure that I want to go back to the theater ever. It's been like a revelation, coming here. I had no idea that being in the theater makes one so apart from other people. I suppose it's because I've never known anything else."

"Hmm, I've always though theater people should stick to each other. Fatal to marry outside. They never understand how it eats you up. Look at your stepmother. Imagine if she'd married a doctor—or a solicitor!"

Sarah chuckled. "The mind boggles!" she agreed.

Daniel's face broke into a puckish grin. "Whereas, my dear, you have enough talent to go to the top, but you're not emotionally involved with the life! I'm glad you're beginning to discover that for yourself!"

Sarah needed all her ability as an actress when she walked through the orchard and across the manor gardens the next morning. She was so nervous that her hands had trembled as she had buttoned up her neat, tailored coat. Strictly speaking, she didn't need to wear a coat, but she had decided that it was suitable for a secretary and had dressed accordingly.

She stood for a long moment outside the front door, tracing out the legend *Invicta* with the toe of her shoe, while she tried to summon up sufficient courage to ring the bell. In the end, she didn't have to. The door was opened wide and Neil stood in the hall, openly laughing at her.

"Well, well, you look the part!" he teased her.

She colored a little. "It's important to me," she began, then she broke off. "I've never done this kind of thing before. I didn't want Robert to think that I wasn't going to take it seriously!"

Neil grinned. "I can see you're going to give an immaculate performance! Lucky Robert!"

Sarah almost flounced past him, sadly put out. "I'm not playing a part!" she assured him tartly.

"Why not?" he retorted. "I expect to play a part every day of my life, standing up there before a whole lot of small boys and trying to din a bit of knowledge into their heads!"

Sarah looked uncertain. "But this is real life," she said.

Neil's laughter rang through the house. "Come on,

I'll show you into the study. Robert was here a moment ago. Shall I go and find him?"

Sarah didn't answer. She had not been in the study before and she gave a gasp of delight as the proportions of the book-lined wall met her eyes. "What a lovely room!" she exclaimed.

Neil perched on the edge of the desk and looked about him. "I suppose I'm used to it." His eyes returned to her face. "It's obvious you've never lived in a village before!" he accused her with mock severity. "You'd be more discreet if you had! And you'd know better than to kiss your boyfriend bang in the middle of the village!"

"I didn't," Sarah protested. "He... he kissed me!"

Neil's mocking look made her blush. "If you say so. Robert and I were on the other side of the river, and despite our best endeavors, we couldn't see much of you—only the back of his head. Who is he, by the way?"

"Alec Farne. He's the producer of the play I was going to be in."

"And what was Smart Alec doing in Chaddoxbourne on a sunny afternoon in the middle of the week?"

Sarah blushed again. "His play isn't going very well."

"My word, and he came all this way to ask you to change your mind and take the part after all?"

She nodded, embarrassed. "I think so. But then my father had an attack of asthma and I was more worried about that."

She was relieved that, at that moment, Robert came into the room and wished her a curt good morning. "I think we can manage without you, Neil," he added. "Miss Blaney has come here to work, not to gossip!"

Neil went obediently, blowing her a light kiss from behind his brother's back. "One doesn't gossip with the people who are being gossiped about!" he said *sotto voce*. "All right, all right, I'm going!"

Sarah pretended that she was looking at the view out

of the window. She couldn't bring herself to look at Robert. It was not only the memory of his kissing her, but Neil's ridiculous joking stood, like something tangible, between them. Behind her, Robert cleared his throat and she jumped around guiltily. "There's no need to look as though I'm going to hit you!" he said irritably.

"Of course, of course not!"

"But you're not taking any chances?"

She made a rush toward the desk, nearly tripping over a small hump in the carpet. With a mounting feeling of hysteria, she sat down on the nearest chair and waited for the blur of embarrassment to clear before her eyes.

"Heaven help you if you're always so clumsy!" Robert barked at her, exasperated.

"I'm not!"

He looked amused. "It's the unfortunate effect I have on you? Why are you looking so frightened? What did Neil say to you?"

"N-nothing much. He said you'd been just across the river when Alec—I don't think he thinks I'm serious about this job either!" She sniffed, aware that she sounded pathetic and who, in Robert's company, would ever want to sound anything so dismal?

"I believe you're serious," Robert said abruptly. "But Neil is right about people gossiping about you and Alec Farne. If you don't want to have everyone talking about you, you'd do well to sort that young man out once and for all!" He studied her pale face and frowned. "Don't look so sick at heart! All you have to do is to tell him that you're not interested—if you're sure you're not!" He put his hands, tanned and long-fingered, flat down on the desk in front of her. "I don't think you're cut out to be a successful sinner," he went on with a hint of a smile. "If you're having an affair with him, it's no business of mine, but I think you'd be much happier married to him."

"But I'm not!"

He regarded her steadily. "No," he said, "I don't think you are. But you'd be a fool to be alone with him again if you don't want him to kiss you."

She gurgled with sudden laughter, her smile lighting up her face. "I don't think I'll condemn him for that. It might lead me into condemning others." She allowed her voice to trail off, as she peeped up at him.

"Are you hoping for an apology?"

Sarah's smile died away. "No," she said quickly. "No, of course not!"

"Good, because you're not going to get one." He stood there, looking down at her, and she knew he was half hoping that she would smile up at him again, because it fascinated him to watch the procession of emotions that flickered across her face, whereas she would have given anything to veil her thoughts from him.

Sarah felt herself going red under his gaze. "I came to work, Mr. Chaddox," she reminded him, folding her hands primly in front of her.

He started, looking disappointed. "All right, *Miss Blaney*, let's get on with it!"

He was very businesslike. Sarah was hard put to keep up with him as they went briskly through the pile of letters on the desk. But when he had gone, she found the work easier than she had expected, and the morning flew past on wings. Robert's housekeeper, Mrs. Vidler, brought her a cup of coffee in the middle of the morning, her deeply tanned face wreathed in smiles.

"Nice to have a young lady in the house! Miss Blaney, isn't it? I've heard in the village that your mother is on the stage? And your poor father is sickly? You have your hands full and no mistake! We weren't a bit surprised that Mr. Robert is taking an interest. There isn't anything that happens in the village that he doesn't deal with. Settling down, are you?"

"Yes, yes, I am," Sara said.

"That's right! Find it a bit lonely, I daresay? Not used to country ways, I'll be bound. Why don't you come to the Women's Institute? We have quite a few young ladies who are members."

"I don't know. I hadn't thought."

"I'll take you," Mrs. Vidler said firmly. "Thursday afternoon at half-past two, down in the Hall. You don't have to make up your mind immediately. You can come along as my guest. You'd do better to come along with me, since I'm to do with the manor, than to wait for anyone else to ask you. It's as well for them to know that you have Mr. Robert standing behind you. That counts for a lot in these parts."

"What about Neil?" Sarah asked, a trifle breathless by the pace of Mrs. Vidler's conversation.

"Him? Ah, Mr. Neil is a fine young man, but he's more like his mother than a real Chaddox. It's Mr. Robert who has all the responsibility, and quite right, too!"

Sarah sipped her coffee. "I'd like to come to the Women's Institute with you," she said, "if my father is well enough to be left."

"Ay, he'll come first with you. You're a good girl, Miss Sarah. There's some of us in the village with eyes in our heads!"

Mrs. Vidler scooped up Sarah's empty cup. "Your mother sings, don't she? Do you do anything of that yourself? It's the competition, you see. We could do with a hand with that. It's not much of a choir as it stands, and that's a fact!"

Sarah felt the first stirrings of triumph rise within her. She was being accepted. She bit her cheek to stop herself from smiling.

"She's my stepmother but I'd like to help, if I can," she said aloud.

Mrs. Vidler gave her a satisfied nod. "Thought I

wasn't mistaken," she said. "We'll be needing a song. There was some talk of our doing 'O, for the wings of a dove,' but what we need is something no one heard before. You'll know all sorts of songs, I dare say. It'll give us a start to have something new to sing!" And, with these ominous words, she departed, leaving Sarah half delighted and half fearful that she couldn't possibly live up to the housekeeper's expectations of her.

She enjoyed her visit to the W.I. that Thursday. The president was a frail old lady whose hold on the meeting was decidedly shaky, but she received such ardent support from all her members that it mattered little when she dozed off in the middle of the afternoon, overcome by the lengthy discourse on wild flowers that was the highlight of the meeting. Mrs. Vidler, with a no-nonsense air about her, became the secretary and read the minutes in a loud, clear voice that made Sarah want to giggle. She sat in front of the piano to play the music for their rendering of "Jerusalem," and then found herself introduced as the person who was going to win the competition for them that Christmas.

Dazed by their kindness and the friendliness that everyone had shown her, Sarah walked home with Mrs. Vidler.

"Not much of a talk, was it?"

Sarah smiled. "I found it interesting. I know so little about the country and I don't know the names of any of the flowers."

"That one would teach her own grandmother to suck eggs! Doesn't charge much, I'll say that for her. Wouldn't ask her otherwise."

Sarah managed to say how impressed she had been with the whole meeting. "But you do so many different things!" she marveled.

Mrs. Vidler smiled her satisfaction. "A bit of everything. It's not just jam-making and remodeling old hats, as they say. Thought you'd like it. Have you thought about a song for us to sing in the competition?"

"Well," Sarah said slowly, "I was looking at Mr. Chaddox's books yesterday. There's a very old one, called Kentish Songs. It was published in 1775. I thought I'd have a look at them. The trouble is, it only gives the words and I don't know where we'd find the music."

"That wouldn't be much trouble. Mr. Neil is always playing on the piano, making up tunes."

"Then you think it's a good idea?" Sarah asked tentatively.

"I wouldn't be knowing about things like that. You get us a song, Miss Sarah, and we'll sing it for you. It's time Chaddoxbourne showed we're alive! In Mr. Robert's father's day he was always one of the judges and we were never allowed to compete because of it. The old gentleman would like us to bring home the prize all the same. Always on about the competition, he was!"

Mrs. Vidler walked with Sarah as far as her gate. "How's your father today, Miss Sarah? Seems better during the week, don't he? Maybe he does too much come Sundays, with your mother coming down to see him."

"He's very well today," Sarah answered.

"That's good! Well, I'll be seeing you in the morning. Goodbye, Miss Sarah."

"Goodbye, Mrs. Vidler."

Sarah stayed on at the manor after her work the next day, poring over the ancient collection of songs hoping to find something suitable for the competition. It was hard to concentrate on the main purpose of exploring the book, however, when there were so many gems to choose from. She tried reading them out loud, listening to the lilt of the words and imagining them being sung by an amateur choir. So intent was she on what she was doing that she didn't notice when Neil came into the study and settled himself into a chair to listen to her.

"Very nice," he commented, when she paused for breath. "I can almost believe that you're the matinee idol of the coastal resorts. Samantha says you are. We haven't seen much of her recently, have we? Robert must be seeing her in Canterbury." He grinned cheerfully. "Reckon the competition is too hot for him when I'm around?"

Sarah shook her head at him. "I doubt it."

"You don't do much to flatter my ego," Neil complained.

"Do you want me to?"

"It would make a change. What's the poetry reading in aid of? They sound as though they should be sung, not spoken."

"That's what I hope!" Sarah's eyes lit with excitement. "Neil, Mrs. Vidler says you compose a little. Would you compose a tune for one of these songs? It's for the competition."

"Good lord, have you been dragged into that? My dear girl, they'll flay you alive if Chaddoxbourne doesn't win this year!"

"They're going to win," Sarah said stubbornly. "They sing quite well."

"When have you ever heard them sing?" Neil scoffed.

"At the meeting yesterday. Neil, will you?"

"If it pleases my lady, I suppose I will. Let's have a look at the book. You know, Robert would be much more help to you than I. I tinker about on the piano, but he really knows his stuff. Does he know that you've borrowed this book, incidentally?"

"No," Sarah admitted. "He wasn't here to ask—and I haven't taken it out of this room." She stifled a qualm of nervousness at Neil's mocking expression. "Will he mind?"

"Probably."

"Oh, then perhaps we should put it back. Only it's just what I wanted! Mrs. Vidler said it would be better if the song could be a local one, and I have been terribly careful with the book."

"Really, Sarah!" Neil picked up the book and began turning over the pages. "Did I hear Mrs. Vidler calling you Miss Sarah, by the way? I hope you're properly complimented?"

Sarah looked doubtful. "Should I be?"

"Mmm, you bet! One of the family!" He smiled at her. "Not quite the prettiest member, I grant you, but I'm beginning to think one of the most interesting."

"I don't think she knows my surname," Sarah said, confused. "Neil, I think we should ask Robert before we borrow his book."

"Never! I can feel a tune coming on! Now, which one are you going to choose? Any ideas?"

"Yes," she admitted. "I was thinking of 'The Man of Kent.'" She was on the point of saying that it reminded her of Robert, but she thought better of it. "It doesn't say who wrote it, but perhaps it was one of those songs that just happened."

Neil turned over the pages and found the song. "Not bad," he approved. "I could write a tune for this fairly easily. You'd better get Mrs. Vidler to okay it before I do much work on it, though, just in case she doesn't like it. I'll ask her, if you want to get home."

"What about the others?"

Neil grinned. "Mrs. Vidler is the one who counts," he assured her.

Sarah could very well believe it. She surrendered the book of songs into Neil's hands, giving him strict instructions to ask Robert's permission for them to use it before he began composing the music.

"Why don't you stay to lunch? You could ask him

yourself and give that tender conscience of yours a rest!"

Sarah gave him a flustered look. It was two days since she had last seen Robert, but she felt that on the rare occasions when he was able to come home for lunch he should have his house to himself.

"I don't think so. I must go! My father will wonder what's happened to me!"

Neil put his hand on her shoulder, his expression kind. "Poor Sarah," he mocked her. "Does Robert know?"

"Does Robert know what?"

He touched her cheek and smiled at her. "What is written, large and clear, all over that expressive face of yours. Poor Sarah indeed! You don't stand much chance with the delectable Samantha around. Never mind, you can always fall back on Smart Alec and bury yourself in the theater."

"Oh, you!" Sarah exclaimed irritably. "You don't know what you're talking about!"

"Don't I? I think I do, but I rather wish I didn't." He turned away from her, still smiling, "I'll bring the music over when I've worked something out. We can try it out on the piano over there."

Sarah only nodded and bolted out of the room, making good her escape while she could.

THE WEATHER changed suddenly at the beginning of August. Heavy showers alternated with thin spells of sunshine, ruining the holiday season. The local farmers, who a few days before had been grumbling about the drought, were now anxious about the harvest. You can never rely on the weather, they muttered. If you thought that, you had only to look out of the window and see for yourself!

Sarah didn't mind the change in the weather as much as most of the other villagers did. She rather liked dressing up in a raincoat and stout rubber boots and walking for miles across the fields with only the rain for company. Even the occasional crack of thunder didn't worry her, though she had to confess that she didn't much like being exposed to the full brunt of a summer storm if there was any lightning about.

As the days ran into one another, she realized that she was more completely happy than she had ever been. It had been a shock to her to realize that she had fallen in love with Robert, but she didn't see very much of him and the spells of wild delight that alternated with intervals of despair, because of course he would never see her in the same way, no longer shocked her as much as they had at first. She was growing used to living from one brief meeting to another and she had even persuaded herself to believe that she didn't want any more, that the knowledge that she loved him was enough for her.

Neil brought the music for the song as he had promised, assuring her that he had sought and gained Robert's permission for them to use his book of songs. Sarah had carefully made copies of the words, propping the book up in front of her on her desk in the study at the manor. Nothing would have induced her to take the book out of the house despite Neil's assurances that nobody would ever miss it.

It was raining again when she tried out the song for her father to hear. Daniel Blaney liked to sit in the circular sitting room, watching the sun set after they had had their evening meal. Sometimes he would hardly wheeze at all and he would be tempted to smoke one of his cigars, but more often he would sit there, doing nothing at all, lost in dreams that Sarah had no share in.

"Neil has been very clever with the music," Sarah told him now. "It varies a bit with every verse, because they're all quite different."

"Why don't you sing it for me?" her father suggested.

"I'll get Madge to try it out on Sunday," Sarah smiled back at him.

Daniel coughed, drawing a deep breath and expelling it slowly through his mouth. "You're too modest. You have a pleasant voice, my dear. What's the song about?"

"It's called 'The Man of Kent.'"

"A piece of local history? Robert was telling me that the kingdom of Kent had a very interesting history, though it sounded to me as though the royal family were more interesting than anything else. They seem to have had more than their share of saints. St. Mildred was the most famous. She and her mother, Domneva, settled in Thanet, more or less where the nuns are now. They came back a few years ago—the nuns, I mean. Then there was Eanswythe of Folkestone, who founded the first nunnery on English soil, and her aunt, St. Ethelburga, who was Queen of Northumbria, who founded another nunnery a couple of years later at Lyminge, I think it was."

Sarah chuckled. "What about the men?" she asked.

"They were the villains," Daniel retorted. "It was their depravity that turned all the women into saints. There has to be something!" A quirk of humor deepened the lines on his face. "I have no idea! You'll have to ask Robert if you want to know about them."

"You've forgotten Queen Bertha, who brought Christianity and St. Augustine to England," she reminded him.

"Another female!"

"At least she converted her husband," Sarah said. "I wonder what it was like in those days, with the Danes plundering the coast and burning down the houses. It must have been rather frightening."

"Is that what your song is about?"

"Not really," Sarah answered. She went over to the piano and spread Neil's music out before her. "I'll play the music first," she said. She played through the whole of the music, delighting in the subtlety of Neil's work and the humor of the variations he had made from one verse to another.

"Well, what do you think?" she asked her father.

"I want to hear the words," he said again. "Sing it through, dear."

Sarah played the introduction again and then began to sing in her low, husky voice:

When Harold was invaded,
And falling lost his crown,
And Norman William waded
Through gore to pull him down,
The counties round, with tears profound,
To mend their sad condition,
Their lands to save, they homage paid,
Proud Kent made no submission.
Then sing in praise of Men of Kent,
All loyal, brave, and free;
Of Briton's race, if one surpass,
A Man of Kent is he.

She looked over her shoulder and saw that her father had dropped off to sleep for a moment, though as she ceased playing he immediately struggled awake again.

"Very nice, my dear," he said automatically.

"Sing it again," another voice commanded from the French window. Robert pushed open the glass door and came inside, removing his raincoat as he did so. "I missed the beginning."

Sarah turned back to the keys of the piano, her nervousness making her fingers stiff and her voice a croak. She made a false start, apologized, and began again.

"I'll play it for you," Robert said abruptly. He sat down beside her on the stool, restraining her with a strong hand as she hastily made to rise. "Neil's done a good job," he commented as he ran through the introduction. "This is the wrong key for you. Try this!"

He played it again, and rather to her surprise, Sarah managed to come in on the right note and made quite a creditable effort at singing at the first verse.

"What are you so nervous about?" Robert asked her. "You sing very well."

"Not really."

"Relax. I won't eat you even if you do sing a wrong note! Shall we go on to the second verse?"

She nodded, not daring to look at him, and waited for the music. But when he didn't begin to play, she was startled into looking up. His eyes met hers, his own full of laughter. She swallowed, feeling as though she had fallen down a precipice, and knowing that he knew exactly the effect he had on her.

"I think I'd rather stand up," she said.

"Much safer!" he agreed.

He smiled at her, giving her time to recover, and then he looked down at the music and started to play again. This time, when she sang, he joined her in a deep, gusty voice that combined with and strengthened her own.

"We make a good team," he commented as they finished the verse.

But only for singing, she reminded herself. She was no match for him when it came to anything else.

CHAPTER SIX

At hunting, and the race too,
They sprightly vigour show;
And at the female chace too,
None beats the Kentish beau.
Possessed of wealth, and blest with health,
By fortune's kind embraces,
A yeoman here surpasses far
A Knight in other places.
Then sing in praise of Men of Kent,
All loyal, brave, and free;
Of Briton's race, if one surpass,
A Man of Kent is he.

Robert broke off, laughing. "This should go down well locally!" he congratulated her. "My father would have loved it! Particularly the Kentish beau bit. He rather fancied himself with the ladies."

"Don't all the Chaddoxes?" Sarah asked demurely.

"It depends on the lady in question!" his eyes glinted dangerously as Sarah colored and edged away from him on the stool. "Tell me how you plan to dress your choir? I imagine tonal variations won't be enough for the good ladies of the village?"

"Certainly not! We're going to have part of the choir in the appropriate costume for each verse, and they'll stand in the front and make appropriate actions while that verse is in progress."

"You'll have your work cut out! Still, Mrs. Vidler says

you have a gift for this sort of thing. I believe you're enjoying it!"

"I am!" Sarah declared. "It won't be so difficult really. For instance, we'll have period English and French uniforms for the verse about Wolfe. That reminds me, I must check and see if they wore anything peculiar when they were in Canada." She made a mark on her copy of the music. "Let's try that verse," she suggested.

"Right. I'll sing it this time and you can listen. Ready?"

She nodded, very aware of his strong, muscular body beside hers. It was tempting to lean back against him and she gasped audibly when he put one arm around her and began to play again.

She scarcely dared to breathe lest she disturbed him and called attention to herself, for she couldn't believe that he wanted so close a contact. While it lasted, though, it was a wonderful moment and one she would treasure all her life long.

Augmented still in story,
Our ancient fame shall rise,
And Wolfe, in matchless glory,
Shall soaring reach the skies;
Quebec shall own, with great renown,
And France with awful wonder,
His deeds can tell, how great he fell,
Amidst his god-like thunder—

The music thundered out under Robert's strong fingers and Daniel started in his chair.

"I didn't know Wolfe was a Kentishman," he said quickly, lest anyone should notice that he had been asleep.

"Not a Kentishman, sir," Robert answered. "A Man of Kent."

"Is there a difference?"

"All the difference in the world. On this side of the Medway we're Men of Kent, on the other they're Kentishmen. Two quite different people, even if we do share a country."

"Then the kingdom of Kent was really the kingdom of East Kent?" Sarah asked him.

He grinned. "Are you disappointed that it was so small? It has a history that can compare with Wessex. They had Winchester, but we had Canterbury."

"And a parcel of saintly women!" Daniel put in wryly. "Sarah says you have some very fine books on Kent in your library. Would you object if I borrowed some of them while we're here?"

"I'll bring you over some," Robert promised. "My father began the collection, and I try to keep it up when and where I can. We have some very fine volumes. Some of them have been in the family for generations. We had more at one time, but Neil's mother sold a lot of them for ready cash."

Sarah was visibly shocked. "Without your father's consent?"

"As she pointed out," Robert said bitterly, "my father had endowed her with all his worldly goods at their wedding ceremony. Just how true that was was rammed home to us by the double dose of death duties I had to pay because she survived my father by a few hours."

"I still think that was a terrible thing to do!" Sarah went on in outraged tones. "Whatever he promised her, they weren't hers to sell! It would have been bad enough if he had sold them, but at least he was a Chaddox!"

"My dear Sarah, most wives consider they belong to their husband's family!"

"Yes, in a way. But the books were a trust for the generations to come."

"I don't think you'd find many people to agree with you!"

Daniel roused himself once more. "Why not?" he demanded. "You don't have to belong to an old family to know that they are the caretakers of our history, do you?"

Robert looked from one to the other of them. "I don't see why you should think that way. Neil doesn't; nor did his mother."

Sarah escaped his restraining arm and went and sat beside her father. "Neil's mother was in the theater," she told her father.

Daniel breathed in and out, beginning to wheeze again.

"There are good and bad in the theater, just like everywhere else," he said with difficulty.

"Not quite the same as everywhere else, sir," Robert contradicted him. "In the theater you become so accustomed to living with makebelieve that it spills over into real life. Anyone in the theater seems able to convince themselves of anything!"

"Is that really how you see us?" Sarah asked sadly.

Robert's expression softened. "I'm not sure about you," he said. "I find it difficult to believe that you ever worked on the stage."

Sarah chuckled. "Because I'm such an unglossy individual?"

He hesitated, then said curtly, "You don't pretend." He stood up and stretched himself. "I must go. Shall I give you a hand upstairs, Mr. Blaney? This sudden change in the weather has made us all sleepy, I'm afraid."

Sarah was grateful to him for his easy way of dealing with her father. She waited downstairs, listening to the sounds above as Robert helped her father into bed. Robert's hearty laughter warmed her, especially when her father's breathless chuckle joined in. She went to the foot of the stairs, wondering what on earth they could be doing. She found to her consternation that they were discussing her.

"You're a poor man if all you want is a pretty face," her father was saying.

"I'm not such a fool. What I do want is to know what lies beneath the face. A pretty face won't last a lifetime. Does any actress want a husband, home, and children, if they interfere with her career?"

"Sarah has always wanted a loving home," Daniel replied. "Unfortunately, I was never able to give her one. She's been on her own, living in digs, earning her own living without any support from either her stepmother or me, ever since she was seventeen. She deserves a little kindness."

Sarah tiptoed away, not wanting to hear any more. She didn't want Robert's kindess, or anything like it. That was the trouble, she wanted nothing less than Robert himself.

Her stepmother arrived just before lunch that Sunday. Sarah thought she looked tired and worried and did her best to cosset her all afternoon, not that Madge seemed to notice, but then she hardly had a word to say to her husband either. By teatime, Sarah was in despair at pleasing her with anything.

"How's the show going?" she asked. "We haven't heard much about it recently."

Madge Dryden shrugged delicately. "It's terrible, but they won't take it off all the while the tourist trade keeps coming." She eyed her stepdaughter through narrowed eyes. "I hear Alec Farne came down to see you and that you didn't make him very welcome. I hope you're not becoming too much of a country bumpkin?"

"I like it here," Sarah admitted.

"Yes, well, I've been thinking that you should have a

little break now and then before all your friends in London think you've forgotten all about them. Why don't you go up next weekend? I'll hold the fort for you here."

Sarah tried not to look surprised. "I don't have many friends in London," she objected. "Nobody who'd want to be bothered on a Sunday night," she added. London seemed suddenly very far away and the thought of leaving Chaddoxbourne even for one night filled her with dismay.

"Alec Farne would like to see you," her stepmother said.

"Alec? He only wanted to talk me into taking the part in his play." Sarah stirred restively. "As a matter of fact, we quarreled. I don't like him much—"

"My dear, one neither has to like or dislike people like Alec! One cultivates them!"

"Does one?" Sarah asked, amused. "I don't think I want to see Alec again."

"But you must! You won't be here forever, darling! What are you going to do then? If you think you can ignore people with as much influence in the theater as Alec Farne, you'll stay in rep for the rest of your life!"

Sarah blinked, trying to find the courage to tell her stepmother how she really felt. "I may not go back to the theater," she burst out.

"What?"

"I like living in the country." Sarah went on apologetically.

Madge was silent for a long, pregnant moment. "I'm beginning to think it was all a horrible mistake sending you down here! Alec said you had been rather unfriendly, but I didn't pay much attention. Now I'm beginning to see what he meant! However you feel about the country, why be unpleasant to him? He was very much hurt by your attitude. I'll tell him you're coming to

London next Sunday and you can apologize to him then. He's fond of you, so he'll probably forgive you, which is more than you deserve."

"I don't think it would work, mother."

"Don't be stubborn, Sarah! Really, you're quite impossible! No, don't tell me what you quarreled with Alec about. I don't want to know. I'm quite sure you were in the wrong, because he's such a reasonable person and you seem to have lost your head entirely! Live in the country indeed! What on, I'd like to know? You needn't think that I'll subsidize you for ever!"

"I don't," Sarah said, sick at heart. "I have a job with Robert Chaddox that pays for my keep. If I lived here all the time, I could find something in Canterbury, I expect."

Madge looked forlorn. "I won't hear another word! If I hear any more of this foolishness, I'll talk to your father about it! And I expect you to go to London next Sunday. You can stay at the house if you want to, or anywhere else you please, but you'll make it up with Alec, or I'll know the reason why. Is that quite clear, Sarah?"

Sarah nodded dismally. At the sound of her stepmother's car drawing up the drive, her father's face had changed to an ashen gray and the awful, forced breathing had begun again. How could she allow Madge to worry him now over her future, or anything else? She couldn't do it. She would have to go to London and explain it to Alec. There was always the chance that he would understand and leave her alone, without trying to kiss her again, or to make her change her mind and go back to the London stage.

The hours dragged by until Madge left to go back to London. Sarah felt guilty when she finally waved her goodbye and knew that she was glad to see her go. They had never had a great deal in common, but she had always been conscious of loving her stepmother before, especially since she had no memories of her own mother. Now, for the first time, she felt only a grudging worry about her father looking so tired. And that was absolutely all.

She stood by the gate for a long time after Madge had driven away. The garden was looking all the better for the rain they had had recently. Some nasturtiums she had put in were running completely wild, a mass of yellows and oranges, and even one or two in a peculiar shade of brown. Then there were tobacco plants and a sweet-smelling mock orange, as well as the usual asters, snapdragons and geraniums. Sarah found she had quite a pride of possession in the garden now and enjoyed the earnest discussions she shared from time to time with Robert's gardener.

"Hullo there!" Robert said from the other side of the gate. "You're looking pensive!"

Sarah started and smiled, very pleased to see him. "I was taking myself to task for not being better natured," she confessed. "It's too nice a place to be small-minded in."

Robert's eyebrows rose quizzically. "What are you being small-minded about?"

"My stepmother wants me to go up to London next weekend."

"And you don't want to go?"

She shook her head. "I haven't any ties in London—except Alec. And I don't want to see him."

"I see," Robert said slowly. "May I ask why?"

She stooped to pick out a weed, uncomfortably aware that she was blushing. "You said I should sort out my friendship with him," she reminded him.

"Perhaps this is your opportunity?"

"I don't think so. Alec doesn't believe in being just good friends with any female," she sighed. "But I have to go, or mother will have a long heart-to-heart with my father and he isn't strong enough to stand it just now."

She glanced up at Robert and was surprised to see he was smiling. "I don't think much of platonic friendships myself," he said. His smile turned into a laugh. "Now what in the world is there to blush about in that?"

"I don't know," she admitted, more confused than ever.

"Sarah, will you come in to Canterbury tomorrow evening and have dinner with me? I'd ask you up to the manor, but Neil is always there, and this time I want you to myself!"

"Why?" Sarah asked baldly.

His smile was very intimate. "Why? To make you blush again, of course! Will you come?"

Excitement sang in her veins, depriving her of speech. She nodded soberly, while the rich color flooded up into her cheeks.

"Come on the bus," Robert instructed her. "I'd prefer you to arrive in one piece, and I want to drive you home myself."

Sarah laughed. "I can drive quite well," she told him.

"Not when you're in a dither, my love!" His eyes twinkled irresistably at her indignation. "As you will be by the time I've finished with you!" he added and leaning forward he kissed her softly on the cheek. "Come to my office at half-past six and we'll start from there."

And long before she ran down the road to catch the bus the next evening she was in a dither. She had tried on and discarded two dresses before she settled for one in old rose silk. With it she wore a white crocheted cape that her father had given her, and it was to him that she turned to make sure that she was looking her best before she set out.

"Mrs. Vidler is going to look in later on," she told him. "You'll be all right, won't you?"

"I feel fine!" her father assured her. "You go out and enjoy yourself." He acknowledged her kiss with a puckish smile. "Robert knows how to bring out the beauty in my daughter! I've never seen you with such a glow, my dear. Don't keep him waiting!"

Sarah hovered beside his chair. "You do like him, don't you?" she brought out in a rush.

Daniel picked up the book he was reading with an air of decision. "Yes, my dear, I do. And now will you please go!"

She went. The bus was a few minutes late, which gave her time to worry about her appearance and whether she had chosen the right dress after all. Just as she was thinking of hurrying home and changing yet again, however, the bus trundled into view and she stepped on board, paying her fare to the waiting driver with shaking fingers.

Once in Canterbury, she found Robert's offices easily. The reception desk was empty, the typewriter hidden beneath its cover, giving it a deserted appearance. Sarah glanced through the few ancient farming magazines that lay on a table between some hard-looking chairs and tried to control the effervescent emotions that betrayed her usual calm. She had worse stage fright than ever before and she tried all the cures that had ever been offered to her before—little tricks of the trade like breathing exercises, sorting out the contents of her handbag, even, in despair, reciting poetry to herself like a lunatic.

She was painstakingly running through a chunk of *Hamlet*, when Robert came and found her. Sarah clutched her purse, spilling most of its contents on to the floor, and with a startled gasp, she bent down hastily to pick the things up, colliding with Robert who was bent on the same mission as herself.

"I-I'm sorry!"

He was very close to her. If he turned his head their lips would meet. Her breath caught in her chest.

"I knew you'd be in a dither," he said.

"Oh!" She bent her head quickly, searching for the elusive objects with a reckless energy that sent them far and wide.

Robert put a hand under either elbow and lifted her to her feet, pushing her gently back on the nearest chair. "Sit there," he bade her. "I'll pick them up." He did so, examining her compact with its unusual pattern on the top, spelling out her initials, before dropping it into her bag. When he was done, he looked up at her and smiled, his eyes very gray. "You'd better see if everything's there."

She swallowed, unable to tear her eyes away from his. She held out a hand for her purse, but he went on holding it himself. "You'd only drop it again," he said against her lips. "Darling Sarah, have you ever been in love before?"

She shook her head as his arms tightened about her. "Not even with Alec?" he queried.

"N-no."

"You don't sound very sure."

She shut her eyes. "I'm quite, quite sure," she told him.

"Because I won't be played with, Sarah. If we go on from here, I want to know that I have all your heart. It won't be a stop-gap arrangement between other interests, to fill in during the time at Chaddoxbourne, so don't say yes unless you mean it. I think you're honest, but I've known too many people falter and break up because one or other of them has been lost when transplanted into another background. You won't have the theater or your family to run home to every time something goes wrong between us." He touched her cheek with a stern finger. "Take your time, sweetheart. I'll wait for your answer."

"But I don't want to wait!"

"Nevertheless, I'm not going to kiss you until after we've eaten, entrancing prospect as it is. I want you to think about it when your wits aren't scattered to the four winds and your heart isn't scudding like a mad thing against mine."

"Oh, Robert," she protested. "I haven't much guile, have I?"

"I hope not."

She pulled herself free of his arms, smoothing down her hair to give her hands something to do. "I've never felt like this about anyone before." She glanced at him shyly. "I wish I were prettier and had more to offer you," she added, and then blushed.

His smile was very tender. "You're not a conventional beauty, but your face is never dull!" he teased her. "Never play poker, my pet. You look as though you've just won a million dollars, and I haven't even started on you yet!"

Her eyes misted over and a smile trembled on her lips. "What's a million dollars?" she demanded. "Robert, I think I'm going to cry!"

"Cheer up," he responded. "You'll feel better when you have some food in you. Shall we drive out into the country?"

She didn't care where they went. Clutching Robert's hand, she followed him out into the sun-filled street, hardly aware of the amused look in his eyes as he handed her into the car. He took her to Chilham, one of the loveliest villages in Kent, though Sarah told herself that she preferred Chaddoxbourne even though it hadn't quite as many old timbered houses. There was a new restaurant that had recently opened near the square where they served old-fashioned country dishes and had a wine list that vied with some of the larger restaurants in London.

"Will this do?" Robert asked her.

"Anything would taste like ambrosia tonight," she answered.

"I think I could do with something more filling myself," he smiled at her.

She laughed. "I only know it as the food of the gods. Does anyone know what it really was?"

"It's rumored to have been some kind of mushroom," he told her dryly. "And, as I didn't have much lunch—"

"Nor did I," she confessed.

"When did you last eat?" he demanded.

She couldn't remember. She supposed she must have eaten something for breakfast, but she couldn't actually remember having done so. She had made lunch for her father, but by that time she had begun to worry about what she was going to wear that evening.

"Well?" he prompted her.

"I'm not sure," she said. Her eyes lit with laughter. "If you must know, I was far too excited to eat anything! There, now I've said it, and you can laugh all you like!"

"I wouldn't dream of laughing," he denied. "But I feel enormously flattered all the same. Never mind, you can make up for it now. If we're going to be foolish, we'll be foolish together in future!"

She sat down opposite him, still unable to believe that it was all happening to her. "I can't believe it!" she exclaimed.

He looked up and his eyes met hers, making her catch her breath.

"What can't you believe? That you'll never work in the theater again?"

"No, not that! I like working for you far better anyway," she told him impulsively.

He lifted an eyebrow, enjoying her confusion. "Good," he said. "I'm used to having you around. I'd miss you if I had to write my own letters now."

Sarah's eyes dropped to her plate. "Wouldn't you miss Samantha more?"

He laughed out loud. "Can I hope that you're actually jealous of the fair Samantha?"

"A little," she admitted. "She's a joy to look at—and I'm not!"

"Little you know, my darling! I find I enjoy looking at you very much indeed. Nor have I ever felt in the least bit romantic about Samantha. I've known her all my life and I like her very much as a friend. Does that satisfy you?"

"Almost," she said. "But, Robert, doesn't that gorgeous, fiery hair give you a jolt when you see it?"

"I remember her hating it when she was ten years old! How we teased her! I'm afraid it's a case of familiarity breeding contempt, my love. I prefer the subtleties of nut-brown hair that glows in the sunlight and is as soft as silk."

It was very strange, but he seemed to mean it. Sarah watched him covertly from beneath her eyelashes as he tackled the steak and kidney pie he had ordered for them both. He had been very pleased to discover that oysters had been included in the recipe, which he could remember his mother putting in her pies when he had been a small boy.

"We must come here more often," he told her.

The idea of going anywhere with him often filled her with delight. She would have been happy to eat anything as long as she was assured of his company. But there was no doubt that the pie was excellent, and so were the raspberries and cream that followed. Robert ordered their coffee to be taken out into the garden, and putting her wrap over her shoulders, he found some white seats under a mulberry tree and suggested they settle there while they waited for the coffee to be brought out to them.

Sarah looked about her and found they were completely alone in the garden. She sat down on the nearest chair, aware that Robert was watching her, and tried not to blush.

"Well?" he asked her, so quietly that for a moment she thought she had imagined it.

She looked up, suddenly brave. "I love you, Robert," she said.

He stood over her, his hands on the arms of her chair. "Will you consider all else well lost for that love?"

She nodded. "Though I wouldn't put it quite like that," she added with a smile. "I liked my work in the theater, but it wasn't life itself!"

"And I am that for you?"

"Yes, I think you are, but I'll try not to let it become oppressive."

He smiled at that. "Don't try too hard. I find I like being the center of your interest. I haven't much time for women who want the dominant rather than the supporting role. I'm selfish enough not to want to compete for your love. I meant it when I said it would be an all-or-nothing relationship, Sarah. If you don't want that, now is the time to say so."

Sarah made a helpless gesture with her hands, wondering how to convince him. "I want it that way too," she said in a low voice.

The look on his face was more than enough reward to her for giving up her freedom and independence into his keeping.

She was wise enough to know that that was what he was demanding, and that there were to be no half measures in her giving.

"Then we may as well enjoy some of the rewards," he smiled. "I've been wanting to kiss you for quite long enough!"

His embrace was a revelation to her. His gentleness

gave way to ardor and Sarah knew a moment's fear as she gave herself up to the pressure of his arms and lips. Then the unexpected passion of her own response swamped all thought and she was aware only of their complete joy in each other.

SUNDAY WAS a sultry, stormy day. Sarah packed the things she would need for her night in London with marked reluctance. She wished that her stepmother hadn't insisted on her going, but all the arrangements had been made and she had no valid excuse for not going.

Even Robert had appeared to think it a good idea.

"You may as well go and see how the city lights look to you now!" he had teased her.

She had chuckled, for he had looked pretty confident that she would come running back to Chaddoxbourne as fast as she possibly could.

"It's such a waste of time!" she had complained.

He had put his hand on the small of her back, smiling triumphantly as she had turned immediately into his arms.

"Never mind, sweetheart. I'll drive you to the station and put you on the train. And it is only for twenty-four hours!"

It was the only nice part of the day as far as Sarah was concerned. Her father was already wheezing badly at the thought of her stepmother's visit. Indeed, he looked so ill that it caught at her heart to leave him to struggle through the weekend without her.

Robert bought her a pile of Sunday papers to read on the train and kissed her lightly on the cheek through the open window of her carriage. In the distance the thunder rumbled threateningly and the lightning flashed, making her shiver just as the train pulled away from the platform. She felt a sudden urge to fling herself out of the moving train into Robert's arms, but of course she repressed it. Instead, she sat down and crossed her legs, opening the first of the papers, and pretending to read it as the pretty scenery of Kent went flying past her.

CHAPTER SEVEN

SARAH STEPPED out of the train and began to walk along the length of platform toward the barrier. What on earth was she going to do with herself all day? She had never much cared for Sundays in London. She remembered them from her childhood as being endless, boring days, when her stepmother had spent most of the time resting in bed and her father had gone out on his own, visiting friends. Later, when she had grown up, she had found work out of London and had spent most of her Sundays by the seaside, or walking in the countryside that surrounds most of the big cities in the Midlands and the North of England.

The ticket collector took her ticket with a languid air and a faint smile. Sarah smiled back at him and then froze, for over his shoulder, she caught a glimpse of Alec Farne.

"What are you doing here?"

"Meeting you. What else?"

She regarded him suspiciously. "How did you know what time I was coming? I didn't tell anyone the time of the train."

He grinned amiably, taking her overnight bag from her. "Madge told me—only last night, unfortunately, or I would have seen to it that I was free to entertain you. As it is, I have rather a busy day ahead of me. You don't mind, do you?"

Considering the terms on which they had parted, Sarah thought it was nice of him to ask.

"Of course not!" she said. "You didn't have to meet me, you know. I quite understand that you have other fish to fry!"

"I wish I thought you minded!" he grunted. "No, that isn't quite true. But I wish we could be friends, Sarah."

"Why not?" She thought she had never liked him so well. "As long as there are no strings on either side."

He looked abashed. "To be honest, I've never felt as comfortable with any woman as I feel with you. Could it be because we're not at all in love with one another?"

Her laughter took the last awkwardness out of their meeting. "I think it might be," she said demurely. "Oh, Alec, I'm so glad! I was rather dreading seeing you again."

"Soft-hearted?"

"More likely soft-headed! I hate quarreling with anyone!"

"You're a quaint little thing," he said. "Most of us enjoy a good battle. It sharpens up our wits. Your stepmother is one of the best quarrelers in the business!"

"Oh, surely not!" Sarah protested.

"She has that reputation," Alec said with a touch of grimness. "I've never worked with her myself, so I can't say. I'm not sure I want to," he added thoughtfully.

"You won't get the opportunity!" Sarah exclaimed. "Madge is very much sought after!"

"Do I detect a touch of sour grapes?"

"Oh no!" Sarah's smile transformed her face as she thought of Robert. "I have better things to do with my time! No, I mean it. Mother is at the top and she's been there ever since I can remember., She doesn't have to look for people to work with her! She never has!"

"Very loyal!" Alec said dryly. "I'll tell you what, we'll go to her show tomorrow and you can see for yourself. Disasterville is how I'd describe it!"

"You've seen it?"

"No. I've talked with those who have. Is it a date, Sarah?"

"Well," Sarah answered, "I want to get back to the country. It would mean rushing for the train and I'd be late back. Daddy would be on his own for rather a long time."

Alec turned and faced her. "I think you owe it to your stepmother to see it," he said seriously. He smiled suddenly. "You can come along to the rehearsal of my play tomorrow morning and see what you're missing. Then I won't feel so guilty about not looking after you properly today."

"All right," Sarah said reluctantly. "Where is it?"

He told her the name of the old music hall they were using for the first rehearsals until the piece was knocked into some kind of shape. "Eleven o'clock. Don't be late, honey!"

She made a face at him. "For once, it won't matter if I am!" She held out her hand to him. "Thanks for meeting me, Alec."

"Think nothing of it! I'll put you in a taxi, okay? Or are you going by bus?"

"I'll go on the bus," Sarah sighed. "I'm not in a hurry."

The bus was a long time coming. People in the line complained that the Sunday service were getting worse and worse, and to complicate things there was another demonstration that was holding up the traffic. The only person who didn't mind was Sarah. She would willingly have put off her arrival at her stepmother's house for as long as possible. It meant nothing to her, except a long, lonely day by herself.

And so it was. Sarah made herself something to eat and wandered about the house like a lonely ghost, wondering what to do. It was evening before she decided to sort out the things that she had left in her room there over the years. There were books and treasured possessions from every stage of her life. Some she remembered with pleasure and amusement; others she had forgotten she had ever had. She had had a phase in her teens when she had spent every spare penny she had on old and rare books, and it was amongst these that she dragged out one she had indeed forgotten all about. She looked at the tooled cover with pleasure, opening it to find out what it was. *A Perambulation in Kent*, by William Lambard and dated 1570. It was not a first edition as she had secretly been hoping, but it was old enough to be valuable.

She sat on the bed for a long time, holding the book close to her. She would take it back to Chaddoxbourne with her, she decided, imagining Robert's face when she gave it to him. How it would light up, and how pleased he would be to have another volume to add to the collection Neil's mother had rifled for her own gain. Tomorrow was too long to have to wait to go home! She shot out of her room and ran down the stairs, dialing the number of the oast house. A minute later and her stepmother's voice answered sounding tired and somehow disheveled.

Madge Dryden wouldn't hear of her catching the train home.

"My dear, you're supposed to be getting a rest and having a gay time!"

"But I'm not!" Sarah said crossly. "Alec wants to see your show tomorrow," she added, "but I don't like to leave daddy on his own for such a long time."

"Daniel is almost his own self!" her stepmother insisted. "Of course you must see the show. I'll leave instructions with the box office for you to have some tickets. I want you and Alec to see it!"

"It will mean catching the last train."

"Darling, you sound like somebody's maiden aunt! It

won't kill you to have a late night for a change! I don't think living in the country is doing you any good at all!"

Sarah replaced the receiver, her mouth dry with disappointment. It was good to hear that her father was all right, though. And it wouldn't be very long before she would be home again and in Robert's arms.

THE OLD MUSIC HALL had once been a handsome building. Relics of its Victorian grandeur could still be seen in the faded decorations and the velvet curtains that hung in dusty shreds on either side of the stage. Most of the seats had long since gone, or had collapsed with old age. Those left were huddled together in the center of the auditorium, as though they were ashamed of their shabby appearance and were seeking a mutual anonymity in the gloomy darkness. The chandeliers had long since fallen from the ceilings and most of the footlights no longer worked.

Sarah sat in one of the seats, trying to pretend to herself that she was not bored. For a mad moment, when she had first come in, she had thought that the old longings to be performing herself would overcome her. But nothing of the sort had happened. She had watched the actors walk their way through the first act, their scripts still in their hands, and her mind had begun to wander almost immediately.

"No, no! Try it again! Take it from the cue, Jacqueline!" Alec's voice recalled Sarah to the rehearsal and she winced in sympathy with the unknown Jacqueline. "Which cue? My dear girl, the last cue!"

Jacqueline began again, the young man beside her shooting darts of rage at her.

"I *can't*!" the poor girl exclaimed. "He puts me off!"

"You're telling me you can't!" Alec said in an audible undertone. He cleared his throat menacingly. "Nor can a professional actress allow herself to be put off by other members of the cast. You're not doing amateur dramatics now!"

The girl, far from pulling herself together, dissolved into tears. Alex ground his teeth and the girl cried harder.

"You all hate me! None of you wanted me to have the part! Why didn't you choose someone else, if you don't like the way I do it?"

"I did," Alec said.

Jacqueline stopped crying for a minute, staring at him across the footlights. "And I suppose everyone else knew all the time!" she declared.

"I did choose someone else, and as a matter of fact, she's here, watching you. Sarah, go up and show this little creature what she should sound like, would you?"'

Sarah sank further into her chair, hoping that he wasn't serious.

"Sarah!"

The peremptory tone brought her to her feet. "It wouldn't do any good, Alex," she whispered fiercely. "She's nervous."

"And you wouldn't be?"

"Yes, of course I would be. I'd be paralyzed with fright, especially if you spoke to me like that! Why don't you use a little kindness?"

He turned on her. "Any rights you had in a say in this production you lost long ago!" he stormed at her. "You forfeited having an opinion the moment you decided to give way to the frivolous satisfaction of feeling virtuous about your father! Unfortunately, you have more idea of what the author intended in your little finger than Jacqueline has in her whole body, so get up on that stage and show her what it's all about, or I'll make mincemeat out of the two of you!"

Sarah tumbled up the stairs on to the stage, deciding it

was the lesser of the two evils. Jacqueline handed her the script, her tearful face blotched and ugly in the wreathed lights that were all that the building provided. "I thought he was a friend of yours," she remarked. "Rather you than me!"

Sarah was beginning to think so too. "Perhaps it's the way he works...."

"Shut up whispering, you two! All right, get on with it, Sarah!"

It was queer how the old magic came flooding back, taking control of her mind and body. The way of walking that kept her in the center of attention without blotting anyone else out; the way of speaking that made her voice carry effortlessly to the back of the hall; even how to stand still and register emotion while another was speaking. She took a deep breath, smiled at the young man who had given her her cue, and began to read the part.

It was just as it had always been. Nothing else was real except the part she was playing until she came to the end of the scene. Sitting in the auditorium she had felt nothing at all, but actually being on the boards again pulled her, making her give the best performance of which she was capable.

"And you want to throw it all away!" Alec shouted at her in disgust.

She blinked at him. "Yes," she said. "Yes, I want to give it all up!"

"Tell that to the marines!"

Sarah handed the script back to Jacqueline, her smile lighting her face. "I want much more than this," she told him, her voice husky with emotion. "I want an ordinary life, with a husband and children."

"You can't! You'd be bored stiff without any challenge."

She silenced him with a gesture. "I think I'll find loving someone challenge enough."

Alec looked at her for a long moment. "I don't know whether to envy you, or brand you traitor!" he said at last. He turned back to Jacqueline. "Think you have the idea now? Then could we trouble you to run through the scene again—just as Sarah did it? With expression, my dear! You'll find, if you take a look, that you're made of flesh and bone, not solid wood! Though we might be forgiven for thinking you were!"

Sarah returned quietly to her seat. The magic had gone as suddenly as it had come. Well, it wasn't surprising. She had spent years diligently acquiring the art of how to appear on the stage. It was unlikely that the knowledge would ever leave her now. It was a part of her, like the school she had been to and the friends she had made. But it wasn't the future, and she was glad of that. The future was Robert and therefore glorious!

She glanced down at her watch. Only twelve more hours to go.

ALEC CAME OUT to St. John's Wood to pick up her in his car for the theater that evening. Sarah was put out to see him in a dinner jacket. "I didn't bring any evening wear with me," she told him. "I really meant to catch an earlier train back."

"I hope you don't expect me to go home and change?"

"No, of course not! Only I feel uncomfortable not being properly dressed. Never mind, while you get the tickets, I'll slip around and ask Madge how daddy is. She said she'd leave the tickets at the box office in your name. It will be quite dark in the theater and we can always pretend that we're not together!"

"Strangers in the dark? It sounds fascinating!" he said sarcastically. "If your father wasn't all right, don't you think Madge would have told you? I wish you wouldn't play the role of the Lady with the Lamp quite so enthusiastically! I could have wept when you read that scene this morning and I knew you were never going to do it!"

"Goodness!" said Sarah.

Something in her tone made him look at her quickly. "Are you laughing at me?" he demanded.

"Only a little," she apologized. "You were so beastly to that poor girl this morning you don't deserve to get a performance out of her!"

"I didn't!" he said moodily. "I don't think I ever will!"

"You will, when she gets used to your snapping at her all the time."

"She's not you!"

Sarah giggled openly. "Thank goodness she's not!"

"I believe you really mean that!"

"I do." Even to her own ears she sounded complacently happy at the prospect of giving up her career forever. In fact she was feeling vastly more cheeful than she had all day—only a few more hours and she would be back in Chaddoxbourne!

The theater was only fairly full. Sarah was surprised at that. She had thought that everything in London was packed, but then it was Monday night and that was not a day that many people came in from the suburbs to see a show. Her stepmother had left them tickets at the box office, bang in the middle of the stalls. That was another sign, Sarah thought, that the play was not being the commercial success that Madge Dryden was accustomed to.

When the curtain went up she saw why. There was no applause to greet the set. Perhaps it was too modern to appeal, with great splodges of colour supposed to represent the sky and the countryside. Such an approach was out of keeping with the simple little story that ran through the music and dancing. And the tunes were sickly sweet and very ordinary. This in an era of experimentation, when people like Burt Bacharach were trying nine or eleven to the bar, and found the old eight, sixteen, thirty-two boring with its constant repetition.

Madge Dryden was the heroine, a young girl who had fallen in love with a man twice her age. As a piece of casting it was a disaster. The man was years younger than her stepmother, and worse still, he looked it. Sarah watched in an agony of embarrassment and wished she hadn't come. It was some years since she had seen Madge in anything, and then she had been as fresh and light as thistledown. Now there was a touch of desperation in her performance. There was too much of everything—too much makeup, too many flounces on her dresses, and far too many pretty little songs that made her look pathetic rather than touching.

As the lights came up for the first intermission, Sarah and Alec exchanged speaking glances.

"Well, well," said Alec dryly.

"She's miscast," Sarah put in quickly.

"You don't say! Even so, not what I would expect from Madge Dryden. The sooner she gets herself out of this the better!"

"I expect they have tied her up pretty tightly in her contract. My father seems to think so. And those awful sets! No wonder he was so upset about not doing them!"

Alex helped her out of her seat, shaking his head at the curtained stage. "Do you want to go around and have a word with her?"

Sarah nodded. She knew that her stepmother had no costume change in the first intermission, because it was then that she often phoned Chaddoxbourne to find out how Daniel was. In the second intermission, she had a complete change and consequently less time to chat.

The whole cast seemed to be assembled in the corridors backstage. Their costumes flashed brilliantly against the somber paintwork that was always such a contrast to the front of the theater. The Catholic Theatre Guild was advertising for support for a party they were giving in aid of some charity. The disembodied voice came over the intercom, repeating the message again and again. Madge's dressing room had her name on the door, which was firmly shut against the clamor and laughter that was going on outside.

Sarah knocked on the door, barely waiting for her stepmother's answer before she rushed in.

"Was daddy really all right when you left?" she asked.

Madge looked astonished. "Of course he was. Dear, please don't fuss! How are you enjoying the show?"

Sarah hesitated. She looked at Alec, but he was examining his already immaculate nails.

"I can't think why you agreed to it!" she burst out awkwardly. "Madge, it's awful!" She broke off, dismayed at the expression on Madge's face. "I'm sorry, but it is. It isn't you, is it?"

"What do you mean?"

Sarah swallowed. "It's too young for you."

"How dare you!" her stepmother snapped. "You're taking it out of me because you didn't want to come! I think you're mean!"

"She's quite right," Alec said brutally. "You should have left after the first rehearsal, Madge. However, I doubt it'll last more than a few weeks. You'd be wise to look more closely at your next part."

Madge sank down on the stool in front of the dressing table. She looked old and raddled in the harsh light from the naked electric bulbs. Over her head bobbed a roll of soft toilet paper that she used for wiping off her makeup and behind her was a clutter of powder and paint and an abandoned wig that was badly in need of being restyled.

"You're quite right. I've been miserable about it for ages! I've even more miserable now you've confirmed that it's a ghastly failure! You'll both have to come out to supper with me afterward and cheer me up!"

"But, Madge, I can't! I'll miss the last train."

"Rubbish, darling. Alec will take you to the station in his car and we'll all keep our eye on the time. You have got plenty of time."

Sarah bit her lip. "I haven't! Truly, Madge. I'd feel much happier if I didn't. Daddy has been poorly recently on Monday nights."

"After my visits, you mean! Why don't you say so?"

"I didn't mean that!" Sarah said wretchedly, well aware that that was exactly what she had meant. "But it would be awful if I missed the train!"

Alec put a comforting hand on her shoulder. "I'll make sure that you make the train. You can rely on me, can't you?"

"I suppose so," Sarah sighed. "But I'd really rather not!"

"Well, darling, I think you might consider me for once," Madge complained. "I'm sure my need is much greater than your father's! He is in the pink of health and I'm perfectly miserable!"

"Oh, all right," Sarah said reluctantly.

Madge gave her a sardonic look. "Don't let your enthusiasm run away with you!" she drawled.

The musical comedy dragged toward its close, with neither Sarah nor Alec paying much attention to what was going on on the stage.

"I wish you'd backed me up about going straight to the station," Sarah said in the second intermission.

Alec shrugged. "Your stepmother looked all set to throw a scene if I had. Whatever I may think of this wretched story, she has to get through it. I'd never do anything to put an artist off during a performance."

It sounded so virtuous, Sarah thought, but what about her? The last thing she wanted was to have to sit through supper with her stepmother when she could have been going home.

The restaurant was within walking distance of the theater. Madge ordered champagne, which none of them much cared for, and made light of Sarah's anxious scanning of the menu in her search for something quick and easy.

"Relax, darling. Alec won't let you miss the train!" Madge looked across the table and winked at Alec. "Not that he'd object if you missed it, I'm sure! You must tell me what you two have been doing over the weekend."

"There's nothing to tell," Sarah said.

"I was busy all day yesterday," Alec let out apologetically. "But we made up for it this morning, Sarah came to one of my rehearsals and saw some of the things I have to put up with."

"Some of the things your players have to put up with, you mean!" Sarah retorted.

Madge quelled her stepdaughter with a glance. "Do you ever produce or direct musical comedies?" she asked Alec.

"I never have. I may do in the future." Their eyes met, and to Sarah's surprise, it was her stepmother who looked away. "I don't think a musical play can get away with a bad story these days," he went on. "There's no future in the second-rate and wishful thinking."

They went on talking about the difficulties of bringing any show to the London stage, how expensive it was, and how things had changed since the provincial theater had begun to come to life again in the last few years. Sarah ate her food in silence, longing to be gone. She looked at her watch a dozen times, but when neither of the other two paid any attention to the time, she stood up.

"I'll have to go!"

To her surprise, her stepmother flashed her a radiant smile and rose too. "We'll take you to the station and come back, my dear. You don't mind, do you, Alec?"

"Not at all," he said politely.

He went to get the car while Madge and Sarah stood on the edge of the pavement and waited. He was a long time gone, though, and Sarah was really worried by the time the car drew in beside them.

"You sit in the front, darling," Madge suggested. "It will be nicer for Alec!"

Sarah was in such a hurry to get out of the car that she opened the door before it had stopped and almost fell as she jumped out, already running for the train.

She was vaguely aware of Alec following her, carrying her bag.

"Sarah, come back!" he yelled to her.

But Sarah was running hard now. She flung herself against the barrier just as it began to close against her.

"You can't go on the platform now!" the ticket collector told her.

"I must!" she cried out. "I *must*!" She flung herself against the iron gates again, but the gates were shut solidly against her. It was the last straw. Sarah put her hands on the iron bars and burst into tears.

"You've missed it," Alec said behind her.

"What am I going to do?" Sarah sobbed.

He turned her to face him, catching her tears with his forefinger. "Is it such a tragedy? Madge says your father is quite all right. You can catch the first train down in the morning. Your father will be asleep by now anyway. He'll hardly know the difference."

"I suppose not," she said pathetically. "But oh, Alec, I wish I'd caught that train! I should never have agreed to have supper after the theater!"

"You didn't," Alec reminded her. "Come on now, Sarah. Do you know the time of the first train in the morning?"

She nodded. Once she had started to cry it was very difficult to stop. The tears flowed down her face, making her self-conscious in the lights of the station, and so she turned her face into Alec's jacket and allowed him to lead her away, out of the station and back to his car.

THE TAXI that took her to the station in the morning was early. Sarah got into the back seat hugging her bag to her, as they traveled through the almost empty London streets.

"Going home with the milk?" the driver teased her.

"I missed the last train last night."

"Bad luck. Actually you're more likely to find the newspapers on the train than the milk. Still, so long as it gets you there, eh, miss?"

"Yes," said Sarah.

The train stopped at every halt on the way down. Sarah found herself willing it to go faster, but it trundled along in its own time, emitting a series of thuds and thumps every time it stopped. At times she thought it would be quicker to walk.

Canterbury Station was deserted. Sarah phoned a taxi and asked him to take her to Chaddoxbourne.

"We're short-staffed early in the morning, madam," she was told. "It will be a few minutes. Will you wait?"

Reflecting that she had little choice in the matter, Sarah said she would. She went outside to wait for the taxi, standing in the mild sunlight and listening to the morning chorus from the birds. She didn't have long to wait and she climbed into the car with a sigh of relief. She had hardly slept at all during the night and her eyes felt sandy from lack of sleep.

She sat forward when the taxi turned off the main road for Chaddoxbourne. The first sight of the village never failed to delight her, and on this particular morning, she thought it had never looked prettier. The church was golden from the early morning sunlight, and the mill stood out in silhouette, with the freckled water going by.

They drew up in front of the oast house without stopping, for the gates stood wide open. Sarah jumped out of the taxi and paid the driver too quickly, spilling a few coins on the drive. For some reason this reminded her of Robert and a great longing to see him welled up within her.

The taxi drove off, and at last Sarah went inside the oast house, willing herself to be sensible and not to give way completely in the face of her relief at being home. She shut the front door behind her and wandered slowly into the sitting room to draw back the curtains and let the sun into the room. As she entered, she saw someone sitting there and leaped to the conclusion that it was her father.

"Daddy?"

But it was not her father. It was Robert. He stood up slowly, his face as bleak as granite.

"Where have you been?" he asked her.

CHAPTER EIGHT

"WHERE HAVE you been?"

Sarah started toward him, but something stopped her. It was only then that she realized that he was bitterly angry.

"What's happened?" she whispered.

"You may well ask! I hope you enjoyed your night out?"

"You know I didn't! It was awful. I missed the last train, but it wasn't my fault—truly it wasn't! Robert, you must believe me!"

The look in his eyes was contemptuous. "Nicely played!" he applauded.

She faced him bravely, only just preventing herself from bursting into tears. It had been bad enough having to spend the night in London, without having him look at her like that! What did he think she had been doing, waiting for the first train home that morning? And why, oh, why did he have to condemn her for that?

"What's the matter, Robert?"

"Need you ask? Do you really need to ask?"

"I can't know unless you tell me," she pointed out.

His lips curled. "You do it very well, Sarah Blaney, but you can't hope to take me in a second time. I told you it was all or nothing as far as I'm concerned. The choice was yours. You've chosen nothing. That's all there is to it. Not such a big tragedy, is it?"

"But what am I supposed to have done?"

He looked really angry at that and she was afraid for

the first time. A cold hand of fear clutched at her as she saw her happiness slipping through her fingers for no reason that she could see.

"Where were you last night?" he demanded again. "Doesn't that tell you in itself? You were unlucky, Sarah. You had every right to expect that I would never know, but by that one chance in a hundred I did."

"Know what?"

"Oh, what's the good of going on about it? I have no inclination to hold an inquest on what might have been!"

Sarah clenched her fists. "I think you owe it to me to tell me what I'm supposed to have done," she insisted doggedly. Her eyes reflected her agony as she stared at him out of a pale and weary face. "I knew you were a hard man," she went on, "but I never thought you'd be unjust."

"Unjust? If you only knew! I spent the greater part of the night trying to think of some excuse for you, but there isn't one! You were seen, Sarah. It's that simple!"

"Seen doing what?"

"Oh, very well, if you must have it, you'd better sit down. Did you see your stepmother last night?"

Sarah nodded. "I saw her show. She insisted on having supper afterward. I didn't want to, but she made it impossible for me to go on refusing. That's how I missed the train."

He whipped around, and for a moment, she thought he was going to strike her.

"Don't lie to me, Sarah! Let's end it with dignity!"

"But I don't want to end it!"

"You should have thought of that last night!"

Sarah sank down on the very edge of the sofa, feeling that her legs were unable to support her any longer. "I didn't want to stay in London! I was counting the hours until I could get back here—to you!"

"In Alex Farne's company?"

"He was there, yes. My stepmother asked him to supper, too."

"For heaven's sake, Sarah! I saw Madge yesterday too, don't forget! She was distraught when she left here. In fact she wouldn't have gone at all if I hadn't said I'd stay here with your father. We both expected you to be home within an hour or so. And then you tell me that she asked you out to supper!"

Sarah's face was whiter than ever. "How is dad?"

"He's still alive," he said brutally. He saw her wince and his expression softened a little. "He's better than he was. I had the doctor look at him and he gave him a shot to make his breathing easier. But his heart is bad, Sarah. Very bad. He can't go on like this, but you know that, don't you?"

"You mean he's going to die," she said tonelessly.

He nodded slowly. "It has to happen sooner or later. Yesterday was a terrible day for us all. Your stepmother was in a dreadful state, for she'd never seen him having an attack like that before. I thought she was going to collapse when she realized how ill he was. She's a very brave woman!"

"Isn't she?" Sarah said with gentle mockery in her quiet voice.

The sympathy that she had glimpsed in his face died and his expression was as hard as ever. "You weren't here," he said unanswerably. "You can't know what she went through."

"I saw her in London," Sarah reminded him. "I went around to speak to her in the intermission and she said that Dad was quite all right. 'In the pink' was the expression she used." She was silent for a long moment, then she added inconsequentially, "She ordered champagne for dinner."

"I don't believe you!"

"Alec took me to the station, but they closed the barrier just as I arrived and they wouldn't let me through."

"Yes, I know. You must have been very disappointed. Disappointed enough to allow Alec to console you by embracing you in public and leading you off arm in arm to his car—*and then where*?" He shrugged. "Wherever it was, it was enough for you both to be overcome with joy!"

"Who told you that?" Sarah demanded. "Some troublemaker tells you something like that and you prefer to believe them rather than me? Perhaps, after all, it is as well if we think again!"

"I'm sure Alec will think so!"

Sarah lifted her head proudly. "Unworthy!" she declared.

"Perhaps. I am not as adept at hiding my feeling as you are. Nor was it some troublemaker, as you put it. It was Neil who saw you."

"Then why on earth didn't he say anything to me?"

Robert laughed harshly. "You were otherwise engaged," he reminded her.

"I see," she said. "And so I'm already condemned and cast off without your even listening in to what I have to say."

"Cast off?" he mocked her. "Your taste for the dramatic is unfailing. I can't imagine why I didn't see it before!"

"And your lack of trust is despicable!" she flared back at him.

"An ill-matched pair!" he agreed dryly.

"Oh, you're impossible! I don't even like Alec!" Her voice broke and she swallowed hard. "But even if I did, I couldn't have left dad."

"That sticks in my gullet too. I've been saying to myself over and over again that whatever you really felt about me, I'd have sworn on my own life that you were sincerely concerned about Daniel. That was truly unforgivable!"

"Yes, it was. But not on my part, whatever you believe. And just in case you're interested, I spent the night at my stepmother's house. You can ask her if you don't believe me!"

"I'm not interested."

The finality of those three icy words struck her like a blow. "Then there's nothing more to say, is there?"

"No."

But, even though she knew it would do no good, she felt obliged to make one more try to tell him the truth.

"Robert, I can explain."

He ran his hand through his hair, looking very tired and defeated in a way that hurt her even though she knew he was doing it to himself, that she hadn't betrayed him.

"I can't stand any more lies," he said at last. "Lies breed very easily, Sarah. Tell one, and before you know where you are you're enmeshed in them. The best thing is not to tell them. I saw your stepmother yesterday and I know she was beside herself with grief and worry. The last thing she would have done would have been to have kept you in London quite unnecessarily to see a show she didn't care a button about beside your father. But even then I might have given you the benefit of the doubt, because I thought you cared for him too. But Neil effectively finished that. I told you that I wouldn't play second fiddle, to keep you entertained in the country until you could get back to London, and I meant it. You'd better go up to your father and see what you can do for him now you are here. Me, I'm going home to breakfast before I start work in Canterbury."

Sarah rose to her feet, ashamed that her knees were still trembling. With as much dignity as she could summon, she escorted him to the door, head held high.

"Thank you for looking after my father," she said formally. "And, Robert, whatever you may think, I don't tell lies. Perhaps one day you'll find that out." She chewed on her lip, shocked by the cold anger that gripped her. "I'm sorry it had to end this way."

She closed the door quickly before her cool deserted her. He had gone and there was nothing left. It was a curious sensation to be dead inside and yet to have to go on living.

Perhaps, later on, she would cry her eyes out and come alive again.

But she doubted it. She doubted if she would ever feel anything ever again.

FACING HER FATHER was another hurdle she had to take before she could go to bed. When she went into his room he was still asleep, his heavy breathing creaking noisily. His ashen face looked unbelievably tired and lined against the pillow. Sarah stood beside the bed and looked down at him for a long moment, her thoughts bitter. That her stepmother was capable of leaving her husband at such a time, she had always known, though she had never admitted to the knowledge. But why? Why did she do it?

She became aware of her father's eyes on her and smiled at him in answer to his own painful attempt.

"Madge was here, wasn't she?" he said.

Sarah nodded. "Yes, she was here."

His face twisted into a grimace that hurt her to the quick. "She didn't stay?"

"It was Monday, dad. She had to get back to London. The show has to go on!"

He shut his eyes. "My show is nearly done. I'm glad of it. You've been a great comfort to me, Sarah, but there are times when a man has need of his wife."

"Hush," she whispered. "Try and sleep."

"Sleep! I could sleep forever, and I probably will!"

Sarah bit her lip. "Oh, dad! Please don't!"

"I'm sorry, love."

She held his hand in silence, listening to his wheezing breath and wishing she could do something, anything, to ease him.

"What time is it?" he asked at last.

She told him. "I missed the last train home. I'm terribly sorry, daddy. Madge asked me to see the show."

"She would!"

"It was ghastly, Alec Farne told her that she would have to be doubly careful before she chose her next part. I don't think she liked it very much."

Her father breathed deeply. "How were the sets?"

"Modern! Splodges of color and very little else. Some of them were badly built as well."

"I thought so!" He seemed to derive a certain satisfaction from contemplating what they were like from her description. "And Madge?"

Sarah stood like a rock. "She was awful too, dad. She's too old to take the part of a teenager. Her leading man is years younger than she is, and he looked it."

Daniel sighed heavily. "Well, it's not worse than we already knew. What are you looking so miserable about?"

"Dad, I wouldn't have left you on your own for anything!"

"I know that. It was Madge."

In a second she was on her knees beside the bed, her hand still in his, her face crumpling at the love she read on his.

"Robert doesn't believe me! He thinks I stayed up deliberately to be with Alec. Daddy, I don't know what to do!"

His heavy breathing contracted her heart and she felt doubly guilty for pushing her own unhappiness on to him. He should be sleeping, not listening to her babbling about something that couldn't be altered. One day she would grow used to the prospect of life without Robert. She had to!

"Robert...is too good a bloke...to bear a grudge for long. He'll come around, darling. He doesn't know Madge. We do. She'll give herself away—when she thinks she's got her own way!"

"Oh, dad! Madge isn't like that!"

"Madge is herself. I've...loved her many years, but still...she left me!"

"And I wasn't here!" Sarah wailed.

"You couldn't help it." Her father broke off, breathing jerkily in an effort to relieve his laboring lungs. "Tell me what else you did. You saw Alec Farne?"

"I went to one of his rehearsals. A girl called Jacqueline has the part I was going to have. He shouts at her all the time, and the poor girl has no confidence at all. At one point, he made me read a scene in front of her, to show her how it should go. It was rather brutal. I'm glad I'm out of it. Whatever happens, I don't think I want to go back to the theater. Will you mind?"

Daniel shook his head. "I always knew that you would choose a person in the end. I did, and your own mother did too. Only your stepmother did not."

"It's so unfair!"

Daniel attempted a chuckle. "Some people manage both to love...and have a demanding career. Must one...criticize because someone isn't...big enough for both?"

"I suppose not," Sarah agreed. But it did seem unfair all the same. Why should her father have spent so many years loving her stepmother with such little reward? And why should her stepmother carelessly reach out and ruin her life, without any reason, but just because it suited her to do so?

"I think I'll sleep now," her father told her. "Don't be too... unhappy, my dear. Robert is a fine... man, and a worthy person to love, even if it... never works out!"

"Yes, he is, isn't he?" she said. "But it hurts that he thinks so badly of me. Never mind, dad. We'll both survive, and we have each other!"

Daniel nodded, closing his eyes. "Bless you," he whispered.

Sarah had thought that she wanted to sleep herself, but now she knew that she wouldn't sleep a wink. The sight of the worn-out shell of her father made her think that she hated her stepmother, but she knew she didn't. Her father was right as always. How could you hate someone for not being what you wanted them to be? It wasn't Madge's fault that she wasn't a dowdy, loving, maternal body. But it wasn't that that Sarah was bitter about, she reflected sadly. It was because her stepmother had shown herself to be unworthy, and she was suddenly passionately glad that Robert was such a different kind of person. He might never forgive her; he might never find out the truth about her, but at least she would never feel ashamed of having loved him with all her heart and being.

She went out into the garden. The rain had brought on a new crop of weeds and the pansies needed attention. It was good to have her fingers back in the soil.

What better than a garden to give one back one's perspective?

She had hardly begun her self-appointed task of weeding the bed by the drive, though, when Mrs. Vidler came walking by and leaned on the gate to have a chat, seeing that neither of them were doing anything in particular.

"We missed you at the rehearsal of the song, Miss Sarah," she began cheerfully. "Mr. Neil came along and played the piano for us, but it wasn't the same without you. I hear your father's not too well."

"Neil played the piano for you?" Sarah repeated, puzzled. "I thought he was in London?"

"Not he! Very particular he is about that music of his. One or two of the ladies were on the point of telling him where he got off with those fancy ideas of his. But then we knew you'd be back soon enough!"

"But, Mrs. Vidler, are you sure that Neil wasn't in London?"

"Sure as I'm standing here. We had the rehearsal in the village hall, beginning at seven o'clock, and we were all there. Nothing suited him, though! The acoustics were bad, and our voices are worse! It was a lively evening, I can tell you!"

Sarah went back to her weeding. "Did it go on for long?"

"Quite long enough!" Mrs. Vidler peered over the gate to see what Sarah was doing. "Don't you take out that columbine, Miss Sarah! That ain't no weed, I'll have you know!"

"Oh," said Sarah, "isn't it?"

Mrs. Vidler sniffed. "You're no better than a child, Miss Sarah, let loose in the garden. You mind what you're doing!"

"I'll try," Sarah agreed meekly.

Mollified, Mrs. Vidler changed her basket from one hand to the other, plainly reluctant to leave. "Had the doctor to your father, I hear?"

"He was sent for last night. He's coming again this morning."

"Thought he might be. Saw his car in the village, and there's no one else who's sick, so far as I know."

Sarah looked up. "My father had a very bad day yesterday," she said abruptly.

Mrs. Vidler nodded. "A good thing you had Mr. Robert to stand by you. Near everyone in the village has had cause to be grateful to him some time or other. Why,

Miss Sarah, you're crying! Now, dearie, don't take on so! Is he that bad? It won't do him a might of good for you to be shedding tears!"

"No, I know," Sarah sniffed. "I'm so sorry, Mrs. Vidler. I'm rather tired, that's all. And Robert *was* very kind yesterday!"

"Ay, he would be, and not only because he thought he should be, if I'm any judge. He has his eye on you, I'm sure of that."

"Mrs. Vidler, I don't think you should say things like that," Sarah interrupted her hastily.

"Mebbe not. But I'll say this, Samantha isn't going to be pleased when she sees how the land lies. Just thought I'd warn you, Miss Sarah. Now I mustn't let you keep me standing here when I have so much to do! Mr. Robert is back to lunch today, but I don't suppose you'll be over to do his typing, will you?"

Sarah shook her head. "I can't leave my father."

Mrs. Vidler went on up the road. Sarah sat back on her heels and watched her go. Oh well, Samantha would have less to worry about in the future! But she was glad that she wouldn't be able to go over to the manor for some days to come, especially if she was going to go on bursting into tears when anyone mentioned Robert.

The doctor came soon after. Surprisingly, he looked strangely like Robert. Sarah looked at him with a feeling of outrage that must have shown clearly on her face, for he laughed.

"I'm his cousin," he explained. "Strange how these things happen, isn't it? I look like Robert's brother, and Neil and he have nothing in common at all."

"Then you're Dr. Chaddox?"

"Dr. Fairfield. We're related on his mother's side."

"Oh, then it isn't so strange really," Sarah found herself saying. "I mean, Robert must have been like his mother."

"A little bit. I was pretty angry with him last night, Miss Blaney. I should have been called in much sooner, you know. There are drugs that can help your father breathe more easily. It doesn't do his heart any good to be left to struggle for hours. You knew his heart was bad?"

"No, I didn't," Sarah said. "Robert told me when I got back."

The doctor nodded, his shrewd eyes studying her face. "Robert said he'd been left in charge. You had to go to London, did you?"

"My stepmother was here," Sarah told him.

"Really? I didn't realize that Mrs. Blaney was here with you too. I had the idea that your parents were living apart, or that your mother—stepmother—was dead?"

"No. My stepmother is in the theater."

"Well, she should be told, Miss Blaney. All we can hope to do for your father is to make him more comfortable when he gets one of these attacks, and to do all we can to remove the emotional anxieties and pressures that bring that asthma on. We can't give him a new heart, or the will to go on living."

"How long...." Sarah broke off hopelessly. "It's a silly question, I suppose. But he looks so terribly tired!"

"So would you if you'd been straining for breath for hours together. Now, I want you to think hard, Miss Blaney. Have you noticed any pattern of events preceding these attacks?"

Sarah looked guilty. "Not really," she stammered.

"When his wife comes?"

Sarah nodded unhappily. "Anything to do with the theater. He wasn't able to design the sets for my stepmother's present show and that seemed to upset him. I don't think he ever had asthma before. But I didn't live at home and I hadn't seen very much of him recently, not until we came down here."

"I see." Sarah was glad that Dr. Fairfield didn't go on about it. She thought that he probably understood better than anyone else of her acquaintance how it had been for her father. "I'll go up and see him now. I'm going to give him another injection and then we'll hope he sleeps for the rest of the day. You won't be going out, will you, Miss Blaney?"

Sarah's eyes widened. "No, no, of course not!"

The doctor smiled. "Don't look so worried," he said gently. "You'll have him a little while yet. But call me the moment he starts another attack, won't you? I'll come at once—even if it's in the middle of the night!"

"Thank you," said Sarah. "And thank you for being so kind."

The doctor's smile grew bigger. "I imagine you're pretty easy to be kind to!" he rallied her. "Are you coming up with me?"

She stood by her father's bed while the doctor carried out his examination and gave him an injection which acted like magic on his stertorous breathing, bringing relief and a smile to Daniel Blaney's face.

"Good of you to come, doctor," he said throatily.

Dr. Fairfield patted his shoulder with a smile. "You'll do now, Mr. Blaney. Try and eat some lunch, but don't be disappointed if you don't feel hungry for a while. You're lucky to have such a charming nurse!"

"Yes, Sarah will look after me."

The doctor ran lightly down the stairs, barely pausing in the hall as he said, "Don't forget, call me any time! Otherwise, I'll be back in the morning. And cheer up, he's looking much better already!"

Sarah stood in the doorway and half waved as the doctor got into his car and drove off down the road. He might look like Robert, she thought, but his driving was quite different. He had an urgent, aggressive manner at the wheel that was quite in contrast to Robert's smooth perfectionism. But she wished he looked a little less like Robert. She didn't want to be reminded of him for a long time to come.

Her father had some soup for lunch which she had made herself. She had discovered the value of having a stockpot to which she could add bits of this and that for flavor. It was one of the many things she had learned from the Women's Institute. Realizing she had had nothing for breakfast, she added an egg to her bowl of soup and took it out into the garden to eat while she read the morning paper. She liked to sit in the orchard, where no one could overlook her, and where she could see the fruit growing on the trees.

When she went into the orchard, however, she found Neil sitting on the gate she shared with the manor. He watched her moodily as she set her lunch out on the wicker table under an apple tree.

"Care for a game of tennis this evening?" he asked her.

"I don't like to leave my father," she answered.

He swung himself over the gate and came and sat down opposite her. "That soup smells good!"

Sarah grinned at him. "Would you like some?"

"No thanks. Mrs. Vidler has given me urgent instructions to be on time for lunch to keep Robert company—as if he cares one way or the other! But I feel obliged to stay on the old girl's right side. Those harridans gave me quite a roasting at the rehearsal yesterday. Quite honestly, Sarah, I'm glad you're doing it and not me! They don't have a clue!"

"They don't have to until next December. It's a social occasion for them, not a class they have to take seriously."

Neil made a face at her. "Point taken, gentle lady."

Sarah hesitated. "If you were taking the rehearsal yesterday, how come you were in London?" she asked.

"I suppose Robert told you," he came back. "Look, Sarah, I didn't mean to cause trouble. I didn't even know that you were that way about each other! Robert was worried when you didn't put in an appearance and he said you might try for the last train. He was looking as bleak as hell, but I thought it was because he was worried about your father. Anyway, he asked me to drive up the highway and pick you up from the station and bring you staight home."

He flushed slightly. "He said I could take his car, as a matter of fact, so of course I went like a shot. It goes like a bomb on the highway."

"I see," said Sarah.

Neil looked increasingly more uncomfortable. "Yes, well, you see I was there in plenty of time for the last train."

"Then why on earth didn't you bring me home?"

"My dear Sarah, I would have thought that was obvious to a moron!"

"Well, it isn't obvious to me! I nearly died when I saw that train going out of the station without me!"

"Oh, come off it! I was there, don't forget! I saw you, Sarah. You and Smart Alec. You took one look at the departing train and rushed into his arms as though you couldn't wait! I followed you the whole way out to his car. You didn't exactly look upset to me!"

"But that's why Alec put his arm around me. I didn't want everyone to see how upset I was!" Sarah sighed. "If you saw me get into Alec's car, you must have seen my stepmother sitting in the back. Couldn't you have told Robert about that while you were about it?"

For a desperate moment she actually thought that Neil winked at her. "If you think it would do any good."

Sarah sat forward, hope kindling in her eyes.

"But you did see her, Neil?"

"Well, between you and me, no," he said. "Come on,

Sarah, I wasn't born yesterday! I know when two people want to be alone, and that was you and that Smart Alec of yours last night!"

CHAPTER NINE

THE WEEK slid by without Sarah seeing anyone but her father and the doctor when he came on his daily visit. Each day her father looked better, and by Saturday, he was well enough to sit up in his dressing gown and take an interest in what was going on.

"Is Madge coming?" he asked Sarah when she took him in his breakfast on Sunday morning.

Sarah threw him a quick look of concern. "I think so," she said.

His lips quirked downward. "Don't worry, I won't upset myself. Madge will come and go as a stranger and I'll greet her as such. Unless—do you want me to try and make her repair the damage she has caused between you and Robert?"

"No. No, thank you," Sarah said with dignity. "I'd much rather Madge didn't know about me."

"Understandable!" her father grunted.

"I don't suppose she meant any harm," Sarah said.

"Probably not. Lack of imagination is a serious handicap in an artist. She would never have got herself tied up with this ridiculous part if she had given a moment's thought as to how she would look as a teenager!"

Sarah chuckled. "Did you warn her?" she asked with interest.

"Again and again!"

Sarah was still laughing as she went downstairs at the irony in her father's voice. Poor Madge! What a lot she had missed by not enjoying her husband as much as she might have done. How could any success compare with that?

She didn't expect her stepmother for several hours, but the sound of a car drawing up in the drive drew her to the kitchen window to see who it could be. She was surprised to see Madge stepping out of the car and ran to the front door to let her in, wondering what could have happened to make her stepmother make such an early start.

"I nearly came last night," Madge greeted her. "I had to know how Daniel is. Telephone calls tell one nothing. I'm sure you don't mean it, darling, but you sound as though you're trying to exclude me from something, you're so noncommittal on the phone. I have a right to know! I am his wife, you know. You are merely his daughter!"

"Yes, Madge."

"Oh, Sarah, really! Now you're upset, I suppose? Well, so am I! I've had a terrible week, and worrying abut Daniel was almost the last straw!"

Sarah said nothing. She had nearly said that her stepmother had shown no sign of worrying about her father last Monday, but then she realized that that wasn't quite true. Her stepmother had been unaccountably depressed, and she had said at least twice that she was miserable. From Madge Dryden that was quite a lot.

"Have you had breakfast?" Sarah asked her.

Her stepmother's eyes lit up hopefully. "I've given up eating breakfast. I have to keep my figure." She trailed off uncertainly. "What are you having?"

Sarah smiled almost maternally. "Bacon and eggs?" she suggested.

"Oh yes, darling. That would be lovely!"

Madge sat down expectantly at the kitchen table, slipping her shoes off her feet and wiggling her toes with a grimace. "I'm tired! Nobody makes any effort to pull their weight in the songs! I have to carry it all on my back! It's too much!"

"It isn't the right vehicle for you," Sarah murmured, breaking a couple of eggs into the frying pan.

"You can say that again! Of course I knew that when I first read the part. I kept telling everyone, including Daniel! But nobody pays any attention to anything I say!"

Sarah thought that perhaps her stepmother really did believe that and she very nearly laughed.

"Dad is much better," she said brightly. "The doctor still comes every day, but I don't think he has to any longer. He's been very kind."

"Which doctor? Is he any good? I think Daniel should see someone in London. It's ridiculous to think that country doctors are any good. They wouldn't *be* in the country if they were. I think I'll arrange for him to see someone next week."

"I don't think he'll go. He likes Dr. Fairfield."

"I don't think it's your decision to make, Sarah. I'm the one to say what should, or should not, be done! Even if I weren't his wife, I'm paying for it after all!"

"Dr. Fairfield is a National Health doctor," Sarah said reluctantly. "Why don't you wait and see him for yourself before you call in anyone else?"

"I'll see." Madge accepted the plate her daughter held out to her and regarded the rashers of bacon and the two fried eggs with satisfaction. "I'll do it for you, darling. There, you can't say I never do anything for you, can you?"

Sarah gave her stepmother a sardonic smile, chastizing herself inwardly for becoming cynical, and went upstairs for her father's tray.

MADGE PROWLED around the house, fingering the ornaments as she went. "Why doesn't he want to see me?" she asked Sarah for the tenth time.

"He's sleeping," Sarah told her tactfully.

"Doesn't he know that I got up at some unearthly hour just to be with him?"

"I suppose so."

"Sarah, you did tell him, didn't you?"

"He heard your car arrive. He has an amazing ear for car engines. He can tell whether it's your car almost before you've got here."

"Well, I think he might put himself out a little to make me welcome. This house is like a morgue! I feel so sad—you know how atmosphere affects me! No, come to think of it, you wouldn't! You've never had any imagination or sensitivity for others."

"No," Sarah agreed, "I'm a hard case!"

"I'm beginning to think you are! Doesn't he come downstairs at all now? I don't think he should be encouraged to be lazy. I expect you find it easier to give him his food on a tray, but it isn't good for him to be on his own so much. I'll make him come down to dinner!"

"Please don't, Madge. The doctor says his heart is very tired after that last attack and that he shouldn't put any extra strain on it."

"But it's so boring!"

"You could go out," Sarah suggested.

"By myself? I wouldn't know where to go! Besides I wouldn't dream of leaving you on your own." Madge looked thoughtfully at her stepdaughter. "Unless you would like to go somewhere?" she hazarded.

"No, thank you. I don't think daddy should be left on his own."

Madge shrugged her shoulders. "You don't want to become a *cabbage*, darling," she remarked.

When the telephone rang, Sarah was aware of a feeling of relief that she didn't have to answer her stepmother. "Shall I get it?" she offered.

"No, I will. It's probably for me anyway. I'm expecting my agent to call some time." Sarah's eyebrows rose. She tried not to listen to her stepmother's end of the conversation, but the temptation was irresistible, and so she knew that it was Robert who was speaking. Madge sounded both pleased and flattered.

"No, no," she was saying. "I was down at the crack of dawn. Yes, much better! I'm sure we all owe you a big vote of thanks for getting that doctor of yours in to see him. Worked miracles in a few days!"

Sarah tasted a bitterness on her tongue. She tried to turn off her ears, but her stepmother's voice was too well produced to be ignored.

"Dinner tonight? Why, how very kind of you! I'd love to, of course. How nice of you to ask me! Are you sure it isn't Sarah you want?"

There was another break and Sarah wondered what it was that Robert was saying.

"You only want me? Well, if you're sure, I think it would be better if Sarah stayed with Daniel. He isn't really well enough to be left on his own yet. No, she won't mind a bit. It's one of the penalties of having a famous stepmother, that she receives more invitations than you do. Poor Sarah learned that at an early age, but she doesn't mind, bless her! She hasn't a glamorous turn of mind!"

Sarah could hear Robert's laughter.

She was hurt that he hadn't asked her, and even more hurt that he should think she was ever jealous of her stepmother.

"Darling, that was Robert! He's asked me to dinner tonight. I think perhaps he realizes how dull it is here for me. Do you think you could press my dress for me? I think something long, don't you?"

"Who else is going to be there?"

"How should I know?" Madge smiled happily, clasping her hands in front of her. "I believe he mentioned his brother and that girl called Samantha. Is that right?"

Sarah pressed her lips together and nodded. He hadn't lost much time, she thought, in turning back to Samantha. And she was shocked by the depths of her own misery. How was she going to survive without Robert? For an instant her courage faltered and she thought she couldn't. But then the moment passed and the mundane tasks of the moment took over. She went and got her stepmother's dress, plugged in the iron and spent the next half-hour smoothing its ample skirts.

For once Sarah had seen both the films that the television offered that evening, and the third channel offered only a selection of very modern, computerized music that depressed her. She spent an hour or so with her father, losing a game of chess to his quicker and more mathematical wits.

"I'd die of shock if I ever won a game of chess!" she remarked as she put the pieces away.

"You're too impetuous to make a good player," he told her. "Nor is it very practical to defend your pawns at the expense of your queen!" He laughed at the chagrin on her face. "I really believe you look on them as helpless children in need of care and protection!" he teased.

"If it were only that, I might improve over the years!"

"What makes you think that?"

"I don't know. I think we all grow more cynical as we grow older."

Daniel glanced up at her. "Maybe. Bitterness is not an attractive quality, my dear. That is something we must all guard against, if not for our own sake, for those who love us."

Sarah bit her lip at the reproof. "I'll try," she said. "I have an object lesson in you that it would be churlish to ignore."

"You don't do so badly!" he smiled. "Would you think me terrible if I asked for a cup of tea?"

She shook her head and went downstairs to make it. It was just nine o'clock, though it felt like midnight. Perhaps she, too, would go to bed with a book, though she doubted her ability to concentrate on the written word.

When her father had finished his tea, she straightened his bedclothes and left his spectacles and his book on his bedside table, adding a bowl of fruit, which she knew he liked to pick at if he woke up early.

"What does Robert say to your leaving his letters? I should imagine he's a stickler for time-keeping."

"It was part of our agreement that I wouldn't go in if you weren't well enough," Sarah answered. "Besides, no matter how angry with me he is, he wouldn't take it out on you."

Daniel smiled. "He's too big a man for that?"

Sarah felt herself blushing. "Yes," she said firmly, "he is."

Daniel kissed her cheeks, openly laughing at her. "Oh, Sarah, don't ever lose that expressive face of yours. And don't worry about Robert! He'll come around!"

It was cold comfort to take to bed with her. Sarah undressed quickly and put on her nightdress, only then deciding to have a bath. The water was blazing hot, ready for her stepmother, but Sarah didn't care. She used most of it, stifling any guilt that she might have felt. She even put in handfuls of bathsalts, a luxury she was usually more sparing with, until the water was syrupy and slippery against the bottom of the bath.

When she lowered herself into the water, she made no effort to wash herself, but lay there soaking, tantalizing herself by imagining what tales her stepmother was telling Robert.

When that occupation became too uncomfortable,

even for the masochistic mood she was in, she got out of the bath again and rubbed herself dry, going into her bedroom. She turned out the lights and pulled the curtains back, watching the moonlight as it cast its white light over the laden fruit trees. If she leaned out far enough, she could see the drive as it made its way up to the manor. She fixed her eyes on the black surface, wishing that she was at the other end of it. Then, just as she was turning away, she saw her stepmother, Robert and Samantha come walking down the driveway toward to the gate of the oast house. Unable to restrain herself, she went into her stepmother's room and watched them approach. Madge kissed them both as she parted from them, her voice coming floating up to the open window.

"Lovely evening! Robert, I'm so grateful to you for all your good advice and I will try not to feel guilty about Daniel, though I can't help a tiny twinge now and again. Good night, Samantha. Don't let Robert do too much! That stepdaughter of mine can do a bit more for him! He shouldn't pay her for doing nothing, I'm sure you agree! Thanks again for a lovely evening!"

Madge opened the front door with her key and came inside. Robert and Samantha turned away, joining their arms together as they walked slowly back toward the manor.

Sarah gave a stifled gasp, ran in her bare feet into her own room and jumped into bed, hauling the bedclothes up over her head. That night was the first night she cried herself to sleep since she had been a tiny child. She didn't care if she felt rotten in the morning. She didn't care about anything!

BY THE MIDDLE of the week her father was well enough for Sarah to leave him for more than a few minutes at a time and she went back to work at the manor. She was almost as nervous as she had been that first time when she had walked through the manor gardens, not knowing what to expect when she reached the other end. This time she had the book she had found for Robert amongst her possessions in London. How much she had been looking forward to giving it to him and now, would he even accept it? She blinked quickly, knowing that she was laying herself open to a snub. Well, if he did, he did, and that was all there was to it. She had to keep hoping that he would eventually believe her, or she would be left with nothing.

The letters she was to type were neatly piled up on the desk in the study. She looked through them, noting Robert's penciled replies on the back. There was nothing there that she would have to ask him about, so she took the cover off the typewriter and began the first letter, wishing that she had the speed of a professional instead of her own rather hesitant method.

She had practically finished when Robert came into the room. To her annoyance, far from remaining calm and dignified, she felt the color fly to her face and her mouth was suddenly dry when faced with having to speak.

"I brought you something back from London," she burst out.

His face was so reserved that she winced. Surely, no matter what he thought she had done, there was no need to look at her like that.

"I thought you'd like it," she added, sounding tearful.

"Oh?" he said cautiously.

"I went through the things I have at my stepmother's house on Sunday evening."

"Indeed?"

"Things I had when I was at school, and other stuff that I didn't want to cart round the countryside when I went into repertory. And I found this book." She gave him a scared look. "I hope you like it."

He made no move to take it from her. "Sarah, don't make it more difficult for yourself," he said.

"Aren't you going to accept it?" she asked baldly.

"I don't know. Are there any strings attached?"

"What an ugly thing to say!"

He admitted the justice of that. "I suppose so. But it's no use clinging on to something that's dead. I won't change my mind, Sarah. You'll have to accept that."

"I do," she said quietly.

"I wonder. I'm not completely inexperienced in these matters. I know there was a spark between us that even you couldn't simulate. It wasn't all boredom, was it? But the temptation of having your cake and eating it was too much for you when you saw Alec Farne again. I'm not blaming you."

"Aren't you? I think you are."

His eyes glinted, icily gray. "I was going to ask you to be my wife. Are you surprised if I'm jealous that you can cast your favors in another man's direction? But I'm not blaming you for that. Different people have different standards in these matters. Where you're to blame was in lying to me about how you felt. For that, I don't think I'll ever forgive you."

Sarah sighed. "Don't you think you could possibly be wrong?"

"No, I don't."

"Then there's nothing more to be said."

"Oh, Sarah! Why did you have to do this to me? I told you I couldn't share you with anyone else! I wouldn't even have shared you with the theater—I saw too much of that with my stepmother."

Sarah turned away from him, suddenly hopeless. "I'm going to give up the theater anyway," she said.

"You have no choice while your father needs you."

"No, but you were right in thinking that he won't need me for very long."

"I'm sorry," he said stiffly.

"Yes, it's an unhappy ending for him. I wish things could have come right for him, but they don't always, no matter how worthwhile the person. I suppose it's a lesson that we all have to learn some time or other. Only he deserved better things!"

"He has a devoted wife and daughter."

She smiled a bitter smile. "Thank you for those few kind words. You do believe that I care for him, then?"

"Of course, I do! You've worn yourself to a shadow this last week looking after him."

"Ironic, isn't it?" she mocked. "I love him but I can't give him the love he wants, because I'm only his daughter and not his wife! And I love you, but I can't have that either because—"

"It doesn't do any good to keep going over the same ground. I've tried to believe you, Sarah, but I can't. And it doesn't do any good to try and shift the blame on to Madge. Why do you suppose I asked her to dinner last night? She's heartbroken about your father. She loves him, as you do—"

"In her way, I think she does."

"You didn't see her face when she had to leave him to go back to London," he said bleakly. "But even so I asked her outright if she had told you about how ill Daniel was. She was so surprised at the idea that she dropped her fork. As far as she knew you were out with Alec and she was unable to get hold of you. As for having supper with you both, she denied it absolutely. What reason would she have for lying?"

"I don't know," Sarah admitted.

"Whereas you have every reason for not wishing to be found out," Robert went on brutally. "You see, I do believe you feel somthing for me, but you were quite prepared to have a little fun on the side if you weren't going to be found out!"

"If our positions were reversed, I'd believe you no matter what!"

"Don't be silly, Sarah. You'd have to believe the evidence of your own eyes!"

"But not Neil's hastily drawn conclusions."

"And your stepmother's evidence? Would you dismiss that too? She denies seeing you at all that evening!"

"Then there's nothing more to be said," Sarah agreed wearily. "But does that mean that I can't give you a book for your father's collection?"

He studied her pale face for a long moment. "I'm not to be bought by a well-chosen peace offering," he said finally.

"Nor would I insult you by offering one." She smiled wryly. "Not that I expect you to believe that. Your opinion of me is quite clear even to one of my limited intelligence. It couldn't be lower!"

"It could be," he told her seriously. "There are many things I admire about you."

"But not enough!" she protested.

"No, not enough. I'm too possessive by nature. If I can't have all of you, then I don't want any of you!"

She knew then that he was hurting himself as much as he was hurting her, and she could have wept for them both.

"I'd like you to have the book," she said. "I'd forgotten I had it. I bought a lot of books at about that time. I was rather lonely, you see, and they made reliable friends."

He looked down at the book she had put down on the desk again. "You didn't buy it when you were in London?"

She shook her head. " I don't suppose you'll believe that either!"

He picked up the book and examined it with the careful delight of the genuine booklover. On the fly-leaf he read her name, written in a clear childish hand and dated some ten years before. "It isn't a first edition," she told him anxiously. "But it is a facsimile, and you haven't got a copy. I know because I looked."

"*A Perambulation of Kent* by William Lambard," he read aloud. "Are you sure you want me to have it? It must have represented quite a lot of pocket money."

"I read it from cover to cover when I first had it," she remembered. "It will feel more at home on your shelves than in my old school trunk, though." She didn't add that she wanted to leave something of herself in the Chaddox domain. She thought she didn't have to. "I must get on with my work," she added briskly. "I don't want to leave my father for long until he's a bit stronger."

"You're not finding it too much, are you?" he asked, noting again how pale and drawn she was looking.

To his surprise her face crumpled and he thought she was going to cry.

"I can keep on coming, can't I, Robert?" she begged. "You don't have to see me while I'm here. I won't come when you're at home."

His face softened as he looked at her, his eyes puzzled. "Do you want to as much as all that?"

If she had had any pride she would have denied it, she thought dully. But, as far as he was concerned, she had no pride. She had no defenses at all. She nodded her head and gulped. "It takes my mind off my father," she said.

He smiled at her and her heart turned right over. "Then of course you must come—when your father can spare you. Thank you for the book."

She attempted a smile herself. "You're welcome!" She began to type madly, knowing she would have to do it all over again. He went on standing there, watching her, until her hands began to shake and she had to grit her teeth to force herself to go on. But when she looked up again he had gone, shutting the door behind him.

SARAH WAS JUST putting the cover back on the typewriter when Mrs. Vidler brought in her cup of coffee.

"I didn't think you'd know I was here," Sarah smiled at her.

"I wouldn't have, but Mr. Robert went out through the back door and he said you'd come in this morning for a little while. Your father must be better. I'm ever so glad for you."

"Thank you. He is very much better, but the doctor says it won't last. He has a bad heart, you see."

"Yes, love, I know. Mr. Robert told me. He was saying that you wouldn't be needing the oast house much longer the way things were going. Still, I expect you'll be glad to get back to London in some ways. Nobody will be asking you to make a choir out of a collection of females there, I'll be bound!"

"I'll miss it," Sarah said sadly.

"Mebbe. You've settled down right nicely. I was thinking you might want to stay around here now you've had a taste of the life, but I suppose you feel more at home in London?"

"I hate London!" Sarah said with such concentrated energy that she upset the pile of letters she had just finished typing. She bent down and began to pick up the scattered pieces of paper.

"Then you'll be staying on here?"

Sarah pretended she hadn't heard. She went on picking up the letters, hoping that Mrs. Vidler would take the hint and go away.

"Of course we'll miss you if you go," Mrs. Vidler went on inexorably. "I'm not going to pretend, Miss Sarah, that I didn't have hopes that *something else* was going to keep you here, but you can't arrange things like that to order, can you? I don't mind saying that I won't stay on here the day that that Samantha sets foot over the threshold."

"Is she likely to?" Sarah asked, jerking herself upright.

"Well," said Mrs. Vidler, "she'd like to."

"How do you know?" Sarah told herself that she had no right to encourage Mrs. Vidler to gossip with her like this, but she had to know, she just had to!

"You're not drinking your coffee," Mrs. Vidler accused her. "It wasn't a secret that Samantha had her eye on Mr. Robert. It's said she has more money than she knows what to do with and that she wanted to be Mrs. Chaddox so badly that she offered to put it all into the estate. Mr. Robert had more sense than to accept. But now he's out with her every night, just as though they hadn't quarreled about the money at all!"

"I think Samantha is beautiful," Sarah forced herself to say.

"Do you now?" Mrs. Vidler's body quivered with indignation. "Beauty is as beauty does, that's what I say! That Samantha never goes out of her way to speak to one, never once. She's been here times without number and she's never so much as said good morning!"

"Perhaps she's shy," Sarah suggested, feeling rather sorry for Samantha.

Mrs. Vidler sniffed. "She's not a lady," she confided. "That's her trouble. Mind you, I wouldn't discuss her outside this house, Miss Sarah. But seeing that you come in yourself to help Mr. Robert out—"

"Oh, quite!" Sarah cut her off hastily.

"Well, it isn't what I'd hope for him, but there, what can the likes of me do about it? If he's set on a pretty face, he won't be persuaded that there's more to living with a woman than that!"

"Mrs. Vidler—"

"Now you, Miss Sarah, would have been just right for him!"

"Mrs. Vidler, I don't think you should say things like that, even to me. Robert—"

"There now! I've upset you, Miss Sarah. I should have thought that maybe you wouldn't want to talk about it. Never you mind, I'll see to it that Samantha doesn't have everything her own way!"

"But you mustn't, Mrs. Vidler! Robert has every right to do as he likes. And he has a right to the privacy of his own home." Mrs. Vidler snorted, her eyes meeting Sarah's. She knew, Sarah thought, she knew exactly how she felt about Robert, so what was the good of trying to pretend that she didn't. She began again.

"I don't think you understand. I mean, you're quite right in thinking that I'm very much in love with Robert, but we've decided that we don't want to become any further involved with each other. We've decided *mutually* that we don't suit each other in any way that matters—" Sarah broke off and busied herself again with sorting the letters she had spilt.

To her surprise, Mrs. Vidler put her comfortable arms around her and held her against her ample bosom in a way that her stepmother had never done, not even when she had been a child.

"Don't grieve now, Miss Sarah. He's hurt you, but I daresay he didn't mean it. Mr. Robert won't see you leave us now, no matter what you've said to him. Now you go home to your father and don't you go thinking about it any more. It'll all come out in the wash!"

It wouldn't, of course, but it was nice to pretend, just for a moment, that it would. Sarah forced a smile and nodded.

"I hope so," she said. "I'll see you tomorrow, Mrs. Vidler."

The housekeeper beamed at her and picked up the now cold cup of coffee. "That you will, Miss Sarah. Hurry home now!"

Sarah went, looking at her watch as she did so. It was unbelievable, but she had only been away from her father for a little less than two hours.

CHAPTER TEN

AUGUST SLIPPED into September and the hops in the field were gathered in. Sarah picked up the windfalls in the orchard and looked for new ways of using up the apples that she and her father couldn't eat. She learned to make chutney and to bottle the best of them, and for the first time she saw the point of having a deepfreeze, for she could have frozen still more and used them at another time.

The children went back to school and Neil departed to take up his teaching post at a school in the suburbs of London.

"I'll be seeing you most weekends," he said as he went. And he was as good as his word, calling in whenever he went past the oast house and giving her news of Robert. Sarah looked forward to his visits with mixed feelings, but she soon came to the conclusion that just to hear about Robert was better than to have him go out of her life completely.

Mrs. Vidler was another source of information. Her efforts to be tactful visibly hurt, but her loyalty to Sarah, as well as to Robert, was never in doubt. She would often do Sarah's shopping with her own, stopping at the oast house for a cup of coffee on the way home.

"How's your father, dearie?" she would ask, plonking herself down on the nearest chair. "Getting along nicely, I hope?"

And the news was good for the most part. Daniel Blaney seemed to have separated himself from his previous worries and anxieties. He accepted his wife's visits more easily and without much interest. More and more he lived in a world of his own in which Sarah felt she was a a stranger and not always a very welcome one. But she, too, was busy growing scar tissue over her lacerated emotions, and she spent much of her time out of doors, taking advantage of the last of the summer. She would walk for miles through the pretty countryside, wearing out her body with grim determination so that she would be sure of sleeping at night. She had had enough of tossing and turning endlessly through the night, wishing things were other than they had turned out to be. Now she fell into bed and slept until morning, when she would be almost as tired as she had been the night before, but that was a small price to pay when the alternative was so much worse.

Then one night she woke suddenly in the small hours. She thought it must have been a noise that had wakened her, but only silence greeted her straining ears. Even the wind, which had been high when she had gone to bed, had dropped soon after midnight, and there was no sign of it now.

Sarah left her bed and went out on to the landing. The silence began to oppress her and she longed for the hoot of an owl, or anything that would break into it and bring normality back to the house. That there was something wrong she was increasingly sure, but she didn't know how to find out what it was.

Instinct took her to her father's room. The stertorous breathing was still and she knew immediately that her father was no longer there. She switched on the light and spent a long moment looking at his quietened, puckish face. Then panic took her and she fled out of the room, hurtling down the stairs, half wondering what it was that she was afraid of. It seemed pointless to phone the doctor, but she did not want to be alone. Without thought of the consequences, she did what she wanted to do most and dialed Robert's number.

It was some time before he came to the phone. "Robert Chaddox," his sleepy voice came over the wire.

"It's Sarah!"

"Yes? What is it?" The quiet sympathy in his voice made her want to weep, but she couldn't, not yet, not until she had told him what was the matter.

"I think daddy is dead."

She didn't know what she expected him to do about it. Whatever it was, she was surprised when he said quietly, "I'll be right over. Don't grieve over him, my love."

And then, almost immediately, he was there, and she had flung herself into his arms, too tired and sad to care whether he minded or not. She buried her face in his shoulder and was warmed by the comfort of his arms holding her tightly against him. "I woke up and he'd stopped breathing," she whispered.

"Hush, love. You knew it had to happen and so did he!"

"I know. He wanted it that way. But I can't stop shivering!"

Robert hugged her closer still. "It's shock, I expect," he told her. "Why don't you make us both a cup of tea while I go up and take a look?"

She nodded, backing away from him. "I'm sorry to have woken you, too, but I couldn't think of anyone else!"

"I'm glad you did," he said gently. "Are you all right now?"

"Yes, thank you." She sniffed, wiping her face with her hands. "I'll put the kettle on."

She had finished making the tea and was sitting at the table with the tea tray in front of her when Robert came back. He smiled at her, his gray eyes warm and affectionate.

"He is dead, isn't he?" she asked abruptly.

"Yes. I think you must have woken up almost immediately."

"I heard him stop breathing," she said flatly.

He took the teapot from her and poured out the tea, pushing her cup close to her hand. "This isn't really the time," he said, "But someone will have to make all the necessary arrangements. Do you want me to do it for you?"

"Oh, Robert, would you? I don't know what to do. We... we never discussd that sort of thing!"

"No, people seldom do," Robert said with a sigh. "Have you told Madge?"

Sarah stiffened. "No."

Robert frowned at her. "She has a right to know."

"Yes, of course she has. Only I don't know what to say to her!"

"Would you like me to phone her for you?" Robert offered.

She was grateful to him even while she knew that he didn't approve of her not contacting her stepmother herself. She sipped her tea quickly, wishing that she could explain how she felt. It was right that her stepmother should be told, but not yet! Not until she had grown used to it herself and could say all the right things, and be ready for Madge's comments on her father's last few months.

"I'll do it now." Robert said. "There's no point in putting it off."

He went out into the hall and she heard him searching for her stepmother's number and then dialing it with impatient fingers.

"Mrs. Blaney? Yes, Miss Dryden, if you like! Will you fetch her, please. This is Robert Chaddox." There was a lengthy pause, pregnant with Robert's suppressed impatience at the delay. "Madge? This is Robert Chaddox. I'm with Sarah at the oast house. I have some bad news."

Sarah wandered out into the hall and stood beside Robert. She could easily hear her stepmother's voice, as beautifully produced as ever.

"Is it Daniel?"

"Yes, I'm afraid it is. I thought you'd better know immediately. I don't know what—"

"Sarah will cope with everything, I'm sure," Madge Dryden interrupted him. "I'm afraid anything like that is apt to upset me! Especially when it concerns someone I love—or should I say loved—like Daniel."

Robert's voice took on a harsher note. "I've already offered to do all that. Perhaps I could speak to you about it when you come down."

"I don't know that I want to!"

"I see," said Robert. "But surely you'll want to come to the funeral?"

"I suppose I must! But it will have to be on a Monday. I can't possibly take off just now. The show is hanging on by a thread and if I were to be away, even for one performance, that would kill it once and for all!"

Sarah held out her hand for the receiver, but Robert had already murmured a brief goodbye and had replaced it in its cradle.

"I'm sorry!" Sarah said helplessly.

"So am I!" he answered.

"She can't help it," Sarah rushed on. "She loved him, really!" She looked at Robert with a kind of impatient sympathy. She knew so well the disillusionment that he was feeling.

"I don't think she needs you to apologize for her!" he snapped.

"I'm sorry!" she said again.

He gave her an angry smile. "It's always the same

when one gets involved with the theater! What is it about it that makes perfectly pleasant people put it first, last and all the time?"

"It's an escape," she said gently, "for some people. They don't have to portray their own emotions on the stage."

"I sometimes doubt they have any!"

Sarah touched his hand with her own, but drew back before he could misinterpret the gesture. "Some of us have," she said. "Actors are people like everyone else!"

"Neil's mother was more like an overgrown child!" he retorted.

This was so apt a description of her own stepmother that Sarah gave him a quick, frightened glance and looked as quickly away again.

He saw the look. "Are you going back to the stage?" he asked her.

She shook her head. "I don't think so."

He grunted. "But you will go back to London?"

"I suppose so." She took a deep breath and changed the subject. "Robert, will you be able to arrange the funeral for Monday."

"Why not? If you agree to his being buried here at Chaddoxbourne. I'll speak to the vicar about it and arrange a time if you like."

"Would he be able to be buried in the churchyard? I mean I wouldn't like him to be buried somewhere else."

"There's plenty of room on the Chaddox plot," he said indifferently.

Sarah went very pale, wondering if this was the olive branch she had been waiting for, but his next words disillusioned her. "I wouldn't want to put a bar in the way of your visiting the grave, but I'd have to ask you not to come too often. It's better that we don't see each other too frequently."

"I don't suppose I'll want to come very often," she

said. It was hard to believe that it was her father they were discussing. It all seemed strangely unreal to her.

"Then I'll let you know as soon as I've made all the arrangements," he went on formally. "You'll want to inform all his friends and anyone else who is likely to want to come. I don't suppose your stepmother will want to involve herself in that sort of thing." His face softened and he put up a hand, running his finger along the line of her jaw. "I'm sorry, Sarah. I'm sorry it had to be like this and that you were here alone. I'll try to make it as easy for you as possible."

She forced a smile. "I know you will."

"D'you think you can sleep a little now?"

She nodded. "I'll try. I'm not nervous, if that's what you mean. I was at first, but I'm not now. You have a wonderfully soothing way with you, Robert."

He gave her a little slap on the cheek. "There's no going back, Sarah. Not even now!"

She did smile at him then, a light jaunty smile that he found unsettling. "There won't be going back on my part until you trust my word, so you needn't look so worried, Robert my darling. One day you'll find out that I wasn't lying and you'll find me waiting for you. But all the time you're despising me, I wouldn't lift a finger to make you change your mind!"

His eyebrows lifted. "You're sticking to your guns then, despite all the evidence against you?"

"Yes, I am."

"Oh, Sarah, Sarah, I wish I could believe you!"

This time it was she who comforted him. "Never mind, you will one day," she said certainly.

"What makes you think that?" he asked heavily.

"Because one day it won't matter and then my stepmother will tell the truth, quite casually, wondering what all the fuss is about."

"Madge had no reason to lie!"

"No reason in the world!"

"Well then?"

Sarah thought he looked so tired and wretched that she wished that there was some way she could comfort him, but there was none.

"She hates to be uncomfortable," she explained.

"That still doesn't explain what Neil saw!" he objected, clenching his fists. "I'm going back to bed. Goodnight, at least for what's left of it!" He glared at her with such dislike that she blenched. And then he caught her to him and kissed her hard. "I'll be glad when you've gone!" he said.

THE FUNERAL was arranged for the following Monday. Sarah had expected her stepmother to come down the day before, but at the last moment Madge rang up and said she wouldn't sleep a wink in the house where Daniel had died.

"I'll come tomorrow," she said. "I'd only be in the way if I came today."

"All right, Madge. But could you give me some idea as to how many people will be coming?"

"Does it matter?" Madge said testily.

"It's a long way for them to come. I thought we should offer them some kind of refreshments before they go back."

"Why don't you get in a caterer?" her stepmother suggested.

"I prefer to do it myself," Sarah said quietly. "If I just knew how many—"

Her stepmother made some swift and audible calculations. "I'd say about twenty of my friends. He didn't have any of his own, so I don't think we need to bother about them. You'd better say twenty-five. Okay?"

"Yes, thank you, Madge. I'll see you tomorrow."

"Here, wait a minute, darling! Have you any black to

wear? I was lucky and managed to borrow a black hat from one of the girls in the cast. I don't want either of us to look unfeeling!"

"I'll do my best," Sarah promised. "Goodbye, Madge."

Her stepmother hated the person she was talking to on the telephone to say goodbye first and she uttered a cross sound in the back of her throat. "I don't think you care about me at all!" she snapped and replaced the receiver with a bang.

Mrs. Vidler kindly helped with the catering. She came early, clutching her shopping bag in one hand. She stood in the kitchen, looking about her with approval at the start Sarah had made on the sandwiches and canapés.

"I'll put on my apron and then we'll be halfway there!" she said.

"Are you sure Robert doesn't mind your helping me out like this?" Sarah asked her, not for the first time.

"A fine thing if I can't give my friends a hand when they're in need of it!" Mrs. Vidler retorted.

"You're very kind to me," Sarah murmured. "I don't know what I would have done if I had had to do everything myself!"

Mrs. Vidler sniffed. "A fine thing!" she repeated darkly. "And when is Mrs. Blaney putting in her appearance?"

Sarah suppressed a smile. It was almost as if Mrs. Vidler knew how much her stepmother disliked being referred to as Mrs. Blaney.

"She said she'd come as early as she could," she answered noncommittally.

"Ay, and be gone in the same way!"

"I don't think she's faced up to it yet," Sarah reproved gently. "She'll keep as busy as she can for the next few weeks to keep herself from thinking about it. But she isn't unfeeling, Mrs. Vidler."

"If you say so, but I have my own ideas about that!"

"Then you'll have to keep them to yourself!" Sara said with a spurt of temper.

Mrs. Vidler's eyes looked like two round marbles. "Well, she is your stepmother," she admitted with a great effort at being just. "All the same, one can't help noticing things. As I was saying to Robert—"

"Could you pass the butter, Mrs. Vidler?"

"I said, that poor girl needs someone to look after her, with them all pecking at her, and him as bad as the rest of them!"

"I think I'll go and check the drinks," Sarah put in firmly. "I won't be long."

"All right, Miss Sarah. Don't you worry none, I can manage here!"

Madge Dryden came with her car overflowing with guests. They poured out of the car and stood on the drive, exclaiming at the quaintness of the oast house and the calm atmosphere of the village.

"I wonder you can resist staying down here for good!" one of them said to Madge.

"It's pretty, but too, too boring for a day or so!"

Alec Farne smiled at her. "Sarah doesn't seem to think so," he said.

"Sarah doesn't know what she wants! She thinks long walks and the Women's Institute are going to keep her occupied for the rest of her life, but it's only a phase. She had to work so hard in repertory and probably needed the rest!"

"Do you think so?" Alec said pointedly. "I thought she'd found something much more to her liking in the country."

"What do you mean?" Madge demanded with a dazzling smile.

"Robert Chaddox."

"Oh nonsense! Whatever made you think such a

thing? I don't want to break a confidence, but I can assure you that Sarah's looking in quite another direction! And now, at last, she can come back to London and you can see a great deal more of each other!"

Sarah caught the end of this remark and came and stood beside her stepmother. Alec raised his eyebrows at her and she shook her head at him. It was not, she thought, a very auspicious beginning.

"Are you sulking, darling, because I didn't get down earlier?" her stepmother railed her. "I wonder if you should have worn black after all, dear. It makes you look so pale and plain."

"I feel pale and plain," Sarah assured her. "You, on the other hand, look terrific!"

Madge was pleased. "It *is* a nice hat, isn't it?" she preened herself. "Do we go inside now, darling? Or straight to the church?"

Sarah looked about her uncertainly. With relief she saw Robert. He came straight up to her and with the ease born of long practice escorted the little group of mourners over to the church and had introduced the vicar to her stepmother, without Sarah herself having to do any more than take her place in the pew.

Afterward she had little idea as to what the vicar had said about her father. She was conscious of Madge weeping a little by her side, but she felt no urge to cry. Dry-eyed and ashen-faced, she allowed the service to pour over her, thankful for Robert's solid presence in the pew behind her, and afterward, when they followed her father's coffin into the churchyard, so close beside her that she could have put out her hand and touched him.

Later still, it was a little like a theatrical garden party. Groups of her stepmother's friends stood and chatted in the garden and the orchard, their high-heeled shoes and formal dress looking out of place in the country scene. Mrs. Vidler passed around the food with a stormy face and Sarah did the best she could with the drinks.

"Why don't you ask Alec to do that for you?" Robert asked her, when he saw her struggling to make more soda, a job that always terrified her.

Sarah looked him in the eyes and replied, "Because I prefer not to."

He held out his hand for the new sparklet and shook the container violently. "Not very handy, is he?"

She bit her lip. "It isn't that. He has to drive home afterwards."

His eyebrows shot upward. "I wouldn't let you nanny me like that!"

"You wouldn't drink and then drive!" she shot back.

"True. Nor do I need mothering by someone younger than myself. Shall I take over the bar for you? Who else is driving? Your stepmother?"

"I expect so. And that man over there. He was a friend of my father's." She pointed out a tall, spare elderly man who stood a little apart from the others. Of them all, he alone was obviously saddened by the occasion.

"Is he in the theater?"

Sarah shook her head. "He's a solicitor too," she said. "He and my father played chess together a lot. I think it's been a bit of a shock to him because Daddy was so...young. He was a friend of my mother too." She broke off, biting her lip. "Would you say something nice to him, Robert? None of the others will be much in his line. They don't like to show their feelings."

"They're succeeding!" he said dryly.

But almost immediately, with a shriek of dismay, Madge noticed the time. "We will have to start back! The traffic was impossible coming down! And I can't be late tonight. I'm seeing.... Oh well, it never does for the star to be late, does it?"

Her leading man seconded this opinion, his arm negligently draped about her. "Though on an occasion like this one might be forgiven," he added.

"Never!" Madge giggled.

"You look more like a child than a widow," he agreed softly. "Doesn't she, Sarah?"

Hotly embarrassed, Sarah turned away and went over to her father's friend. From the look in his eyes he had seen the whole exchange and he smiled at her. "Well, Sarah, how are you?" he greeted her.

"Sad," she said frankly. "But I'm very well, and that's something, isn't it?"

"Hm. You're looking tired. Daniel said you'd had the whole burden on your shoulders. What are you going to do now?"

"I don't know, Uncle Edwin. I'm not going back to the theater."

He looked surprised. "Marriage?"

"No, not that either!" she said as though she had been stung. "Are you going home with the crowd, or can you stay on for a bit?"

"I'm staying on. I have something to say to you about Daniel's will." He glanced across the grass toward Madge Dryden. "I suppose your mother is going straight back?"

"Right away, I think."

"Pity. What I have to say affects her too. Never mind, I can call and see her some time in London. It isn't the way I like to do things, but I suppose she is going on tonight regardless?"

"Yes," said Sarah.

Edwin Wymer looked disapproving. "I saw her show. Terrible! And to think I drew up the contract for her! Once I'd seen it, I expected to hear from her daily to get her out of the thing, but she seems determined to stick it out!"

Sarah laughed. "I think they're going. Uncle Edwin,

may I introduce you to Robert Chaddox while I see them off."

"Chaddox? I seem to have heard the name."

"Chaddox as in Chaddoxbourne," Sarah told him pertly. "He's the local lord of the manor!"

Mr. Wymer's eyes twinkled. "And one of the leading attractions?" he teased her.

"You'll have to judge that for yourself!" she retorted tartly.

She introduced the two men and left them discussing the differences between a town or country practice. Before she left, she thought she caught a glimpse of envy in Uncle Edwin's eyes as Robert spoke of local property values and the conveyancing fees that were coming in to his office.

"You should try a fashionable practice in London, my boy, and then you'd know what worry is! We have our share of property exchanging hands, of course, but we have a lot of other work. Both Daniel and Madge were among my clients."

Sarah slipped away, hoping to have a word with her stepmother before she went, but she was already too late. Madge was already in her car and busy encouraging as many other people as possible to travel with her.

"Of course there's room! You came with me, didn't you?" She barely looked at Sarah and then only to turn away again. "Do hurry!" she urged her guests.

"Madge, when will you be down again?"

"Soon, darling. You may as well stay and use up the tenancy. It will be somewhere for me to visit when I want a breath of fresh air. I'll give you a ring!"

"Yes, do." Sarah pleaded.

"Don't worry, darling, it's over now! You've earned a little holiday for yourself. Enjoy it! I'll send you some money some time to help out."

"But, Madge—"

"'Bye, darling! 'Bye, everyone!" With a last flurry of activity, the fleet of cars followed her stepmother out of the gates and away through the village.

Sarah turned on her heel and marched into the house, secretly hoping that Mrs. Vidler would not be there wanting to discuss the funeral blow by blow. She felt too exasperated and battered to talk to anyone for the moment. But if she was lucky as far as Mrs. Vidler was concerned, the voices coming out of the sitting room told her that Robert and Mr. Wymer had come in from the garden and were probably waiting for her to join them.

Unconsciously she squared her shoulders as she went into the room almost as though she were facing a firing squad.

"Have they all gone?" Mr. Wymer asked her.

She nodded, sitting down quickly as far away as possible from Robert.

Mr. Wymer fingered his breast pocket and drew out a document which he spread out on his knee. "This doesn't seem the moment to be bothering you with your father's will, my dear, even if it is traditional to spill the contents straight after the funeral." He put his spectacles on his nose and peered at the paper in front of him.

Robert rose to his feet. "I'll be going if you have business to discuss," he began.

"No, no, sit down, my boy. This concerns you too."

Sarah's eyes widened. She had never thought about her father leaving a will, or even that he had anything much to leave. She had a horrid thought that he might have left her in some way in the care of Robert and the idea brought a burning blush to her cheeks. Surely, he wouldn't have humiliated her in such a way!

"Ah yes," Mr. Wymer went on. "His share of the St. John's Wood house has been left to Madge—"

"I thought it was her house!" Sarah exclaimed, startled into speech.

"No. Your father actually bought the house just after the war. Later on he included your stepmother's name on the title deeds to avoid death duties."

Sarah blinked. Like everyone else she had always thought it had been her stepmother's money that had kept them all, and she thought miserably of all the pin-pricks her father must have suffered on that score through the years.

"He also leaves your stepmother certain sentimental objects—we needn't bother about them—and ten thousand pounds outright, as her earning power is extensive and she is unlikely to ever be in need. The rest of his estate is left absolutely to you, Sarah. It's a considerable sum, my dear, and he hoped that it will provide you with a modest living for life."

"But Daddy wasn't a rich man!"

Mr. Wymer glanced at her over his spectacles. "He sold some paintings very well over the years. He was an artist of repute in some circles. And your mother was well off too, you know, and all that she had went to him, in trust for yourself. And that leads me to the last bequest, added recently in a codicil to his will." A smile flickered over his lips as he looked at Robert. "'To Robert Chaddox of the Manor House, Chaddoxbourne, I give the portrait of my daughter, Sarah, painted by myself and at present hanging in the hall of my house in London, because like myself, he too finds beauty in my daughter's smile.'"

Sarah found herself gripping the arm of her chair until it hurt. "But you won't want that!" she declared.

"Why not?" Robert returned.

Sarah looked at him, completely forgetting Mr. Wymer's presence in the room. "You're only accepting it to annoy me!' she declared wildly. "Well, don't think that I'll fetch it from London for you! I'll have nothing to do with it! If you want it, you'll have to go and get it yourself!"

CHAPTER ELEVEN

IT WAS MICHAELMAS, still summer, but with the first hint of autumn adding a nip to the air in the morning and evenings. It was also rent day and Sarah was uneasily aware that the rent on the oast house was due. It was only two weeks since her father's death and she had not seen Robert since, though she was often at the manor, typing the letters he left for her. Then, on the evening of St. Michael's Day itself, Robert asked her to dinner.

"I have your portrait hanging in the dining room," he told her. "I thought you might like to see it in its new home."

So he had been up to London and had brought it back already. Sarah was intrigued to discover how he had found her stepmother's address, but she wouldn't have dreamed of asking him.

"Why did you accept it?" she asked instead, knowing that she had no right to ask that either.

"Why not?" he drawled. "Daniel wanted me to have it."

"He may have done once," she objected.

"I don't think he changed his mind," Robert said maddeningly.

"Well, I'm surprised you want it! I don't think Samantha will like it much! If you ever sell it, will you sell it to me?"

"I won't sell it. I like it. It goes very well on my wall. Your father is a very interesting painter. I'd like to see more of his work."

"Oh," said Sarah, hurt. "You mean you like it as a portrait of anyone?"

"Come and see it for yourself. I'll expect you for dinner. About seven-thirty?"

She agreed that that would be very nice, but she couldn't help wondering why he had asked her. Whatever reason, her spirits lifted dramatically at the thought of an evening in his company and Mrs. Vidler, who called in soon after, told her that she must be getting over her father's death because she was looking so much better.

She spent a long time dressing that evening. In Canterbury she had bought a long dress in a clinging manmade fiber that had a bright, bold pattern and an underskirt that swished against her legs with an agreeable crackling sound. Over it she wore a black velvet cape that fell straight from her shoulders to the ground in a dramatic sweep that appealed to the more extroverted side of her nature.

Robert had changed too. He wore his dinner jacket with an air and she thought he looked very fine as he took her cape and led her into the sitting room.

"Sherry?"

She nodded, a little shy of him. Her hand trembled as she accepted the glass and she tried to hide it from him by half turning away and taking a hasty sip of the wine. She wished she were better at reading his expression, but his face was completely enigmatic as he stood in front of the fireplace, watching her closely through narrowed eyes.

"Have you decided what you're going to do?" he asked.

She colored a little. "N-not really. Robert, why did you ask me here?"

"I wanted to compare the original with your portrait. Also, I thought we should part on a civilized note—"

"Part?"

His smile was insolent. "Did you think I'd changed my mind and was going to let you have a second bite at the cherry?"

She had thought so, or to be more accurate she had hoped against hope that that had been his reason for asking her.

"I thought..." she began. She shrugged. "I don't know what I thought! So this is in the nature of revenge, is it, Robert? Somehow I thought you were a kinder person than that."

"I've never felt kindly toward you, but I didn't mean to hurt you. You've been hurt enough recently. I couldn't think of any other way of telling you that I'm not going to renew the lease on the oast house. It doesn't give you much notice, but I think you must have been expecting to leave Chaddoxbourne anyway."

"I see."

He moved across the room and poured himself another drink.

"Where do you plan to go? Will you live with your stepmother in London?"

She shook her head. "I haven't lived there since I left school."

He looked surprised. "Why not?"

"I prefer my independence. I'll probably get a room, as I did before. I think I'll take some kind of training and then go abroad somewhere. I've never been anywhere much."

"What makes you think Alec Farne will agree to that?"

"Alec has nothing to say to anything I choose to do!"

"Another passing fancy?"

She winced, but she knew that he was as badly hurt as she was and that took much of the sting out of his taunts. "I don't see why I shouldn't have friends," she said.

"And lovers?"

She put her head on one side, her eyes challenging him. "Perhaps one day, a long time hence. Will you?"

"I dare say. Neil doesn't care for the place and I wouldn't like it to leave the family."

"Poor girl!" said Sarah.

"Why do you say that?" he asked sharply.

She twisted her hands together, wishing the comment unsaid. 'I didn't mean it. I expect I'm jealous of her, but you did make it sound as though she would be more mother than wife." She stopped helplessly, suddenly aware that she couldn't bear to think of Robert living with anyone else, whatever role she had.

"And that wouldn't be enough for you?"

She shook her head silently.

"It will have to be enough for me," he said abruptly. "Would you like to see the portrait now?"

She consented with a quick incline of her head, blinking away the unshed tears in her eyes. She preceded him out of the door, her skirts swishing madly around her ankles in her hurry.

"Look out!" he called out to her.

But he was too late. She caught her foot in the mat in the doorway and fell headlong into the hall. In a second he was beside her, holding her hands tight in his. "Are your hurt?" he asked in a strained voice.

"I don't think so," she said, resigned. "I'm always clumsy when you're anywhere in the area."

His hands grasped hers more tightly still. "Why, Sarah? Why did you have to lie to me?"

She gulped. The temptation to rest her head against him and to beg his forgiveness was very strong. His defenses against her were not as strong as he liked to pretend and she thought that if she accepted the role he had given her, he would give way. It was the lies that he thought she had told that had put her beyond the pale as far as he was concerned. But she had not lied! And she could not say that she had, no matter what the immediate reward.

"Why couldn't you believe me?" she whispered.

"I wish to God I could!"

"Then why don't you! Is it so very difficult to understand that my stepmother is Madge Dryden all the time, and hardly ever Mrs. Daniel Blaney?"

"No," he said. "But there's still Neil."

Sarah sighed. She pulled her hands out of his and, rejecting his help, climbed stiffly to her feet.

"If you want to know I was *crying* because I'd missed the train! But you don't want to believe that, do you, Robert? You made up your mind about me and found me wanting, and that was that! Well, all right, that's your privilege, but don't expect me to be cheering you on. I won't apologize for something I haven't done, but neither will I accept your estimation of me. I have to go on living too, you know!"

He put out his hand to her, but she ignored it, turning on her heel, and made a quick rush for the dining room before she disgraced herself by throwing herself at him on any terms he cared to think up.

In the doorway she came face to face with her father's portrait of herself. It was beautifully lit and looked, to her startled eyes, alive and on the point of speech, the smile breaking across her face like a shaft of light in her eagerness to live life to the full.

"It looks different," she exclaimed inadequately. "I've seen it often before, but I never knew it was like that!"

"It's a very good likeness," Robert told her.

"Then why do you want it?" she snapped.

"To remind me that even a smile that breaks across a face like a transformation scene at a pantomime is not always all it seems."

She put her head on one side and looked at the painting of herself again, ignoring the cruelty in his words. "Beauty is in the eye of the beholder," she remarked.

"You have flashes of beauty. I've seen you blaze up like a furnace and thought you the loveliest thing I've ever seen."

She was astonished. "I've never seen it!" she said.

He was amused. "I don't suppose you have. You don't stare at yourself in the looking glass immediately after you've been kissed! In fact, you're not a conceited person, are you?"

"Sometimes. Sometimes I'm as proud as the devil himself!"

"That isn't quite the same thing," he smiled. "You must have been told you're an attractive person before now!"

She considered this soberly. "I don't think so. Daddy used to think so, but then he was prejudiced. I can't think of anyone else!"

His face shut down and became completely expressionless. "Perhaps you're too obtuse to recognize a compliment?" he suggested smoothly.

"Very likely!" she agreed, her eyes flashing with sheer temper. "One has to have practice to be good at that sort of thing. I'll stick to typing! At least you've never complained about the work I've done for you!"

"Why should I? You're neat and accurate. It would be different if you had pretended you were a professional, but you didn't, and it was very much better than having to type my own letters."

She turned on him with an angry look. "You're insufferable!"

To her surprise, he smiled. "I prefer you angry to looking like a hurt animal in search of comfort. I'll miss having my letters done for me."

"Oh."

"You can hardly come all the way from London to type a few letters for me," he reminded her sardonically.

A cold wind of loneliness blew around her heart. "You don't intend to see me again, do you?"

He shook his head. "I want you too much for that. It will be better when we don't see each other. You must see it's better, Sarah!"

"For whom?"

"For both of us! Neither of us could blind ourselves to the fact we would be building on sand."

Sarah held her head very high. "I don't want to hear any more!" she said grandly. "You asked me to dinner and I intend to enjoy it—*if* you don't mind?"

He laughed. "I love you when you come the *grande dame*!"

"No, you don't!"

His eyebrows lifted. "What made you want to be an actress?" he asked her. "Was it because your stepmother's one?"

She thought about it. "I don't know that I ever considered anything else," she told him. "I never heard anything else except the joys and trials of the theatrical life. It was second nature to me. And I'm quite a good actress. That helped me to think that I had to go on doing it. It never occurred to me not to."

"But you never acted with your stepmother?"

Sarah gurgled with laughter. "Heaven forbid! Can you imagine me kicking up my heels and singing pretty little songs as she does? I'd die, if I had to do that sort of thing in public!"

Robert grinned. "I saw your stepmother's show when I picked up the portrait," he said, straight-faced.

"Oh." She was disconcerted. "She's better than that!" she said quickly, leaping to Madge's defense.

His eyes twinkled. "I think I'd die if I had to watch

you cavort your way through something like that!" he teased her.

"Oh, I'm strictly a straight actress." She stirred uneasily, still hating the thought that he nad seen her stepmother in such a bad vehicle. "You must see Madge Dryden in something more worthy one day," she pressed him.

"I might. You're a strange mixture, Sarah. Why don't you want to live with your stepmother?"

She flushed. "I don't think I want to tell you that."

"Why ever not?"

"Because you won't believe me. You see, as a child I never noticed anything except that she was the great Madge Dryden. I had my father to talk to and that was enough then. It was only later that I saw other things, things that I didn't want to be a part of, and so I decided to find my own place. I think daddy understood, though we never discussed it. I hope he did, because he was rather lonely these last few years."

Robert studied her face as she ate. He saw the flicker of pain that came and went as she mentioned her father, and the coolness with which she referred to her stepmother.

"You can be pretty uncompromising yourself," he commented. "What was it that drove you away from Madge?"

"She makes use of people," Sarah said flatly. "It sounds like a small thing, but it leads to all sorts of other things."

"And you didn't approve of that?"

"I tried not to disapprove," she answered, "but I didn't want to live like that myself. I do have some standards!" she added with a spurt of anger.

"Tell me about them," he invited. "And tell me the truth."

She shook her head. "Isn't it enough that I understand why you don't want to have anything more to do with me?"

"I don't know. Almost you persuade me that I may have been mistaken about you."

A flicker of hope rose within her. "Almost?"

"I won't live with a lie under any circumstances!"

She sighed and changed the subject, finding that she couldn't bear the hurt look in his gray eyes any longer.

"Where's Mrs. Vidler?"

Robert took his cue from her. "I told her we'd cope for ourselves. Do you mind a spot of washing up? You're not really dressed for it."

"I expect Mrs. Vidler has an apron. I'll wear that."

She rather enjoyed her moment in the kitchen. The china they had used was particulary pretty and she was domesticated enough for the action of restoring it to it former pristine state to appeal to her. Robert stood by her side, drying the occasional article and remarking with smug satisfaction that it was really much more hygienic for most of the things to be left to dry on their own.

"Can you also make coffee?" he asked her, when they had done.

She laughed. "I think so. Why don't you come back and have coffee with me?"

He hung up the cloth he had ben using and looked at her over his shoulder. "I'd like to, but I don't want to raise your hopes that there'll be anything more."

Sarah blushed faintly. "I wasn't expecting anything."

"But you can't help hoping?"

"I think that's my business," she retorted.

"Perhaps it is, but I don't like hurting you, Sarah."

"I know you don't," she said immediately. "I don't blame you, Robert!"

"Then you're more generous than I am!"

She was in a position to be, she thought, as they walked across the manor gardens and through the orchard to the oast house. Because she understood why he wouldn't give way, whereas he couldn't understand why she had double-crossed him. The oast house had become very dear to her and the thought of leaving it chilled her to the marrow. There was so little time left for him to find out that she hadn't lied!

"Are you nervous of going into an empty house?" he asked as they reached the small garden that she now thought of as her own, she had worked so hard in it.

"No," she answered.

"Then why do you leave all the lights on?"

She came to a full stop, staring at the lit-up house. "But I didn't, " she said, her mouth dry. "Oh, Robert, could it be burglars?"

"I doubt it. Still, I'm glad I came back with you. Will you wait here while I go in and see?"

She put her hand in his, trembling slightly. It had to be burglars. There was no one else it could be!

"No. I want to come. They might come out by another door!"

"And bop you on the head?"

"Laugh all you like, I'm not going to be left alone!" she told him.

He gave her hand a squeeze. "All right, we'll be intrepid together. But stand well behind me, Sarah!"

The back door had been left on the latch and fell open in response to the touch of his hand. The light from the kitchen came flooding out into the darkened garden making Sarah blink. But the room was empty, and so was the hall beyond.

"There doesn't seem to be anyone here," Robert whispered. "Are you sure you didn't leave the lights on yourself?"

"Of course I'm sure! If I did leave a light on, I'd remember! Besides, I wouldn't have left them on all over the house!"

Robert braced himself and walked down the hall, throwing open the door into the sitting room. He stood stock still, with Sarah peering over his shoulder with frightened eyes. Then slowly Madge, swaying a little, rose to her feet.

"I thought you'd never come," she said.

Sarah felt her breath leave her with the suddenness of a pricked balloon. "Madge!" she gasped.

Madge turned and looked at her, a hint of disapproval on her face as she took in the dress Sarah was wearing. "It isn't quite what I had expected you to be wearing so soon." Her voice trailed off dramatically. "No one wears *black* any longer, but such *bright* colors, darling? People are old-fashioned in the country, you know."

Sarah said nothing, but she couldn't help her eyes straying over her stepmother's scarlet and white linen coat and skirt, crushed from traveling, but as vivid and startling as it had been when she had first put it on.

"Shouldn't you be at the theater?" Robert asked her stiffly.

Madge laughed. "Are you worrying about the rent? One night's truancy wouldn't make any difference to that, my sweet, sweet landlord!"

"I didn't think Madge Dryden ever played truant!"

The harshness in his voice caught Madge on the raw. "Perhaps that's why I'm the one who always does pay the rent!"

"Robert isn't renewing our lease!" Sarah put in, hoping to divert her stepmother.

"Oh?" Madge cast Robert an arch look. "Has Sarah been stepping on your preserves?"

Robert looked bleak. "I think I'd better be going," he said. "We thought you were a burglar, Mrs. Blaney."

"And instead you found me celebrating my latest triumph all on my own! Were you really going straight home, Robert? I'm sure Sarah wouldn't allow it!"

"Madge," Sarah began with a touch of desperation, "if Robert wants to go—"

"Of course he doesn't! I have something to celebrate and the more people to celebrate with me, the better I like it! It's been worth it, all of it! Going on with that dreary play night after night! Everything!"

"I'll make the coffee," Sarah said abruptly.

Her stepmother giggled. "Not for me, darling. Nothing but champagne for me tonight!"

"I'm surprised you're not celebrating with your friends in London," Robert put in.

Madge's smile wavered. "I wanted to include Sarah!"

"Why?"

Sarah had a sudden vision of how Robert must appear to a recalcitrant client. It was not an aspect of him she had seen before and she was not sure that she liked it. She leaped to her stepmother's defense with a defiance that had nothing to do with Madge Dryden's hurt, bewildered expression.

"Why shouldn't she want me to celebrate her success with her?"

"That's what I want to know," he said dryly.

Madge pouted. "I don't like your friend," she said to Sarah. "I much prefer Alec Farne!" She raised her glass of champagne. "Don't you?"

"I'll make the coffee," Sarah said again.

"Nonsense! We'll all have champagne! Alec wouldn't come with me, but he told me to tell you that everything would come right. Silly, because it already has! I *adore* Alec, though!"

Robert's gray eyes flickered over Sarah's astounded face.

"Do you adore him too?" he asked. "Or is Mrs. Blaney a minority of one?"

Sarah gave him a speaking look. "Why aren't you on stage, Madge?"

"Because the play folded last night!" Madge declared, triumphant.

Sarah bit her lip. "But you knew it had to happen, didn't you? It was so bad, and you can't have enjoyed it very much."

Madge shrugged. "I hate doing nothing, and nothing was the alternative when I was first offered the part. Daniel told me something else would turn up, but it never does unless you make it happen. And you didn't mind, did you, Sarah?"

"It was your decision," Sarah said gently.

"Daniel thought I should have come down here with him. But once you're out of the public's eye, you're dead!"

"I didn't mind that!" Sarah exclaimed.

Robert's quizzical look brought the color flooding into her face. "But there was something that you did mind?" he suggested sweetly.

Sarah made an odd noise of protest and rushed out of the room. In the kitchen she filled the Cona coffee machine and lit the paraffin wick underneath it, bitterly conscious of her shaking knees and an aching longing for Robert's touch.

She put off going back into the living room for as long as possible, but when the coffee was made and would only become cold if she delayed further, she put the cups and some cream and the coffee on the tray and carried it into the room, her face averted from the interested looks that both Robert and her stepmother cast in her direction.

"Are you feeling all right?" Madge asked her.

"Yes, thank you. Why?" She sounded completely poised to her own ears and allowed herself to relax a little.

"You haven't asked me why I'm celebrating!" her stepmother complained.

Sarah smiled at her. "Have some coffee and tell us all about it," she invited.

Madge made a face. "I'm sticking to champagne! I told you, darling!"

Sarah poured out two cups of coffee and handed one to Robert, offering him the cream and sugar, neither of which he accepted.

"I'm going to be in a new play!" Madge announced with suitable drama.

"What is it?" Sarah asked. Her caution made her stepmother frown. "Have you discussed it with anyone?"

"I've never discussed my parts with anyone but Daniel, and he isn't here!" A faint smile played about Madge's lips. "I've talked it over with Alec."

"I think his advice would be pretty sound," Sarah agreed, satisfied.

"I don't think I'd care to follow his advice about much!" Robert snorted. "If I ever saw anyone out to feather his own nest, it's he!"

"About some things," Sarah agreed. "But he knows about the theater."

"He's a genius!" Madge breathed.

Revolted, Sarah frowned. "He's been fairly successful." To her surprise, Robert threw back his head and laughed. "What's the matter with you?" she demanded, her eye kindling.

"Not a very loverlike assessment!" he taunted her. But if he had hoped to embarrass her, his barb missed its mark. It was Madge whose eyes widened in dismay, two tears perched on the lower lids and waiting to fall.

"Oh, darling! You're going to be so cross!" she confessed. "Though why you should be, I don't know, because you never were very successful with boyfriends, were you?" She turned mournfully to Robert. "They all came flocking after me," she explained. "Poor little Sarah used to get so cross! She left home because of it!"

"Madge!"

"You never admitted it," Madge went on. "But I knew! You can't hide your feelings about things like that from another woman, can you? I mean, I knew that you didn't like Alec much, but I truly thought that he was interested in you, or he wouldn't have offered you that silly part." She frowned. "I wonder why he did? I must ask him." She brushed the question aside like a tiresome fly. "I'm sure he must have felt *something* for you, though he absolutely denies it now. Sarah, did you tell him that you were my stepdaughter? That would explain everything if you did!"

"No, I didn't. But I never hid the fact either."

"Well, it doesn't matter. The thing is that I've been *longing* to work with Alec for more than a year now, and I couldn't resist encouraging his connection with you because I thought it might be useful. How else was I to keep in touch with him if not through you? You *had* to go up to London to keep his interest alive, though I don't know when I've spent a more miserable evening, thinking about poor Daniel all the time!"

Sarah turned her back on her stepmother, her cup of coffee in her hands. "Did you see Neil at the station when I missed the last train?" she asked quietly.

"Robert's brother? Yes. What was he doing there? He was running about like a halfwit, and he followed you and Alec right back to the car! I was afraid that he would see me, so I hid in the shadows while you climbed in."

"I could have come back to Chaddoxbourne with him," Sarah said tonelessly.

"Oh, darling, I'm sorry about that! But you do see that I had to keep in touch with Alec? It hurt like anything when I discovered that it had all been unnecessary because he would have contacted me anyway just as soon as that dreadful show folded. But I didn't know that then! It *was* important, wasn't it?"

"Then Sarah did have supper with you," Robert said from a long way off. "I particularly asked you if she had, Madge, and you denied it."

"I thought you'd be cross because I'd landed you with looking after Daniel," Madge explained casually.

"So I was!" Robert remembered grimly.

"But I had to have Alec as my next producer!" Madge said tearfully. "I just had to! And he's going to find me something that will put me right back on top, so it was all worthwhile, wasn't it? I was beginning to think I was over the top. In fact I know I am, so I have to have a bit of his glory to keep me going, or it will all be over, and what will I do then?"

Robert said nothing. He swallowed his coffee down with a gulp and walked slowly out of the room. A long time later Sarah heard the front door shut after him and, if her stepmother had not been there, she would have run after him. But Madge was there, crying as if her heart would break, and out of habit, Sarah comforted her just as she knew her father would have done.

"It will be so exciting doing a new play!" she said.

Madge sniffed and looked more cheerful. "I'm not over the top! There are years more in me yet! You do think so, don't you Sarah?"

"I know so," Sarah said.

CHAPTER TWELVE

MADGE HAD ALWAYS been resilient and in a few minutes she was as gay as ever. "Darling, it is so exciting! Alec will be so good for me! At last I'll be allowed to grow up. He says one doesn't have to be young all the time. Ethel Merman doesn't take young parts, so why should I?"

A little startled by the comparison, Sarah murmured some suitable response, but her thoughts were with Robert. She wished he had stayed. Why had he gone so quickly? Was he still unconvinced? Her stepmother watched her. "You're not listening, Sarah. What bad manners that young man of yours has. By the way, I suppose he is your young man? He's not very loving, is he? Have you failed to keep your man again?"

"At least I haven't lost him to you!"Sarah snapped.

"You won't. Not him. Didn't he say his stepmother had been in the theater? I think she must have given him a bad time, because he disapproved of the lot of us, which is very boring of him."

Sarah was surprised by the shrewdness of Madge's comment. "I think his father was unhappy—"

"Probably wanted to be first, last and all the time with his wife. Be careful, Sarah. The son is very like his father in that."

"I'm not afraid," Sarah said gently.

Her stepmother looked at her as though she were a stranger. "You've never had much time for me, Sarah, but don't grow too far away from me. I need you, especially now. I can't help the way I am."

Sarah grinned. "You wouldn't change anyway! You like being the beautiful Madge Dryden—and why not?"

Madge preened with obvious pleasure. "I am still beautiful for my age! And now Alec is producing me, it's all been worth all the trouble. Tonight, I think I'm truly happy! Have some more champagne, darling, and be happy too!"

It was late when they went up to bed. Sarah went around the house turning out the lights and then she followed her stepmother slowly up the stairs.

"By the way," Madge said when they reached the landing, "did Daniel leave you much money?"

"I don't know yet. It wasn't a set sum, and all his debts and other bequests have to be paid first."

"But it's more than ten thousand pounds—apart from what your mother left him?"

"It may be. Does it matter?"

"Not to you evidently. It does to me. I think Daniel should have left it all to me. I was his wife!" Madge stood in the doorway of her bedroom, actually smiling. "I don't think Edwin will help me upset a will he helped to draw up, but I think I may get Robert to act for me. What do you think of that?"

Sarah met the malice in her stepmother's eyes squarely. "You can have the money," she said, suddenly tired. "Uncle Edwin need never know."

"Don't you want me to employ Robert?"

Sarah turned away, feeling sick. "Why do you want to humiliate me, Madge?" she asked. "I can't believe that the money means anything to you."

"Humiliate you? Darling, what an idea! I only want what is right. Daniel had no right to leave it all to you over my head like that!"

"He left you ten thousand pounds. Isn't that enough?"

"No, it's not! So don't take that holier-than-thou attitude to me, my girl! You're like your father in that, just like in everything else. But I won't be looked down on by you! What makes you think you're so much better than I am?"

"Oh, Madge, I don't!" Sarah protested.

"You think you'll marry Robert Chaddox, don't you? He won't have you! He doesn't like *your* stepmother any more than he liked that stepmother of his! You think you're too good for the theater now—"

"I don't! I don't want to go on with it as a career, that's all!"

"Nor will you ever be Mrs. Robert Chaddox! You can't change what you are. If he looks down on me, he'll look down on you. Once I've used him to contest the will, you won't even have Daniel's money to offer him!"

"Please don't, Madge."

Sarah went into her own room and shut the door firmly behind her. What a fool she was, she thought. She had been so sure that when Robert knew she hadn't lied to him, everything would be all right and she would marry him and live happily ever after. Whereas he had walked out without a single word to her, and her stepmother's spite would see to it that he never wanted to again!

More than ever, Sarah missed her father that night. She lay awake, trying to make up her mind why Madge disliked her. The only answers she could find distressed her, but she thought they were probably the right ones, and her father was the only one who could have taken the pain out of the knowledge. Sarah knew that she was a better actess than her stepmother and how unbearable that was to her. It was still worse now that she wanted to give up the stage, and she thought it possible that Madge saw that as a rejection of herself, rather than the honors and the exclusiveness of being always amongst theater people.

The other answer was her stepmother's dislike of feeling uncomfortable. She had been obliged to admit—and with Robert there too—that she had deliberately made use of her stepdaughter and had ignored her husband's illness merely to keep in touch with a producer she thought would be useful to her career. She wouldn't like them to think badly of her no matter what she had done. If she thought they despised her, her revenge would be as terrible as she could make it.

Sarah winced from the ugliness she had discovered. It was hard to believe that life would go on just the same despite the burden of her new knowledge. In a few weeks she would find she was able to accept her stepmother as she was.

It was only now, when the discovery that someone close to her could be so petty had exploded over her, that she was shocked and humiliated. It had been all the worse because Robert had witnessed the shock and humiliation. By dawn she had begun to think that she could never face him ever again!

Long before her stepmother was awake, Sarah pulled herself out of her crumpled bed and dressed in jeans and a sweater, slipping out of the house and away from the atmosphere that had become intolerable. She walked down the road toward the center of the village, not sure where to go, but one of the acorn signs of the North Down Way to Dover caught her eye and she turned down the lane to the path, glad to have a positive destination to aim for.

She didn't hear the car coming down the lane behind her until it was only a few feet away from her. She flattened herself against the hedge, barely looking up and was all the more surprised when it pulled up beside her and the door opened for her to get in.

"Sarah, are you going my way?"

She nodded briefly, without looking at him, knowing

only that she was pleased to see him whatever he thought of her, just because he was Robert.

"Are you always going to be so forgiving?" he asked her somewhat wryly.

She didn't answer immediately. Then she said, "Which way are you going?"

"I don't know. I caught sight of you trudging along as though your life depended on it, and I hopped into the car and came after you."

"I was going to walk to Dover," she told him.

His eyebrows rose. "What about your stepmother's breakfast?"

"I don't see that as any of my concern," she retorted. "Besides, she's asleep."

"Why aren't you?"

"I couldn't."

"You shouldn't let her upset you."

She wriggled uncomfortably. "You're a fine one to talk! How often did Neil's mother succeed in upsetting you? And without witnesses!"

He smiled, amused. "More times than I care to remember. And there usually were witnesses, especially at the beginning, before I grew a hide tough enough to deal with her. Your skin isn't very thick, is it?"

"I thought it was," she began impulsively. "I thought I was immune because I hardly ever saw her. Do you know I think I'd forgotten...." She broke off, uneasily aware that she had said more than she meant to. "It doesn't matter."

"On the contrary, I think it does. A lot of things were made clear to me last night."

"Oh?"

"Yes. I learned a lot about Sarah Blaney."

"And I suppose you didn't like what you learned?" she snapped.

He was surprised. "What makes you think that?"

"The way you just walked out without a single word. You didn't even say goodnight!" She tried to sound bright, but she wasn't at all successful. It seemed to her that she had revealed far too much of the agony he had caused her. It wasn't fair! He looked as calm as ever, and more than a little pleased with himself!

"Would you rather I'd stayed?"

"No, of course not," she whispered. "It was bad enough as it was!"

"That's what I thought, my love. Nor would it have done for me to be rude to Mrs. Blaney, and I would have if I had stayed."

Sarah uttered a little giggle. "She hates being called Mrs. Blaney."

He slowed down, turning off into a little group of trees. A few hundred years farther on the road petered out at the foot of a rounded chalk hill on which grazed a few sheep.

"Feel like climbing up to the top?"

She accepted immediately, glad to be out of the car. In the open, she thought, she could stand back from him and think before she spoke. Perhaps there would be no need to speak at all, and that would be better still.

He started off ahead of her, pausing whenever the path grew rough, or slippery from the morning dew. Once he took her hand and pulled her up the slope toward him, apparently thinking of something else. Only afterward he didn't let go her hand again, and she didn't like to reclaim it herself in case she reminded him that she was there when she was practically certain that he had forgotten all about her.

When they reached the top of the hill, she saw that the ground fell away far more sharply on the other side. In the far distance, lit by the early morning sun, she caught a glimpse of Canterbury Cathedral and some buildings that she took to be the new University of Kent. Nearer to her, in the valley below, was an Elizabethan farmhouse, with bulging walls and wavy roof, supported by a more modern wing that had been built on at the end. It was a peaceful scene and one that caught at her heart when she thought of London and the life she had led there.

Robert spread his jacket on the ground and gestured an invitation for her to sit down on it. She did so, twisting nervously away from where he was sitting. In silence, he put an arm around her waist and pulled her back beside him.

"Are you ready to talk?" he asked in her ear.

"What is there to talk about?"

She felt rather than heard his laugh. "My dear girl, if you want to pretend you don't know, you shouldn't tremble whenever I come near you!"

She stiffened and flushed. "I don't think that's kind!"

"I'm not a kind person," he said. "Especially not where you're concerned. You can only afford to be kind when you are indiferent to a woman. And I'm not indifferent to you, my Sarah. Far from it!"

She stole a glance at him and looked away again. "I told you I would be there waiting, but I'm not going to ask again," she muttered crossly. "Besides, I'll quite understand if you find you don't want to start again. It wasn't very pretty. You don't have to have anything more to do with either of us." She tried to struggle free from his restraining arm, but he tightened it about her until it hurt her ribs and interfered with her breathing.

"Tell me about your stepmother."

"I can't, Robert."

"Then I will. She's bone selfish about that career of hers and you and your father have encouraged her to wipe her pretty shoes all over both of you! I can understand why Daniel did it, but you, Sarah, why did you allow her to get away with it?"

"I don't think I allowed anything," she said slowly. "You believed her and there didn't seem to be much I could do about it. Daddy said that one day you would find out, and although I didn't really believe him, I held on to that. There wasn't anything else I could do!"

"I wasn't talking about this last incident," he said. "What about when you first left home? Wasn't that because you came up against the same kind of thing?"

She nodded unhappily. "I'd hate her for a while, but never for very long. The theater is the only real thing for her. She's the most dedicated person I've ever met. It's rather frightening to see someone totally given to anything. I think that was one of the things that hurt most, that she had nothing left over for anyone else, certainly not for me, who wasn't even her real daughter!"

"Nor for Daniel. She's a better actress off the stage than on it," Robert added bitterly. "I believed in her all the way until the night your father died."

"I know. It was bad luck that Neil didn't speak to me at the station."

"Yes, I had some pretty violent thoughts about him last night. In fact my view of myself as a pacific sort of person had to be radically overhauled one way and another. There was a moment earlier when I knew that I couldn't let you go, no matter what you were. I even considered threatening to take a stick to you if you ever looked at another man again, or told another lie. Your father's portrait is a poor substitute for the real thing."

Her laugh rang out, startling them both. "Oh, I'd love to have seen that!" she gurgled. "You'd never bring yourself to lay a hand on any woman! And if you did, you'd be so apologetic about it, I'd probably argue you out of it!"

"That's all you know!" he said grimly. "I've felt violent about you for weeks!"

Her eyes met his and her flesh tingled with what she

took to be fear. She tried to laugh. "Behold me in terror!" she joked. But he didn't laugh with her. He put up a hand and traced the outline of her jaw with his forefinger, slipping it into the neck of her jersey and jerking her toward him. His lips closed on hers and she could feel the violence that was still within him. He was hurting her, but she didn't care. With a murmured protest, her arms went up behind his neck and she pulled him closer.

After a few minutes he pushed himself away from her and she was surprised to discover that she was lying on the wet grass and in danger of falling down the slope into the valley below. She sat up and brushed the dew off her jersey. It didn't matter, for the sun would soon dry both her and the grass.

Robert lit himself a cigarette. She couldn't see his face, as he had turned away from her, but she could imagine exactly how he was looking. She plucked a blade of grass and examined it closely, annoyed because her fingers were trembling.

Civilization was a very thin veneer, even in someone like Robert, but who would have suspected that he too would ignite like a bomb and need time to recover? Certainly she had not.

He turned suddenly and smiled at her. "Convinced?"

"I didn't know..." she began.

He touched her face again, still smiling. "I know that. It's never happened to you before, has it?"

She shook her head, not looking at him in case she saw, not him, but a stranger. But he turned her face toward him and he was just the same after all, and his expression was very gentle.

"We'll have to do something about it," he said. "Will you marry me, Sarah?"

She was silent for a long moment, then the dam within her broke. She flung her arms around his neck.

"Oh, Robert, yes, please!" she cried out. And the tears came thick and fast, rolling down he cheeks in a new, exquisite agony of feeling.

"Darling Sarah, must you cry like that?"

She thought she would always be grateful to him for his gentleness as he wiped her tears and chided her tenderly for making him feel a brute.

"I'm sorry. I thought I'd lost you, and then, last night—"

"At least the truth came out."

"It was worse still after you'd gone. I thought you'd never come back! And Madge said she was going to upset the will and she'd ask you to act for her. She may yet," she added.

"I don't think she will," he comforted her. His mouth tightened. "Madge isn't likely to want to tangle with me for a long time to come."

Sarah's eyes opened wide. "Why not?"

He smiled faintly. "You remember the night I asked her to dinner?"

Sarah nodded. "I was terribly hurt that you didn't ask me too," she confessed. "I still think you might have done! You made me very unhappy!"

"Did I?" His eyes glinted and she thought he was going to kiss her again. "I was pretty unhappy myself!"

"Madge was terribly pleased that you asked her," she murmured.

"Yes, well, I asked Samantha, too,"

"I know that!"

He laughed. "Did Madge tell you?"

"No." she blushed. "She was with you when you brought Madge home. You saw her into the house and then you walked back to the manor with Samantha. You had your arm around her!"

He did kiss her then. "I hope you were jealous," he teased her.

"You shouldn't wish jealousy on to your worst enemy!" she sighed. "I hated both of you!"

"Samantha," he said dryly, "doesn't see well in the dark. Unlike you, my darling."

"I watched you from Madge's bedroom window."

His hand tightened on hers, but he made no other comment. "Your stepmother intrigued me. The only other actress I had known intimately was my own stepmother, and she was such an obvious fraud that I could only despise my father for being taken in by her. Yours is different. She has the same driving ambition, more of it in fact, but she had attracted and married a man like Daniel and she brought you up, so she had to have something else as well. I thought she was honest with herself." He gave her a quick kiss, silencing her protest. "You and Daniel were very loyal, my darling. Neither of you gave any sign that you weren't a completely happy family, temporarily at a loss because Madge couldn't see your father through his illness. Your father mentioned that he wished you'd had a happier home life, but that could have been caused by anything."

"I told you that she had asked me to supper after the theater, but you didn't believe me."

He looked at her seriously. "You haven't quite forgiven me for that, have you? The trouble was I wanted to believe you too much. I was equally sure that Madge would tell the truth if I asked her outright if she had had supper with you that night."

"Is that why you asked her to dinner?"

"I asked her twice," he said flatly. "Once directly, and once when we were talking about her show I slipped in some comment about your reaction to what she'd said to you about it on Monday. I drew a blank."

"Oh, Robert!"

"I know, I should have known better. But I kept remembering that you were in the theater too, and how your thoughts flit across your face. There was always the possibility that it was an act for my benefit."

"I know," Sarah said gently. "You were afraid of that from the beginning, weren't you?"

"I kept remembering how Neil's mother ran rings around my father. It wasn't a pretty sight."

"No," Sarah agreed. "I learned that last night, in a way. Personal relationships are not easy to put into perspective. I realized last night that I'd always believed all the clichés about them. Family feeling, and loving the child because she loved the father, and even that loving one's family was a happy feeling."

"Yet you left home and went off on your own?"

"That was different." She hesitated, not knowing quite how to tell him. "I wanted to go on the legitimate stage, and I didn't want to be crowded by the great Madge Dryden. But I still thought we loved each other. I suppose we still do—in a way, mixed up with a whole lot of other things. Some of them aren't very nice. Maybe I didn't want to see them before."

"Poor Sarah! Yet you kept you head better than I did, insisting that you'd be vindicated in the end."

"I didn't always believe it."

"But you didn't give up. You gave me some uncomfortable moments when you kept insisting that I was wrong about you. There was all the evidence against you, unanswerable, as I thought, and all you had was hurt bewilderment that I wouldn't believe you. It was such an uneven battle that I found myself wondering why you didn't admit that you'd been with Alec. You never did."

"I might have done if I hadn't understood how you felt," Sarah said gruffly. "But I couldn't help agreeing with you that one can't compromise with the truth. If I had been playing games with Alec, I'd have thought you were right." She smiled fleetingly. "Now that you know the truth, I find it comforting that you think it important.

We may hurt each other, but it will be a clean hurt."

"I'll try not to hurt you," he promised. "Will you mind being nothing more exciting than Mrs. Robert Chaddox?"

She took a quick breath, her face white and solemn. "Oh, Robert, I hadn't thought—I haven't much to bring you, but I will try to be worthy of your name!"

And she wondered why he let out a whoop of joy, completely overcome by delighted laughter.

MADGE DRYDEN went straight back to London when she heard that Sarah intended to marry Robert.

"I'm not going to encourage you in this foolishness," she said as she climbed into her car. "I won't have anything to do with it! When you want to come back to the theater, let me know, and I'll do what I can to help you."

Sarah ignored that. "You'll come to the wedding, won't you, Madge?"

Madge screwed up her face while she thought about it. "I don't think so," she said. "You're too old to be my daughter—even my stepdaughter—and if I came, there would be a whole lot of publicity about us and my age would be bound to come out."

"I see," said Sarah.

Her stepmother looked her straight in the eyes. "You won't miss me," she said wryly.

Sarah felt both guilty and inadequate. "I'll send you some wedding cake. And you'll always know where to find me."

"I suppose so," Madge sighed. "I might come and visit you after a year or two. Robert's bound to insist on children and they may be glad to have a famous stepgrandmother. It will counteract some of the worst effects of their country upbringing, and you never know, one of them may have a yen for the theater later on."

Sarah blinked at this pat presentation of a readymade

family when the idea of children—Robert's children—had scarcely crossed her mind. She felt decidedly foolish, especially when she realized that her stepmother knew exactly what she had been thinking.

"Come whenever you can!" she said.

"We'll see," Madge nodded. She revved up the engine and blew a kiss in Sarah's direction. "'Bye, darling!"

Sarah watched the car disappear down the road. She still felt guilty and knew it was because she was glad that her stepmother had decided not to come to the wedding. It was not a moment that she wanted to share with Madge Dryden, either in the guise of famous star or of her stepmother. She wouldn't enjoy being outshone by Madge's dazzling charm herself, but worse still Madge would be bound to annoy Robert on a day when she wanted everything to be perfect for him. Then she laughed at herself for the conceit of that particular desire and went through the orchard to find him.

Robert greeted her with a smile. He held out a hand to her and she slipped into the circle of his arm with a sigh of relief.

"Has she gone?"

She nodded. "It wasn't as bad as I'd expected. She says she'll come and visit us when we produce some grandchildren to appreciate her!"

"I hope you carried it off with an air," Robert said, enjoying the expression on her face.

She chuckled. "You would have been proud of me," she teased him. "I'll never learn to act off a stage! I'm afraid it was only too clear that the idea came as a shock to me. Rather a delightful shock," she added. "Ridiculous because you as good as told me that you would marry to have an heir to leave the house to rather than have it go out of the family!"

"You sound very willing to oblige me," he retorted.

"Yes, I am," she said frankly, acknowledging the

pressure of his arm with a smile. "Madge won't come to the wedding. I think it's just as well, don't you?"

"I'd have preferred you to have someone to support you, but as long as you don't change your mind about marrying me, I don't care what happens."

Sarah looked thoughtful. "I think I'll ask Uncle Edwin. He'd like to stand in for daddy, and he'll approve of my being married in a village church in the place where I'm going to live."

"Good idea. Neil will be my best man. That leaves the reception."

Sarah gave him an embarrassed look. "I think that's all been arranged," she told him. "The Women's Institute choir is going to sing for us, and the rest of them, led by Mrs. Vidler, are going to make the food."

Robert kissed her cheeks. "I'm ashamed to say I was worried about your lack of family, in case you minded, but with the whole of Chaddoxbourne on your side of the church I'd better look to my own laurels!"

"Darling, you don't have to! It's only because I'm going to be your wife and they're pleased for you. They've all been so kind to me that I'd like it to be a day to remember for them."

His arms tightened about her and she turned to face him, reaching up for his kiss. It would not be many days now until she was Mrs. Robert Chaddox, and if it seemed long, it was all too short for the multitude of things that had to be done.

"Happy, darling?" he asked her.

She answered him with her lips. She was indeed totally happy and she had no fears for the fuure, for together they would guard their happiness well, working at it all the harder because it had so nearly fallen through their fingers. His kiss deepened and her heart thudded against her ribs with the new familiar magic that his touch produced in her.

THE RED PLAINS OF JOUNIMA

The Red Plains of Jounima

Dorothy Cork

Fate held out a string and Pippa followed it from England to Australia, to the outback sheep station of Skye Bannerman.

The invitation, made without the owner's knowledge, had been vague; Pippa had jumped at it only as a chance to escape her cousin's manipulation of her life.

The country was vast and exciting, different from anything she had imagined. Yet her reception at Jounima was cool. Skye was a formidable boss, and was unimpressed by her appearance and reason for being there. Pippa had no wish to be indebted to him.

But she found her independence and determination to control her own destiny were of secondary importance once she'd fallen in love!

CHAPTER ONE

PIPPA WAS RELIEVED and didn't pretend to herself to be otherwise when at long last she was alone in the train coach. *I am a dill*, she thought, looking ruefully at orange-juice stains on cotton jeans that had started the day—some sixteen hours ago—sparkling white. Children attacked her soft heart every time, and she had recklessly taken a small boy on her knee while his mother fed the baby. The small boy had brought his orange with him and wiped sticky hands on Pippa's pretty pants, then devoted some time to lovingly stroking the gay little flower-sprinkled patch on her right knee that said warmheartedly, "Have a nice day."

For Pippa, it had not really been a nice day. Now she looked through the train window into darkness—the utter darkness of the Australian outback. In a half hour or so she would leave the train at Jounima Siding, and she would be very, very thankful. It had been a long and tiring journey and she had not counted on making it alone. It would have been cheerier in every way if Bronwen Lightfoot had been on the coach, too, but, mysteriously, Bron had not appeared. Pippa hadn't a notion why not, and she tried not to consider the possibility of Bruce Lightfoot's not appearing at Jounima Siding, either. That would be a disaster! All the same, as she glanced upward at the luggage rack where her big suitcase, which contained everything she had brought out from England, rested, she felt reassured. If for some reason the two Lightfoots had disappeared into thin air, she would resign herself to that fact and find some sort of a job at Jounima Siding as a start. *A good typist*, she told herself firmly, *can get a position anywhere.*

Later knowledge of Jounima Siding proved that thought laughable, but just then it was a steadying one. In actual fact, a job was what she most needed at the moment, if she was eventually to pay her return fare to England. There was no desperate hurry about that, particularly since she had met Bruce, but she wanted to be able to go when it suited her, for through her own softheartedness, she had been put in an awkward position.

She relaxed back against the seat and her fingers, playing idly with her long golden brown hair, began to weave a thin plait that started at the temple, as her mind strayed bemusedly over the events of the past few weeks.

Pippa was an orphan, and although she was only nineteen, she had had to fend for herself for some time. That was no hardship, for she was an independent girl with a proud spirit. Her cousin Lalla, wealthy to begin with and now married into still more money, could not understand this, and had never abandoned her efforts to patronize Pippa and to use her. "I can get you a cushy job with Tony's firm any time you like, Pippa, and in return I ask only that you come and live with us and make yourself reasonably useful." Pippa was not tempted. She was a good typist and definitely in line for promotion from the typing pool. In next to no time she expected to become a private secretary. It had, in fact, been about to happen when her tender heart got the better of her, and for once she gave in to Lalla. Tony was being sent to Sydney for two years to open up a new branch of the firm, and the whole family—Lalla, the two small children and the baby—was organized for the move when little Christopher was unexpectedly whipped off to hospital for an urgent appendectomy.

"Pippa, you've got to help me out," Lalla had begged

over the telephone. "We can't turn all our plans upside down for one small child. Chris adores you, Pippa. If I knew you'd stand by him at the hospital I'd go away without a worry."

"Of course," said Pippa immediately. "Of course, I'll visit him every moment I'm free, Lalla, but...."

There was a pause. Then Lalla said firmly, "And Pippa, I want you to bring him out to us in Australia as soon as he can travel."

"But my job!" protested Pippa, dismayed. Only yesterday she had been sent for by Mr. Phillips whose secretary was leaving to be married, and she had been as good as told that she would be asked to take over.

Lalla said airily, "Your job? You'll get another job, Pippa. It's not as if it were anything special you were doing—typing."

Pippa held out, but only till she had visited Christopher that evening. After that, she knew that of course she would see him safely to his parents in Sydney. He was old enough to understand and to be rather frightened by what was happening, but if "Pippy" was looking after him, then everything was all right.

So Pippa did her good deed without any regrets. Christopher's small, trusting face, the little hand reaching constantly for hers, were her assurances that she had done the only possible thing.

And then she discovered the catch. There was no return ticket waiting for her when she reached Sydney. Trust Lalla!

"You must stay with us, Pippa, now that you're here," her cousin said. And she said it after she had shown Pippa the lovely bedroom with its own bathroom that she was to have in the house Tony had rented in Killara. It was a huge house—almost a mansion—with a beautiful garden, a small swimming pool, a double garage and masses of space for entertaining.

"It's been a headache getting staff," Lalla said. "And it's practically impossible to get anyone to mind the children. Anyone I could *trust.* But they love you, Pippa, they know you and you'll have a wonderful life here. No more dreary little basement flats or getting up in the dark of a winter morning to go to work. Lots of sunshine, freedom whenever you want it and of course you'll be one of the family and meet all our friends. Look, I've already put by a whole heap of clothes I want you to have." She opened the door of an enormous built-in wardrobe, and Pippa stared at the array of dresses and skirts and pants and blouses that hung there. That long slinky, silky greenish gold affair...

She turned her eyes resolutely aside as Lalla said persuasively, "They're all as good as new, but I went on a buying spree before we left London, and now I've found a wonderful little boutique up the line with the most ravishing sunwear."

Pippa said resolutely, "No, Lalla. I'm not staying."

Lalla bit her lip. "Then what am I to do? The children love you, Pippa, Chris will miss you—"

"It's *you* they should love," said Pippa, refusing to have her heartstrings torn, refusing most of all to be bribed or coerced or bulldozed into a life-style she had resisted for years. "*You're* the one who should be there when they need loving. *You're* the one Chris should miss...."

NEVERTHELESS, for the following three days she minded the children while Lalla busied herself with the beginnings of a new social life. Tony simply refused to discuss the possibility of paying her fare back to England, having been well and truly briefed by his wife. "Of course you must stay with us, Pip," was about all he contributed. "We'll love to have you here, and you can help with the children."

It would have been so easy to give in. Everything in that house was so beautiful and luxurious, and Lalla had managed to get hold of an excellent housekeeper who cooked "like a goddess!" The line of least resistance. *But I'd be a sort of parasite,* Pippa reflected dispassionately. *A cross between a parasite and a slave.* She had no illusions about the extent of the freedom that would be hers: she would be worse off than a bird in a gilded cage, and she rapidly decided that if Tony wouldn't pay her fare back to England then she would find herself a job, move out of Killara into some less-exclusive suburb and set to work to save up the money herself.

The fourth day, she told Lalla she was going out. There was quite a scene. Lalla had a luncheon date, she had guests coming to dinner, she would need a respite from the children when she came home, and she couldn't possibly cope without Pippa.

"I'm sorry," said Pippa firmly. "You didn't tell me your plans, Lalla, or ask me if I'd be available."

Lalla was almost speechless, and Pippa hurried away feeling mean and guilty, to spend an aimless day wandering about the city, window shopping, getting lost, looking at beautiful clothes she could never afford. She lunched in the cafeteria of a big department store, wandered into an arcade and was attracted by a "hip" shop full of young people and pop music and rose and purple lights. There she succumbed to temptation and bought herself a pair of white jeans with a heart-shaped flower patch on the knee and sleeveless green top that sparked up the latent green in her gray eyes. She walked out of the shop wearing this gear and feeling like a different person, her neat blue summer suit folded in tissue and popped into a carrier bag that was gay with flowers.

If she was going to be reckless with what little money she had, she decided not to be reckless all on her own account, and in a toy shop she bought a red truck for Christopher, a fluffy koala for Samantha and a bright mobile for the baby.

Feeling a bit overladen, she headed for the quay and took a ferry ride. When it grew dark and she had eaten fried fish and chips at a beach café and was feeling tired and lonely, she found her way to an amusement park.

And that was where she met Bruce and Bronwen Lightfoot.

Pippa had installed herself and her parcels on a bench, and was watching the crowd with eyes that were becoming glazed with weariness. There was a shooting gallery nearby, and soon her attention became riveted on a fair-haired, good-looking young man who was knocking down prize after prize and causing quite a degree of interest. Pippa's eyes became alert, fascinated. He had three dolls, a set of steak knives and a toy rifle, and as she watched in disbelief, he shot through yet another string and won a pair of binoculars. He certainly was a crack shot. He had very blue eyes and a curving, laughing mouth; he was with a girl so like him she simply had to be his sister. They were dressed alike, in blue jeans and shirts.

I'll die if she's anything else, thought Pippa fatuously, weariness having demolished some of her usual disciplines.

Presently, these two, laughing themselves into fits, staggered with their trophies over to the bench where Pippa was sitting and sank down near her.

"What'll we do with them?" the young man asked with an explosive laugh. He held up one of the big kewpie dolls and fluffed out its nylon net skirt. "I can't take all this stuff back to North Star—Skye would tear a great strip off my hide if he thought I'd squeezed a bit of play into my study program, even if it is a final fling."

"Skye's an ogre," said the girl. She put the wrong end

of the binoculars to her eyes and looked along the bench at Pippa. "Bruce, these glasses are crazy! This bench is two miles long and there's a girl away off at the other end, almost out of sight."

"Bron, you're an idiot." Bruce looked at Pippa, too, but without the aid of the binoculars. He grinned at her in a friendly way. "Hello there! I suppose you wouldn't like a doll?"

Pippa's eyes widened. She thought of three-year-old Samantha. "I have a little semi-neice who would," she said promptly.

"Terrific! Take your pick."

The dolls were dressed in different colors, and while Pippa chose, she knew that Bruce was studying her. She looked up suddenly and caught his eye, and she thought, *I like him—he's fun.* She knew a pang of regret that they should meet like this and then part—forever. She chose the doll with the pink dress and remarked, "I could do with an extra hand, now. All these parcels to carry!"

A brown hand reached out to take hers. "You're welcome to help yourself to one of mine. I'm Bruce Lightfoot, and this is my sister, Bronwen, by the way."

"Hello! I'm Pippa Shaw."

They all smiled at each other, and Pippa felt she had suddenly acquired two Australian friends.

After that they spent about two hours together. They went on the ferris wheel and the water dodgems; they went on the ghost train, and Pippa shrieked and hung on to Bruce's arm. Somewhere along the way she lost her nice blue suit, and Bruce lost his rifle, and they laughed hilariously about it all as they drank ice-cream sodas at a high counter and shouted to each other over the blare of hectic, mad fairground music.

"I'll have a headache," shouted Bron.

Pippa thought she would have, too, and was regretful that soon a headache was all that would be left of the evening—apart from happy memories. They were heading with unspoken agreement for the exit when Bruce halted suddenly, turned to look at Pippa, and exclaimed, "Pippa, I adore you! So what are we going to do? I simply must see you again, but I have to get back to the bush in the morning."

"Must you really?" protested Bron. "Isn't Skye holding the fort? An extra day or two can't do any harm."

"No?" Bruce raised his eyebrows. "Skye's all ready to take the first opportunity that crops up to boot me out and get his precious sister and her husband back on North Star. Now that Adrian's back in circulation...."

Pippa listened curiously. Skye must be Bruce's boss, and he didn't sound like a particularly amiable one. North Star must be where Bruce worked and....She gave up trying to conjecture further when he said, "Anyhow, how free are you, Pippa—jobwise?"

"Free as the air," replied Pippa promptly.

"Great! Then suppose—" he screwed up his blue eyes and looked measuringly at his sister "—suppose the two of you come out west and we get a party rolling. Bron's got a birthday coming up, he added for Pippa's benefit. "Her twenty-first. Pretty important!"

"Mother's already got something worked out for *that*," said Bron.

"Yes, but what's wrong with two parties? We'll have a preview in the sticks. How about it, Pippa? A week from tomorrow. That will give me a chance to prepare the ground, as it were."

Pippa, a little bewildered, said carefully, to make sure she had it straight, "A week from tomorrow. Is that right? And where is the...the Styx?"

He laughed. "Not the Styx. The sticks, the bush, the outback. And you're invited not just to a party, you must come to stay."

"For how long?" Pippa wanted to ask, more bewildered than ever. It was all so vague, so casual and informal. Of course she would go—if they ever got around to being more specific. And of course she was insane, because she should be looking for a job, instead. But *she was going.* She was following a hunch, and she had a feeling that right then that was a good thing to do. She was in a strange land and was virtually alone. And she liked Bruce—and Bron—very much. So why not?

Bron was asking, "Shall we fly, Pippa? Or shall we take the train?"

"Say you'll take the train, for God's sake," exhorted Bruce. "My sister's scared stiff of planes. But be warned—the train trip's an ordeal, no less."

"But it's cheaper by rail," said Bron.

Pippa confessed, "That's a deciding factor with me. At this stage of my life, I have to count my pennies."

The next few minutes were more practical. Bron produced a ballpoint pen and a scrap of paper. "Right. We take the train a week tomorrow. That'll be, um, the thirteenth! Better make it the fourteenth, in that case. Not that I'm superstitious...."

"But it doesn't do to take chances," said Bruce with a grin.

"We'll take the day train. You must buy a ticket for Jounima Siding, Pippa." She wrote the name down carefully under the date. "The train leaves central at six-thirty. Where are you living, by the way?"

"Killara," said Pippa. She tore a narrow strip from the paper and wrote Lalla's address and telephone number on it.

"Lucky you," said Bron. "You'll get an extra half-hour's sleep. Seven o'clock at Hornsby for you, Pippa. I'll be on the train already and I'll look out for you. I'll hop out on the platform and wave a red flag if necessary."

"And I'll be at Jounima Siding with the red carpet,"

said Bruce. He hugged Pippa and kissed her goodbye, and Bron kissed her, too, and she went back home to her lovely bedroom in Tony's and Lalla's house feeling happy and slightly dazed.

She hadn't heard anything from Bruce since, or from Bronwen either, but then she hadn't expected to, and she had refused to listen to Lalla's exclamations of disbelief that Pippa should be taking off into the blue just when everything she could possibly desire was there in Killara. Pippa packed her bag on the night of the thirteenth, and with a feeling she was betraying her principles just the tiniest bit, she included the slinky golden green dress—because after all she was going to a party—and a yellow bikini because she couldn't resist it. She felt excited and she felt nervous, too. The night at the amusement park seemed as unreal as a dream, and she wished that she had asked a dozen questions so that she had something a little more solid to think about than a fair-haired brother and sister who were loads of fun and who had befriended her so spontaneously.

"Pippa, I adore you." Had he said that? Pippa didn't adore him—not yet. But who could tell? If she came to know him better.... Once or twice she thought of passing up the party, but the idea of a secretarial job in the city failed to excite her, and besides, she didn't want to be within Lalla's easy reach. Better to find herself a job at Jounima Siding or somewhere in the vicinity. And get to know Bruce better, if she felt that way about him and he felt that way about her....

When Bron failed to show up on the train, her high spirits received a serious blow. This was the right day, and this was the right train, and she clung doggedly to the belief that there was some simple explanation and that Bruce would be waiting to welcome her at Jounima Siding.

Pippa stirred on the seat and glanced at her watch. Almost there. Her busy fingers had by now made a plait at each side of her brow, and she brought them across her forehead and tied them together at the back of her head. Like a Red Indian girl. All that was lacking was a feather. Bruce would laugh.... She stood up and heaved her suitcase down from the rack and glanced at herself in the mirror over the seat. Ruffled, tired, nervously bright-eyed; a pale, heart-shaped face, black-lashed eyes that looked plain gray in the rather dull electric light; a slightly tilted nose sprinkled with pale freckles, a mouth that was too wide. Would he still adore her?

She picked up her suitcase and staggered along the corridor and reached the door just as the train came to a halt. The guard was shouting, "Jounima Siding!" and Pippa opened the door and looked out into the night, blinked hard, and stared.

Instead of the railway station she had expected to see, with lighted office and waiting room and refreshment stand, there was virtually nothing. The guard, swinging a lamp—the only light in the darkness of the night apart from those of the train—stood on a rickety wooden platform just about big enough to hold him and his lamp, and Pippa and her suitcase.

Stepping down beside him, she asked faintly, "Did you say Jounima Siding?"

"That's right, miss. A special stop for you. And here's your party coming now, by the look of it. You'll be all right."

He was back on the train and it was sliding away into the night before she had fully gathered her senses. The train lights flicked over a row of trucking yards, a wooden ramp. She could smell sheep and fresh earth and grass. But when the train had gone, she couldn't see a thing. Except the headlights of a car. Bruce's car. Pippa bit hard on her lip and managed a smile. A job at Jounima Siding! She would certainly have to rethink that part of her plan, she reflected ruefully. At least she had enough money to get back to Sydney or to some other town. She stood waiting while the car, a station wagon, came closer, and in a couple of minutes pulled up on a track a few yards beyond the platform on which she stood, looking, she supposed, rather ghostlike in the darkness, in her white jeans and pale green top. Well, the night was warm, the stars were bright in a black sky, and here was Bruce and everything was going to be all right. Pippa heaved a sigh of relief.

But the man who climbed out of the station wagon and came up the ramp toward her was not Bruce. She realized that in no time. He carried a large flashlight, and he flicked it upward so that it shone on her indirectly, and as she came closer they could both see each other. Pippa saw a tall, wide-shouldered man with black brows and eyes that seemed black, too—a man years older than Bruce, who smiled at her distantly and politely with no pretense of welcome or friendliness, so that her own smile faded from her lips and she simply stood and stared and waited.

Had he even come for *her*?

He looked her over quickly but thoroughly. At the two narrow plaits brought across her forehead, Red Indian style, at the golden brown locks that lay across her bare shoulders. At her stained jeans and the patch on her knee. At her suitcase, which seemed so enormous on the tiny platform. For just a second she wanted to giggle. It must have looked as though she had come for a month! Unless he decided she had brought a crinoline to wear to the party!

He said at last with frigid politeness, "Good evening. I presume you're Pippa Shaw."

Pippa breathed a faint sigh of relief. At least she was the right person!

"Philippa Shaw,"she said, trying to look dignified despite her jeans and her hair and her sneakers. "I beg your pardon. Philippa Shaw." He didn't smile. "I'm Bruce's cousin, Schuyler Bannerman. Will you come along to the car? He picked up her suitcase and lit the way down the ramp, and somehow or other she didn't dare ask him where Bruce was, but followed him as meekly and unquestioningly as a child. He saw her into the front seat in silence, disposed of her suitcase in the back and climbed in beside her.

Pippa said, with an effort at composure, "I suppose you think I've brought a lot of luggage just to come to a party. In actual fact, it contains all my worldly goods, because you see, I thought I might get a job at Jounima Siding." She sent him a sidelong glance, but he was plainly not amused. His lip curled a little in the faint light of the dash, but it was not in a smile.

As he started up the motor and the car moved smoothly forward, he said distantly, "Your hopes of a party are groundless, I'm afraid, so it's perhaps as well that you don't have only what you stand up in plus your evening finery."

Pippa, chilled, digested that. No party! Was it taking Bruce longer than he had anticipated to prepare the ground, whatever that had meant? Or had he simply not told this Schuyler Bannerman about the party? Pippa thought she wouldn't be surprised if that was the case. He didn't appear to be what you would call a party-goer. She had an uneasy feeling that she should apologize for coming—the man beside her had that effect on her—and she had to bite back any apologetic words. After all, she had been invited, so there was no reason to apologize for accepting an invitation. The station wagon was speeding along a narrow dirt track that ran through wide grassy paddocks, past occasional groups of tall trees; there was no sign of a town or even of a house anywhere at all, as far as Pippa could see. Not a light showed anywhere.

She asked presently, "Perhaps you can tell me why Bronwen wasn't on the train, Mr. Bannerman."

"Skye," he said automatically, and she felt a shock. Bruce had talked about Skye. "Skye wants to boot me out." And Bron had said, "Skye's an ogre." Pippa decided she was right. She was secretly frightened of him already and hated herself for being so. He continued briefly, "We've more to be doing around here just now than to be playing about with parties. Hence there was nothing to bring Bronwen here."

"Oh," said Pippa, dashed. She added coldly, "If she had let me know, I wouldn't have come, either."

"She would have let you know if she'd had your address. However, it appears nobody had that, Miss Shaw—Philippa. A little fact I find rather hard to follow. So the wheels of fate couldn't be stopped and I had to come to meet you."

He spoke, Pippa thought, as though there were something disreputable about the whole setup, and she decided it was beneath her dignity to tell him that she had given Bron both her address and her telephone number. Why, after all, should she explain herself? Bron must have lost it, and that was easy enough to understand. She had used such a small scrap of paper. She said, distant, too, "You should have let Bruce come."

"Bruce has gone out to the back paddock," she was told briefly.

"What for?" Pippa wondered aloud, unable to help herself.

"To bring in a herd of sheep from a drought-stricken area."

"Oh," said Pippa. She peered out into the darkness. "Is this a sheep farm?"

He sent her an odd look. "A sheep station," he corrected her. "Didn't you even know that?"

"No," said Pippa. She knew perfectly well that his

opinion of her couldn't have been lower: a girl whose address was unknown, who didn't even know she was coming to a sheep station; who had talked of working at Jounima Siding; who had brought all her worldly goods with her to a nonexistent party. And now she saw him send a lightning glance downward at the heart-shaped patch on her knee.

He touched it briefly with a hard brown finger. "What does that say?"

"Have a nice day," said Pippa faintly.

For the first time he laughed.

But Pippa wanted to cry.

SHE DIDN'T KNOW how much later it was when the homestead came into sight. There was a great grove of trees shadowing the dark skyline ahead, and then they entered a long, gravelled, tree-lined driveway that wound up the slope of a low hill. Finally the headlights picked out a white house, two-storied and set in lawns surrounded by flower beds. There was a haunting fragrance all about, and the air was soft and warm and motionless. The man beside Pippa said, "Here we are," and braked to a standstill before wide steps that led up to a gracefully pillared veranda. Light fell across the gravel from wrought-iron lamps, and a flower-starred vine moved almost imperceptibly in a light stirring of the air.

Pippa climbed down and stared up at the house. She had not had the faintest notion that North Star would be like this! She thought of her meager wardrobe with a slight feeling of panic, then thanked heaven for the green gold dress. Only of course, there was no party.

The wide front door stood open, and Schuyler Bannerman took her suitcase from the station wagon and ushered her up the steps and inside. Pippa could see at once that this really was a luxurious home. The splendors of Lalla's Killara place paled in comparison. But what a shocking contrast she must make in her casual, mussed up gear! She stopped staring around and refused to be overawed or intimidated. Through glass doors at the far side of the big square entrance hall, which was as large as Lalla's sitting room, she could see into a sort of lighted courtyard. She saw dark orange trees and the glitter of a pool, and a beautiful dark-haired woman in a one-piece swimsuit lying back in a swing seat. Nearby a small blonde girl was playing with a big rubber ball, and Pippa thought automatically, *She should be in bed* and then she thought, *That must be his wife and child.*

She became aware that she had been left alone at the very moment Schuyler Bannerman rejoined her from a side door. He stood looking down at her narrowly in the light from an elaborate and beautiful overhead lamp, and Pippa looked back at him curiously, for the first time seeing him properly, as he was seeing her. His eyes, she noticed immediately, were not black. They were sharply, darkly blue. His face was tanned and hard, his hair almost black, thick and inclined to be unruly, ruffled by the drive through the night. He wore pants of light colored fine cotton and a cream silk shirt open at the neck, and just now the lines of his mouth were relaxed and softened. She had thought he had a hard mouth, to go with that firm jawline, but now a smile touched its corners. Sudden color flew to her cheeks. Of course! In a superior way he was amused at *her.* No doubt he thought she had spilled orange juice all over herself.

"I suppose you're hungry, Philippa," he said.

Pippa turned away slightly. "No," she said indifferently. Dinner must have been over hours ago, and she was not looking for favors from anyone, be it cook, housekeeper, wife or Schuyler Bannerman himself. She had eaten a rather horrid dried-out cheese sandwich and drunk scalding tea from a thick white cup at a railroad restaurant way back in the distant past, so she would not starve. She would wait for Bruce, and if her hunger pangs were bad, then he would get her something. Meanwhile, she was going to be no trouble to anyone. She added, "But I am tired."

"I guess you are. Well, there's a comfortable bed awaiting you. Eve will take you up."

A fair-haired woman of thirty or so, tanned and capable-looking as well as attractive, appeared at that moment and sent Pippa a smile before she asked, "Did you want me, Skye?"

"Yes. This is Philippa Shaw. Look after her, will you, Eve? She's spent the day on the train; she's tired and probably hungry."

"I'm not hungry," said Pippa furiously, but he ignored her.

"Are the children in bed?"

"Except for Annabel. She needs to be tied down, I think," said Eve, laughing a little.

"Don't worry about her. She can stay around a little longer." He glanced at Pippa and nodded briefly. "Sleep well."

Pippa said nothing. Eve turned to her. "Come along, Philippa. Here, we can carry your suitcase between us. It is a large one, isn't it? Whatever have you got in it?"

"All her worldly goods," said Skye sardonically, pausing on his way to the courtyard.

Eve's eyebrows shot up and Pippa said defensively, "It's true. I thought I could find work at Jounima Siding."

Eve laughed and they climbed the graceful, carpeted stairway together. Pippa felt slightly soothed. Eve, who struck her as being friendly, showed her into a large and beautiful bedroom that had both a bathroom and a dressing room off it; wide windows opened onto a small, shaded balcony. Pippa stepped out on it for a moment.

She could see a side garden, tennis courts, and what looked like stables. But no outhouses. Eve was switching on soft lights, inspecting towels and bed linen and opening drawers. Pippa, inside again, asked her, "Are you the housekeeper?"

"No, I'm the governess. My name's Eve Arnold. Skye didn't really introduce us, did he? He's not in the best of moods at the moment."

You can say that again, thought Pippa.

"Hang up your clothes, Philippa, and freshen up, and then if you come downstairs you can have a snack in the sun room."

Pippa opened her suitcase. Apart from the party dress, what she saw didn't look impressive—in surroundings like these.

"I'm not hungry, thanks, so I'd rather not come down. And please don't call me Philippa. I'm Pippa."

"Now come on, Pippa. You must be hungry. I know the sort of meal one makes do with on trains. Please come down. I'll wait for you, shall I?"

"No," said Pippa stubbornly. No fuss, no trouble—particularly as she wouldn't have been there at all if Bronwen hadn't mislaid her address.

Eve left, and Pippa hung up her clothes. She took off her sneakers, changed her jeans and blouse for a short housecoat, then washed her face thoroughly at the pretty blue basin in the bathroom. It was a super bathroom. Everything you could possibly want was in it—bath salts, body lotion that smelled divine and must have been very expensive, scales, a magnifying mirror, a hair dryer....

Pippa was still looking around and opening cupboards and drawers in what she thought of as her suite, when Eve knocked on the door and entered with a tray, which she put down on a small, glass-topped table with gilded legs. She indicated a low, satin-brocaded chair and told Pippa, "Sit down and eat this up. It's very light and will do you good." She raised the lid from a silver dish, and Pippa sniffed and felt immediately hungry. Creamy chicken soup garnished with parsley, thin slices of bread and butter, a goblet of white wine.

She sat down and started eating, quite ravenously.

"When will Bruce be home from the, er, back paddock?"

"I don't really know," said Eve, who had sat down on the divan.

"I'm going to stay up and wait for him," Pippa decided.

The other woman looked surprised. "He won't be coming back *here*, Pippa. He lives out at North Star."

Pippa blinked her gray eyes. "Isn't this North Star?"

"No, of course not. This is Jounima. Surely everyone's heard of Jounima...and Skye Bannerman."

Everyone but me, thought Pippa. In a reflective silence, she finished her soup, bread and butter and wine, every bit of it.

After the first shock of surprise, she felt much better. She decided that Eve couldn't have told her anything that pleased her more. This wasn't North Star and so she wouldn't have to stay here—with Schuyler Bannerman, where she hadn't been invited—any longer. She could move over to North Star and she hoped it would be a simple, unpretentious sort of place—her kind of place. Bruce must still want to see her, and Bruce was her kind of person. Schuyler Bannerman most definitely was not.

She let Eve say good night and sweet dreams and take away the tray, and then she slipped into a clean blouse and a clean pair of jeans and went downstairs. Whether Schuyler Bannerman was sitting out by the pool with his wife or not, Pippa was going to talk to him. She was going to demand to be taken to North Star as soon as possible. She just wasn't going to be an unwanted guest in this house a moment longer than necessary.

She was so completely absorbed in planning exactly what she would say that she walked straight into him at the foot of the stairs.

He gripped her by the arms as she stumbled and asked her sharply, "Are you walking around with your eyes shut or are you sleepwalking, for heaven's sake?"

"Neither," said Pippa, unnerved. "I'm sorry. I was looking for you. I want to talk to you, to ask you...." She stopped. Everything seemed suddenly to have gone from her mind leaving it bewilderingly blank. Schuyler Bannerman still held her by the arms, and those dark, inky blue eyes held her almost mesmerized.

"Yes?" he said. "You want to ask me what?"

Pippa bit her lip, furious that he had this effect on her. "Please let me go." He did so, and she pulled herself together with an effort. "Mr. Bannerman—"

"Skye."

"Mr. Bannerman, I'd rather not stay in your home any longer. You didn't invite me, and I know you don't like me or my clothes or...."

He leaned against the polished banister of the staircase. His dark brows were drawn and his eyes, narrowed and still, watched her intently. "You appear to know a great many things, Philippa. But you must imagine yourself something of a mind reader if you think you know what I like or don't like."

Pippa said stubbornly, "About this I do know. I happen to be sensitive to feelings. You think I'm riffraff."

There was a moment of silence while he continued to study her. Then he said quietly, "You must think what you like, of course. But I'm not in the habit of making hasty judgments. I assure you, you wouldn't be here at all, if I were.... What's more, in my book there are certain conventions to be observed. I'm certainly not prepared to engage in any kind of a squabble with a girl I've only just met."

Pippa felt herself whiten. She said with a touch of hysteria she couldn't hide, "Please let me go to North Star. Bruce wants me, even if you don't."

He was suddenly impatient with her.

"Quit acting like a melodramatic girl in a novelette and thank heaven you're somewhere comfortable and civilized. You can't go to North Star—it's not just around the corner—and that's that. Now please excuse me. I'm tired, too."

She watched him go and she hated him for his hardness, his remoteness, his superiority. He was like some Olympian god looking down on the stupid, empty follies of weak mortals. He made her feel infinitely small and insignificant.

She called after him on an impulse. "I'll talk to your wife in the morning. She may be more approachable and human than you. Because she couldn't possibly be less."

He turned back with a look of amazement on his face. "My wife?" he repeated. Then, mockingly, he added, "Your sensitivity—your intuition—has failed you there. I don't happen to be married yet, Philippa."

He continued on his way, and Pippa felt more frustrated than ever. She felt she was in a hall of mirrors, unable to tell the real from the reflection. Who, she wondered, was that glamorous, dark-haired woman she had seen beside the pool? Whose were the children? And even though North Star was not just around the corner, why shouldn't she go there?

CHAPTER TWO

When she awoke in the morning, she could not wait to be up and moving. She jumped out of the big bed and ran across to the balcony. The sun was well and truly up, the sky was blue and deep and cloudless, and stretching away beyond the gardens and the stables was mile upon mile of plain, its green pastures interspersed with stretches of bare red earth. Pippa could see the line of a fence, wavering, climbing a faint rise, intersecting another fence, disappearing here and there behind dark clusters of shade trees. A few horses cantered friskily beyond the stables, but otherwise nothing moved.

No, she was wrong. She narrowed her gray green eyes and looked harder. A long way out on the shimmering plain was a great mob of sheep, a creamy straw-colored blur that surged smoothly over the red earth toward the green of pastures. And she could make out, too, the figure of a man on horseback! Her pulses leapt. It had to be Bruce out there, bringing in the sheep from the back paddock! In no time at all, he would be there to fetch her.

Oh, frabjous day, thought Pippa jubilantly. The scene before her seemed utterly entrancing, and everything was wonderful. So this was the outback, she thought, and this was a station homestead. How different it all was from anything she had ever imagined! Not that she had ever dreamed for one moment that she would actually one day be in the outback. Her eyes roved once more over garden and the never-ending plain before she turned away. Not an outhouse or a shearing shed "within cooee," she thought, and was rather pleased with her use of the Australian phrase for "within shouting distance."

As she danced off to the bathroom to take a shower, the lovely dress she had accepted from Lalla caught her eye through the half-open door of the wardrobe. Of course there would be a party! Bruce would arrange it, now that she was here. It suddenly seemed that all the mix-up of the previous day was no more than a horrid dream. Everything would come right now....

It was only later, after she had dressed and was combing her hair in front of the long mirror that another thought struck her. If that was Bruce she had seen—and could still see—from her window, then where was North Star in all that empty countryside? Not just around the corner, that Bannerman type had said the night before. When she tossed down her comb and went to the balcony again, the sheep were still there, but now there were two horsemen, and they were moving away from the homestead, not toward it.

She met Eve on the stairway a couple of minutes later.

Eve said, "Good morning, Pippa. I hope you slept well. I was coming to see if you would like some breakfast."

"Am I too late? It doesn't really matter; I can go without."

Eve laughed. "You don't have to go without. The children have just left the table and it's an ideal time for you to come." She turned about and went downstairs with Pippa. "I'll keep you company while you eat," she said, as they crossed the hallway and entered an airy room with walls papered in soft yellow. Sunlight filtered through wide windows shaded by a vine-covered trellis, and on the flagstone walk flowers spilled luxuriously from green-painted tubs. The sun room had a green tiled floor, and indoor plants made patterns against the walls. The whole effect was one of cool greenness. A long table covered with a yellow cloth and set with shining silverware and blue and white breakfast china stood to one side. Beside a basket of fresh rolls, another of oranges and a tall coffee pot, there were two covered dishes, one containing piping hot lambs' fry and bacon, the other scrambled eggs. Pippa, who was hungry, helped herself lavishly to lambs' fry and was relieved to learn that Skye Bannerman had already eaten. Outside on the flagstones, the children played—three little girls and a small boy. Inside, there were only Pippa and Eve, and Pippa wondered again about that dark-haired woman.

She began to eat, relishing the delectable fry, the crisp curls of bacon. Reaching for the coffee pot, she asked Eve, "Do you have to start lessons with the children soon?"

"It's Saturday," said Eve. "We don't do lessons at all on Saturdays. They're such babies still, I'm really more of a nanny than a governess, I suppose."

"Who are they?" asked Pippa, as she poured the coffee into her blue and white cup. "The children, I mean."

"Charles and Joanne and Sara belong to Skye's brother, Adrian," Eve explained. "And Annabel belongs to Angela Glas." She said the last name as though it needed no further qualification, as though, thought Pippa, she expected her to know who Angela Glas was. But Pippa hadn't a notion.

"The one who was out by the pool last night?" she suggested.

"That's right," replied Eve. She put her hands behind her head and leaned back in her high-backed chair and looked at Pippa. "But don't you know *who* Angela Glas is, Pippa?"

"I haven't the faintest idea. Who is she?"

Eve made a comical face. "Of course, you're English, aren't you? How long have you been in Australia?"

"About two weeks," said Pippa.

"Then that explains it," Eve sat up and reached toward the table for cigarettes. She took one from the packet, lit it and relaxed again, her face turned a little away.

"Angela Glas has made quite a name for herself on television. She has the leading role in a series that absolutely everybody watches—'Heads You Win.'"

Pippa took this in. "But why is she here?"

"On Jounima? She was invited to stay. Do you need more coffee, Pippa? More of anything?"

"No, thank you. I'll just have an orange."

"Very good for you. I always encourage the children to eat an orange after breakfast."

There was a moment's silence, but finally Pippa was unable to restrain her curiosity, though there was no reason she should feel so curious about somebody she had so far caught no more than a glimpse of. She asked, "But why here? Why was she asked to stay here?"

"Angela? Oh well, she was on location on this property for the filming of the last episode of this particular series. Skye gave permission for the production group to stay here for two weeks. They had the most elaborate caravans, but it was a strenuous affair and when it was finished, Angela was ready for a rest." Eve said no more, and her expression puzzled Pippa. She had spoken pleasantly, casually, and yet Pippa had the distinct feeling that Eve didn't like Angela Glas... and didn't like her staying on Jounima. She gathered that Schuyler Bannerman had asked the actress to stay, and she wondered exactly what that implied. She had certainly looked to be a very beautiful woman, and so very sophisticated. *Not at all like me,* thought Pippa.

She finished peeling her orange and glanced at Eve. "I saw a lot of sheep from my window this morning. Would they be the ones Bruce was bringing in?"

"Oh, dear me, no. That would be the herd Skye and Adrian are shifting over to the yards for drenching."

Pippa's spirits took a dive. So the two men she had seen had been Skye and Adrian Bannerman. She started to eat her orange. "Oh well, I suppose Bruce will be back today, and will come to Jounima for me."

"I'm afraid you're going to be disappointed, Pippa," Eve said apologetically. "He took off only yesterday and he has to move those sheep a good many miles. Didn't Skye explain?"

Pippa shook her head. Skye Bannerman had not bothered to explain a thing and had left her completely up in the air. "And when he's moved them," she asked, "Then do I get to see him?"

Eve shrugged and flicked her cigarette. "You'll have to ask Skye."

"Why? Does Bruce work for Skye?" Pippa decided despairingly that it was no use pretending she knew all about Bruce. There were some things she really had to know, and the only way to find out was to ask.

"Not exactly," said Eve slowly. "You see, North Star, which is part of the Jounima estate, belongs to Bruce's mother. She was Elizabeth Bannerman, Skye's aunt. But she married a surgeon and went to live in Sydney. I suppose you knew that, though."

Pippa tried to look as if she had known without actually telling a lie. But the fact was, she knew nothing at all about Bruce Lightfoot, except that he was fun to be with. It was rather absurd, when you considered it, that she was here in the outback, all mixed up with people like Schuyler Bannerman and a television star! Eve Arnold at any rate was just an ordinary person and Pippa was thankful for that.

"Skye managed North Star for years," Eve went on. "But when his father died, he had to come back and take over Jounima."

"And what happened to North Star?"

"Skye put in a manager, Ken Martin, who eventually married the only Bannerman girl—Skye's sister Caroline. Then when Bruce decided that he'd like to take up sheep farming, things had to be reorganized."

Pippa groped in her mind. She remembered Bruce's saying something about Skye wanting to get his precious sister back on North Star—now that Adrian was back, he'd said. She sighed, wondering where Adrian fitted into it all. It was such a complicated setup!

"It sounds like a game of chess," she said resignedly.

"Don't worry. It will all come clear when you've met everyone," comforted Eve. "At any rate, Ken and Caroline are on the third part of the estate just now—Cedar Creek." She stood up and stretched, and Pippa reflected that she had said nothing about Adrian. "I'm taking the children for a picnic at the billabong today. Would you like to come, too?"

"If you're sure Bruce won't be coming for me...."

"I'm sure."

"Then I'd like to come very much."

"Good," Eve looked at her watch. "Can you be ready in half an hour?"

"Of course."

Pippa went upstairs with a sense of purpose. She felt grateful to Eve for making her feel less like an uninvited guest, but she decided that she would tidy her room and pack away all her belongings so that she would be ready to leave at a moment's notice. She couldn't quite understand why Bruce had gone away to the back paddock when he had known she was coming. Was it so urgent? Or had he thought that Bron had contacted her and told her everything was off? She wondered if he had cared much about that—if the invitation had been simply on impulse and he had been sorry afterward that he had issued it. And now she, Pippa, by using a silly scrap of paper to write down her telephone number, instead of using a card or something, had made it impossible to stop the wheels of fate from turning, as Skye had put it. So here she was, possibly not wanted by anyone, waiting; like a parcel, to be dealt with.

But not, she determined, with a swift return of her usual independent spirit, ready to wait in meek silence. Maybe fate had brought her here, but she, Philippa Shaw, was going to take over again, regardless of fate.

When she went into her room, it was already immaculate. One of the maids had been at work: the bed was made, fresh towels had been laid out, the bathroom tidied. The windows were open and the clothes she had left lying about had been put away—some of them, a brief search revealed, had been taken away, evidently to be laundered, including her white jeans and green top. Her suitcase was on a low shelf in the dressing room.

Feeling as if too much had been taken out of her control, Pippa brushed her teeth and applied a little makeup to her fair skin. She decided that what she was wearing was right for a picnic, but as Eve had said something about the billabong, she hunted out her yellow bikini.

She was downstairs, ready and waiting, before Eve put in an appearance, and rather cautiously she went through the entrance area to the courtyard where the orange trees and swimming pool were. Two sides of the square were formed by angled walls of the homestead, and the other two were enclosed by a white wall that was draped with cascades of glowing crimson bougainvillea. The waters of the tiled pool shimmered blue green in the morning sunlight, and the black-and-white-striped swing seat, where Angela Glas had lounged the previous night, moved faintly in trellised shade, as if pushed by an unseen hand.

Pippa stood bemused, feeling as if she had walked onto a stage set, when she heard footsteps behind her. She turned quickly and saw Angela Glas coming toward her or, rather, toward the swing seat, which she sank into without a word.

Pippa said awkwardly, "Good morning." She smiled politely but received no answering smile.

The actress, who wore a long white caftan edged with silver braid and a matching turban that hid her dark hair, curled herself gracefully on the seat and tucked her sandalled feet beneath her gown.

She fitted a cigarette into a long black holder that was inlaid with mother-of-pearl, lit it, inhaled and looked at Pippa.

She had beautiful brown eyes and high cheekbones, and she certainly must have been very photogenic; but Pippa thought she wore too much makeup, and she noticed that the bright sunlight was not kind to her tanned skin, which looked a little coarse. The woman's long, hard, studied look was unnerving.

Pippa tried again. "I'm Philippa Shaw. Did you sleep well?"

Angela Glas closed her eyes. She kept them closed as she enunciated on a pained, weary note, "No civilized person should have to exchange...civilities with anyone before eleven in the morning."

"Oh." Pippa looked at her watch. She was almost an hour too early. Silently, while Angela Glas's eyes remained closed, she left the courtyard, and once inside, almost ran toward the sun room.

What an infuriating, unfriendly person, she thought. *She didn't even say good morning, didn't even look at me as if I were a human being.* She thought she understood now why she had received the impression that Eve didn't like the dark-haired woman. Pippa didn't much like her, either.

IT WAS A LOVELY PICNIC. The children—Sara and Joanne who were twins, and the younger Charles—were delightful. The little blond girl, Annabel, was a handful and a somewhat precocious child, though that was more or less to be expected, since she had a mother like Angela Glas! Pippa thought the Bannerman children treated Eve as if she were their mother, and was not surprised to learn that she had been looking after them for almost two years. Pippa was about to ask her about the children's mother when Charles, who was four, marched over with a complaint. He had left his "motorbike" under a tree and Annabel had taken it. She didn't know how to drive and she would "smash" it. His "motorbike" was a stout piece of stick about fifteen inches long, which he held like handlebars, and it was his most important and valuable bit of equipment. By the time Eve had settled the dispute and organized a dam-building project on the bank of the pond, the time for Pippa's question had passed.

Early in the afternoon they began the long, leisurely walk back to the homestead, and during that walk, Pippa discovered that the wool shed, the shearing shed and shearers' quarters were hidden behind a low ridge on the other side of the river. She told Eve, "I hope Bruce will come soon. He did invite me, you know, and I feel so awful having to stay at Jounima."

"You mustn't feel that way," Eve assured her. "There's plenty of room in the homestead. Nobody worries. Not even about me and the children."

"But the children live there," said Pippa in surprise.

"Not permanently. Their home's at Cedar Creek—that's Adrian's part of the estate. I brought the children to Jounima when he went overseas for a trip. There's more room here. I expect we shall move back soon now."

Pippa hoped silently that it would not be too

soon—not while she was there, anyhow. She liked Eve and she believed Eve liked her—which was more than could be said for the two other people she had met. She had yet to meet the children's father, Adrian.

And when she did, he was something of a surprise. She didn't know why, but she had expected far more of a father figure.

She had stayed upstairs in her room for as long as she dared that evening, but finally she had to come down to dinner. She deliberately skipped the pre-dinner drinks that Eve had told her would be available in the courtyard. For one thing, she was not used to alcohol and would have no idea what to ask for or accept; and for another, she felt like an intruder. She went to some trouble with her appearance. Eve had said they didn't dress for dinner, but Pippa knew better than to come down in jeans and have Skye Bannerman mark her down as ill-mannered. She settled for one of the crease-resistant cotton dresses she had brought from England—a lime green affair with long cuffed sleeves, a high round neck and pin-tucked bodice. She dressed it up a little with burnt orange beads and sandals and tied her hair back with one of its own strands.

When she saw Angela Glas she knew she must have looked like a little girl dressed up for an afternoon tea party.

She stood rather hesitantly in the dining-room doorway. Skye was at the sideboard dealing with the food, which was in covered dishes over a long warming plate, and Eve was helping by his side. The other two stood near the table talking.

Skye was the first to notice Pippa. He turned and nodded to her.

"Come on in, Philippa," he said politely. "Did you have a nice day?"

Pippa looked at him warily. Was that a reference to the

words on the patch of her jeans? But his face showed nothing but the politeness of a host, so she answered with equally deadpan politeness, "Yes, thank you, Mr. Bannerman."

"Skye," he said. "You'd better sit over there—" he indicated a place at one side of the long narrow table "—by Eve."

Pippa did not discover until later that it was not only by Eve. It was also by Skye and, almost as uncomfortably, opposite Angela. As she moved to stand by her chair she felt them all looking at her—Eve with gentle friendliness, Angela with eyes that were darkly and dramatically made up as if to match her black turban, her black sequinned dress with its long side split. And Adrian....

Skye made the introductions without elaboration. "This is Philippa Shaw. Mrs. Glas, Philippa. And my brother Adrian, whose children you've already met."

Angela gave her an artificial smile, but Adrian came and took her hand. Slighter than Skye and not as tall, he was still devastatingly handsome with his lean, rather craggy face, dark hair and blue eyes. Sexy, Pippa found herself thinking uncomfortably, as he held her hand longer than necessary and looked down into her face. He almost seemed to be challenging her as if, because she was a female, sparks were to be expected to fly between them.

"A houseful of lovely women," he said lightly. "I'm dazzled."

Pippa said nothing. She knew she was neither lovely nor a woman. Angela was the only one present who would dazzle anyone, though for Pippa, Eve with her charming unobtrusive maturity and natural friendliness was the winner in every way.

She got through dinner somehow and hardly knew what she was eating. The two men and Angela Glas, a dynamic threesome, did all the talking, while Pippa uttered an occasional monosyllable and Eve kept an eye on everyone's needs.

"Eve, we need mustard with this; French mustard," Adrian said once, and Eve rose obediently and brought it from an ornate compartment at one end of the big sideboard. Angela wanted iced water, and Eve made a move to fetch that, but Skye said sharply, "That should be on the side table. Sit down, Eve. Nora must fetch it herself."

He rang a small silver bell. The maid, when she appeared, was reprimanded pleasantly and the omission rectified.

Pippa, who had drunk a glass of chilled white wine too quickly in her nervousness, felt a little light-headed. She was there and yet she was not there, and the lights were so soft that presently she felt herself relaxing. The table talk ceased to bother her, and she gave up the effort to appear alert and intelligent. Nothing they spoke of—station affairs of the day, the film Angela Glas had been making (that seemed to be the favorite topic)—had anything to do with her. She was sure that if anyone had mentioned Bruce's name her ears would have picked it up at once. But no one mentioned North Star or Bruce Lightfoot. Pippa wished a little that she were invisible, yet in a way she felt that she was. Just invisible enough to begin to enjoy her dinner by the time they had reached dessert—a fresh fruit salad decorated with ornate pyramids of heavy whipped cream and little feathery meringues.

Skye said jokingly, "Need I warn you that cream like that can add pounds overnight."

Pippa had actually parted her lips to say that nothing added pounds to her weight, no matter how much she ate, when she realized that of course he was talking to the actress.

"I don't care. I'm going to indulge myself for once,"

Angela said. She had a theatrical accent, not at all Australian, but certainly not English. Artificial, thought Pippa. "I can forget all about 'Heads You Win' for two marvelous months, so I can forget dieting. To tell the truth, I'm a little tired of that series. I haven't altogether made up my mind that I want to continue playing in it. Though who they'd find to take my place I simply cannot imagine."

She was still talking about her indecision, her popularity, the other offers she was continually receiving, when they left the dining room and went out to chairs ranged near the pool in the cool courtyard. With a murmur, Eve slipped away to fetch the coffee before Pippa had a chance to offer to accompany her, so that she was more or less shepherded out with the others. It was for her a relief from tension when the small pajama-clad figure of Annabel appeared, and Angela's daughter said firmly, accusingly, "I'm having a nightmare. I've had too much 'citement, and I can't go to sleep. I want someone to tell me a story."

"For Pete's sake!" exclaimed Angela. "I haven't had my coffee yet, Annabel. You'll have to grow out of that business of wanting a story now that Grandma's holidaying. When she's back, you may have stories all night, for all I care."

The child stood, small legs apart, looking belligerent rather than forlorn, and Pippa found the situation rather funny. Annabel refused to move and so did her mother; plainly it was a battle of wills. Though so different physically, the two were very alike. Both were theatrical, both determined to have the limelight and their own way.

The situation hadn't been resolved when Eve appeared with the coffee.

"I want a *story*," Annabel demanded as Eve set the tray on a low, wrought-iron table with an enameled top. "*You* tell me a story, Eve. That's your job, isn't it?"

Pippa saw Eve's breast heave with a sigh, and suddenly she heard herself saying, "I'll tell Annabel a story."

Nobody accepted or refused her offer, but Angela, sounding bored, said, "There you are, Annabel. You've got your own way again. You always do."

"I always do," repeated the child placidly. She lay on her stomach by the pool while Eve poured the coffee, and Pippa observed a little bit of byplay.

Angela had seated herself in the swing seat and Adrian had sat down beside her. Skye, still standing, started to hand around the cups, which made Pippa feel that she, by far the youngest adult present, should be doing just that. He said to Angela, "Come over here where you can smell the orange blossom, Angela. Orange blossom and our own special blend of coffee, plus a small mandarin liqueur—the combination has to be experienced to be believed. Come along." He kept her cup in one hand and held out his other hand to her. "I'm going to indulge myself the same way."

Adrian, whose arm was along the back of the seat, raised his eyebrows slightly.

"Are you going to fall for my brother's musical-comedy wiles, Angela?"

Angela was smiling mysteriously. "I think I am, Adrian. I'm stage-minded and incurably romantic as well. Do you know, I adore musical comedy." She put her hand in Skye's and allowed him to draw her to her feet. Pippa tried not to stare, but she was thinking, *My oh my, isn't she popular, and doesn't she love it!* She was sure that if there were half a dozen men present, they all would have eyes for no one but Angela Glas. And then she thought of Bruce, and she was sure that Angela Glas wouldn't have much to offer *him.* And neither, the unwilling thought followed fleetingly, would Bruce have much to offer the actress....

She drank her coffee rather quickly, refusing a liqueur, and then she took Annabel upstairs. She told her the story of the Three Bears, and she apparently told it satisfactorily, for in no time the child was fast asleep. And, wondered Pippa, now what? Should she go meekly to bed and possess her soul in patience? Or should she go downstairs and demand that Skye Bannerman treat her seriously, as a resonable adult, and tell her exactly what was going on and what she could expect to happen in the next twenty-four hours or so?

Meekly to bed did not appeal at all. Pippa went downstairs quickly before her courage failed. She was longing to see Bruce, longing for her visit to the outback to turn into the sort of visit she had imagined, even if she hadn't known it would be quite such an outback place as this. Sitting down waiting would make her feel fidgety in the extreme.

Down by the pool, Angela was sitting close to Skye. Adrian was alone in the swing seat and Eve was gathering the coffee cups.

Pippa drew a deep breath, clenched her fists for steadiness, and said rather more loudly than she had intended, "Mr. Bannerman...."

He looked across at her, his dark brows lifting quizzically, his eyes black and bright in the soft lamplight, where a few large pale moths fluttered languidly. "Skye," he said. "What is it you want, Philippa?"

"I want to talk to you." She felt as demanding and unreasonable—and as unbudgeable—as Annabel. She knew she was intruding, that he would not get up and leave Angela whom he had deliberately lured away from his brother, and she blinked in disbelief when he rose to his feet.

"Very well," he said briskly. "We'll go to the study."

In a minute, Pippa was hurrying across the entrance hall at his heels, her heart hammering, her mind busy.

What exactly was she going to say? What was more, what was he going to say to her? And why had he chosen the study for their talk?

However, the study proved to be a far more attractive room than she had envisaged, and she was not frightened into memories of her schooldays. It was a small room, as rooms went at Jounima, and it was well equipped with filing cabinets and with bookshelves full of books about sheep breeding and so on. But there were blue curtains at the windows and a bowl of roses on the desk; a *mille-fleurs* paperweight that held down a small sheaf of papers. Skye Bannerman waved Pippa into a chair and seated himself behind the desk. On the wall to one side of him, a bracket lamp lit the room softly.

Pippa, determined not to be intimidated into nervousness, said in a rush, "Why doesn't anyone tell me what's happening? I came here because Bruce invited me, and everyone seems to ignore the fact. I certainly don't want to go on staying here—"

"Hold on," interrupted Skye gently. He leaned back in the chair behind the wide, leather-topped desk and looked at Pippa hard, seeing every bit of her that was on view. She thought with a small sense of triumph that she looked very nice, very presentable, very respectable. There was nothing for him to raise his eyebrows about that night!

But her appearance apparently didn't impress him all that much, she was soon to find out. He had formed his opinion of her.

"Now," said Skye. "Let's get this quite straight without any hysterics. To begin with, you have been told what's happening as far as Bruce is concerned."

"That he's gone to the back paddock to get some sheep!" flared Pippa. "I can't see that's any reason why I should be a prisoner here."

"A prisoner fed on milk and honey," he suggested

pleasantly. He leaned his arms on the desk, moving slightly toward her so that the lamplight struck blue fire from the darkness of his hair. "Have you really very much to complain about, Philippa?"

Pippa flushed deeply. She had nothing to complain about except her deep instinctive feeling that she was not wanted there, that Skye was not only unconcerned about her not yet having seen Bruce, he was even determined that she should not see him at all. She said aggressively, ignoring his question, "Did you send Bruce to the back paddock, Mr. Bannerman?"

For once he didn't murmur the mildly corrective "Skye." He shifted the glass paperweight slightly, then drawled, "Well, let's see. I certainly suggested that it might be wise for him to go."

"Because you didn't want him to see me again—before you'd ever even met me," cried Pippa accusingly, and saw his eyebrows go up.

He said sardonically, "Not for that reason at all. For the very good reason that if he didn't go, then he would most assuredly lose some valuable sheep. We've green grass and good fodder over most of Jounima just now, Philippa, but North Star hasn't been so fortunate this season, and in the far paddocks it's so bone dry that now there are not even pickings." He let her digest that for a moment, then continued equably, "As for not wanting Bruce to see you again.... How long have you known each other?"

Pippa colored even more deeply. Two hours or so seemed a ridiculously short time to admit to, but she said with a defiant honesty, "Two hours." And added for good measure, "We met at an amusement park."

She saw his lips compress and knew what he thought of that. And then she remembered too late that Bruce had said, "He'll tear a strip off my hide if he knows I've been to an amusement park." But Skye merely said clinically, "And that was long enough for you to make the journey here—to pack up all your worldly goods with the apparent expectation of staying in the vicinity? I think you must have been reading the social columns very assiduously, Philippa, or else you plowed through a lot of questions in your two hours, despite the rides." He pushed back his chair and rose to his feet. "There's a train back to Sydney in the morning if you're interested. And now, if you'll excuse me, I'll get back to my guest."

Pippa was on her feet, too, her heart hammering. She said tensely, her breath coming fast with anger, "I'm not remotely interested, Mr. Bannerman. I'm going to North Star."

He had crossed to open the door and turned back momentarily to face her. "I'm afraid it's not convenient to take you there just now. Besides, it would be quite pointless. There's no one at the homestead apart from the housekeeper and her husband, and I can't promise you when Bruce will be back."

Pippa stared at him in silence. She felt trapped, helpless. He made it appear that there was nothing for her to do but take that train in the morning. And if she did that, thought Pippa, she would have to go back to Lalla. She hadn't enough money to do anything else until she had found a job. She bit hard on her lip, aware that tears had flown to her eyes—tears of anger and frustration and helplessness. Despite them, she looked straight at Skye Bannerman, hiding nothing. And he said unexpectedly, "You may continue to wait for Bruce at Jounima if you really want to, Philippa. Feel free to make my home yours."

Pippa's mouth fell open. He had spoken formally, politely, and yet she was sure he meant what he said. For an instant she was tempted to retort, "No, thank you, Mr. Bannerman, I can't get out of your hourse fast enough," and to sweep past him with scathing dignity.

Instead, she heard herself answer cooly, "That's very civil of you. I'll take you up on that, Mr. Bannerman."

"Skye," he said, a smile touching his lips. He held the door open and waited for her to go ahead of him. Pippa went up the stairs to the room that was hers for as long as she wished to stay, and Skye...Skye Bannerman went back to join Angela Glas.

CHAPTER THREE

THE NEXT DAY WAS SUNDAY, and Sunday on Jounima was different from other days. The sheep were not worked, but Skye went out riding early in the morning, and so—to Pippa's gratitude—was missing from the breakfast table. Angela was missing, too, but that was because she had not yet risen, not because she was out with Skye.

Eve, Adrian and the four children were at the breakfast table when Pippa came down, and as she entered the sunny room she was struck by the thought that they looked very much like a family group. Eve could have been the mother of those children—all four of them—and at the moment even the unruly Annabel was intent on cracking open the brown egg in its Peter Rabbit eggcup.

"Sleep well?" Adrian greeted Pippa, his eyes taking her in quickly. She was back in the green top and white jeans that had been laundered and folded away in her drawer. She didn't have an extensive wardrobe, but she could have worn a cotton dress, yet had put on the jeans as a gesture of defiance, if she were honest with herself. A sign, a flag, for Skye Bannerman to see and interpret; a reminder that Pippa was a girl his cousin had picked up at an amusement park. Now Skye was not here, and Adrian's reaction seemed to be one of casual and even pleasurable acceptance. He told her, in fact, that she looked delightfully young and fresh!

He left the table first, and presently Eve took the children outside to play in a big sandheap shaded by cedar trees. It was in a corner of the garden that could be seen from the kitchen quarters, so that Nora or one of the other maids could keep an eye on the children.

Eve told them, "Now for goodness' sake, see if you can play together agreeably. And don't any of you forget that Annabel is a guest here and must be looked after."

"She can't have my motorbike," Charles said instantly. "It's in the toy cubbid."

"Then that's fine," said Eve. She went inside and started up the stairs, and Pippa, following a little diffidently, asked, "What are you going to do now, Eve? Is Sunday your day off?"

"I don't have a day off," said Eve. "Except occasionally when Nora minds the children and I go all social. But just now I'm going to start on the packing. Adrian has decided to go back to Cedar Creek this evening." She sounded happy, but Pippa was disappointed. She had not expected Eve to depart so soon and couldn't think how she would manage without her reassuring company. She stayed and helped her for a while in the big room where the children's toys and clothing were kept. Presently from the window she saw Skye striding from the stables, the sun shining on his black hair. And later still, when Eve had begun to pack her own things and Pippa had gone to the balcony outside her own bedroom, she saw a Land Rover arrive. It swept around the corner of the house and was out of sight before she could see who was in it, and she turned and raced downstairs, because, of course, it would be Bruce.

And, of course, it was not.

Skye was greeting a man and a woman, who had a Dalmatian dog with them, when Pippa reached the foot of the stairs, and defeatedly she slipped across the hall and out to the courtyard where the pool was. Eve was there, as well as Adrian, Angela Glas and the four children, and she realized it must be nearly lunchtime. The dog bounded out and was greeted exuberantly by the children—with the exception of Annabel, who had apparently never encountered such a creature before and was uncertain whether he was dog or some sort of wild animal. Angela, draped gracefully on a huge, low, outdoor divan in the shade of a vine-covered trellis, her dark glamour enhanced by the bright fall of bougainvillea in the background, watched her small daughter dispassionately. Hand to mouth, her small frame shuddering, the little girl shrank from the friendly, tail-wagging overtures of the dog, whom the Bannerman children called Roddy. It was the first time Pippa had seen Annabel in any role other than that of aggressor or conqueror, and after waiting for a second for Angela to take action, she joined the little blond child and tried to persuade her that Roddy wanted no more than to make friends.

"You must pat his head and say hello," she said, squatting and taking the reluctant child's hand in her own. While she was thus engaged, Skye and the two visitors came out to the courtyard.

The woman exclaimed, causing Pippa to look up, "Why, hello, Angela! I hadn't expected to find you still here. In fact I was about to make the most frightful *faux pas*. I was on the verge of exclaiming how marvelous it is to have peace reigning once more, Skye back from his exile—self-imposed though it was—on North Star, and all of us able to move freely about." She dropped down into the swing seat, a woman in her late twenties, with thick, wavy dark hair, blue eyes, and a strong resemblance to Adrian. She reached a negligent hand toward her husband, an agreeable-looking man with sandy hair, who obligingly handed her a cigarette and flicked on his lighter. They must have been the Martins, Caroline and Ken, thought Pippa. She brought her attention back to Annabel as Caroline continued, "It can be totally aggravating, you know, Angela, even in the interest of dramatic art—if you can possibly place 'Heads You Win' in that category—to be asked by some autocratic cinema operator or production man or whatever, kindly not to appear anywhere within a half-mile radius of your favorite swimming place on the river, for fear of ruining some marvelous sequence, and thereby causing the waste of invaluable time, not to say thousands of dollars of hard cash. What happened?" she concluded. "Has someone ruined a sequence? If so, then it simply must have been Roddy. Of us all, he's the only one who was neither intimidated nor overawed. But tell me quickly. Is it all to start over again?"

"Calm down, Caroline," said Skye sardonically. "It's all over and Angela is staying on at Jounima in the capacity of guest."

"Thank heavens for that!" His sister sounded genuinely relieved. She looked at Pippa in a kindly way and nodded to her. "Hello to you. I take it you're here to mind the child now that Mrs. Thompson's gone."

Pippa saw Angela's malicious smile before Skye said briskly, "Just don't jump to any more conclusions, Caroline. Pippa is a guest on Jounima, too."

It was the first time he had called her Pippa since he had met her at the Siding, and Pippa gave a little blink of surprise.

"Oh! Whose?" asked Caroline.

"My guest," said Skye. "She's a friend of Bruce's." He left it at that.

After that, Pippa was left more or less to herself. Drinks were poured; Eve took the children to wash their faces and hands and tidy up for dinner; Caroline joined Angela on the divan, and the men stood in a group and talked station affairs. Pippa sat pensive, alone, sipping the lemon squash she had asked for and wishing it could have been Bruce who had arrived. She listened to snippets of conversation, only one of which really caught her imagination and aroused her curiosity. That was when Ken Martin remarked, "So Percy Daylight got that dingo out at Wilga Plains. What's the news on the north boundary, by the way?"

"Bad," said Skye. "I'm checking on that again tomorrow."

Pippa heard no more. Percy Daylight, she thought. What a fantastic name! She would have loved to ask about him, but would not have dared to interrupt the men for anything. Caroline, who would surely have been able to enlighten her, was deep in conversation with Angela Glas, with whom she appeared to be on very comfortable terms despite the fact that they were completely different from each other. Pippa envied Caroline her self-assurance and poise, and wondered if she would be as confident of herself in eight or ten years' time. *Where will I be then,* she wondered. The answer should have been "in England" and probably married to some nice Englishman if she were lucky. But such an answer just didn't occur to Pippa right then. She simply couldn't imagine herself back home and married to a nice Englishman. Maybe she would be married to Bruce Lightfoot and living on North Star! Wouldn't that surprise them all!

Sunday dinner was a traditional meal of roast lamb, carved skillfully at a side table by Skye and served with a variety of vegetables brought around the table by Nora. Fruit, salad, ice-cream and coffee completed the meal, and by the time it had been demolished everyone was feeling languid. Eve still had to finish packing, but Pippa went to her room to lie on the bed and read one of the novels that stood in a row at the back of a cedar chest, supported by dark wooden bookends carved in the shape of merino sheep. She soon fell asleep, and when she went downstairs again late in the afternoon, it was to find everyone gathered around the pool again, where some of the adults and all of the children except for Annabel were swimming.

"Fetch your swimsuit, Pippa," suggested Caroline, as she pulled herself streaming from the water to sit on the tiled edge of the pool beside Skye. Pippa, moving off to do as she had suggested, heard her ask her brother, "What's Bruce up to these days? Was your conscience easy when you left him alone at North Star?"

Pippa loitered so that she could hear his answer. Her back was turned and she pretended to be watching the children. Skye said, "More or less. He's learning. But it all takes time, and I'm keeping a pretty strict eye on things."

"Where is he today? How come he's not here?"

"He's shifting the herd from that back paddock. He should be in tonight."

Well, that was good news! Heartened, Pippa continued on her way. She thought that Skye might have told her that, instead of leaving her to find out for herself.

She had her swim, and though she was not a wonderful swimmer, she could at least acquit herself creditably. She tried to persuade Annabel to come into the water, but without success, and she suspected that Annabel's inability to swim and her desire to shine were what kept her out. The other children swam like frogs, fearlessly and agilely.

"No luck?" Skye strolled across to ask when she finally abandoned her efforts. Pippa shook her head and he said nothing more, but she had the feeling he had been watching her for a long time, and it made her uneasy. She didn't like being watched when she wasn't aware of it. The trouble was that she had been so intent on her efforts with Annabel.

Presently, Eve asked from the shadow of the house, "Adrian, are we leaving before tea or shall I see about something for the children's supper?"

Adrian looked at Angela, now back in her favorite position in the swing seat and wearing a one-piece, chalk white swimsuit, that was beautifully molded to her curves.

"Me?" The actress looked back at him blankly. "I don't quite get it."

Skye said lazily, "You're surely not planning to carry Angela off to Cedar Creek, Adrian."

"That was the idea," said Adrian, looking rather coldly at his brother.

"It's unthinkable," said Skye lightly. "We haven't even had that game of tennis yet." His glance went to Angela, and she smiled at him and made a little face.

There was a second's pause. Then, "I asked Angela to stay," Adrian said, "and of course I intend for her to come to Cedar Creek."

Pippa heard what he said with surprise. So it was Adrian who had invited Angela Glas to stay at Jounima! She had taken it for granted that it had been Skye himself. The pieces were slowly falling into place, though as yet still somewhat incomprehensibly. Skye had been on North Star while the film unit was on location on his property—Caroline had referred to that fact—and quite possibly, reflected Pippa, he had barely met Angela before he came back home to find her installed as a houseguest.

And then—this was certain—he had been attracted to her himself. Both he and Adrian were obviously more than a little in love with her, and right now, at this very minute, it looked as if they could start having a row about her.

With cold and deadly deliberation, Adrian said, "You knew that, Angela. I told you quite plainly that this was not my home ground." He stood, hands on hips, looking at her hard.

She said brightly, "Of course you told me, darling. I

wouldn't dream of disputing it. What you didn't tell me was that you intended I should uproot myself today. I'd love to come, but I'm simply not adjusted to having surprise moves sprung on me, darling. Besides, as Skye says, we haven't had our game of tennis."

"You see?" There was an odd smile on Skye's lips. "Angela is perfectly happy here."

Pippa saw Adrian's fists clench and unclench and a muscle in his jaw tighten. He looked as if he would like to take a swing at Skye. Skye was looking at him, too, his eyes narrowed. "Why don't you stay on a while longer yourself?" he asked with a kind of indifference. He raised his voice to call to Ken, who was in the pool. "Does it upset any of your plans if Adrian stays on Jounima a while longer, Ken? Without Jeff, and with North Star still demanding my attention, I can do with an extra man. But of course—" he turned back to his brother "—It's entirely up to you, Adrian. If you're in a hurry to get back to Cedar Creek, I won't hinder you."

Adrian glared at him. "If Angela stays, then I stay," he said shortly.

Pippa's eyes went to Angela Glas. She looked perfectly composed, as if nothing that was being said concerned her, and yet Pippa sensed that she was in her element—that she liked nothing better than to be the cause of contention this way between two extremely handsome men. She leaned back in the swing seat, her painted lids and long darkened lashes hiding her eyes, her hands, adorned with heavy rings, idle and graceful, one on the armrest, the other curved over a smooth brown knee. Pippa thought acidly, *She certainly hasn't been in the water. That getup is purely decorative....*

KEN AND CAROLINE left after tea, and when they had gone, Skye organized tennis. Angela refused smilingly to play that night, and Eve said she was too tired and would have to be excused. She was certainly looking pale and upset, and Pippa thought it was no wonder with all that strenuous packing she had done to be undone again. More than that, Pippa thought she was disappointed not to be going back to Cedar Creek. She had been so happy when she had told Pippa they were going.

Nobody asked Pippa to play tennis, and Skye and Adrian decided on a game of singles.

Angela will see it as a kind of tournament, thought Pippa, *with her favors to be won.* She walked out to the garden, refusing to stay and watch, and hoping that Bruce would hurry to Jounima once the sheep were in—if he knew that she was there!

Whether the sheep were in or not, he didn't show up that night or the next day, and nothing was said about him. Nothing at all. But Pippa had dug her toes in; she was staying and would continue to stay, and sooner or later Bruce simply had to materialize. Meanwhile she could at least help Eve with the children, particularly with Annabel, who was apt to stir up trouble and appeared to delight in creating little rebellious or turbulent scenes. In that, she was probably like her mother, thought Pippa, and decided it might be a good idea to teach the child to swim and that it would be kindest to do it when the other children were not around. She consulted Eve about this, and found her in wholehearted agreement.

"Should I ask Mrs. Glas for her permission?" Pippa wondered.

Eve smiled a little. "I wouldn't bother. Angela leaves her child with me quite unconditionally." She spoke ironically, and Pippa more than suspected that nothing had ever been said about Eve's looking after an extra child. She had simply been allowed to do it. Or, if one took the less charitable view, the task had been foisted on her. It made Pippa's blood boil, but it was Eve's business, not hers. So, while Eve took the Bannerman children for a walk to the billabong, Pippa took Annabel to the swimming pool and set about teaching her, first, not to fear the water, and then, gently and persuasively, how to keep afloat and how to swim. She was going to learn fast, for once she felt secure she was a very determined little girl, and in an astonishingly short time she had managed six dog-paddle strokes without the support of Pippa's hands. Pippa praised her wholeheartedly, but decided not to prolong the lesson. Angela was likely to appear at any minute, and Pippa had no desire to spend any more time than was necessary in that woman's company. She got Annabel out of the water, wrapped a large towel around her and told her firmly, "Now put on your shoes like a good girl."

Annabel licked her lips and looked at her wickedly, her amber-colored eyes, so striking with the blond hair, calculating. Only that morning, Pippa had heard Eve tell her to put on her shoes and socks and she had heard the child's naughty refusal. "I won't! That's your work, Eve." Eve had sighed and, rather than waste time when she had three other children to supervise, had done the task herself. Pippa wondered if Annabel was going to tell her that putting on her shoes was her work also, and was ready to assure her that it most definitely was not. The child was still staring at her and trying to make up her mind; then, as she opened her mouth to protest, Pippa got in first.

"Come along now," she said briskly. "Putting on your shoes is *your* work, Annabel. I've been helping you to swim, and Eve has taught you how to build dams at the billabong and all sorts of interesting things."

Annabel gave in. She sat down on the flagstones and proceeded to tug on her sandals, and Pippa looked up to find Angela Glas at the other side of the pool watching her. She began to walk slowly and gracefully toward

Pippa. Her lovely dark eyebrows were raised superciliously, and the expression on her beautiful face was cold and unfriendly.

"You're forever meddling with that child. I suppose you hope eventually to impress Skye Bannerman with your busy, virtuous little ways—just as Eve Arnold hopes to impress Adrian. Well, I wouldn't bother if I were you, Pippa. Skye is hardly likely to develop an interest in a scruffy little Cinderella type like you."

Pippa looked back at her, the color surging into her cheeks. How dared she! She felt absolutely speechless with indignation, but to her amazement she heard herself flash back, "I'm not the one who's trying to impress the men in this household, Mrs. Glas."

Angela's eyes widened and her nostrils flared angrily.

"Why, you jealous little cat! How dare you suggest...?"

Pippa didn't wait to hear any more. She was appalled at herself for saying what she had and could think of only one thing to do, and that was to walk away, and this she did as quickly as she could. She could hear Annabel pattering along in her wake like a little dog until her mother called to her sharply, "Annabel, come back here this minute!"

Well, that was the end of the swimming lessons, reflected Pippa, her temper cooling rapidly. It was a pity. She was beginning to grow fond of Annabel.

By the merest chance, Pippa caught Skye on his own that night before dinner and decided to tackle him about her situation. She felt she had to make sure that Bruce knew she was there. She had come downstairs expecting to find everyone gathered for pre-dinner drinks when, through the open front door, she caught sight of Skye walking in the garden. Scarcely pausing to think, Pippa hurried outside and chased after him as he paced beneath a row of flowering trees that were unfamiliar to her—trees whose small creamy, bell-shaped blossoms fell in slow drifts on the warm night wind, like showers of scented confetti. "Well?" she demanded, as she caught up with him at last, and he turned in surprise to face her in the near-darkness. "Is he back yet? And does he know I'm here?"

"Is *who* back?" His voice was infuriatingly casual and amused. Of course he knew whom she meant!

Pippa rushed on, ignoring his question, "Or have you sent him somewhere else now, to keep him away from an impossible girl like me?"

Skye took hold of her arm and gazed down at her searchingly. "What's this idea you have about me, for God's sake? That I'm some sort of a judge, a meter for injustices? You're behaving like some silly little girl chasing after a pop singer."

Pippa frowned. True, she had run after Skye, but....

"You think you're like a pop singer?" she asked scathingly.

"I certainly don't," he said sardonically. "I was referring to your attitude to Bruce. But forget it. If Bruce isn't back now, then it's damned time he was. Believe me, I've plenty of worries without cooking up pointless things for him to do, or rounding him up so you can have your reunion with him. We're sheep farmers here, Philippa. We're not running some kind of a lonely-hearts bureau for adolescents."

Pippa stiffened. His fingers were still on her arm, and as the sky darkened and the stars began to glitter brilliantly, his form looming over her became little more than a dark silhouette.

"You must think I'm an idiot," she breathed.

"Maybe I do at that," he agreed infuriatingly, after a second's silence. "But I'll admit you've handed out a few surprises. I believe you've been teaching young Annabel to swim."

Pippa stepped away from him a little and the movement brought down a cloud of perfumed flowers. They fell lightly and softly as feathers, temporarily diverting her. Then she said, "Who told you that?" She could see his face smiling down at her, and then he reached out a hand and negligently, lingeringly, brushed some of the fallen flowers from her silky hair. "Angela?" breathed Pippa, her voice husky, unnerved somehow by the contact with his fingers.

"Annabel," he corrected her, amused now. "You would appear to have quite a way with children, Pippa. I'd never have believed it."

"Wouldn't you?" Pippa began to move slowly beneath the trees in the warm darkness. She didn't know why, but she simply couldn't go on standing there with the shadow of that man overwhelming her, feeling his fingers brush against her hair, hearing his voice call her Pippa. "I've always been fond of children, Mr. Bannerman. Like Eve, I suppose."

He was walking beside her, and his arm touched hers momentarily.

It was like the touch of a flame and she walked a little more quickly.

"Like Eve," he agreed. "Eve is a treasure."

"I'm glad you realize it," said Pippa. "But she has too much to do," she added wildly. "I don't think it's fair...."

They had come clear of the trees, and away out over the rolling paddocks she could see the moon rising softly from a soft, warm, colored mist. A golden, shining, beautiful moon that slowly flooded the plains with such a flow of liquid ambient light that Pippa half expected to hear a nightingale sing. She stood stock still and asked the man beside her in a hushed voice, "Do you have nightingales here?"

"I'm afraid not." He sounded amused. "The best we

can do for you is a curlew, or a mopoke owl. Melancholy rather than romantic, unfortunately." He had lit a cigarette and stood motionless beside her, and Pippa could feel herself softening, relaxing, all her defences disappearing, all her resolutions to be demanding and practical and hardily matter-of-fact fading away. It was so beautiful here. She wondered if Skye Bannerman had come out into the night specifically to look at this scene, maybe to be calmed by it as she was being calmed....

Well, she was not going to be soothed and calmed a moment longer. With an effort she withdrew her gaze from the beautiful plains and the brilliant sky. What had she beeen saying? About Eve....

"I don't think it's fair that Eve has to look after Annabel. Annabel has to be watched all the time. If you'd been out at the billabong the other day you'd know something about it. You'd know she's a very spoiled little girl. She makes trouble just like—" She broke off abruptly. Skye had turned slowly and was regarding her intently in the moonlight, and Pippa knew that her petulant, childish words must have grated on his ears. They grated on her own ears, come to think of it, and she wished them back.

Skye said thoughtfully, "So Annabel is a spoiled little troublemaker. And here was I thinking you were fond of the child." He paused, turned imperceptibly, and began strolling back the way they had come. After a mere second's hesitation, Pippa stepped along with him. "Here's something for you to ponder on, Pippa," he continued evenly. "I'm inclined to think you exaggerate the child's failings, but if she is a little spoiled, a little demanding, then no doubt it's because she's spent a great deal of time in the care of a doting grandmother." Pippa's aggressive mood was still uppermost. She recalled Caroline Martin's reference to Mrs. Thompson, and said swiftly,

"And now that the grandmother's not here, Mrs. Glas expects someone else to take over—just like that. She's the same as all wealthy women—she doesn't want to look after her own child." More words she wished instantly that she could recall! It was hardly good tactics to speak so cattily about the woman with whom this man was quite obviously in love.

Skye said chillingly, "I don't know that Angela is what you could call wealthy, Pippa. Besides, I'd say that anything she has, she has come by the hard way. The acting world is a cruelly competitive one, as you'd know if you were not quite so obviously young and inexperienced, and for Angela it's been even harder than for most. She had to battle her way back into the ranks after her husband was drowned in a yachting accident at Palm Beach a couple of years ago. It was essential for her to have someone help take care of her child. In my opinion, she's to be admired on several counts, and if you'll give the matter a little thought, you may even come to agree with me."

I may, thought Pippa. She knew she had been hasty, that she had judged without knowing the facts, but it really didn't alter her basic opinion of Angela Glas. Mrs. Glas wasn't engaged in any battles now. She was on holiday, and she should be showing her child that she was loved and wanted instead of glancing her way only occasionally and not caring in the least if she grew up afraid of dogs or unable to swim. Skye Bannerman might like and admire Angela Glas, but Pippa Shaw most definitely did not. However, for the sake of dignity, she withdrew from the discussion and fired only one parting shot.

"Why should Eve have to look after Annabel?"

"Eve doesn't have to. Eve draws children like a magnet. And so, apparently, do you."

They had reached the house and he let her go inside ahead of him. The bright lights recalled her to another world, and she wondered suddenly what had got into her that had made her let go of her reserve so completely. She had the strange feeling that, despite the fact her temper had flared and she had said nothing that could have pleased Skye—and that he had said little to please her—they had still made an encounter with each other at some deep, strange level.

It took her ten minutes to recover from her oddly bewildered state and to realize that she had found out nothing—not even whether or not Bruce knew she was at Jounima.

However, that particular question was answered shortly after dinner. Adrian and Skye had been talking about a dingo out on one of the far boundaries. A number of sheep had been killed the previous night, and something drastic had to be done about it.

"That trapper from down south's not worth a brass farthing," she heard Skye saying, and at that moment Nora came out to the courtyard where they were taking their coffee to say that Miss Shaw was wanted on the telephone. Pippa's heart hammered fast. And thirty seconds later she was talking to Bruce.

"Bruce, you're back!"

"Pippa, you're there! If I'd known, I could've been in a day earlier. Is everything all right?"

"What do you mean?" Pippa asked cautiously.

"I thought Skye might have tossed you out. Obviously he hasn't."

Pippa was puzzled. Had Bruce really thought that Skye might toss her out? And if so, why? Surely Bruce didn't think she was the type of girl that respectable people tossed out.

"Why should he?" she asked.

"It's the sort of thing he does. Anyhow, it's marvelous you're there. When do I see you?"

"As soon as you like," said Pippa.

"I could kick myself for taking my time with those sheep! But I thought Bron was going to tell you not to come. What happened? Or am I just so irresistible nothing could keep you from me?"

"Something like that," said Pippa gaily. "I think Bron lost my address," she added. "As I remember, I wrote it on a piece of paper about the size of a bus ticket."

"You did, too. That was a fabulous evening, wasn't it? I'm sorry about the party, by the way. Skye jacked up completely when I suggested it—too much work to be done and all that. And I can't ask you to North Star without Bron being here. Skye says you must stay on Jounima."

"Skye says!" exclaimed Pippa. "Have you seen him today, Bruce?"

"No, I just got in. He phoned a message through to old Allie, the housekeeper here, about your being there and my place being more or less out of bounds."

Pippa's heart began to race. "But that's surely not his business," she said angrily.

"Sorry, but it is. I want to stay here, and he wants me out. And as I may have told you, he has my mother well and truly intimidated. This is still her place and what Skye says goes, though I'm working on it. However, more of that later. What are you doing tomorrow?"

Pippa's head was whirling. She was trying to remember exactly what Bruce looked like. His fair hair, his laughing mouth, his voice—those things she recalled. And that he had been fun. But he was still very much of an unknown quantity. Had she really thought that something big might develop between them? And if so, then why, at the exact moment they renewed contact, should she find that an astonishingly ingenuous thought? After all, one has to meet one's future husband for the very first time. *It happens to everyone,* thought Pippa confusedly.

"Pippa, are you still there?"

"Yes...yes." Pippa pulled her thoughts back to this conversation. Only a few minutes before she had been called to the telephone Eve had suggested a picnic tomorrow at Redrock Gorge, wherever that might be, so she told Bruce, "Tomorrow we're picnicking at Redrock Gorge."

"*We* are? You couldn't possibly mean cousin Schuyler's going picnicking!"

"No, of course not. Eve and the children and I."

"Oh. Only Eve. That's great. Well, I'll be along, too."

"Marvelous!" enthused Pippa. "We're leaving in the morning—taking a picnic lunch—but I don't know exactly what time we'll be there. We're taking horses." She felt excited in a nervous way, almost as though she were arranging a blind date. "Will you be able to come for the picnic part—for lunch, I mean?"

"I sure will! Just try to stop me."

"I can't believe it," said Pippa, "that I'll actually see you tomorrow."

The words were barely out of her mouth when a hand reached over her shoulder for the receiver, and Skye's voice said commandingly, "Tomorrow's out, Philippa. Say goodbye, there's a good girl. I want a few words with Bruce."

CHAPTER FOUR

SKYE DIDN'T WAIT for Pippa to relinquish the telephone chair. Too surprised to do anything else, she said a stunned "Goodbye for now, Bruce" into the mouthpiece, and at once, before she had even heard Bruce's reaction, the receiver was whipped out of her hand and Skye had taken over.

"Skye here, Bruce. You can forget about picnicking tomorrow. First thing in the morning, get into the jeep and go out after Percy Daylight. He's heading northwest beyond Wilga Plains toward the Centre. I want you to grab him and bring him back here, but fast." There was a pause while Bruce said something that Pippa did not hear, then Skye rapped out, "Don't try to teach me my business! Skinner's been there close on a week and we're still losing sheep. There's only one man for this job and that's Percy Daylight. Your social life will have to take second place. I expected you in last night, by the way. Doesn't an extra day mean anything in your life?" Another pause. Then wearily, "I know all that. I know also that we're in danger of losing valuable stock. So quit arguing and do what I say."

He slammed down the receiver and turned to stare down at Pippa who had remained seated in the low chair, listening with a feeling of rising resentment. She stared back at him, knowing that her emotions were written plainly on her face.

"Why couldn't *you* go and get Percy Daylight?"

He considered her, his dark eyes wandering from her

eyes to her lips and back again, in a ruthlessly disconcerting fashion. One hand groped in his pocket for cigarettes.

"I could," he said finally, laconically. "But Bruce can save me the trip." He added, sending her a cynical smile, "You haven't landed yourself in a holiday hotel, you know, Pippa."

As he spoke, Angela Glas appeared in the doorway of the small telephone-room. She looked more glamorous than ever in one of the glittering turbans she affected. This time it was of a deep amber color to match her high-necked golden gown. Amber earrings with long gold tassels swung from her ears, and a cigarette in a gold and amber holder made a flourish in one long graceful hand. Pippa thought wryly that such a vision would surely fool anyone into thinking this was a holiday hotel. She looked quickly at Skye and bit back the little smile provoked by the thought. He had seen her lips tremble and he knew... but he didn't smile back.

Angela said in her carefully pitched carrying voice, "I'm missing you badly, Skye. Are you coming?"

"Sure, honey. I'm on my way. Coming, Pippa?"

Pippa rose quickly from the chair. "No, thank you. I'll leave you to your social life," she added pointedly, and saw his lips compress with displeasure. She went quickly away and upstairs to her room, but feeling restless and disturbed, she wandered out to the small balcony that looked across the garden to the moonlit plains. It really hadn't been fair of Skye to do that. To have listened, to have known they were picnicking tomorrow, and then to have taken the telephone over and smashed their plans to atoms. It was autocratic and it was mean. Moreover, he had admitted he could have gone after Percy Daylight himself. He had no intention of letting the urgency—or otherwise—of station affairs interfere with *his* social life, that was plain. He was so enamored of Angela Glas that he stopped his own brother, whose guest she really was, from taking her to Cedar Creek.

I hate him, thought Pippa, leaning into the night and catching the unbearably evocative scent of orange blossom on the warm air. *He's unfair to everyone.* The only thing that puzzled her was why he hadn't tossed her out, as Bruce had suggested he might do. But he hadn't. In fact, he had said she must make his home hers. Obviously, as she had discovered, it was going to be on his conditions, and obviously he was going to make it very hard for her to contact Bruce. Pippa more than suspected he was trying to wear her down. He thought that if she had to wait long enough for Bruce, and if she were made to feel herself a misfit at Jounima, then she would ask to be put on the train.

Well, that was what *he* thought. But Pippa had other ideas....

THE DAY OF THE PICNIC was hot, but a pleasant breeze was blowing. Pippa expected to see clouds tossed across the sky, but it was a peerless blue. In fact, it was a perfect day, and the disappointment and frustration she experienced when she remembered that Bruce would not be coming to Redrock Gorge refused to remain with her. Despite everything, she felt happy and excited, and full of high spirits. She enjoyed Eve's company, and she liked the children. She had even grown fond of the aggressive and strong-willed Annabel, despite the impression she had given Skye of thinking her a spoiled little miss.

Pippa was no rider, and neither was Annabel, so that created a peculiar bond between them in Annabel's mind. No doubt she was relieved to find someone else who couldn't do what the other children took for granted! Annabel decided, seeing a laughing Pippa helped onto the back of a quiet and amiable little mare, that it was safe enough, and allowed Eve to heave her on to the back of a fat pony called Louie.

"Louie always goes to Redrock Gorge," Sara told Pippa as they set off. She and her twin, Joanne, had appointed themselves Pippa's protectors and rode one on each side of her. Eve rode ahead with Charles on her left and Annabel on her right.

"Louie's mother was a wild horse—a brumby," Joanne explained. "She escaped when Louie was very little and went back to Redrock Gorge and disappeared forever. Louie goes to look for her."

"And there's only her ghost left," Sara concluded. "If you listen, you can hear her neighing in the water under Redrock."

"She's calling Louie," her twin said. "Louie always wants to go to Redrock, and you have to be very strong like Eve to force your will on her. That's what Uncle Skye says. He never rides her. She's too fat and lazy and stubborn for him to be bothered."

Eve looked back over her shoulder and called, "We'll head toward the river now, but keep on this side, children."

After that, they followed the line of the river, moving in the shade of the great, towering red gums or in the lesser and feathery shade of wattles, covered with fluffy golden blossoms, and of peperinas whose rose pink berries hung in clusters among the light green foliage. Pippa loved it all. The ponies moved at a gentle, easy pace, a slight breeze tempered the fierceness of the sun, and the green of the plains was soothing to the eyes. There was very little water in the river bed, and the trees shaded a twisting, brown, slow-moving stream. They passed the turnoff to the billabong, and Eve instigated a competition to see who could spot the first black cockatoo, the first kangaroo. It kept the children alert and interested, and only Annabel, intent on mastery of the single-minded Louie, failed to take part. Galahs were spotted by the dozen—pretty pink and gray cockatoos that flew from the trees in flocks, screeching and circling and settling again. Charles saw a sleepy mopoke camouflaged against the strips of bark peeling from the trunk of a gum tree. And Pippa saw a kangaroo bounding off into the scrub away off across the plains and couldn't believe her own eyes. The 'roo had gone before anyone else saw where she was pointing, and she was disappointed not to have her sighting confirmed.

"I'm sure it was a kangaroo. It was just *flying* through the air," she exclaimed.

"Kangaroos don't fly. It must of been an eagle," said Charles.

They reached Redrock Gorge without anyone catching even a glimpse of a black cockatoo, and here the competition was forgotten. The banks of the river had suddenly grown steep and rocky, and Pippa realized that without her being aware of it, they had been climbing steadily, and that the river had cut a deep channel between the hills. The trees grew thicker and the country wilder. The grass had gone and the red earth was littered with chunks of dark rock, so that the track they were following became indistinct. Soon they reached a clearing among the trees, and they all dismounted and tethered the horses. Then, with Eve and Pippa carrying the picnic baskets and the swimming gear, with Charles importantly in the lead and Annabel scrambling beside him and only just restraining herself from going ahead, they made their way down a steep path that led to a strip of sandy beach at the river's edge. It was a cool and shady spot, with the steep sides of the gorge towering overhead and the tall gums casting their shadows across the water. The river was wide here, slowly moving but deep on the far side where it ran close to the bank and there was no beach. A little upstream, where the river disappeared around a bend into a narrow gorge, Pippa could see a large flat red rock jutting out from the almost perpendicular cliff to form a precarious-looking ledge. The water below it looked deep and dark and dangerous and almost black in the shadow of the great rock.

Eve, seeing the direction her glance had strayed, told her, "That's the rock that gives the gorge its name, Pippa. Long ago, the Bannerman boys used to dive from it into the river below—it's very deep there when there've been rains farther out. Skye won't allow it now. We've all been strictly forbidden to go on the rock at all."

"Why?" Pippa wondered briefly if this were just another example of Skye Bannerman's autocratic ways. As she spoke, she was absentmindedly helping Annabel to struggle out of brief denim overalls into a minute swimsuit.

"There's a good reason," said Eve dryly, as if she guessed Pippa's thoughts. "We had the most tremendous flood a couple of years ago. The water came down that gorge in wall, pushing tons of trees and branches and junk ahead of it. Masses of stones and boulders crashed down from the banks and you can see how the red rock's balancing there! We've only to have a big storm and it will go. It's just not good sense to play games with it. Agreed?"

"Agreed," said Pippa soberly.

The children were now in their swimsuits and Charles was clamoring for his string and the jar of bait.

"I'll catch some yabbies for your lunch," he told Pippa.

"Yabbies?" repeated Pippa.

"Freshwater crayfish," Eve explained.

Pippa watched the yabbying with interest before finally succumbing, and when she was in her bikini, joined in herself. A small piece of raw meat was attached to a string and trailed well out in the water. The minute a yabby was sighted, he was played along much as a donkey is drawn by a carrot. The tricky part was to scoop him up quickly, once he was close enough, with a small plastic bucket. Charles was the most successful at the sport, though Annabel was soon coming a close second. The twins were inclined to shriek and splash and let their prey escape, and Pippa lost more yabbies than she caught.

A long happy time was passed in this way, and when finally they left the water, the children ran around collecting twigs to make a fire on the beach. Soon the yabbies were cooking in a billy can of water, and the rest of the picnic was spread out—bread and salad and cold milk, a thermos of tea for the adults, and a big basket of fresh fruit.

Pippa was intent on watching the crayfish being scooped into a large dish when a voice said, "Hi, Pippa," and, startled, she looked up to see Bruce jump the last few feet down from the path and land on the sand beside her. Her mouth fell open in surprise, and he seized her by the waist, whirled her around and kissed her soundly. Pippa, in the yellow bikini that had been Lalla's, was left breathless.

"Forgotten who I am?" His blue eyes laughed into hers.

Pippa began to laugh. "Oh, I didn't think you were coming. I'd... I'd...." She broke off. She'd been about to say, "I'd forgotten all about you." She asked instead, "How did you manage it? I thought Skye said—"

"That I had to go and chase up Percy Daylight. I was lucky. I got hold of someone just as good, a fellow called Ten Bob Willie."

The name made Pippa smile. She felt sure that anyone with a name like that must be the equal of Percy Daylight. She glanced at Eve, busy supervising the children's lunch, and Eve looked up and pushed a strand of fair hair from her intelligent forehead. She said quietly, "Hello, Bruce. Are you going to join us for lunch? I think we've plenty. Not too many yabbies for either of you, though, if you don't hurry up."

From then on, the day, for Pippa, assumed a completely different aspect. Into its lazy, pleasurable feminine atmosphere, Bruce's young male personality obtruded disturbingly. Pippa no longer felt relaxed and easy. She wanted to go on helping Eve with the children, but she wanted to please Bruce, too, and to rediscover his attraction for her. She felt torn in two when finally he said, "Let's go for a stroll along the river bank, Pippa."

Pippa hesitated. "I'm helping with the children."

"For the lord's sake, *you* aren't the children's nurse," exclaimed Bruce. "Come on."

Eve looked up from the pile of picnic plates she was gathering. The Bannerman children were trying to skip stones on the water and as yet none of them had succeeded in doing so. Annabel was obviously wondering what it was all about, and for her part she was quite satisfied with creating a big splash.

"Everything's under control," Eve said. "You mustn't think of tying yourself down with us. You've been waiting for days to see Bruce."

A little reluctantly, Pippa strolled off with Bruce. She had pulled on a blouse and shorts over her bikini and Bruce put his arm around her waist. They walked slowly along the sandy beach and he said, "Poor old Eve. She works hard at it, doesn't she?"

"She works hard at what?"

"At making herself indispensable."

"Well, isn't she?" said Pippa reasonably. "I can't think what Adrian—or the children—would do without her. What happened to their mother?" she asked after a moment.

"Oh, Leonie ran off with someone else. She was never what you'd call a one-man woman. I don't know what's happened to her now, except that Adrian has divorced her. He went overseas to cleanse her from his mind or something. We never hear of her now."

"How could she bear to leave her children?" Pippa wondered aloud. "Didn't she love them?"

"Apparently not as much as she loved herself. She preferred to let Eve take the hard work out of mothering. And poor old Eve keeps hoping Adrian will marry her."

Pippa frowned. She didn't care for the phrase "poor old Eve." She said slowly, "I think it could be a good idea." And she thought, *A lot better idea than marrying Angela Glas.*

"Well, I don't suppose it's ever occurred to Adrian," said Bruce. "After all, a nurse or governess or what have you...." They had left the beach and started climbing the bank as they talked, and now they reached a flat grassy patch shaded by wattles. Pippa felt vaguely troubled, though she couldn't have said why. From far off she could hear the children's voices as they shouted to each other, and she allowed Bruce to pull her down on the grass beside him without being fully aware of what was happening. He kissed her and then released her.

"You're very quiet all of a sudden, Pippa. What's the matter? You were a laughing girl when we met in Sydney."

"I know," said Pippa. She smiled ruefully and sat up, hugging her knees. She wondered why she was feeling so flat when she should have felt happy and elated. Perhaps it was walking out on Eve like that, or perhaps.... "Are you sure it's all right about that dingo trapper, Bruce?" she asked unexpectedly.

"Is that all that's worrying you? Sure it's all right. This Ten Bob Willie's a real old-timer—the best when it comes to trapping dingoes. He's been working up and down the dingo fence for centuries. He knows all the tricks."

"But Skye said—" began Pippa

Bruce scooped up a handful of fallen wattle blossom and threw it at her so that her hair appeared to be sprinkled with gold dust.

"Skye's a bit too keen on laying down the law. You've got to watch it. I have to take the initiative sometimes, Pip. I did just that today, and it's saved me a long, dreary drive. There's no certainty I'd have caught up with Percy Daylight anyhow. Just don't worry. Willie will trap that dingo and Skye won't have a thing to complain about. All he wanted today was to get me out of the way. He's trying to stop anything from starting up between you and me—that's obvious. Probably doesn't think you're good enough for anyone who's half a Bannerman." He spoke flippantly as if it were all a musical comedy thing that would come right in the end, but Pippa was aware of instant and surprising hurt.

She had a natural pride in herself and didn't take kindly to the thought of being considered "not good enough." She wished that Bruce had not said that, and though she longed to retort, "I'm far from ashamed of my family," she kept silent, fearing that she might sound too serious.

He said after a moment, as though continuing a conversation, "Just the way he tried to cause a break between Vicki and Jeff. Well, he didn't manage that." He rooted out cigarettes and offered Pippa one.

She shook her head. She was groping in her mind. She had heard Jeff mentioned before, somewhere along the line. By Skye, of course. Hadn't he said he needed someone else on Jounima with Jeff gone?

"Who is Jeff?" she asked Bruce. The hot sunlight, filtering through the mass of golden wattle and flickering, feathery leaves, shone on his hair making him look very young and very good-looking. For the first time she wondered just how old he was.

"Jeff's the youngest of the Bannermans—Skye's youngest brother. He's about my age, twenty-three. The family used to call him an afterthought, though there's not all that much age difference between him and Caroline."

"And who's Vicki?" Pippa persisted. She must sound curious, for the Bannerman family had nothing to do with her. Yet she wanted to find out about them, though she didn't know why.

Bruce had no inhibitions. "Vicki is Jeff's wife. Skye didn't approve the marriage, said they were too young and all that. But Jeff was twenty-one, and Vicki's parents—as you might imagine—had nothing against her marrying *him,* so it all went ahead, and when the honeymoon was over Jeff came back to Jounima to start work. He'd been to agricultural college the same as me and of course he wanted to make a go of it, put his knowledge into practice. But Skye was breathing down his neck all the time, trying to drag him and Vicki apart by keeping Jeff's nose unnecessarily to the grindstone. All work and no play is Skye's rule for anyone except himself. The trouble I was in because I took a breather or two and didn't spend twenty-four hours of every day at the junior sheep farmers' conference just recently! That's one reason why no party, believe it or not. Anyhow, for no good reason that I can think of, Skye just decided he couldn't stand Vicki, and he made it so uncomfortable for them they eventually moved off, though he'd have been more pleased if Vicki had gone and Jeff had stayed."

"You can't *know* that," said Pippa uncomfortably.

She wished he hadn't elaborated on his explanations so much. She didn't really want to know all the high-handed and damaging things Skye had done, and when Bruce said, "*You* don't know Skye," she jumped up.

"I'd like a swim in the river. Did you bring your trunks, Bruce?"

"Did I what!" said Bruce, jumping up, too. "They're back in the jeep. Come on."

From that point, they had fun. Back at the picnic spot they were soon wading into the water. It was faintly warm and dappled with sunlight. The children and Eve had gone for a walk and Pippa could see them a little farther downstream where they were evidently looking for pretty pebbles. Bruce and Pippa swam and splashed each other and had hilarious races, and it was all tremendous fun. Pippa came out of the water only when she suddenly discovered that Eve was back and packing up to go.

Bruce called after her, "Stay another half hour, Pippa, and I'll drive you back in the jeep."

"Do that," Eve told Pippa. "And you don't have to look apologetic about it. We've all had a good time, and that's what we came here for, isn't it? I can lead your pony home."

Bruce and Pippa stayed not just half an hour longer but more like two hours. When they were dressed they sat on a log and looked at the reflections in the water, and Bruce became rather romantic. He stroked Pippa's hand and pretended to read her palm, telling her she had traveled far and had met a young, fair-haired man who was madly in love with her.

"Should I beware of him?" asked Pippa, laughing.

"You must trust him completely," said Bruce solemnly. "It's the dark-haired men you must beware of, Pippa."

Ridiculously, Pippa felt herself coloring, and Bruce asked teasingly, "Which of my cousins has been making a pass at you, I wonder? I thought they were both too taken up with that tarted-up actress to bother about you. Skye was like a bear with a sore head when he went back to Jounima and found Adrian had staked out the first claim. What's the score now?"

Pippa had a feeling of faint distaste. She shrugged lightly. "I don't know a thing about it."

"Then find out, will you, and keep me up to date."

She didn't know if he meant it or not and gave him a quick upward glance through her dark lashes to find him looking at her ardently.

"You're so pretty, and your eyes are so green." He pulled her into his arms and kissed her again.

By the time he had driven her home, it was sundown.

"Are you coming in?" asked Pippa. But he didn't get out of the jeep.

"I don't think I will. There are one or two things awaiting my attention at North Star." He gave her a grin, and she had barely climbed out of the jeep and shut the door when he shot off again. Pippa turned toward the house and saw Skye standing at the top of the steps. Even from several yards away, she could see that he looked furious. He was white about the nostrils and his jaw was set in anger.

"Well?" he said, as Pippa nonchalantly climbed the steps toward him. The way he rapped out the word was enough to make her shake. She knew that she was not a prepossessing sight. Her long hair was a mess after its soaking in the river, and Eve had accidentally packed up her comb and makeup with the rest of the gear. And one of the children had trodden on her yellow shirt so that it looked soiled, to say the least. Nevertheless she looked Skye Bannerman straight in the eye and kept her head up, wondering inwardly how her stock was now, if he had started off by thinking her not good enough for someone who was half a Bannerman.

"Well?" he repeated, more emphatically.

Pippa stopped in her tracks and wished she were not so many inches shorter than him. "Well what? I'm sorry, but I don't know what you mean, Mr. Bannerman." He didn't say the corrective "Skye."

He said, "Where have you been?"

Pippa widened her eyes. "To a picnic. At Redrock Gorge."

"And Bruce?"

She blinked slightly. "He came too." Those eyes that were so dark a blue they were virtually black seemed to cut through her like knives, and Pippa began to feel herself grow very weak at the knees. She felt idiotically frightened and despised herself for it. "You've got to watch it," Bruce had said. "Skye is too keen on laying down the law." He had no right at all to lay down the law as far as she was concerned, and so Pippa put her chin up and marched past him, despite her wobbly legs.

At least, she attempted to march past him. She hadn't gone very far when his hand shot out and she was pulled back and held prisoner before him while his eyes continued to rake her.

"Bruce was supposed to be out after that dingo trapper, not messing about with girls by the river."

"He got a dingo trapper." Pippa's voice quavered despite her defiance.

"Percy Daylight?"

"Ten Bob Willie," Pippa said, in a husky, giveaway whisper, though she had meant to speak clearly and fearlessly.

"My God!" She barely heard the low exclamation. "And now he's sneaked off without waiting to see me." His eyes, which had closed momentarily, opened again and returned to her. There was no mistaking the fact that they took in the whole of her bedraggled appearance. "All right," he bit out. "You can get upstairs and tidy yourself up. I'll have a talk with you later." He released her arm abruptly, and shaking and white-cheeked, Pippa half stumbled away.

By the time she reached her room her breath was almost normal again, and her mind was teeming with all the things she ought to have said. She muttered under her breath, "I'm not going to do everything he says. And he's not going to have a talk with me later as if I were a schoolgirl. I'll just...walk out on him if he so much as attempts it."

But she didn't have to walk out on him, for he didn't attempt it. In fact, he scarcely glanced at her or addressed her during the remainder of the evening.

The following morning after breakfast she took a walk in the garden and came upon him unexpectedly by the stables. Pippa had taken it for granted that he would be out working the sheep, but here he was under the peperina trees talking to a man who wore elastic-sided boots and a stained gray shirt with tight cord trousers. He had a greasy-looking hat tipped back on his head, and somehow Pippa knew instinctively that he was Ten Bob Willie, the dingo trapper. She loitered about for no good reason, feeling the sun growing hot—too hot—on the top of her head, and wondering how much longer she could stand it. Then at last she saw the man lope over to a horse that was tethered to a rail near the stables, swing himself into the saddle, and with a casual wave in Skye Bannerman's direction, ride away.

Pippa thought of the fairy stories in which unanswerable riddles were asked or impossible missions set, and in which the contender who failed invariably had his head chopped off. She watched Skye stride toward her, and as soon as he was near enough, she asked, her head high and color in her cheeks, "Is that Ten Bob Willie you've sent away?"

"It is," he said briefly. Then, "I hope you're not planning to shed any dramatic tears over his dismissal."

"No," said Pippa. "But I don't like seeing people have their heads chopped off after only one day's trial."

His dark brows lifted. "It sounds like a Grimm's fairy tale. I presume I've been given the role of the wicked king. Well, if it will comfort you, Pippa, Willie's been paid handsomely for exactly nothing. It's not his fault he was engaged against my orders."

"But you didn't give him a fair trial," argued Pippa. "One night—"

"One night was too long. We've lost fourteen more sheep," he said dryly. Somehow or other he had taken her arm, and they were walking along past the stables. Pippa, who had been stunned into temporary silence by his revelation of new sheep losses, managed to rally.

"One dingo couldn't kill fourteen sheep. You could hardly expect to trap all the dingoes in one night. I still think—"

"Hush," he said peremptorily. "Just stop thinking until you really have something to think about. What do you know about dingoes and their killing habits, Pippa?"

"Nothing," Pippa admitted after a fraction of a second.

"Well then," he shifted his hand from her arm and rested it on her bare shoulder.

Pippa felt her flesh, her nerves, tingle. *I must be crazy,* she thought, *to be walking along with him like this when I should be taking him to pieces.*

He said mildly, "I didn't talk to you last night, Pippa. I apologize for that as I'd promised that I should. But I thought it best to wait until I'd calmed down."

Pippa was disarmed and couldn't think of a thing to say. They had reached the orange orchard and began to walk into the trees. Bees hummed in the waxy blossoms, and a ripe golden orange fell at Pippa's feet and rolled into the grass. The heat of the sun made the exotic scent of the flowers so heavy it was almost tangible, and Pippa drew a deep breath and knew an unexpected and intense moment of pure delight.

"This is what I wanted to say to you last night," the tall dark-browed man whose hand still rested upon her shoulder said from above her head. His voice was deep, faintly drawling, somehow intimate, and it affected Pippa strangely. Or maybe it was just that they were in the orange orchard. Pippa made a conscious effort to tense herself ready for attack. She was certain she was not going to like what he had to say to her. It would be about Bruce, about girls who let themselves be picked up at amusement parks, who came to outback sheep stations and tried to interfere with the work. It would be—

"We're pitting our wits against a very cunning dog," Skye Bannerman said. "*One* dog, Pippa, but a killer dog. He's been prowling about a certain section of our western boundary for more than a week and we've had a trapper there all the time. Now Fred Skinner's worth a dozen of Ten Bob Willie's kind, and he hasn't managed to trap that dingo, either. So you see it's not just for some whimsical reason that I want Percy Daylight on the job. And it's not for the purpose of keeping young lovers apart, either," he added sardonically. "Can you follow me? Or am I talking to someone who doesn't want to hear?"

Pippa didn't want to be disloyal to Bruce, but she knew that what Skye Bannerman said must be true. She said reluctantly, "You could have gone yourself, all the same."

And now, she thought, waiting for his wrath to descend, *he'll be furious. He'll tell me more than to hush!*

He was silent for a few seconds, and feeling like Marie Antoinette, she waited for the ax to descend. And then he said concisely, "The sheep that have been killed are Elizabeth Lightfoot's sheep, Pippa. And Bruce is supposed to be running North Star." His voice hardened suddenly. "It will pack up fast if he doesn't look after it. It's a good station, yet he wastes valuable time, is incredibly careless of his stock, doesn't bother to carry out my instructions.... Well, that's enough of that. I'd like you to come along with me and have your eyes opened."

Pippa was silent. Uncertainly, she walked along with him, not knowing where he was taking her or why; wondering if what he had said about Bruce was true, wondering if that word "instructions" was a substitute for "command."

Wondering who was right, Bruce or Skye, and having an uneasy feeling that maybe, after all this time, it was Skye.

CHAPTER FIVE

IN NOT MANY MORE MINUTES, Pippa was sitting beside Skye in the Land Rover, and they were traveling at a singularly fast rate away from the homestead, past the turnoff to the billabong, past the long, low ridge beyond which she knew were the shearing sheds and the shearers' quarters. Past Redrock Gorge and through numerous gates that had to be opened and then meticulously closed, because it was essential to keep the mobs of merino sheep in the right paddocks.

Pippa's long, golden brown hair flew out behind her in the breeze created by the swiftness of their passage, and she soon forgot how hot the day was. Suddenly, Skye reduced speed. At the far side of the paddock they were crossing, a huge mob of sheep was going through the gateway. Two kelpie dogs ran around the outskirts, urging and rounding up, shepherding the sheep through. Pippa saw two men on horseback, one already on the other side of the fence. The other she recognized as they drew closer as the handsome Adrian, a wide-brimmed hat tilted well forward over his brow. He was riding leisurely behind the merinos, and presently he glanced around and sent Skye a brief salute as the Land Rover slowed almost to a standstill.

Pippa watched the sheep surging through the gateway, a rolling turbulence of golden fleece, pressing forward, crowding and tumbling, some of them leaping in the air as the mob loosened up beyond the narrow gateway and spread out over the green pasture land ahead. A haze of dust hung above them, golden in the burning sunlight, and their hundreds of feet made a continuous pattering, like the sound of rocks showering the ground.

It was a fascinating sight, and Pippa watched with enjoyment.

At last the Land Rover was able to move forward again, and Adrian waited to close the gate after them. He leaned down from his shining chestnut to say good morning to Pippa and good day to his brother as they passed through the gateway. He didn't ask where they were going, and Pippa supposed that was because Skye was the boss.

As they drove past the sheep, Pippa said reflectively, "They make a lovely sight, don't they?"

"I think so," agreed Skye. His eyes narrowed and after he had picked up speed again he began to talk.

"The dingo is the sheep farmer's enemy, Pippa. He's Australia's only indigenous dog—the fox was introduced here, but the 'yellow dog dingo' is our own—and he's a menace. Have you ever seen a dingo, Pippa?"

"No," she said at once. Where on earth would she ever have seen a dingo?

"I thought not." He turned to her with a smile that showed the whiteness of his teeth, and she was aware very strongly of his male charm. He had never smiled at her like that before. At Angela Glas, yes, but at Pippa Shaw never. "He can be very handsome," said Skye. "In a lax moment, I'll admit I've even caught myself admiring him. I've had to remind myself that he's our enemy." He braked and pulled up, and nimbly Pippa hopped out to open a heavy, five-wire gate. When the Land Rover had passed through, she closed it with a clatter, fastened it and rejoined Skye, who didn't even say thank you but waited until she slammed the door and then drove on. Even from that brief contact with the sun, Pippa could feel her skin burning.

"Have you heard of the dingo fence, Pippa?"

Pippa said yes. Bruce had told her that Ten Bob Willie had worked up and down the dingo fence, and although she hadn't the remotest idea what it was, still she had heard of it.

Skye couldn't have heard her say yes, because he began to explain. "It's a fence—a wire fence, hundreds of miles long, that's been erected along certain parts of the state boundaries in an effort to keep the dingo out of the sheep country. The fence has to be constantly supervised and repaired and kept clear of drifting sand from inland deserts—otherwise the dingo can cross it. It's an immense project and to a great extent a successful one, but we still haven't found a way to rid ourselves of the dingo menace entirely. Right now we have a killer on North Star, and if we don't exterminate him pretty quickly, then we may suffer heavy losses."

"We?"

"Elizabeth Lightfoot is my aunt. North Star is part of the Jounima estate, just as Cedar Creek is. We're all tied up together, dependent on each other in various ways. Besides," Skye concluded, groping for the inevitable cigarette and then unexpectedly handing it to Pippa to light for him, "I've managed North Star for so long, been responsible for North Star for so long, it's as if it were still mine."

Pippa, who had never smoked, was having some difficulty in lighting the cigarette. It was idiotic of her to try, of course, and she couldn't think why on earth she should want to please him. Or for that matter why he should so casually expect her to perform for him what seemed so intimate a task. Angela Glas, Pippa reflected, would have had no problems at all. But she doubted whether Angela had ever been out in the Land Rover with Schuyler Bannerman. And this reflection prompted another thought: exactly where were they heading?

Skye reached across for his cigarette. "For God's sake, are you such a child you can't light a man's cigarette for him? Give it to me. Can you take the wheel?"

Pippa couldn't drive, either, but she grabbed wildly at the wheel, and he laughed at her. With the greatest of ease, he steered the vehicle over a series of ruts, dodged a number of trees and at the same time lit his cigarette. Pippa thought he had made a fool of her and subsided against the seat, which was growing hot as the day progressed. The question she so badly wanted to ask—*Where are you taking me*—died on her lips and she remained stubbornly silent.

When they stopped for a drink from the water bag, and Skye produced biscuits from a tin box on the back seat, she steeled herself and asked, "Where are we going?"

"What do you think? To fetch Percy Daylight, of course. That's the most pressing thing on my agenda at this moment."

Wide-eyed, Pippa stared at him. "It's going to take all day!"

"So? Don't tell me you had an appointment with the hairdresser."

Pippa knew he was joking, but her hand went instinctively to her hair. She had washed it the night before and it was soft and silky and flowed against her neck caressingly.

Skye said, "It looks remarkably pretty today. Full of lights.... Well, we'd better be on our way or we'll get lost in the dark."

Pippa had no idea what time it was when they finally caught up with Percy Daylight. She had even dozed for a little, and woke up wondering where on earth she was. Ahead of her she could see a stark, red plain, and isolated in the middle of it, a group of trees—stunted trees with branches twisted into weird shapes. In the shade of the trees was an old rattletrap of a car, and beside this car a man sat on his haunches, his back against a tree trunk. A few feet away a camp fire burned and his blackened billy hung over it. Smoke wreathed eerily about him.

"Who is it?" Pippa half whispered.

"Percy Daylight." Skye's voice sounded amused. The sun poured from a high blue sky, shadows were indigo stark on the ground; all the colors seemed too bright, too high in tone, too dramatic to be real. Pippa blinked to clear her vision, but it still looked the same. And the man who sat beneath the tree....

At the sight of the Land Rover, he rose unhurriedly to his feet, and Pippa saw that he was an aboriginal, a grizzled old character in sagging, once-blue trousers and a gray shirt that appeared to be made of flannel. Skye braked to a stop and climbed out of the Land Rover.

"Hi, Percy."

"G'day, boss." The man grinned, showing big teeth that were unexpectedly white. His nearly black eyes were screwed up as he asked, "Dingo trouble?"

"That's right, Percy. Big trouble. A cunning old dingo too knowing to be caught. How about packing your swag and coming along to see what you can do about it? Leave that old heap of junk here in the shade—it's not going to fall apart any faster because you're not here to look after it. Put out your campfire and we'll be on our way."

Pippa watched and listened with fascination. The old man nodded, and that was the end of any business talk. She was amazed at the quickness and thoroughness with which the campfire was extinguished and amused to see the aboriginal swill down what looked remarkably like boiling tea from his billy before he tossed the dregs on the ground. Skye returned to the Land Rover and a few minutes later, Percy Daylight, with his rolled swag and, of all things, a fur rug that he had taken from his "heap of junk," had climbed into the back seat. Pippa didn't know how he disposed of the bulky swag that looked as if it contained all manner of things, but one end of the fur rug appeared over the front seat between herself and Skye.

Skye said laconically, "Say hello to Percy Daylight, Pippa."

Pippa turned in the seat and found the bright black eyes watching her shrewdly. She said shyly, "Hello, Mr. Daylight," and smiled at him, because her senses told her that he was a nice old fellow. She noticed that, despite his somewhat disreputable clothing, there was an odd air of dignity about him. She thought, *He knows a lot of things I'll never know, not in a lifetime.* A thought that was later proved to be correct.

Skye said no more, and once the Land Rover got going, they began to tear across the plains at a literally rattling pace. Red dust rolled out behind them creating a small dust storm, for this was bone dry country with not a blade of grass to be seen. Pippa thought how good it would be to see the green paddocks of Jounima again. Meanwhile, Percy Daylight's fur rug was making her feel hotter than ever. It appeared to be made of irregularly shaped skins stitched together and backed with moth-eaten green felt. She had the feeling that in its day it must have been a beautiful rug, but that day was far behind, and now most people would have thought it fit only for the scrap heap. The fur was thick and wooly, soft, brownish gray on the surface, a deep cream where the underneath showed through in partings. She became aware of Skye's quick glance in her direction and then he shot back over his shoulder, "Shift that precious rug of yours into the back, will you, Percy. Pippa and I can do very well without its comforting warmth right now." The rug disappeared, and Skye told Pippa, "That's possum fur, if you were wondering, Pippa. Long ago all the outback people had such rugs. Now it's illegal to shoot the possum—except for the aboriginals, who need them for tucker." He raised his voice slightly. "Where did you get your rug, Percy?"

"Old missus from Mahogany Creek. Long time ago now. Keeps me warm at night."

"See you don't wrap yourself up in it too soon tonight, then. I don't want any more of my sheep butchered for the crows."

The Land Rover bounced and bounded on, dodging trees and boulders, and still the dust flew. At last they went through a gate and followed a five-wire fence for how many miles Pippa did not know, and then they were out of the dust. There was grass—not the green grass that Pippa had seen at Jounima, but grass all the same. And there were sheep that merged into the red and straw colored background, and the round strewn boulders of the plains. After some time, Skye pulled up on the edge of a belt of low scrub from which rose scattered clumps of hardy, dark-leafed trees.

"This is it." He was grim and businesslike now, and Pippa saw him look around with hard keen eyes. "Out you get, Percy, and take a look."

The old man climbed onto the ground and stood for a moment, his broad nose wrinkled, his eyes narrowed to slits, and then he moved slowly and deliberately to the edge of the scrub. Pippa watched him. He looked at the ground, and sometimes he looked up into the trees. He wove an erratic course, now doubling back on his tracks, now standing and staring.

Pippa was intrigued and puzzled. "What's he doing?" she whispered to the man who sat beside her, watching too.

"He's looking for dingo tracks," said Skye laconically. "What else would he be doing?"

"I can't see any tracks," said Pippa.

"And neither can I," agreed Skye. "But even I can

see where Ten Bob Willie was blundering about yesterday, laying his traps. It's no wonder at all that murdering dingo went on another foray last night."

Pippa looked hard. All she could see was dry-looking grass, plenty of scrub, some red earth scattered with rocks. She wondered if Skye could really see what he said he could, and she wondered if Percy Daylight was really discovering anything or if he was just looking and hoping for the best. But she decided that for the moment at any rate she would say nothing.

After some minutes Percy sauntered back to the Land Rover. He leaned in the front window and took one of the cigarettes Skye offered him. His black eyes were crinkled up, and when his cigarette was alight and he had taken several apparently enjoyable puffs, he remarked, "That plurry dingo plenty smart. Mebbe too smart for this old fellah."

"He'd better not be," Skye said threateningly, but with a glint of humor in his eye.

Percy's wide mouth opened in a grin. "I reckon that dingo laugh plenty good at Ten Bob Willie. I reckon he stood on that rock and laugh his head off."

"Hmm," said Skye. "That's not all he did. Well, Percy, when you've got that dingo's scalp you bring it in to Jounima and show it to me. Think you'll make it by the weekend?"

"Too right I will." Percy stuck the cigarette in the side of his mouth and reached into the Land Rover for his swag and his rug, and in another minute, Skye had swung the vehicle around and they were heading across the plains with the sun behind them.

Pippa found herself worrying. She liked Percy Daylight and she very much wanted him to catch that dingo. But she couldn't really see why he should succeed where others had failed. Hadn't Skye said that Fred Skinner was worth a dozen of Ten Bob Willie's kind? Yet Fred

Skinner had not trapped the dingo. She sat and worried silently while Skye, equally quiet, drove on. And presently it struck Pippa as odd that she should be so wrapped up in the fate of an old aboriginal and a dingo. She couldn't seem to get her mind on to anything else. For a change, she tried thinking of Bruce, but that did not work. Back into her mind came Percy Daylight—his smile, his big teeth, his dark shining face, his battered old rug that kept him warm at night....

"What's the matter, Pippa?" Skye asked. "Are you having mental images of Percy Daylight losing his head?"

Pippa gave a start of surprise. This was so close to the truth it was absurd, yet now all her thoughts were scattered. She was aware only of Skye. She could feel his eyes on her face and she knew that her cheeks had crimsoned. That the color raced away again, leaving her pale. She stammered, "Yes...yes, I am."

"I thought so. Well, you can quit worrying, I promise you. I have."

"You have?" Almost compulsively, she turned slightly and looked at him—at his strong profile, the little upward curve at the corner of his mouth, at the darkness of the thick hair that fell forward across one side of his forehead.

"Sure I have. I've got an expert on the job now—a trapper who'll leave no signs to tell the dingo he's about, who'll obliterate every disturbance he's made setting his traps. He'll bring in that scalp like a trophy and there'll be great rejoicings on Jounima."

He smiled as he spoke, and Pippa, reassured, sighed. She settled back in the seat again, but now she thought not of Percy Daylight but of Skye Bannerman and of how kindly he had spoken just then. She wondered why she always thought of him as a dominating, unfair sort of a man who tried to force his will on everyone. He had convinced her that he had had a good reason for asking Bruce to go after Percy Daylight, but all in all he had not been as condemnatory of Bruce as he had every right to be. Pippa didn't want to think about Bruce. Her mind was suddenly overtaken by a pleasant torpor. She felt physically exhausted, too, and all she wanted for the moment was to relax there in the car beside Skye Bannerman while he took her back to the green fields of Jounima.

But when at last they reached those green pastures, the sun had gone down and the moon had not yet risen. The outback was cloaked in darkness; not a light shone anywhere except those of the Land Rover, and they lit up briefly the pale trunks of the gum trees, the huddled backs of sheep, the long slope of a low hill. *We could be anywhere at all,* thought Pippa drowsily. The night air was soft and warm—warmer than it would be away out where Percy Daylight was laying his traps and waiting for the dingo....

"Not cold, are you Pippa?" Skye's voice seemed to come from a long way off and she started slightly.

"No, I'm comfortable, thank you."

"But tired, I think. And you must be very hungry."

Pippa laughed aloud. So she was! She had forgotten all about eating. They had had nothing during the day but a couple of drinks of water and a few biscuits.

"And you must be hungry, too," she told Skye. "Far hungrier than I am."

"Don't tell me you couldn't eat a hearty meal of steak and eggs if it were set down in front of you," he joked.

"Don't," said Pippa weakly. Her mouth had begun to water. "I could eat an ox!"

"I haven't looked after you very well, I'm afraid."

"Still, I've had a nice day," Pippa said reflectively. And now it was Skye who laughed, and Pippa realized what she had said. Those jeans of hers!

"Well, you're a nice child," he said lightly and added, "but a reticent one, in many ways. I doubt whether any of us knows much about you. I certainly don't. How about filling me in tonight? We've a good many miles to go yet."

Pippa was silent, suddenly still. What was the idea of this? Was he vetting her? Trying to find out whether or not she was good enough for Bruce, his cousin? Somehow it seemed an unworthy thought, and she stifled it quickly.

"I'll help you make a start," said Skye. "You're an English girl, of course—I know that much. Have you been out here long?"

"About three weeks."

"Is that all?" There was surprise in his voice. "And your family—they're still back home?"

"Well, I haven't any immediate family," said Pippa.

"I'm sorry. You're very young to be here all on your own and a free agent, aren't you?"

That was surely a dig at her for allowing herself to be picked up at an amusement park, Pippa reflected wryly. It put her a little on her mettle. It hadn't been anything as cheap and ordinary as being picked up—it had been a sort of warm and immediate attraction between herself and the Lightfoots.

It had been spontaneous and good. But perhaps Skye Bannerman was too old to understand that kind of attraction.

She told him defensively, "I'm not all that young. I'm nineteen. I've been managing my own life for quite a while now and I haven't come to any harm yet. How old are you?"

He laughed. "I can see what you're thinking," he said quizzically. "I'm thirty-five, Pippa, but I haven't quite forgotten what it's like to be twenty. All the same, I still think it's risky for so young and appealing, shall we say, a girl to be making her way around the world alone. Did you come out to Australia by yourself?"

Some devil entered into Pippa. She said with a pretense at reluctance, "Well, actually, no. But the young man I came with—" She paused provocatively and waited for his explosion of reproof.

Surprisingly, he didn't explode. He said sharply, "Well, let's hear it all, about this other man. What happened?"

Pippa was suddenly abashed, ashamed of her flippancy that might be taken for coquetry. She admitted hurriedly, "I was fooling. Christopher is five, and he's my cousin Lalla's little boy. He had appendicitis and was left behind when Tony and Lalla and the two little ones moved to Sydney."

"I see," he said dryly. "You had me worried for a moment. I thought there was some other heavy admirer lurking in your background."

Some other admirer? Then Pippa realized he was referring obliquely to Bruce. She shook her head in the darkness. "No, there's only Bruce. He's my only admirer."

"You're quite sure of that?" he asked cryptically.

"Quite sure," said Pippa, rather wishing she could somehow make herself appear a little more worldly and experienced.

"All right. We'll let that pass. Go from there. How is it you're not staying with your cousin since you brought young Christopher all this way to rejoin his family? Doesn't your cousin want you?"

"Oh yes, she wants me. But I just don't want to live with Lalla and Tony."

"I'd have thought if there were small children about you'd have been in your element."

He paused for an explanation and Pippa said economically and discreetly, "I prefer to work things out for myself." She didn't think she need tell him that Lalla was trying to use her, to patronize her, to bribe her—in the nicest possible way. That she was too independent to like the idea of being a cross between a parasite and a slave in the home of a woman who had too much money.

For a while Skye said nothing. He slowed down, though he had not been driving fast, and lit a cigarette. Both their faces were illumined as he flicked on his lighter, and his eyes found Pippa's unerringly, searchingly. She was aware of sudden shock, of the quickening of her heartbeats.

"So you found your way out to Jounima," he said musingly, and now she could see only his dark profile and the faint glow of the cigarette. "And you had plans to get work at Jounima Siding," he added mockingly.

Pippa grimaced. "I explained about that. I thought it was a country town. Anyone could make the same mistake. Coming here was... a lead to follow."

"Hmm. Tell me, what was your particular star? Was it this nonexistent job? Or was it Bruce Lightfoot?"

Pippa drew in her breath sharply. It was a direct question and one that she didn't much care for. She said evasively, "I do want a job. I'm a typist, and a good one. And I want to earn enough money to pay my fare back to England."

"I'd have imagined your cousin would have donated that, under the circumstances," he commented dryly. "However, I won't pry into that aspect of your affairs. Let's have your angle on Bruce."

Now there was no evading this issue. But Pippa was on her mettle. "You mean that I came here hardly knowing him? But I *liked* him—I nearly always know straight away whether I'm going to like a person or not. We all got on so well together—we had terrific fun! And when he asked me to come to a party, of course I said yes. Because you never know, we could have—" She stopped suddenly. She would be out of her mind if she admitted to Schuyler Bannerman that she had thought perhaps she and Bruce might discover they were made for each other, that Bruce just might turn out to be the man she would eventually marry. She said with a sigh, "Here we are, back at the beginning again. You think I shouldn't have come. There's no party and no job—no anything. I guess I've made myself look like a fool and wasted my time as well."

"No," he said consideringly, "I don't think that at all, Pippa. It's too bad about that job at Jounima Siding, but I hope you'll spare us a bit more of your time before you set about earning your fare back to England."

Pippa almost gasped in surprise. "I would like to," she said cautiously. She was aware that he had said nothing at all about Bruce Lightfoot. And she wasn't at all sure whether what he had offered her was an invitation or a truce.

They were both silent after that, and when at last she saw the homestead lights shining from the top of the rise ahead, she felt a pang of disappointment. Disappointment that the day was over, that there was no more, that it had all come to an end. She wasn't sure exactly what had prompted her to think that way....

But finished it all certainly was. She knew that the moment she saw Angela Glas come through the front door and heard her call huskily, seductively, to Skye, "Darling, I was beginning to think we lost you...."

Pippa didn't wait to hear any more. She got out of the Land Rover and mounted the steps like someone in a dream. Half of it was playacting, the sort of playacting that would have done credit, she was sure, to Angela Glas herself. She breathed, "I'm bushed!" and continued on past Angela and upstairs to her bedroom.

And she did feel bushed. Her appetite had miraculously disappeared. She wanted nothing more than to throw herself on the bed and fall into a deep sleep.

Only one thing stopped her from doing exactly that. It was the note propped up on her dressing table. She didn't recognize the handwriting, but the note was for her. "Pippa Shaw," the envelope said. Pippa tore it open and read the enclosed letter through eyes blurred with weariness, and even, oddly, a hint of tears.

Dear, Pippa, What's the idea letting Skye dictate to you? I came in specifically to see you—cousin Schuyler knew I was coming. Why the hell did you go out with him? I thought you had more spirit than to be intimidated. Yours, Bruce.

Pippa read the words again, and slowly, slowly, her anger rose. So that was why he had taken her out for the day! To keep her away from Bruce. Not to show her his country, to give her a nice day. Well, he had fooled her completely. She had been played along as easily and as stupidly as one of those yabbies the children caught at Redrock Gorge. And then, thought Pippa bitterly, they came home and Angela was waiting. And Pippa went to her room to be forgotten, empty stomach and all.

At that exact moment there was a gentle knock at the door. Nora's voice said clearly, "Miss Shaw, would you like to come down and have some supper?"

No, thought Pippa emphatically. She was burning with fury. But she called back brightly, "Is Mr. Bannerman eating supper, Nora?"

"Yes. He's in the sun room."

"Then I shall be right down," said Pippa.

She looked up and saw herself in the mirror over the dressing table. Her eyes looked furiously green and that was fine, but her freckles were standing out—golden freckles on her fair English skin. Slowly, deliberately, Pippa powdered over them, leaning close to her reflection. Slowly, deliberately—though in a way it was not deliberate at all, for she was certain she hadn't thought of doing anything of the kind—she touched her lids with the green eyeshadow she seldom used, and then only for special occasions. But maybe this *was* a special occasion. Her pupils looked enormous and black. She looked—and felt—like an angry cat.

In ten seconds she was stalking down the stairs. She reached the great hallway, and glancing to one side, looked into the courtyard. Eve was not there, but Angela Glas was. And so was Adrian. Pippa wondered what they were saying to each other as they sat together on the gently rocking swing seat. Adrian had his hand on Angela's wrist, and her head was slightly bowed. Oh, the actress certainly had everyone eating out of her beautiful hands!

In the sun room, Skye Bannerman sat eating at the table. He looked up as Pippa entered and whatever he had been about to say was never said. The smile faded from his lips. His eyebrows rose fractionally as he stood up and asked Pippa formally, "What would you like, Pippa? There's—"

Pippa couldn't have been less interested in what there was. She stood accusingly in the doorway and didn't hear what choice he offered her. She burst out angrily, "You took me out today because you knew Bruce was coming, didn't you?" She wanted to add, "I hate you. I loathe you," but she couldn't quite manage it, not while he stood looking at her with those strange, watchful dark eyes that almost frightened her in their burning intensity.

He left the table and walked toward her.

"What on earth are you talking about? Come on now, out with it. Don't stand there spitting at me like a little cat and expecting me to understand it all. Give it more words."

Pippa clenched her fists and stood her ground. She gave him more words. She said slowly and distinctly, though her breath was coming fast, "Bruce came. You knew he was coming. You didn't want him to see me. That's why you took me out with you today, isn't it? And to find out all you could about me before.... I suppose you think I'm just not good enough...." She broke off, her voice breaking, becoming incoherent.

He was standing two feet away from her. His eyes, black and glittering in the soft lamplight, took in every bit of her—the pallor of her face, her green eyelids, her soft, trembling mouth. He said flatly, almost harshly, "None of that is true. None of it. I hadn't a notion what Bruce was up to. As for the questions I asked you—" his voice grew mocking "—you haven't much to hide, have you? So quit jumping to crazy conclusions. Now come along, all that's wrong with you is that you're hungry. There's no point in starving yourself to death, and once you've eaten you'll see it all differently."

"I won't," said Pippa childishly. She didn't know whether to believe him or not. She was afraid to trust him and even more afraid of her own growing sense of confusion. She went on wildly, "I'd...I'd rather starve to death than eat with someone who drags people apart as insidiously as you do."

"You stupid little girl!" The words were spoken on an exasperated breath and were so low that Pippa only just heard them. They made her blood boil just the same. Skye looked at her hard. "Do you really imagine that your beautiful budding friendship with my cousin Bruce is going to be ruined just because I took you out on a little jaunt? Do you?" he repeated when she did nothing but stare back at him. He took her firmly by the arms and she thought he was going to shake her. Instead, he looked down into her face and asked her uncompromisingly, "Supposing that you'd known Bruce was coming today. Would you have passed up the chance to come out with me? Come on now, Pippa, think."

"To...to fetch Percy Daylight?" stammered Pippa, confused. He was maneuvering her some way, she was sure of it, and she knew that she was no match for his tactics.

"Put it that way if you like," he said exasperatedly, his regard intense—far too intense. Pippa's heart began to beat hard. She stared back at him and half a century seemed to pass. And then, somehow or other she was held tight and close in his arms, and his lips were hard against hers.

When it was over, she felt dazed. Every bit of color had left her face and she could scarcely breathe. She asked huskily, "Why did you do that?"

"Why do you think?" he said, his hands sliding down the smooth, slender length of her arms to clasp her wrists. "Did you enjoy it?"

Never in her short life had she experienced a kiss such as she had just been subjected to, and when he began drawing her close again, she reacted instinctively.

"Let me go! You're hateful! I don't know what you mean!" She knew somehow that she had to resist the charm he was deliberately—for what reason she could not imagine—exercising on her.

His eyes narrowed, and he glanced over her shoulder. Suddenly she was freed. And while she stood there feeling completely lost, completely helpless, he returned to the table and calmly began to drink a glass of wine.

Pippa turned and rushed headlong from the room, narrowly missing a collision with Angela Glas, who stood in the doorway. Pippa wondered how much she had seen, and heard, of that little scene. And what she and Skye Bannerman would now say to each other about it.

CHAPTER SIX

DESPITE EVERYTHING—despite her hunger, her anger, her bewilderment and the vague realization that something drastic was happening to her life that she would very soon have to sort out—Pippa slept soundly all night long.

She awoke late in the morning and rose almost as late as Angela Glas. Eve was giving the children lessons in the big playroom upstairs, and after she had breakfasted, Pippa went out to the swimming pool. The water looked green and cool and inviting, and the day was hot. She was tempted to run upstairs and fetch her bikini.

But I won't, she thought. *I'm not going to swim in his pool ever again.* Instead, she sat in the swing seat and rocked it gently. She was going to concentrate hard and sort out a number of things—her confused mental state as well as all the more practical details of her life. One thing she was strangely sure of this morning: her relationship with Bruce was not going to develop into anything more than friendship. He was fun, and that was all. Absolutely all. She couldn't fool herself into imagining she would ever want to stay in Australia because of him.

Somehow, with the sun slanting through the dark leaves of the orange trees, with the bees buzzing in the blossoms and the water glittering in her eyes, Pippa felt too bemused to think logically. The memory of one thing kept floating tantalizingly into her mind.

Skye Bannerman had kissed her.

He had held her hard against the strength of his body and kissed her as she had never been kissed before. And because of it something had happened deep inside her.

She could feel her heartbeats quicken. The memory of that kiss made her feel a strange restlessness. It was as if she had not before emerged from the darkness of night to stretch her wings in the splendor of the day. She began to wonder why on earth she had got into such a state last night. Why had she run away? Why hadn't she stayed to eat her supper and drink a glass of wine with Skye, instead of acting so melodramatically and even childishly? Of course he had told her the truth. He hadn't known that Bruce was coming, he had simply wanted to take her out to find Percy Daylight. He wasn't the kind of man to lie. He was like no other man she had ever met.

Pippa stretched out her legs along the swing seat. *He was right,* she thought. *I was hungry. I wasn't thinking straight. And that woman calling him "darling" the minute we came back....* She bit her lip hard. She had forgotten about Angela. And now, with an odd inevitability, Angela herself came sauntering across the flagstones toward her. For a change, she wore brief white shorts with a white halter top and gold sandals. Her dark hair was uncovered and it had the sheen of a bird's wing. Her skin was brown and smooth, though Pippa thought that she was just a tiny bit overweight, and that her makeup was too heavy.

"I suppose you're dreaming about your passionate little interlude with Skye last night, you poor innocent," said Angela with a pitying smile. She pushed Pippa's feet aside and sat down on the end of the swing seat and casually fitted a cigarette into one of her long holders.

Pippa's cheeks crimsoned. It was as if a stone had been thrown into the clear pool of her thoughts and the ripples were widening into waves that obliterated all her mind's clarity. Nevertheless, she stared unblinkingly at the actress and said cooly, "You're Adrian's guest, not Skye's. It's not anything to do with you."

"Ah, but it is," said Angela complacently. "Simply for your own protection, aren't you aware that Skye's in love with me—madly?"

"Is he?" said Pippa, determined to concede nothing. And yet hearing it put into words like that with such positiveness did something terrible to her heart. She had seen Adrian leaning so close to Angela last night. He was certainly in love with her. Why not Skye, too? And why should she care?

"He is indeed," said Angela, leaning back and blowing smoke. Her beautiful brown eyes grew dreamy.

Pippa thought, *What's one kiss, and a ride out to the red plain, and the offer of a truce?*

"He's terribly in love with me," Angela went on. "And so," she added musingly, "is Adrian. I shan't pretend I'm not enjoying being in such a heavenly situation. Any woman would. Wouldn't you?"

Pippa said nothing. A simple yes or no wouldn't answer a question like that, and about one word was all she felt capable of at the moment. The thought of stammering or faltering in front of this polished actress was simply unbearable.

Angela watched her discomfiture with obvious amusement, then remarked thoughtfully, "As for my being Adrian's guest, everyone on Jounima is Skye Bannerman's guest. Even you, Pippa Shaw. Don't you realize that? And that's why you were given your little sop last night. Skye's a polite and considerate host who sees his guests get what they ask for, no matter what it is."

Pippa answered that with amazing speed.

"You should try applying that statement to yourself, Mrs. Glas." She slid her feet to the ground and with a swift movement was heading for the house. "Excuse me. I don't want to talk to you any more."

She was shaking when she reached the coolness and shadows of the hall. She had certainly scored a point against the worldly and sophisticated creature out there—that was not to be denied. But it had got her exactly nowhere. Pippa walked halfway up the stairs and had to stop to gain control of her breathing. She felt as winded as if she had run a mile. She stood on the landing and looked through the long, elegant window, over the garden and the trees toward the wide sweep of the red and green plains of Jounima. She thought about that kiss again. What had it really been all about? Exactly what had happened last night?

Think clearly, she told herself desperately. *No more flights of imagination.* Exactly why had Skye Bannerman kissed her?

"Would you have passed up the chance to come out with me," he had asked her, "even if you'd known Bruce was coming?" And then he had kissed her. And certainly, though she hadn't had it then, Pippa had her answer to his question now. She would not have passed up the chance of a day alone with Skye Bannerman for anything in the world. She was in love with him. And he knew it. He had kissed her to point up two facts: that she had fallen victim to his charms; and that he was aware of it. He had been very clever—just a little too clever for Pippa, who was a poor innocent. "You're not in love with Bruce," he had implied. "If you stay here, it's not for Bruce's sake." And if she stayed here for *his* sake, then she was indeed a fool! It had taken Angela Glas to force her into an understanding of Skye Bannerman's kiss, and now she was sickened by herself. She was no match for a mature man like Skye, just as she was no match for a mature woman like Angela. They were better suited to each other.

Pippa turned blindly from the window and continued on up the stairs. It was time to go, she thought. But before she went—oh yes, before she went—she would make sure that Skye Bannerman knew he hadn't charmed her, not one little bit. He was not going to have another opportunity of giving *this* guest what she asked for!

As for Angela Glas, she was welcome to him—or what she could salvage from among the splinters of himself that he tossed around so wantonly. Maybe Skye was madly in love with Angela; maybe he wasn't. Pippa didn't know and she didn't care. She was through. Angela Glas was a mature woman and a very different kettle of fish from Pippa Shaw, nineteeen and painfully raw.

When Bruce called her at lunchtime, she had sorted herself out.

"What's the big idea disappearing with Skye when you're supposed to be my girl?" he greeted her.

His girl? That, in Pippa's present frame of mind, was going just too far. She wasn't anybody's girl, and she was through with all this Bannerman lot. She said unpenitently, "I'm sorry, Bruce. But how was I to know you were coming here? And what do you expect me to do? Sit around twiddling my thumbs? All that happened was I had a ride out with Skye while he fetched the dingo trapper. It was scorchingly hot and I almost starved to death, and I really don't know what you're making such a fuss about."

She waited for him to protest that Skye had known he was coming, but he didn't. He said, "It *is* pretty grim out there, isn't it? Can you wonder I managed to talk myself out of chasing up Percy Daylight? Dust and heat and monotony—those are the things that get under my skin in this life. I need someone like you around, Pippa, to brighten my days."

Pippa made a face into the mouthpiece. "All the same, I think it's time I went back to Sydney, Bruce."

"Good lord," he protested, "you can't possibly go yet! I'm sorry if you feel I've neglected you, but I've explained all that, and I did think Bron would be here when I invited you to come. And I'm still determined to have that party I promised you. You'll have to stay for that."

"There just doesn't seem to be a party coming up," Pippa said. "Don't think I'm blaming you, but...."

"Things certainly haven't been my way," he agreed. "There hasn't been a moment fit to work on Skye. But I'll tell you what. I'll get Bron to see what she can do. I'll phone her tonight."

"Don't bother," said Pippa wearily. She felt about one hundred years old and Bruce seemed to be about ten. "I don't think I'll wait around. I should be in Sydney hunting for a job, anyhow. If you come down, I'd love to see you."

There was a long moment of silence, then Bruce protested, "Don't do this to me, Pippa. Please. You can't pretend you need to rush off and get a job. It's not costing you a penny to stay on Jounima."

"That doesn't make it any better," said Pippa ironically. "I'd just as soon get on the train in the morning."

"Without even saying goodbye?"

Pippa almost said, "We can say goodbye now." But she was a kindhearted girl and didn't want to hurt Bruce's feelings. Besides, she knew that right now she was seeing everything with a rather jaundiced eye, so she said, "You can come and put me on the train, Bruce."

"I'm blowed if I will," he protested. "Just give me till tomorrow, anyhow. Will you do that? I hate telephone conversations."

"All right," said Pippa resignedly. But when she had hung up, she wished she had been firmer. Nothing would have given her greater pleasure than to tell Skye when she saw him again that she was leaving in the morning.

She was so engrossed in her own thoughts that afternoon she was unaware that Angela Glas had been absent from her favorite sunbathing spot by the pool until she saw her returning to the house with Adrian. It was shortly before dinner, and Angela was hanging onto Adrian's arm and they were laughing happily together.

Pippa had just come down the stairs with Eve, and the other two passed them without a glance.

"Where have they been?" Pippa wondered aloud.

Eve didn't answer, and when Pippa glanced at her, she saw there were tears in her eyes and that her lips were pressed firmly together. Pippa felt a pang of pity. She had been so wrapped up in her own silly little hurts and imaginings that she had forgotten that other people had worries far graver and more serious than her own. She had worked it out for herself, and would have done so without the help of hints from various other members of the household that Eve was in love with Adrian, but it hadn't been real to her until this moment. Eve had put her hand across her eyes to hide her tears, and Pippa didn't say a word. She wasn't sufficiently intimate with Eve and hadn't known her long enough; besides, she didn't think Eve would welcome such an intrusion.

They continued on their way together to the courtyard where the pre-dinner drinks were usually served, but now, instead of thinking of herself, Pippa was thinking about Eve and Adrian. If he preferred Angela Glas to a marvelous woman like Eve, she thought, then he was a terrible fool. Besides, if he were in competition with Skye, then she didn't think he would have much of a chance. She couldn't imagine Angela, who was too lazy or selfish to look after her own child, taking on the responsibility of three small children belonging to another woman. Eve had only to hang on, she thought, and eventually everything would work out.

No one else was by the swimming pool yet. Eve poured herself a drink—a small brandy and water—and drank it quickly. Pippa had never seen her do that before. Then she said, "They've been to Cedar Creek. Didn't you know?" She still looked upset and seemed unaware of any time lag. She sat down and stared into the pool, where the water glimmered in the last of the daylight. "Of course he would want to show her Cedar Creek. She's never been there before. It's a lovely old homestead—nothing like Jounima, of course, but beautiful all the same. And the garden is.... She stopped in midsentence.

Pippa said nothing. Her heart ached for Eve. Eve had known that homestead, had probably helped plant the garden.

Eve looked across at Pippa and her face was white except for two spots of red that burned in her cheeks. "She's so lovely to look at...and so talented. I suppose it's natural he should fall in love with her. Do you know, Pippa, I think it's time for me to go. I'll talk to Skye about it tonight. He'll know what's best."

"You do that, Eve," said Pippa comfortingly. She was sure Skye wouldn't let Eve go. He knew that Angela would never marry Adrian. He would tell Eve to hold on a little longer. She didn't envy Eve, and she didn't know if things would ever come right for her—love is so unpredictable. She just hoped Adrian would come to his senses for his own sake as well as for the sake of his children. As for Angela, maybe Skye wanted her for himself....

The unbelievable thing was that Skye advised Eve to go. Pippa couldn't believe her ears when Eve broke the news to her the following morning. How mean and heartless he could be, she thought, and her own decision to get away from Jounima was strengthened. She had told Bruce she would hang on until he contacted her, but that didn't matter any more.

For some reason, Skye returned to the homestead at midmorning. Pippa saw him from her window, saddling up the black horse, Kurrajong, his favorite mount, at the stables. She ran down the stairs quickly, with one aim in her mind: to tell him what she thought of his advice to Eve. Incidentally, she would be gratified to let him know that he had seen about the last of *her*, too. Not that he would care a cent about that, but it would afford her quite a lot of satisfaction and cancel out the way he had softened her up with that dose of made-to-order passion the other night.

When she reached the saddling yard he had gone. Her angry eyes soon discovered him galloping over the grassy paddock toward the river flats behind the homestead. Pippa had not been that way previously, but as there were sheep on those flats she supposed it must be something to do with them. She looked around the stable yard helplessly. She couldn't have saddled up a horse had her life depended on it, and in any case she had no time to be fiddling around with such things. Maybe she would have to ride bareback—she didn't see that it would be all that difficult. At least she was wearing jeans, and that was a good start, but even so, she was not at all sure how she was going to get herself on to the back of one of the two tall and beautiful horses now trotting playfully around the yard. Her heart quailed, but not to be beaten, she began to run after them.

It was a hopeless chase. She couldn't even catch up with the horses, and then, just as she was exasperated almost beyond endurance, a small, friendly-looking pony appeared, ready saddled and actually trotting up to her! Pippa felt like Cinderella and wondered who the fairy godmother was that had turned a pumpkin into a coach for her so opportunely.

It was not until much later that she learned that her fairy godmother had been the stable boy, and that he had saddled the pony for Charles—on Eve's request—and sent him trotting out, he thought, to meet the small boy.

Pippa had no trouble climbing onto the pony's back, and in thirty seconds she was out of the yard and heading toward the river and Skye.

All went well for a few minutes. Pippa pressed her heels into the pony's flanks and urged it impatiently to get a move on. She thought she must look rather quaint trotting along on the back of a small, rather fat pony; she wished very much that she could fly across the ground bareback on one of those splendid horses that was a match for Kurrajong. But one can't have everything, and if Skye Bannerman laughed at her, she just didn't care. She didn't expect she would impress him anyway. She was too young, and a stupid little girl to boot.

Pippa suddenly pulled hard and angrily on the reins. The pony had taken it into its head to about-face and begin to canter at a spanking pace in the opposite direction to which Pippa wanted to go. Pippa was furiously impatient. She pulled on the reins determinedly, but it was a stubborn little beast. It tossed its head and kicked up its heels and very nearly unseated Pippa, who thereupon lost the little control she still had. She had to hold on tightly as the pony broke into a gallop and raced determinedly across the paddock and away from Skye as if it were possessed of some demon.

And then Pippa realized. Of course! This was Louie! And it was true what the girls had said. Louie was going to Redrock Gorge to visit the ghost of her mother.

Pippa could have wept with rage. She was not going to Redrock Gorge—positively not! Why did her plans have to go so wrong?

"Stop, Louie," she began to shout commandingly. "Stop, I say! Stop, stop, *stop!*"

But Louie merely galloped on, and Pippa actually did begin to weep. She simply hadn't enough muscle power to force her will on this beast. She collapsed forward on the pony's neck and gave way completely to helpless tears. And Louie slowed down and suddenly became a docile and repentant pony, standing with hanging head while Pippa wept against her neck. She was weeping not just with rage now, but for a number of things: for Eve, who was going away, for the children who would be lost without her; for Skye who was madly in love with Angela Glas; and for herself because her life, like the pony, had somehow become completely out of hand.

There was a flurry of hooves beside her, and Pippa straightened guiltily. She was in the shade of some trees by the river. It was not Redrock Gorge, for the banks here were low and flat and the river wide and meandering. And of course it was Skye, on his towering black horse all dappled with sunlight and shadow, who was beside her.

"What's the matter, Pippa?" he asked quizzically, even a little kindly.

Pippa wiped her tears away fiercely with the back of her hand. She no longer felt abject and weepy, and she whipped up her temper as quickly as she could. Skye had sprung to the ground and tossed the reins over Kurrajong's head with a careless, "Stay there, old boy," and then in two long paces he was beside Pippa. Clumsily but determinedly, she disengaged her foot from the stirrup, aware that he must have noticed how absurdly short the leathers were, and dismounted, too. She, too, tossed her reins over Louie's head, but the pony began at once to move off briskly in the direction of Redrock Gorge. Pippa opened her mouth to order her back.

"Leave her," said Skye, before she could speak. "She'll come back. Now let's hear what's reduced you to tears so early in the day."

Pippa's eyelashes were stuck together in points, her hair was mussed and there were tear stains on her cheeks, but she said distinctly, "I haven't been reduced to tears. I was coming to see you."

"Then you were going in the wrong direction," he said humorously, hands on his narrow hips, his dark eyes glittering with mocking laughter. This did nothing at all to soothe Pippa's ruffled feelings, as it put her at even more of a disadvantage.

Then, unexpectedly he relented and said quite seriously, "Well, you were coming to see me. So let's hear what you have to say for yourself."

"Eve's leaving," Pippa said.

He looked surprised, his dark eyebrows peaking. "I know that, of course."

"Yes, you know, of course," agreed Pippa, "because you told her to go."

He looked displeased. "I certainly didn't tell her to go. She came to me for my advice and I gave it to her."

"And everyone has to take your advice, or else!" Pippa flung at him. She saw one hand move convulsively from his hip, and she thought with a strange feeling of pleasure, *He would like to strike me for saying that. Well, let him. I can hit back.* But of course he didn't touch her, and she stormed on, "Just how selfish can you be! *You* know perfectly well Angela Glas will never marry Adrian, but Eve can't stay and have a chance. I suppose a governess isn't good enough for one of the mighty Bannermans!" It was not exactly what she had meant to say, and it was unpardonably rude, but she was glad she had said it. It made Skye Bannerman look as dangerous and as furious as she herself was feeling deep inside. She raced on, "Well, I'm leaving too—just as soon as I can. I'll find someone to take me to the train in the morning, and I'm sure you'll be only too pleased to see the last of me, Mr. Bannerman."

He looked at her in silence—a silence that lasted so long it made Pippa wonder what on earth could be going on inside his head. She searched her mind for more things to hurl at him, but strangely all her words seemed to have dried up, and she was beginning to feel frightened.

But when he spoke, although there was still the glitter of fury in his eyes, it was courteously rational.

"If that's the impression I've given you, Pippa—that I'd be glad to see the last of you—then I must apologize for it. I had imagined—quite wrongly, I see now—that I was contributing something toward making your visit to Jounima Station an enjoyable one."

Pippa felt a quick prick of shame. But she reminded herself instantly of what Angela Glas had said. "Skye is a good host who makes sure his guests get exactly what they ask for." He needed disillusioning if he thought Pippa was asking for a synthetic romance with him! Maybe because she had been over it so many times in her mind, she said with extraordinary glibness, "You mean you've occasionally acted as a stand-in for Bruce. Let me assure you I'd far rather have spent my time at North Star, and it's only because of your *machinations* that Bruce has been mainly out of the picture."

His eyes narrowed still further and his lips curved in a humorless smile. He removed his hands from his hips and folded them across his chest. Pippa, fists clenched, stood with her head thrown defiantly up.

"You've surely been doing some clever thinking for a girl of your tender years," he drawled, then disconcerted her by shooting out, "Who put you up to it?"

Pippa was silent, though she felt the blood surge to her cheeks, then ebb away again.

"Bruce?" he suggested.

Pippa shrugged. "I can think for myself, despite my tender years. Besides, what does it matter? I'm going tomorrow."

"Where to? Back to your cousin in Sydney? I thought that didn't appeal for some reason."

"It appeals now," said Pippa coldly, implying an

unflattering comparison. "I'll stay there until I've found myself some work, at any rate." The thought was not a cheering one. She was going to have to battle hard to escape Lalla's pleas and demands, particularly when Christopher was there to soften her already soft heart. She looked straight at Skye Bannerman and tried to hide her reluctance. "You've convinced me I'm too young and inexperienced to be threshing around on my own, in any event," she told him cynically.

A smile flickered away back in the darkness of his night blue eyes as he said thoughtfully, "Why be in such a hurry to run away and rush headlong into something that evidently doesn't appeal to you? I seem to recollect your saying that you hoped to find work in the country—at Jounima Siding, to be exact," he added, his smile, which Pippa resolutely refused to answer, in the open now. "Come to think of it, by a strange coincidence, there's a job tailor-made for you ready and waiting at the homestead. Three children—four if you count Annabel—soon in need of direction. They know you and like you already. The pay's more than reasonable, and you'd have your keep. You'd have to see Adrian to get all the details. Some people might find the conditions hard, but would you, I wonder?"

It was an attack—a turning of the tables—so sudden that Pippa was having trouble taking in the full sense of what he was saying. Take Eve's place! Stay here! It was the last thing she would think of doing. She said almost violently, "I'm not interested."

"That's a very hasty answer. Why not?" One eyebrow shot up quizzically as he looked her over. "Maybe it's not good enough for you," he suggested mockingly. "Maybe you have some immeasurably higher target in mind. You think a governess's job is way beneath you. Is that it?"

"That's not it at all," said Pippa hotly. Her mind was

in a turmoil. There was absolutely no question of her staying on at Jounima. No question at all. And yet... and yet....

Later, she tried to convince herself it was his final taunt that made her change her mind, but deep in her heart she knew that it was something else altogether, something against which she seemed to be completely powerless, something that had to do with this man's overpowering charm.

"I'll see," she said distantly. "I'll ask Adrian. He mightn't want me. And after all, they're his children, aren't they?"

"They're his children," agreed Skye reasonably. "And now," he continued briskly, dropping the subject and not knowing, Pippa hoped, that he had won, "I must get back to my sheep. Do you want a ride back to the homestead?"

"No, thank you," said Pippa ungraciously. "I'd rather walk." A decision she regretted when he didn't insist, but left her to it. It was a long hot walk in the burning sun.

ADRIAN WAS AGREEABLY CASUAL that night when she was presented as a possible new governess for his children. Skye had obviously partially prepared the ground, and the interview, if it could be called that, took place in the brief interval between dinner and coffee. It was a windy night and for once too cool and unpleasant by the swimming pool, so the coffee tray had been taken into the sitting room. Pippa, about to follow Eve and Angela, was detained at the dining-room door by Skye's hand on her arm.

"One moment, Pippa. I've told Adrian you're interested in that position."

Pippa's heart began to pound. She had worried all afternoon because she had not said no and stuck to it. She was allowing Skye to force his will on her. She was being manipulated like a string puppet. Now it was too late—or so she told herself.

"Eve's dealt me a very nasty blow by deciding so suddenly to leave," said Adrian with a wounded air. "I thought she was perfectly happy here with my children, but it appears she's finding outback isolation disagreeable all of a sudden. God knows what's at the back of it all. You'll be an angel, Pippa," he continued, "if you'll fill in the gap until I can get hold of a more permanent replacement. I know it's not very fair to ask it of you, when you came here to enjoy yourself."

"Don't let that aspect of it tear at your heartstrings," said Skye sardonically. "The fact is, Pippa needs a job. She was going to run away back to Sydney if this hadn't turned up. Weren't you, Pippa?"

Pippa refused to answer him or even to look at him. She simply ignored him.

"Oh," said Adrian. "Well, of course she must be kept here at any cost!" He smiled down at Pippa and she thought him just as devastatingly handsome as Skye, in his particular way, and not nearly so hard. But his smile didn't make her heart turn with even the beginning of a somersault. "I'll offer you the same as Eve gets, of course, and we'll try to see you get a little extra free time. Talk to her about all the more sordid details, will you, honey? And if you've any complaints or queries, come to me. Okay?"

"Okay," said Pippa thinking how weak-minded she was to be falling for this at all, and wishing that at least she could have been treated in a businesslike way instead of as a sort of family friend. One more thing she did manage to say as they all made their way to the sitting room. "The moment you find someone else, I'll go."

"Of course," Adrian agreed.

Skye said nothing at all, and Pippa, who had shot him

a fiery glance, found his silence aggravating in the extreme. Though what could he be expected to say?

By some means or other he managed to get to the telephone when Bruce called her later on before she did. What was he putting a stop to this time, she wondered cynically. No doubt Bruce was being given a new set of orders that would keep him out of the way. Skye was certainly going to be kept busy with his maneuvers if she was to stay at Jounima any length of time. He would have to be thinking up vitally important things for Bruce to do every single day! She waited passively and finally he emerged from the telephone room.

"It's all yours, Pippa."

"You're too generous," she said sarcastically.

Bruce greeted her, "Hello, Pip. Cousin Skye says you've got great news for me. What is it? The party coming up at last? Don't tell me you've charmed him into changing his mind about that?"

He sounded a little cynical, and Pippa said, "I haven't said a word about it. It's not my department."

"Then what? Couldn't possibly be that he's letting you join me in my bachelor establishment! I don't think he's got much faith in old Allie as a chaperone. While he might not be so Victorian about his own morals, he keeps a pretty strict eye on mine."

Pippa broke in, "It's nothing like that." She was turning over in her mind the fact that Bruce had thought of the party first and it occurred to her that it was rather trivial to set so much store by a party. Even she, who was only nineteen and rather green if some people were to be believed, didn't get her values quite as cockeyed as that. A party was only a party, and she would not have come all the way to Jounima Siding just for an evening of fun with someone she hardly knew. She had come because she had liked Bruce so much. It had been as if fate had held out a string and said, "Follow this and see where it leads you." Silly, maybe, but it had led her to Jounima Station and to a job as governess to three—or possibly four—little children. All this ran through her mind with lightning speed before she said, "The news is that I've changed my mind about going."

"Marvelous! That's really great! Who persuaded you? I didn't seem to be having much success. Not Skye, by any chance?"

"Not by any chance," said Pippa emphatically, though of course it was not actually true. "It happened through a combination of circumstances and necessity."

"Like what?"

"Eve Arnold is leaving and I'm taking up her job."

"What?" His exclamation was one of utter incredulity.

"I can't just go on staying here indefinitely," said Pippa. "I need a job, and here's one ready made."

"Oh no," said Bruce, most decisively. "I'm not going to have that. I'm not going to have you a paid help on my cousin's property. Wiping little kids' noses, sewing on their buttons.... It's just not good enough."

"For whom?" asked Pippa coldly, shocked by his reaction. She could almost feel the hairs on the back of her neck prickling. "How do you know I didn't do exactly the same sort of thing back in England, Bruce? You've never asked." No, her mind echoed. He had never asked. He didn't know the least little thing about her. And it followed pretty clearly from that that he had never thought of being serious about her. It was a chilling, revealing deduction to have made, and one that must have been made long ago by Skye Bannerman. Why she felt so positive on that count, Pippa didn't know, but she had a strong certainty that Skye was very well clued in as to what Bruce's intentions were. She quickly reined in her runaway thoughts. "Actually, I was a typist, Bruce. I'm not qualified to be a governess, or a nursery teacher. So when you think about it, I'm lucky Skye suggested me for the job."

"Skye did? I thought they were Adrian's children."

"Well, the simple fact is I'm staying until Adrian finds someone else."

"You're going to be so tied down! When does it all start? Eve can't have gone yet. I just can't believe it," he went on, leaving Pippa no time to utter a word. "You're a guest—my guest! It's not as if you're desperate for work. It's not costing you a cent to live here...and to live well."

On *Skye's* bounty, thought Pippa. As *Skye's* uninvited guest. She held the earphone a little away from her head, for Bruce was talking loudly and emphatically.

"I just didn't know you were so weak-minded, Pippa, to fall for this sort of thing just because Skye asked you. Don't imagine he'll respect you for it. My cousin's not like that. He's just making use of you, trading on the fact that you've fallen victim to his charms. Well, I'm not going to have it."

Pippa cut in sharply and clearly. Here was someone else wanting to dictate to her! "Bruce, it's all settled. I need the job and I'm taking it, and that's that." When a minute later she said goodbye, Bruce was still protesting loudly and vehemently, and she became aware that Skye was standing in the doorway. Her cheeks reddened and she rose with a feeling of utter confusion. He put his cigarette in the ashtray on the telephone table and reached for the receiver.

"I'm sorry to have been so long," said Pippa formally. "Were you waiting to make a call?"

"Don't apologize," he said briefly. "Everyone has a right to his private and personal life."

"Even a governess?"

"You're not a governess yet, Pippa," he said, a hint of exasperated amusement in his dark blue eyes.

As she turned away and left him to it, Pippa thought, *I'm being melodramatic again. I'd better hush and try to behave like an ordinary uncomplicated human being.*

But that was a task that became a difficult one when she was in any way involved with Schuyler Bannerman.

CHAPTER SEVEN

LATE THE FOLLOWING AFTERNOON an old rattletrap of a car panted and groaned up the homestead driveway and around to the back of the house. Pippa, looking down from her balcony, saw that Percy Daylight had arrived. She wondered how he had made his way back to his car which had been left under a group of trees in the middle of a plain. (It was something she never discovered, as a matter of fact, and she was inclined to think it must have been done by witchcraft.) But the question that was uppermost in her mind was, had he gotten the dingo's scalp? He must have; he would surely not have come to report disaster! She had been dressing for dinner, and with her hair streaming she raced down the stairs and flew across the graveled yard to find out what had happened.

The old man had climbed out of his car and was carefully readjusting the door, which was hanging off its hinge and had to be fastened in place by a complicated tangle of strings and wires. He wore the same faded blue trousers and heavy gray shirt she had seen him in before, and there was a battered old felt hat pushed well back from his broad forehead. He turned around to beam at Pippa, his dark eyes alight.

"G'day, miss. Boss home yet?"

"I think so," said Pippa. She watched him as he began to roll himself a cigarette, slowly, carefully, being very frugal with the tobacco. Then she could contain herself no longer. It might not be proper to find out before the boss, but Pippa was going to do so all the same. "Did you trap that dingo, Mr. Daylight?"

His grin widened and in the red sunset light his whole face seemed to light like a beautiful, friendly lamp. "Too right I did, miss. That plurry dingo won't kill no more sheep again."

"Oh, I'm glad!" exclaimed Pippa. Impulsively she seized his hand and shook it. "I'm so glad!"

"Is that a fact?" said an amused voice from behind her. It was Skye. She had missed the sound of his footsteps on the gravel, as she had been so wrapped up in her congratulations. "What makes you so glad, Pippa? Is it the thought that our sheep will be safe, or are you thinking of a certain scalp other than the dingo's?" Pippa blushed scarlet, and Skye went on to tell the trapper, "The little lady here thought I'd have your scalp, Percy, if you didn't trap that dingo. I don't believe she'd have let me touch a hair of your head, though—she has a soft spot for you. By the way, let's have that scalp now and we'll settle our business."

He whistled when Percy produced the scalp. "By heaven, he must have been a mighty brute! Well, he had to go. Want to look, Pippa?" But Pippa had stepped back and averted her eyes. She didn't at all want to look.

The business transaction completed, the two men shook hands, and then Percy shook hands with Pippa. Before he got into his car, he rooted in his pocket and produced a small, flat stone, smooth and black and shiny, which he presented to Pippa.

"That stone will bring you good luck."

Pippa, surprised, examined the stone. She saw that on its smooth surface a skeleton lizard had been meticulously scratched, and the fine grooves filled with ocher-colored paint. The strange pattern glowed in the sunset light, and to Pippa it had a touch of magic about it.

When the old man had rattled off in his vehicle, Skye

said cryptically, "You've made a conquest, Pippa. That could be a museum piece. May I see it?"

As Pippa handed it over, his glance flicked over her face and the veil of golden brown hair that fell glintingly over her shoulders.

"What became of your Pocahontas hairstyle?" he asked lightly, negligently lifting a stray lock.

Pippa looked at him uncomprehendingly, startled that he should have the faintest interest in her hair.

"Have you forgotten?" he quizzed. "Those natty little braids you had bound across your brow the night I met you at Jounima Siding?"

"Oh." Pippa colored in confusion. Instinctively she pushed her hair back and her hand brushed against his fingers accidentally, unnerving her all the more. "I don't usually do my hair that way. It was, er, sort of unintentional."

He studied her amusedly for a moment. "That's the first time I ever heard a girl admit a becoming hairstyle was unintentional! I imagined you must have worked over it, and imagined the devastating effect it was going to have on Bruce. Instead of which, it had a devastating effect upon me."

"I doubt that," said Pippa wryly.

"You'd be surprised." His attention returned to the black stone, then he looked into her eyes. "Do you like it?"

"The...the talisman?" Pippa held out her hand to receive it and he let the small stone slip through his fingers. She said slowly, "I think there's magic in it, or perhaps witchcraft. Good witchcraft. It gives me a prickly feeling just to hold it."

"Thinking of other hands that have held it?"

"And the hands that made it," said Pippa. "How long ago? And the primitive faith that has maybe been put in it. I don't know anything much about the aboriginals, but I have the strangest feeling—like being in touch with something supernatural."

"Your fingers tell me that. They're trembling," Skye said. He put his hand briefly over hers and his touch seemed to burn her and to stir her even more than the touch of the stone. She literally jumped when Angela Glas appeared floating like a black shadow from the house. A creature of evil, thought Pippa fancifully. Gold earrings shaped like tiny bells tinkled softly as she walked, and her head was covered by a black turban.

"Who was that filthy old character who just drove off?" she asked Skye, linking her arm through his. "Do you have many tramps of his sort hanging about the place?"

Skye said, "That was no tramp, Angela. That was the dingo trapper, and a very clever old fellow. He's killed our dingo for us and earned himself a handsome reward."

"Well, that's a blessing," said Angela, not at all embarrassed by her mistake. She looked at Pippa. "What's that in your hand?"

"It's a good-luck stone," said Pippa reluctantly.

"I thought it must be an injured bird at the very least." Angela peered at the stone with some distaste. "Don't tell me the dingo trapper gave it to you."

"Yes."

"Then if I were you I would get rid of it as fast as I could. It's probably alive with germs. I hope you'll keep it out of my child's reach, at any rate."

Pippa felt infuriated. She simply couldn't take to Angela Glas, not one little bit. And she couldn't understand how Skye Bannerman could be so tolerant, so blind, so admiring and maybe more. He and his infatuated brother. *Men!* thought Pippa, as she took her gift upstairs and put it on her dressing table. Skye had touched it, admired it. *He* hadn't thought it was filthy.

NOW THAT IT HAD BEEN ARRANGED for Pippa to take over, Eve had decided to go in three days' time. She had relatives in Narrabri and she would visit them for a while. "Give myself a holiday," she said with apparent cheerfulness.

"Long overdue," said Skye, though Adrian said nothing. He had a displeased and martyred air as if he had been dealt an unnecessary and unsportsmanlike blow.

"I'll have to rethink my life," Eve told Pippa later.

"Perhaps I should have refused to look after the children," said Pippa, feeling guilty and miserable.

"Nonsense," said Eve. "It's better I make the break as soon as I've made the decision. Otherwise I might weaken and stay. And as Skye said, there's no future in that. At least I know the children will be happy with you."

"They'll miss you," said Pippa.

"I know," said Eve simply and turned away.

And so it was Eve's last weekend on Jounima. On Sunday, Ken and Caroline—and the Dalmatian, Roddy—came to visit, as did Bruce. It was a scorchingly hot day, and late in the afternoon they all drove to the billabong to loll in the shade of the trees or swim in the coolness of the water. Bruce took Pippa out in a rowboat that had been brought on a trailer behind one of the cars, and they drifted across the water in the shadow of the tall river gums.

Bruce had said no more about her taking Eve's position, and Pippa was relieved. It was her business and hers alone what she did with her life—she was quite positive about that.

She had the feeling, too, that Bruce's initial enthusiasm about her had worn off until now she was no more to him than any other passably pretty girl who happened to be on hand. Which was just as well.

Perhaps they were all the same, these Bannermans

and half Bannermans, Pippa thought, trailing her fingers in the water. They blew hot, then cold, considering themselves too good for working girls, like herself and Eve. Bruce was as silent and perhaps as thoughtful as she was, and she wondered what was going on in his mind. Her own thoughts drifted to the group they had left behind them—still in sight, but receding every minute. Pippa could see Eve splashing and swimming with the children, tossing a big red rubber ball for them to catch. The others—the Martins, Angela, Adrian and Skye—were still lying about on the thick cotton rugs that had been spread on the ground. As Pippa watched, she saw Skye's long form unwind itself as he stood up. He reached down a hand to Angela, half-reclining near Adrian, and pulled her to her feet. Then the two strolled off together. How did Adrian like that, wondered Pippa, moving restlessly. She was aware of a deep disturbance in her own mind, something very like jealousy, and she despised herself for it. She was well aware that she meant nothing to Skye. He had stirred up emotions in her simply by giving her guest treatment. It was as simple as that. She was aware, too, that he was making use of her in so adroitly maneuvering her into the position of stopgap and that she would have been far wiser to do like Eve and go. It was a relief to keep in sight of things about Skye that rankled. There were other things, as well. His heartlessness where Eve was concerned; his casual annexing of Angela Glas whenever it suited him to do so. What was the strength of that, she wondered, not for the first time.

Did he have serious ideas about Angela, or was it simply that he couldn't resist proving his charm superior to that of his brother?

And Adrian was a very handsome man. It hardly seemed sportsmanlike to take a girl from one's own brother! Certainly he had prevented Adrian from taking Angela to Cedar Creek. Pippa had heard that scene herself. He had had no trouble at all; Angela was a victim of his charm just as much as he was a victim of hers.

Pippa interrupted her thoughts wretchedly. How complicated life was becoming! And how involved she was becoming in the affairs of the household at Jounima. She knew only too well why she had rejected the idea of leaving as soon as a legitimate excuse to stay was found.

She made the discovery now that Bruce had brought the boat into a small break in the bank of the billabong—an inlet shaded by the green and swaying fronds of weeping willows, cool and secluded. His purpose, it seemed, was to kiss her, and he set about it without any preliminaries.

"At last I've got you to myself, my pretty Pippa. You're the best prize I ever won at an amusement park, do you know that?" He moved carefully in the boat until he was able to sit beside her, put his arm around her and kiss her. Pippa submitted rather than upset the boat. And besides, one part of her mind reminded her half-comically, wasn't this the reason she had come to Jounima? To be kissed by Bruce and see how it appealed? It was a fact. She had wanted all that time ago to be kissed by Bruce. She had imagined she would enjoy it considerably and that she would learn a lot about Bruce—and he about her—in between kisses. As fate—or was it Skye—had arranged it, there hadn't been opportunity for many kisses, but what she had learned between them was quite considerable.

Now she discovered she positively did not enjoy having Bruce kiss her. She didn't find it interesting, and it was certainly not stimulating. Politely and gently, but nevertheless firmly, she freed herself from his embrace and discovered that the boat had drifted from the shelter of its leafy green veil and was now floating in the open.

Straight across the water, on the opposite bank, she could see Skye and Angela. They had paused in their walk, Skye with his arm around Angela's waist, and they were looking across in the direction of the row-boat. Pippa felt an instant and overwhelming annoyance with Bruce and an equal annoyance with Skye—for a reason she didn't understand. She struggled to sit upright and to tidy her hair with an irritated exclamation. "Let me free. It's too hot!"

"What's up?" Bruce followed her glance. "Don't worry about those two. They're quite wrapped up in each other—one more conquest per person. Anyhow, it would be weird if I'd brought you out on the billabong and not kissed you, if you think about it. Everyone knows why I took you in the boat on your own—without any kids."

This might all be true, but it didn't make Pippa feel any less annoyed. She felt she had made herself look cheap. She said briefly, "I just don't like it, that's all."

"You don't like what? My kissing you? Or people looking?"

"People looking," said Pippa after a moment. It was weak, but she couldn't say the other thing. His kisses were harmless and she had come here at his invitation.

Bruce looked at her, his blue eyes thoughtful. Finally he said, "Okay," and took up the oars. He began to row back toward the others. "I thought you were a with-it girl," he said presently, "not a shrinking violet."

Pippa said nothing.

When they reached the others, he threw himself down on the rug in a way that Pippa thought was rather sulky. Or perhaps he couldn't be bothered with her now—a girl friend who was too reserved. Adrian had gone into the water to join the children, and Eve, instead of staying with him, had come on to the bank. She stood rubbing her hair dry and talking to Caroline and Ken about her future plans. "I need a change," Pippa heard her say. "I've been happy here, but all things end." They knew the truth, of course, and they were discreet and sympathetic and bracing. Angela and Skye were still off on their own—probably kissing, thought Pippa, and found the thought unbearable.

She refused to recall the night when Skye had held her in his arms. She sat listlessly on the rug beside Bruce, feeling very much of an outsider, and soon Ken sat down nearby and asked, "Settling down well on North Star, Bruce?"

Bruce grunted and kept his eyes closed. He lay flat on his back, his hands behind his head. "I'd settle down better if Skye would leave me alone and remember that I'm in charge now."

"You want to learn the hard way, eh?" said Ken. "You should count yourself lucky to have Skye's interest. And you might remember that any losses you make are not yours alone. We're still a family unit as far as the estate is concerned."

"We?" queried Bruce. He opened his eyes the merest slit. "Oh, of course. You married a Bannerman, didn't you? You'd like to have North Star, wouldn't you, Ken? I guess it's what everyone would like. Maybe my mother would hand it over but for me. Then Adrian could reign at Cedar Creek, Skye would have me out of his hair, and everyone would be happy. I'm certainly the fly in the ointment hereabouts."

"That's a lot of garbage," said Ken imperturbably. "None of us wants to take North Star from your mother. And you needn't worry about my having an eye on the place. I may have married into the Bannerman family, but I'm an experienced sheepman, too, and don't you forget it. I've had the offer of the managership of a property down south a few miles—Noorima. You'd know it, of course."

"I wouldn't," said Bruce. "I'm not well up in country affairs."

"I'll probably take it," said Ken. "I'll get Skye's advice first, of course." Of course, thought Pippa. Quietly she got to her feet, thinking she would take a walk. She knew well enough that feeling out of it wasn't what was making her restless and edgy. It was the nagging knowledge that somewhere, Skye was alone with Angela....

Adrian and the children had come out of the water, and Charles was throwing a stick for Roddy to fetch. Pippa said to no one in particular, because nobody was listening to her anyway, "I'm going to take a walk." There was maybe an hour left before sunset, and she would come back in time to help clear up the picnic. She walked away rather slowly, choosing the opposite direction in which she thought Skye had gone.

She discovered three minutes later that somebody had been listening to her after all. Behind her came trotting four children, Annabel in the lead. And alongside of them Roddy lolloped, practically smiling his delight. They didn't ask if they might come with her, they simply took it for granted that she would want them, and they were all remarkably full of energy and good spirits. Annabel stopped now and again to squat down to examine a beetle or an anthill or some tiny bush flower. Charles was throwing sticks for Roddy to fetch, and the twins were making a collection of peculiar stones. They offered each one silently for Pippa's inspection, and finally they had so many she had to help carry them.

Pippa kept a watchful eye on them and reflected soberly that this would be her work in a couple of days' time. It was a job with a lot of responsibility attached—to look after three motherless children. And to take under her wing a fourth child whose mother was a dedicated actress...or temptress, she ended unkindly. Roddy made wild rushes ahead after the sticks Charles threw and brought them back eagerly; presently Charles achieved a more skillful throw than he had managed before. The curved stick he had found flew high through the air, "just like a boomerang!" Sara shouted as it whizzed overhead. "One of the killing sort that doesn't come back."

It caught momentarily in the branches of a tree, then dropped into the scrub, and Roddy bounded after it. He leaped around in the bushes, disappeared from sight and suddenly bounced out again as if pursued by a devil. There was a great commotion in the scrub behind him, a loud grunting and snuffling and roaring. The children stood staring and Pippa felt herself tense. Roddy had pulled up, his legs braced, facing back into the undergrowth, and then something huge and dark and bristly and tusked came blundering out.

"A boar! A wild boar!" the children screamed. The Bannerman children made a dash for Pippa, but Annabel, who was a little ahead, stood as if rooted to the spot. The boar came into the open, snorting, his small eyes gleaming as he looked this way and that. Then to Pippa's horror, he turned and made for the thing that most caught his eye—Annabel in her little red swimsuit. She had a small, straggly bunch of bush flowers in her hand, and as the boar made for her she dropped them and ran—not toward Pippa, but stumblingly into the scrub, screaming loudly with fright.

Pippa, with no time to think, with time only to act instinctively, ran, also, pelting the stones she held in her hand at the great lumbering beast and shouting to Roddy. The dog came to join the chase and finally the boar turned after Pippa scored a lucky hit on its tender snout. Annabel, finding herself no longer pursued, for she had stopped and looked behind, began to jump up and down screaming louder than ever, though whether it was from fear or from excitement, Pippa didn't know.

The boar was hesitating, undecided between Pippa and Roddy. She kept her eye on him and told the children, "Go and get help. Quickly now! *At once!*" She knew there was a rifle in Bruce's car—she had seen it earlier on. And of course he was a crack shot—she had seen him in action at the amusement park. The children began to run, the twins dropping their precious stones, Charles catching Joanna's hand. *If he chases them,* thought Pippa wildly, *I'll throw myself in his path.* But he didn't chase them, just stood there grunting and snuffling.

Annabel came cautiously from the scrub and with a sudden scuttle joined the other children and took Sara's hand. She shouted, "He'll kill you, Pippa. Run!"

Pippa had no intention of running until the children were out of the way, and then she wasn't sure just what she would do.

The boar made up his mind with disconcerting suddenness. He chose Pippa and charged at her, while Roddy rushed forward, barking furiously. Out of the corner of her eye Pippa saw a tree and began to run for it. Roddy's tactics were unsuccessful—the boar was distracted for no more than three seconds. Then he was after Pippa again, and she could hear his angry snorts as she leapt for the lowest branch and with stunning agility caught hold of it and swung her legs to safety. It had been years since she had climbed a tree, but she was very nimble right then and in no time at all she was six feet from the ground, standing on a slender bough, holding tightly to another and looking down at the angry boar, ranting below. Such tusks! Such ferocious little eyes, thought Pippa. But at the same time she thought, *Poor boar, poor old fellow, to be routed out of a rest in his own scrub by a lolloping, laughing dog, for no good reason at all. He doesn't know what a rumpus he's started.*

Meanwhile, it was Roddy's turn to be undecided. Quite plainly the boar was staying put, and Roddy dashed around in the background barking half-heartedly and making little sallies that were not altogether courageous. Pippa wished he would desist. She had no desire to see Roddy go into combat against those cruel tusks. She called sternly, "Roddy, stop it! Go and fetch Ken. Go on, there's a good dog." He stopped still and looked at her inquiringly. Pippa repeated, "Go, Roddy." But it was too much to ask. Roddy might not be able to act the knight errant, but he would not desert a lady in distress. He sat down on the ground, eyes alert, tongue lolling, waiting for the boar to make the next move.

And the boar stood waiting for Pippa to come down out of her tree and kept his eyes fixed on her.

If someone doesn't come soon, I shall fall down, thought Pippa. *Like a rotten apple.* She could afford not to be really frightened, because she knew that soon someone *would* come.

It was Skye who appeared eventually, not Bruce. He had a rifle and he walked cautiously and he was alone. Pippa learned later that the children had brought him part of the way and then he had sent them back. He stopped some distance off and said quietly, "Hang on, Pippa. And don't come down until I tell you to. I'm going to shoot."

The boar turned with a loud snort at the sound of his voice and, head down, began rushing toward him. Skye took aim and fired and Pippa shut her eyes as the big animal fell and rolled on the ground.

"Stay where you are, Pippa," came Skye's command, and it seemed to Pippa to come from a remarkably long way off. Her eyes were still closed and she held tightly to her branch, which had begun to sway wildly, as had the whole tree. This seemed so unlikely that Pippa opened her eyes for a fraction of a second. Certainly everything was spinning around, but she realized it was simply because she was dizzy. She heard another shot, heard Roddy bark excitedly, then Skye's sharp order, "Stay!"

A long time seemed to pass before she half fell and was half pulled from the tree into Skye's arms. She stood limply against him, letting him support her, resting her head on his hard, solid, steady chest.

"It's all over now, Pippa," he said softly against her hair. One hand stroked her hair, the other held her close and comfortingly. "You needn't be frightened any more."

"I'm not frightened," protested Pippa. She discovered she was weeping and she was upset that Skye should think she had been frightened. "I knew someone would come. I wasn't frightened." It seemed important that he should believe her and she said it insistently.

"I believe you, Pippa. It's physical reaction, that's all. You're not responsible for that. You did well with the children. They told me how you lured the boar away from Annabel and let him chase you, instead."

"There was nothing else to do," said Pippa. She moved a little in his arms, found her handkerchief and wiped her eyes and her drenched cheeks. Skye did not release her and she did not want him to. "The poor boar," she murmured. "He wasn't doing anything. We disturbed him, and now he's dead."

"Well and truly dead. He'll make a great feast for the aborigines."

Mention of the aborigines made Pippa think of something. Her hand went urgently to the back pocket of her jeans. Had she thrown Percy Daylight's magic stone at the boar? No, it was still there, smooth and flat and hard, and she took it in her hand. "I was afraid I'd thrown my good-luck charm at the boar."

"You've been lucky, anyhow."

"And the children. I was so afraid for Annabel. The boar could have killed her, couldn't he?"

"Could have, but didn't."

"Adrian will never trust me with his children. He won't want me now. Eve will have to stay."

Skye laughed and held her a little away from him. "More melodrama, Pippa?" He looked down into her tear-stained face. "It's all turned out fine. Excitement for the children, a heroine's role for Annabel, sport for Roddy, and a feast for the aboriginals. What's more, a chance for me to take you in my arms."

"And for me?" said Pippa wryly. Those quizzical blue black eyes gave her such a melting feeling in her bones she couldn't look away. She was very conscious of Skye's hands on her bare arms, and then she was being pulled back only too willingly against his chest.

"For you, Pippa, this," he murmured and set his lips against hers in a long kiss that left her trembling and exhausted.

For Pippa, it was a kiss from the only man in the world whose kisses she desired. And of course he knew it and of course that was why he kissed her.

She looked up at him.

"Lucky me," she said ironically.

His eyes looked deeply, searchingly, into hers, and his lips twisted slightly. "Lucky you, Pippa. Two men kissing you within an hour of each other."

"And you," countered Pippa swiftly. "Lucky you—kissing two girls within an hour of each other."

His eyes grew thoughtful, one eyebrow was cocked inquiringly.

"Angela," said Pippa. She pushed the hair back from her cheek. "I saw you," she added calmly.

"You saw me what?" he asked sardonically.

"Kissing Angela," said Pippa, and then colored deeply. She had not seen it at all—she had only imagined it, but oh, how vividly and painfully! She admitted quickly, "Well, I didn't actually see you. But you did, didn't you?"

"Of course I did," he agreed lazily.

Of course. Pippa pulled away from him and stooped to take off her sandal and tip an imaginary pebble from it. The sun was going down and there was a fiery light on the ground and the shadows were long and purple. "We'd better get back," said Pippa huskily, "or the others will think—"

"That I'm making love to you?" he suggested amusedly.

"No," she said, crimsoning. She fastened her sandal and looked at him through her lashes. "They would never think that. I was going to say they'd think something awful had happened." As it has, she added to herself. It was a drastic thing to discover you had fallen so hard and hopelessly in love with a man who had no heart. Or if he had, it was the sophisticated kind of heart that would appeal to a worldly woman like Angela Glas. She began to walk ahead of Skye, but he was at once beside her, his hand laid lightly on her shoulder.

She said, "I thought it would be Bruce who would have come to my rescue."

"You'd have preferred that?"

"Bruce is a crack shot," she prevaricated.

"How do you know that?" he asked in surprise.

"You must have forgotten," Pippa said. "We met at an amusement park. He'd won a heap of trophies at a shooting gallery."

She saw his look of displeasure. "I see. Well, I pass as a marksman, too, and there were surely no problems this evening."

"Poor boar," said Pippa for a second time.

"Would you have liked it spared? I shot the creature rather than have it gore me, or the dog."

"Or me?"

"You were safely up your tree," he reminded her mockingly.

"What else was I to do?"

"My dear girl, I'm not criticizing you. I'm praising you. You showed remarkable presence of mind in a number of ways. I have nothing but admiration for you."

She bit her lip. It was a crazy conversation, and his hand still rested caressingly on her shoulder. Nothing but admiration.... She would have left it alone, but she said, "I don't really think you admire me, Mr. Bannerman."

"You can still be formal? Come along now. Can't you manage to call me Skye?"

"Skye," she said unwillingly. "I'm quite sure you don't admire me."

"Is that the amusement park image still rankling? Frankly, it's been puzzling me what you were doing at such a place, presumably on your own."

Pippa said smartly, "I went along to see if I could pick up a rich squatter for myself, of course."

"Then you did very well," he said smoothly. "I'd say you were as good a marksman in your way as any of us."

They were now in sight of the others and his hand dropped from her shoulder. Pippa felt in a ferment of confusion. Did he really believe that she had gone to the amusement park to pick up a boyfriend? What a stupid, childish thing it had been for her to say. And now she could not straighten it out. She managed a murmured, "You like to think the worst of me, don't you?"

"If I did, Pippa, then I shouldn't have suggested you take over the supervision of four small children."

"I don't think I have done that," countered Pippa. "Adrian has only three children. And I don't think he's going to marry Angela Glas."

"I don't think so, either," agreed Skye smoothly. "But I do think you've taken on the care of four children." He gave her a casual little push in Bruce's direction. The odd conversation had ended, they were back in the midst of the picnic.

The sun had faded and it was almost dark, and a camp fire had been lit. Everyone wanted to hear what had happened, and the children told the story over and over. Pippa asked Bruce, who was busy pouring out glasses of the cold beer that had been brought along in a cooler, "Why didn't you come to my rescue, Bruce?"

He shrugged. "Skye got in on the act first. He said it was his boar and for him to decide whether to shoot it or not." He didn't ask Pippa if she had been afraid or express regret that he had let her go walking on her own.

. Later Angela spoke to Pippa. She didn't thank her for looking after Annabel. She said, "It seems to me you're just not a sufficiently responsible person to look after children."

"You'd better tell Adrian that," said Pippa. She was standing by one of the cars after fetching a cardigan to put around her shoulders and Angela had deliberately followed her. "Of course if you're worried about Annabel, Mrs. Glas, I'm not contracted to look after her, you know."

She expected the other woman to retort that she would certainly not let her do so, but she merely said coldly, "You'll wake up to yourself one of these days, Pippa, and discover what an immature little nonentity you are. You do love limelight, don't you? All that drama over nothing! I can't understand why you didn't come back with the children—staying there and waiting to be rescued, trying to impress us that you're some sort of a heroine."

"Oh no," said Pippa with a little smile. "Annabel was the heroine."

"Annabel?" Angela's voice sharpened suspiciously.

"Skye said so," said Pippa lightly, walking quickly back to the fire.

CHAPTER EIGHT

A COUPLE OF DAYS LATER EVE LEFT. The children wept, and somehow Skye consoled them before handing them over to Pippa. But in the days that followed she had very little time to think about herself and her emotional problems. Those problems had to be shelved and Pippa hoped they would simply disappear. She had taken on a responsible job and she was determined to do it well, as much for her own satisfaction as to prove herself worthy of the generous wage she was being paid.

At that rate, she reflected, she'd soon be able to save up enough money for her fare back to England. The thought did not make her feel particularly jubilant.

Hers was certainly a full-time job. She had not realized before how hard Eve worked, though perhaps it came easier when one was used to it. Pippa was a little young to act as mother to three children, and she could not, no matter how hard she tried, compensate them for the loss of Eve. Young Annabel was quite satisfied with the change—it was really no change at all for her—but the other three missed Eve badly.

The days passed quickly, and Pippa saw next to nothing of Bruce. The men were busy dipping and drenching and shifting sheep and were away most of the day. Pippa steered clear of Angela Glas and neither of them said a word about Annabel. Pippa would have been heartless had she refused to look after the child, for whom she had developed a real fondness. She learned some kitchen lore from the housekeeper, who had always cooperated with Eve over the children's meals and was now prepared to cooperate with Pippa. Adrian, in the evenings, showed more concern over his children's happiness than she had somehow expected, and she thought he felt an inner guilt at depriving them of Eve. She could not help wondering why he didn't marry Eve. Eve was attractive, intelligent, sufficiently mature. She loved the country and she loved the children. It was a mystery to Pippa. Of course it was as plain as could be that he was infatuated by Angela Glas, and there seemed to be two completely different facets to his character. With Angela, he was the handsome, reckless, charming man; with his children he was the tender though sometimes impatient father.

"When's Eve coming back, Daddy?" Sara asked one night, her arms twined around his neck as he stopped to give her a good-night kiss.

And Joanne echoed, "Why can't Eve look after us?"

"You have Pippa to look after you now," said Adrian, straightening up and smiling at them both. "She's very kind to you, so stop complaining." Despite his smile, he looked exasperated and unhappy, and Pippa silently helped him tuck the children in. Sara said in a small voice, "We do love you, Pippa, but we love Eve best."

"*Is* she coming back?" Joanne asked.

"Of course she is," said Sara. "But Daddy, when?"

"We can't talk about that tonight," said Adrian, exasperated. "Now go to sleep like good girls."

Outside the bedroom door Pippa said, "They love Eve. They miss her badly."

"They'll get over it. It just takes time."

Pippa wondered if it had taken time before—after his wife had left him. And how he had reassured his children then. She wished she had the courage to ask him why he didn't marry Eve, but the answer to that must be, of course, that it was not Eve he loved.

Now he changed the subject abruptly.

"What about a game of tennis, Pippa? I promised Skye I'd bring you down to make up a foursome. And don't say you're too tired or I'll feel I've been overworking you."

Pippa reluctantly agreed to tennis. Her heart had leapt when he had mentioned Skye's name, and as she changed into tennis gear, she couldn't help wondering if Skye had suggested she should be asked to make up a foursome. Then she pulled herself up. She was only wanted so that Angela Glas could play. No one cared much who the fourth was. But, logic reminded her, Angela was hardly an asset on the tennis court. She couldn't pretend that either Skye or Adrian, both of them good tennis players, would be breaking their necks to get Angela onto the court. They must surely prefer to have her on the sidelines looking decorative and admiring their male superiority.

When she descended the stairs, Angela was waiting.

"Skye and Adrian have gone ahead to have a few practice shots," she explained with a critical look at Pippa's getup—white shorts and sleeveless shirt. Then, without a pause, she went on, "What were you up to all that time, closeted away with Adrian? And don't try to tell me you were discussing the children's welfare."

Pippa said in surprise, "Adrian came to say good night."

"To whom? To you or the children?"

"To the children, of course," said Pippa, flushing. Her heart had begun to hammer. This woman did nothing but bring out the worst in her, with her suspicions and her evil mind. And now, as on other occasions, Pippa joined in the verbal battle. "If you suspect he came to say good night to me as well, is it any of your business? Have you any particular claim on Adrian?"

Angela achieved a brittle laugh. "Why don't you say

what you mean? Rest assured I don't mind in the least if Adrian amuses himself with you. I'm not quite as ingenuous as you are, you know. Adrian is a good-looking man, and the company of good-looking males invariably goes to the head of pretty little girls like you. As for Adrian, he's young and virile, and frankly, I'd think there was something wrong with any man who didn't grab what he could get."

"And something wrong with a girl—or a woman—" said Pippa hotly, "who didn't give what she was asked for?"

"Are you hinting that Adrian or maybe Skye has been trying to seduce you?"

Pippa bit her lip. She hadn't come off best in that encounter. The whole squabble was distasteful, and if she had any sense she wouldn't engage in any more verbal battles with Angela Glas.

Perhaps it was her heated feelings that made her play a lively and spirited game of tennis that night despite the hot weather. Angela was hopelessly outclassed and none too pleased about it, and both Adrian and Skye were more than a little surprised to find Pippa such a good player. As for herself, the strenuous game drove away all her confused and angry feelings, leaving her exhausted but cleansed.

Adrian, who had partnered her—and of course they had won—said emphatically, "I think that deserves a long, cold glass of beer, Pippa." He put his arm casually around her waist and as they left the court Pippa was aware of Skye's look of displeasure. Pippa let Adrian's arm stay where it was because she knew it was no more than a friendly gesture. They had made a good team together and he was pleased with her and with himself. They all went in to sit by the pool and Adrian fetched glasses and beer. He also fetched gin and squash for Angela, who didn't care for beer.

"What about you, Pippa? Beer for you, too? Or will you have some of Angela's tipple?"

"I'll have beer, thank you," said Pippa blithely. She had never drunk beer, but she thought it might be less potent than gin. Besides which, she didn't want to ally herself with Angela in any way.

In her thirst, she began to drink the beer that Adrian handed her quickly, a fact that made him open his eyes wide. "Well, it's a thirsty night," he commented, "and if I'm not mistaken there's dust in the air. Let me top your glass up." He did so, and Pippa was aware of Skye sitting back watching her thoughtfully through half-closed eyes. In his white tennis clothes he looked more tanned and handsome than ever.

"Go easy, Pippa," he warned. "I don't want to have to carry you up the stairs."

At this point Angela decided that Pippa had had enough of the limelight, and she launched into a story.

"That remark reminds me of an episode in 'Heads You Win'. I don't know if either of you saw it—it was one of the early ones. I was playing Anna, of course, and these two men at the nightclub made a bet...."

Pippa stopped listening. Her eyes were fixed on Skye and she didn't seem able to shift them. She was tired, it had been a long day, and she had played a strenuous game of tennis. She raised her glass to her lips, then hesitated. Had Skye shaken his head at her? She must be imagining it. Pippa took a mouthful of beer. Now that she was not so thirsty, she realized she didn't really like the taste of it very much. But all the same, she was not going to have Skye order her about by no more than a shake of his head. She took another mouthful, and he rose to his feet and in a few strides had reached her and taken the glass out of her hand.

"No more of that," he commanded. "You're not a beer drinker, Pippa, and you're not going to become one. If you're thirsty I'll pour you a glass of squash."

"No, thank you," said Pippa coldly.

"If you're pouring squash, Skye," said Angela, "you can pour some for me with a dash of gin to give it a kick."

Skye took Pippa's glass away and poured a drink for Angela. Adrian was sitting beside her in the swing seat, and Skye stood three or four feet away.

"If you want your drink you must come and get it."

Angela looked at him in laughing exasperation. Her coloring looked dramatically lovely against the stark white of her beautifully cut tennis outfit, and the white band around her head gave her an air of distinction. *I haven't a hope,* Pippa thought dismally. She felt she was watching a play as Skye stood there, with the glass in his hand and Angela laughing up at him and showing her lovely white teeth. Adrian, handsome enough for any actor, and looking now just a little savage, reached out and pulled her toward him.

"Quit fooling, Skye, and give this girl her drink."

"I said she could come and get it," said Skye. He backed slowly away and Adrian kept a firm hold on Angela, whose eyes had a peculiar brightness.

"You're an idiot, Skye," she said. "You'll want me to beg for it next. I'm thirsty. Please give it to me."

"That's better," said Skye. He moved toward her again and as he came he raised the glass to his own lips and drank from it before he finally handed it down to Angela. She took it keeping her eyes on his face as she drank, too, and Pippa fancied that she deliberately drank from the same side of the glass as Skye.

Why this should sicken her so much she did not know, but she felt suddenly that she could stand no more of it and she got to her feet. A little unsteadily, she said, "I'm going up to bed. Good night, everyone."

"Better help the girl up the stairs, Adrian," Skye said.

"It's your fault she's in that state." Pippa heard him with amazement. In that state! She was no more than tired and upset by the scene that had just been enacted. And she was certain he knew it.

But Adrian didn't know it, and he actually came to grip Pippa firmly and concernedly around the waist and help her across the courtyard. In the hallway she glanced back and saw that Skye had taken Adrian's place on the swing seat and was kissing Angela's neck. She felt utterly sick and disillusioned. He had used her that way to clear the field for himself. How could she be in love with a man like that?

She told Adrian, "I'm perfectly all right, Adrian. Just tired. You don't have to see me up the stairs."

"Are you sure?"

To her relief, he went back to the others and left her to climb the stairs alone, and though she tried not to think of it, she simply could not erase from her mind that picture of Skye and Angela and the oddly sordid scene that had preceded it. She wondered, too, what was happening now that Adrian had gone back.

She climbed into bed quickly, but she could not sleep. She lay restlessly, listening to the sounds in the house. Long after silence had taken over she was still awake, tossing uneasily in the big bed, feeling the air unbearably hot and oppressive. At last she climbed out of bed and went to the window. The night air was excessively warm and the sky had a murky purplish look about it, and the stars were hidden, though not by cloud. Pippa thought she could smell dust. She thought of taking a cold shower and then she had a better idea. She would go down to the pool and have a swim. She simply had to take action of some sort, and the exercise might help her to sleep.

She slipped into her yellow bikini and tiptoed into the hall and along to the carpeted stairway. It was pitch dark, but she felt her way safely down and groped her way across the hallway with no trouble. A faint glimmer of light came from the courtyard where it was not as heavily dark as it was inside. The door was unlocked and she opened it silently, closed it behind her and walked barefooted across the stones. She could see the water and felt a shiver of excitement. In a second she had dived neatly and cleanly into the pool and came up with her hair streaming back from her face and a feeling of exhilaration coursing through her body.

She had swum the length of the pool twice before she saw the glow of the cigarette. Her heart gave a leap of fright. Who was it sitting there smoking in the darkness? And did they know it was she, Pippa, swimming in the pool? Silently, she pulled herself out onto the tiles and sat for a moment to wring out her hair. For the first time it occurred to her that she had forgotten to bring a towel with her. How was she to get inside again? She couldn't stay here with the silent unknown watcher in the shadows, but she couldn't go traipsing across the carpets dripping wet. There was a shower and dressing room at one end of the courtyard, but it was sure to be locked. Pippa glanced over her shoulder at the dark figure in the shadows, and as she looked the glow of the cigarette disappeared and she could hear the soft sound of footsteps approaching.

A low voice said, "Is that you, Pippa?"

"Yes," whispered Pippa. It was Skye's voice, unmistakably, and her heart began hammering.

"What are you doing down here at this time of the night... or morning, I should say?" He sat down next to her on the tiles and she could see faintly the darkness of his eyes and the whiteness of his teeth.

"I couldn't sleep. It's so hot and strange somehow." She was still whispering.

"It's the dust flying over. I couldn't sleep, either. Can

you smell the dust, Pippa—the red dust of the plains?"

"Yes. Are we going to have a dust storm?"

"I don't think so. It's blotted out the stars and the moon and the whole of the heavens, but it's high up and I think we've missed out. They'll have had it at North Star, but we're right on the edge of it. It's just enough to be disturbing."

"Yes, it's very disturbing," said Pippa.

He gave a faintly mocking laugh. "Have you finished your swim, or do you want to go in again?"

"Are you going to swim?" she asked. She realized now he was wearing only his bathing trunks and that was why he was almost invisible in the darkness—his skin was very dark. She, in her yellow bikini and with her fair skin, seemed to almost glow.

Skye stood up and reached down a hand to her. "I think I will."

Pippa hung back, vaguely frightened. "I didn't bring a towel. I shouldn't get wet again. I'll drip all over the carpets."

"There are towels in the dressing room," he said easily. "And the key's in the door."

Pippa succumbed and they both dived into the water and swam silently, side by side, the length of the pool and back again, over and over, Skye measuring his pace to her slower one. Pippa was aware of the sound of his breath mingling with her own and she was acutely aware of her physical self in a way she had never experienced before. This man's powerful and domineering personality seemed to permeate her being almost mystically as they swam together in the darkness of the night with not a star to be seen. The white walls surrounding them were darkly stained with the leaves of jasmine and bougainvillea, and the scent of orange blossom combined suggestively with the smell of dust.

It was a long time before she breathed, "I've had

enough, Skye," and pulled herself exhaustedly from the water. As she stood wringing out her hair once more, he left the pool saying, "I'll fetch a towel." He disappeared silently, and she saw the glow of a light as he opened the door of the dressing room and switched on the lamp; then it disappeared and he came back to her.

As he placed the huge soft towel around her he drew her swiftly against the bare, still wet coldness of his body and bent to kiss her lips.... Then she was wrapped in the towel and was hugging it around her. Her minute bikini was almost dry, her long hair hung against the thick towel, and she felt the warm night wind drying her legs quickly. Skye said a strangely austere, "Good night, Pippa. Can you find your own way upstairs? I'm going to take a shower."

At Pippa's murmured "Yes" he was gone far too suddenly. Pippa felt a little bereft, a little cheated, somehow frustrated. She found the door into the house and was soon climbing the stairs. What had happened? Had it all been a sort of dream? A strangely beautiful dream that had ended too soon, too abruptly? She was not at all sure.

In her room, she towelled her hair dry, got into her short cotton pajamas and fell upon the bed and slept exhaustedly.

In the morning there was not a trace of the dust storm, but the housekeeper told Pippa it had been all through North Star. Skye had been on the telephone to Bruce early in the morning. It was getting very dry over there, and only a few big drops of rain had fallen in the wake of the dust. Some trees near the homestead had been blown down and without a doubt some of the fences had been damaged.

"Bruce will have to drive out and look at them today and arrange for repairs."

Pippa heard this with a strange feeling of relief. Somehow she was glad to know Bruce could not possibly come to Jounima that day. She was busy all day with the children, but now and again she remembered the previous night and that secret, silent swim in the pool, and the moment when Skye had embraced her so simply and so closely. What had it all meant? That she loved him despite everything, she knew. She couldn't help herself. It might be a hopeless love and one best forgotten, but she couldn't forget it. Surely he must have *some* kind of feeling for her, or he could not have made her a gift of that hour. Or had it been a deliberate scene, an act calculated and carried out with the intention of upsetting her equilibrium and making her forget Bruce? Though if he only knew it, he had made her forget Bruce long ago. Now she was dizzyingly and hopelessly in love with Skye himself. Was that what love was all about? Was it as easy as that for a girl to fall in love? And could she love Skye this way despite all she knew about him—his autocratic and impossible ways, his heartlessness, his intolerance? And if so, then what had become of common sense?

She should have been repelled, but instead she was racked by jealousy, when she recalled the way he had been engaged in a suggestive and tantalizing scene with Angela Glas, kissing her in a peculiarly intimate way despite the fact that they were not in the least private and that she and Adrian could have turned—as Pippa had—and seen what was happening. Pippa wondered again what had taken place when Adrian had returned to the courtyard. Something surely that had made Skye too restless to sleep. A row over Angela, of course. After all, whose girl was Angela? Both Adrian and Skye were obviously more than half in love with her. She would hardly still be there on Jounima otherwise.

Pippa was badly disturbed by her thoughts. She ached to see Skye again and yet she was afraid to have to abandon her mad hope that the previous night might have meant something special to him—to have to suffer again his civility, his politeness, his indifference.

Tidying herself before dinner that night, before Skye came home, Pippa studied herself in the long mirror in her room. Her eyes were bright and gray green against the pale green of her soft dress. Her heart-shaped face had acquired the palest of tans that minimized her light freckles. Her mouth was too wide for real prettiness, and she was undoubtedly too slim. She scarcely had a suspicion of Angela's ample curves. Was there anything about her at all that could possibly beguile a man like Skye Bannerman? The night before had been nothing but a freak streak of gold in common rock. And yet her whole life now seemed turned toward Skye as a sunflower turns its face to the sun. She was staying on at Jounima for no other reason than her need to be near him.

She went downstairs that night with a feeling close to despair. Nora was supervising the children who were eating their supper in the sun room, and Pippa went slowly to the courtyard. She felt nervous these nights now that Eve had gone and only herself, Angela and the two Bannermans were left. Angela's habit of ignoring her made her feel an outsider—Angela would far sooner have had the two men to herself. Pippa wondered how long the woman was going to stay there. Was she waiting for them to make a move, or was she trying to decide which of them she wanted?

This night was no different from other nights. There sat Angela, exotic in black and gold, smoking, sipping a martini, looking exceedingly decorative while the two men talked. When Pippa appeared, it was Adrian who greeted her first.

"Ah, Pippa. How are the little monsters tonight?"

"They're as good as gold," said Pippa with a smile.

Skye turned and sent her an unrevealing look from his

dark eyes. "Lemon squash for you, Pippa?" he asked courteously.

"Yes, please." She felt color fan over her cheeks. Her hand shook as she accepted the glass from him.

"Have a nice day?" he asked, a faint smile lifting the corners of his mouth.

Pippa nodded and smiled back warily. That query, framed in those particular and evocative words, shook her. Yet to him it probably meant nothing.

"What did you do?"

"Nothing exciting. I gave Annabel a swimming lesson and—" She suddenly caught the tail end of a distinctly chilly stare from Angela and hurried on to tell what the other children had done. She didn't think Skye was really listening, though he watched her closely, nodded once or twice and smiled a little. By the time they went in to dinner, she felt unnerved and jittery.

She felt herself hardly present at the dinner table. Adrian asked Angela to take a walk down by the river with him later, and Pippa half expected Skye to offer some counter-proposition, but he didn't. In fact, after dinner when she was about to go upstairs to put the children to bed, he surprised her by saying, "I'll see you when you come down again, Pippa. All right?"

Pippa nodded and her heart leapt. She felt madly and unreasonably exultant.

She was away for maybe half an hour. She got the children ready for bed, tucked them in and kissed them good night, waited a while for Adrian to put in an appearance and when he didn't told them that maybe he would be up later. She thought it likely that he had taken Angela to walk by the river and hoped he had. She ran to her room to check up on her appearance before she went downstairs again. Her eyes were very bright, and she flicked a brush through her shining hair, dabbed a touch of powder on her nose, decided against lipstick, and went on winged feet to the stairs. She passed Angela in the hall and thought she must be going to fetch a coat or a scarf, and that she hadn't after all yet gone for her walk.

Then as she reached the foot of the stairs, she heard Adrian's voice say angrily, "Why the hell do you always have to interfere? Just what are you up to? Why must you make some counter-suggestion the minute I go to fetch a packet of cigarettes? Why do you have constantly to push your frame in, order people about? Am I never to get Angela to myself? I don't want to come along in the car while you investigate some fictitious lights. I don't want to stand by while you go through some act with her as you did over the drinks last night. I don't...."

Pippa had halted, frozen into immobility on the last step of the stairway. It sounded very much as though the two Bannermans were having a tremendous argument over Angela. Pippa stood undecided and shaken. Should she go back up the stairs or should she go ahead and interrupt, thereby letting them know that she had heard them? In actual fact, she did neither. She stood where she was and listened.

Skye said in a controlled voice, "I've heard what you don't want. But what the hell do you want? Whatever it is, go ahead and take it, say it, do it. I'm not stopping you, God knows. If you want to marry the girl, then ask her. Maybe she'll even say yes, provided I don't ask her to marry me first. But married to you or not, Adrian, she'll still do whatever I ask of her, at any time. She'll turn her back on you whenever I smile at her. She'll come from your kisses right into my arms. I'm the other man this time, and I happen to be right here."

Pippa felt herself go cold with shock. What on earth was Skye saying? She thought she hated him—she *had to* hate him for talking like that, for being like that. He had said, "I'll see you when you come down, Pippa," and then he had somehow or other managed to smash Adrian's plans to pieces, to invite Angela to—Pippa didn't know what.

Turning suddenly, sickened, not wanting to hear any more, she missed her footing and fell clumsily.

Skye appeared in a matter of seconds. His mouth was grim, he was white around the nostrils and his dark hair looked as wild as if he had been in a fight.

He said, "What the hell do you think you're doing, Pippa!" He took her roughly by the wrist.

Pippa's breathing was uneven. "I'm eavesdropping," she said faintly. "You said you'd see me when I came downstairs. But you can forget it, Mr. Bannerman. I gather you're taking Angela out, no matter what anyone else has planned—"

"So?" said Skye. "She's free to say no if she wants to, isn't she? You can come along, too."

His fingers were hurting her wrist considerably and Pippa struggled against him.

"I can say no, too," she panted. "And that's exactly what I do say. No, Mr. Bannerman. I'm not the sort of girl who'll do anything you ask of her, and if I did come from Bruce's kisses right into your arms it wasn't my choice, no matter what you may imagine—"

"Oh, hush up!" He looked suddenly and unutterably tired. Pippa could hear Angela descending the stairs, and below in the hallway Adrian had appeared. Skye released her wrist abruptly.

"Let's go and take a look at those lights."

"All of us?" Angela sounded and looked displeased. She had thrown around her shoulders a flimsy black silk shawl with a long fine fringe, and she looked dramatically and unexpectedly Spanish. Her brown eyes were hard and suspicious.

Skye said briefly, "Those lights I saw need investigating. But of course you can do as you please."

"Will o' the wisp," said Adrian tautly. He, too, was white about the nostrils. The two brothers looked at each other for a second and Pippa thought they were more handsome than they had any right to be. But it was plain that Skye was the stronger character, and right then there was something black and devilish and determined about him.

He ignored Adrian's exclamation and said, "Do as you damn well like!" and gripping Pippa's shoulders began to propel her toward the door.

"Well, *I'm* curious," said Angela sharply. "Are you coming, Adrian?"

Finally they all went out of the house through the darkness to the garage. Pippa thought it was crazy, but with Skye's grip on her arm she had no option but to go. She was convinced he had invented some story about lights to lure Angela away from Adrian, and now there was tension in the air. She had a strong feeling that Adrian would have liked to settle his argument with Skye by a simple primitive fight. But that, apparently, was not Skye's style.

When Skye had backed the car out of the garage, Adrian took the initiative and practically pushed Angela into the back seat before she could follow her own inclination, which was obviously to occupy the place next to Skye. Pippa heard him say grimly, "You promised to take a walk with me. Remember?" She had never heard him use that tone to Angela before.

Angela however, merely laughed theatrically. "Oh, darling, do you think I'm going to miss out chasing up a mystery intruder just for a walk? This is far more exciting."

Pippa got into the front, but she sat well away from Skye who for his part was now ignoring them all. He drove fast away from the homestead through the dark paddock in the direction of the ridge behind which, Pippa knew, lay the shearers' quarters and the shearing sheds. She could see no light anywhere, and her inner agitation and the emotional turbulence that Skye had roused in her made her feel almost nauseated.

Angela leaned forward to ask brightly, "What was it you saw, Skye? Is there a ghost around the billabong—the original ghost from 'Waltzing Matilda,' maybe?"

"I hardly think so," said Skye. "They were car lights I saw—dimmers. It's somebody who knows the property and the general layout. I'm not making any predictions; I'm just going to find out the facts."

Pippa tried to shake herself free of her emotional turmoil, to forget those words that had upset her so drastically. She began to believe that Skye had seen lights, and she had an odd feeling that he knew whose car they belonged to. If he didn't, if he believed there was some sinister character lurking around, then he would hardly have brought her and Angela along.

They rounded the long spur and the shearing sheds came into view. Pippa could make out the dark shape of a car, and in a shaft of soft yellow light that fell from a low window, she could see two figures with a large suitcase.

Adrian exclaimed, "My God, that's young Jeff's car! What the devil is he doing here?"

Skye said nothing. He slowed to a stop alongside the other car—a shabby dark sedan—threw open the door and got out. He shot over his shoulder, "Leave this to me," and walked purposefully toward the two intruders, who had dropped their suitcase and now stood close together like a couple of guilty children.

"Who is Jeff?" asked Pippa in a low voice, forgetting that she had already been told.

Adrian answered her tersely. "Our young brother. He and his wife wanted to run the show at Jounima, and they really got in Skye's hair. They shot off to Queensland and haven't been heard of since. I'd like to know what's brought them back. They hardly look like conquerors, do they?"

Poor things, thought Pippa sympathetically. They looked to her like Adam and Eve who had been banished from the Garden of Eden.

She wondered what treatment the lordly Schuyler would accord to them now.

Skye had uttered an uncompromising, "Well?" and now stood hands on hips waiting for them to speak.

The girl said quietly, "We've come back, Skye."

"So I see. What's happened to your job, Jeff? Did you quit or were you thrown out? Let's have the truth."

Jeff said with a sort of dignity, "A little of each, Skye. I couldn't handle it. I just haven't the knowledge or the experience—only a lot of theories piled up in my head." He paused and looked straight at his brother. "I'd like to start again at Jounima. At the bottom."

He was a good-looking young man, rather thickset and muscular. Pippa thought he looked years older than Bruce, who had said they were contemporaries at agricultural college. The girl was small and pretty with a round face and bright auburn hair. It was curly and cut short and gave her a cherubic air.

"Why didn't you come up to the homestead and talk to me about it?" Skye asked.

"Vicki thought we should get ourselves cleaned up first. We've been on the road since sunrise."

"Hoping to make a good impression?" Skye sounded skeptical, and Pippa saw the girl flinch slightly and catch her lower lip between her teeth as though she were biting back a retort. "Well, Vicki, unfortunately I've spoiled your well-laid plans. Zero hour's right now. Get your gear back in the car and come over to the homestead. You'll make a better job of cleaning yourselves up there than you will here."

He didn't wait for anything further, but having issued his orders returned to the car, got in, started up the motor and drove off. He tossed over his shoulder to Adrian, "Did you hear that? Rebels and runaways and now, it seems, repentant. Well, we shall see."

"Your worry, not mine, thank God," said Adrian cooly.

"Seems like I attract trouble," said Skye dryly. He hunted out cigarettes, handed the packet and matches to Pippa and told her casually, "Light up for me."

Pippa was too stunned to refuse, and despite herself, she managed very efficiently and didn't even cough as she drew on the cigarette. She handed it over to Skye silently, with a feeling that was a mixture of wild adoration and smoldering resentment. Here she was, meekly doing whatever he asked of her. But it was because of those two behind, she told herself. This was not the time to defy, to protest, to be difficult. To make mountains out of what were undoubtedly in Skye's mind mere molehills.

They drove back through the silent darkness of the night and Pippa could see the light of the other car as it followed at a distance. Skye waited outside the house, and Pippa, going slowly inside because she didn't want to make a threesome with Angela and Adrian, heard him speak to the other two when they arrived.

"We won't have it out tonight. I'll see what you have to say for yourselves in the morning, and you'd better prepare a pretty good case! Garage your car and get what you need from the kitchen. The flat's still there for your use so install yourselves. Good night."

Not exactly a warm welcome. But at least he wasn't forcing "zero hour" on them now, and Pippa supposed that that was something. He caught up with her as she started climbing the stairs.

"And now you, Pippa Shaw," he said, his voice so close that she could feel his breath on her hair.

"Now what?" said Pippa distantly.

"Where do we stand, you and I?"

Pippa felt a sort of shock go through her, and then she began to shiver. But she refused to stop or to turn around. "You can forget about me," she said scarcely audibly. Then belligerently she added, "What are you going to do about those two?"

"Jeff and Vicki?"

"Are you going to throw them out again?" She had reached the lower landing and he put a hand on her arm and effectively detained her from going farther. Reluctantly she turned to face him. The light from the wall bracket softened the lines of his face and enhanced its deep tan, but could not hide the look of weariness and disillusion in his eyes.

He said wryly, "Did I ever throw them out? Who told you that?"

"Bruce told me," said Pippa. "I know all about it."

"What do you know?"

"That you don't like Vicki, that you never wanted the marriage, that you tried to break it up—"

"Well, that's a harsh summary." His jaw had set and his mouth had hardened. "So I'm a tyrant, am I?"

"I think you are," said Pippa slowly. "You want your own way about everything, regardless of other people's feelings." She could feel her color rising under his steady scrutiny, but she went on. "You sent Eve away. And right from the start you've tried to keep me and Bruce apart."

"Are you still clinging to that belief? I thought I'd convinced you I wasn't pushing Bruce around without good reason."

"I don't think it's as simple as that," said Pippa. She reflected that intentionally or not, he had certainly succeeded in breaking up any romance between herself and Bruce before it had ever had a chance to develop. But for him and the effect he had on her—and she was certain that he had played on her emotions quite cruelly and deliberately—she might easily have fallen at least a little in love with Bruce. She looked at him accusingly. "I'd believe almost anything of you, after what I heard you say to Adrian tonight. I think that was...despicable. Why should you try to stop him from marrying Angela if that's what he wants? And threaten that you'll seduce her if—"

He laughed suddenly, harshly. "Do you call that a threat?"

"Oh!" exclaimed Pippa. "You're so arrogant and overbearing and conceited! You should have kept out of it when Adrian wanted to take her to Cedar Creek ages ago."

"Then everything would have been lovely," he said sardonically. "Is that the way you see it, Pippa?"

"Yes, that's the way I see it," she flashed. She made a sudden deft movement and escaped him, running on up the stairs. She didn't want to talk to or listen to Skye Bannerman a moment longer. She called back, her voice low pitched and husky, "I think you're altogether hateful!" And she was sure she heard him laugh.

When she had shut her door behind her, she leaned against it, breathing hard, her heart filled with a strange despair. *He could fire me for saying that,* she thought, and she almost wished he would.

But of course, she reminded herself, it was Adrian and not Skye who was hiring her services.

CHAPTER NINE

WHATEVER SKYE HAD TO SAY to Jeff and Vicki was said in private, and all that Pippa knew was that the young Bannerman couple were installed in the "flat"—a small suite of rooms closed off from the rest of the homestead. Jeff plunged instantly into work on the property and Vicki apparently occupied herself putting the flat into order again. Pippa encountered her late in the afternoon when the children were picking oranges in the orchard.

"Hello. I'm Vicki Bannerman. Are you Eve's replacement?"

"I'm filling in temporarily," said Pippa. "I'm Pippa Shaw."

Vicki began to peel an orange and told Pippa casually, "Oranges are supposed to be awfully good for mothers-to-be, and I'm expecting a baby. Not for six and a half months though!"

"How lovely," said Pippa. She couldn't help wondering if this had something to do with the return of the young Bannermans, and she felt vaguely sorry for Vicki. She asked, "How did you get on with Skye this morning? I was in the car last night and I heard what he said to you."

A shadow crossed the other girl's pretty face. "Oh, we passed. I guess the baby did it. Skye's very family minded; he loves children. Whose is *that*?" she added as Annabel pranced by, her small skirt full of oranges.

"That's Annabel Glas."

"Angela Glas's daughter?" Pippa nodded. "Good

lord, what's she doing here? I did hear talk about Jounima being used as a setting for 'Heads You Win,' but Jeff and I haven't kept in touch." She gave a slight grimace. "Anyhow, tell me."

"Angela was invited to stay here after the filming was over," said Pippa briefly.

"By Skye, I suppose. Well, she's beautiful enough to make a suitable wife for the handsome Schuyler, I dare say. What's she like?"

"As you said," replied Pippa cautiously, "she's very beautiful."

"And that's all you're saying," commented Vicki shrewdly. "Well, I shall judge for myself when I meet her. But Jeff and I are not mixing too much. We're aiming to live kind of privately and quietly till we've... readjusted. I must be off to the kitchen now and see what I can scrounge for tea. Wish I had my own vegetable garden! See you later, Pippa."

After that Pippa saw her occasionally, and of course she met Jeff, though as Vicki had said they were not mixing much. But, in the main, the homestead life continued much as usual. Yet Pippa had an odd feeling that everything had changed subtly, that there was a sort of quickening of tempo as if everything was moving toward a climax.

This feeling was heightened by the memory of the argument she had heard between Skye and Adrian. Since the night of Jeff's return there had been no more outward friction, although Pippa thought she discerned a distinct coolness in Adrian's attitude to Skye. As for Skye, he appeared to go out of his way to leave the field clear for his brother. In the evenings, he disappeared frequently, presumably to the small flat to talk to Jeff. And occasionally, as an alternative, he sought out Pippa's company, challenging her to a game of tennis or inviting her out join him for a swim in the pool.

Pippa wasn't sure that she liked being made use of in this way, but the only way she could escape him was to go upstairs to her room. Her main defense against him and against giving herself away was to pretend an interest in Bruce.

"You don't have to entertain me," she told him one night when he asked her to come for a walk by the river. "I'm not a guest any longer. And any spare time I have," she continued recklessly, for despite her protests he had taken her arm and they had begun to walk toward a side gate through a hedge of oleander trees, "I'd rather spend with Bruce. But *that* seems to be impossible. He doesn't get here to see me very often, does he?"

"Is that an accusation?" Skye looked down at her in the bright starlight, his brows lifting quizzically. "Are you trying to blame that fact on me, Pippa? If Bruce really wanted to pursue you, he'd be here, regardless of everything and everyone. I imagine you're the one who knows best what's holding him back. As I see it, we've two choices: one, he's cooled off or two, he's found you unreceptive. Which is it?"

Pippa blushed scarlet. She told Skye furiously, "Neither! Right from the start he's just had so many orders from you he hasn't been a free agent."

"Well, that may soon come to an end, and then we shall see," said Skye cryptically. Pippa instantly thought he was planning to get rid of Bruce.

The next evening Skye did not come home to dinner.

"A night out alone for Skye?" Angela queried, a disagreeable note in her voice as the three of them—herself, Adrian and Pippa—sat at the dinner table. She was restless these days, and Pippa had seen her feverishly reading through what appeared to be television scripts that she had received in the mail, wearing glasses and looking hard and businesslike, and no longer the glamorous star on holiday.

Adrian shrugged. "Probably discussing something with Bruce. He went over to North Star today, left before sunup. Some of those top paddocks are little but dust bowls. Bruce and Alf have been shifting stock all week. It's certainly not the pick of the property. A good manager can handle it. Skye had it flourishing, and Ken knew what he was doing when he took it over after the old man died and Skye came home to Jounima. But Bruce—" he threw Pippa an apologetic glance "—is raw and it's hard work. However, he has a right to be there. It's his mother's place."

Angela, bored, was obviously barely listening, but Pippa took it all in thoughtfully. So Bruce really had his hands full. And that was why she saw so little of him, no matter that Skye implied he could have come to Jounima had he really wanted.

It was nearly eleven that night when Skye came home. Adrian and Angela had taken one of the cars and gone to Cedar Creek straight after dinner, and Pippa was sitting in the courtyard under the vine-covered trellis pretending to read by the light of a small table lamp. She told herself it was too hot to go up to bed, and she did not have the energy to change into her bikini and take a swim. But the truth was—and in her heart she knew it—that she was waiting for Skye to come home.

Her heart leapt when she heard a car door slam, but she warned herself it might be only Adrian and Angela. And then she heard his footsteps and knew it was Skye. She raised her head and looked at him with studied carelessness as he spoke to her from the doorway.

"Still up, Pippa?" He came toward her slowly and when the light fell upon him she saw that he looked profoundly weary. His dark shirt was rumpled and there was dried mud on his boots.

Even his hair looked dull and dusty. He threw himself down in a chair beside Pippa's, his long legs stretched out in front of him, his head thrown back and his eyes closed.

Pippa asked concernedly, "Can I get you some coffee, Skye?"

"You can pour me a stiff whisky if you will, Pippa." He opened his eyes suddenly and the corners of his mouth tilted in a tired smile. "Or should I say if you know how?" With an abrupt movement, he hauled himself to his feet. "Don't worry. Stay there and look decorative. I can fetch it myself."

Pippa, who had risen, continued to stand where she was, biting her lip in vexation. She watched him cross to the small table where crystal glasses, a bottle of whisky and one of gin had been set out. There was a silver ice bucket that had once held ice, and he remarked over his shoulder, "I could do with fresh ice if you'd like to run and fetch me some."

Pippa literally ran to the deserted kitchen to do as he had asked. She returned breathless with ice cubes in the bucket she had taken with her. He said, "Good girl," tonged a single cube into his glass and splashed in a liberal shot of whisky. Pippa watched him knock it back, and then he smiled at her. "Now come and sit by me and tell me what's been happening in your little world today, Pippa."

When you are spoken to as if you are a child it can be difficult to refuse to do as you are asked—unless you want to appear like a naughty child—and after a brief hesitation Pippa joined him on the swing seat, though she kept deliberately to one end of it. This caused him to comment sardonically, "You think I'm not particularly nice to be near tonight, and I don't blame you. Let's hear what you've been up to."

"Nothing exciting," said Pippa helplessly. He could hardly want a recital of the doings of the children, and she continued quickly, "What have you been doing?"

She saw the muscles about his jaw tighten. He reached into his pocket for cigarettes before he answered her.

"I've been hauling dying sheep out of the mud, Pippa." His eyes, dark and burning, met hers, and Pippa felt a strange shock of fear go through her.

She said huskily, "How horrible! But why? What happened?"

"What's happened is that the dams are drying up. There's been a cloudburst that's put just enough water into them to turn them into death traps. The sheep get bogged down in the black mud in their endeavors to get at the water. There they die slowly in the heat unless someone comes and uses his muscles to haul them out. I was too late."

Pippa's face had whitened, and he reached out and put a sun-browned hand on her forearm. His fingers were strangely cold and felt rough against her soft skin. Troubled, she looked at him.

"I've told you a grim story when I wanted you to tell me a pretty one," he said lightly. He dropped his hand from her arm and stood up. "Don't let it keep you awake, will you? I'm going to take a hot shower and go to bed. I'm not fit for anything else tonight. Where's Angela?"

Pippa's throat was dry. "Adrian took her to Cedar Creek."

He made no comment, though his eyes narrowed. Then with a brief, "Good night, Pippa, and sweet dreams," he was gone.

Pippa looked after him helplessly. He would have liked to find Angela here after such a day as he had spent. Someone beautiful and feminine and diverting, who would ask no questions but would without effort take his mind off the sordid business of the day. And instead of Angela, he had found Pippa, who could not even be trusted to pour him a whisky and who obviously had provided him with neither diversion nor comfort—if a man of Skye's strength could possibly be in need of comfort.

As she went up the stairs five minutes later, Pippa wondered about the stricken sheep. Were they North Star sheep? And was Bruce to blame in any way for what had happened? Skye had not said so, in fact, had not even mentioned Bruce's name. Pippa decided it must simply be one of the inevitable but tragic things that sometimes happen on a big station when there is a drought.

But now she felt too disturbed to sleep. It was getting to be a habit with her, she thought pensively. She had a quick look in at the children, then decided she would take a swim and tire herself out. She changed into her bikini, slipped on her cotton robe and, taking a towel, went quietly downstairs. She was crossing the hallway when she heard Angela Glas's low but beautifully carrying voice come floating through the sitting-room door from which fell a shaft of light.

"Darling, I adore Cedar Creek, and I'd really love to marry you, honestly I would. But Adrian, all those children! I just couldn't cope with them."

"Skye?" Adrian's voice was taut and meaningful.

"We-ll, I guess I'm in love with both of you, darling," said Angela. "And Skye just doesn't happen to have any children. It's a fact, isn't it? I know you think I'm heartless, but...."

Pippa discovered she was walking on across the hallway. She must have stopped dead in her tracks and listened for those few seconds without even being aware of it. And now she was on her way again to have her swim.

So it's happened, she thought vaguely. *He's asked her to marry him and she has refused. Because of Skye. What comes next?*

What came next happened soon—on Sunday afternoon after another family dinner. This time Bruce was not present but Jeff and Vicki were. Jeff seemed very much at ease, but Vicki was quiet, amusing herself sometimes with her small nieces and nephew, occasionally talking to Pippa. The favorite topic of conversation among the others—with the exception of Angela—was station affairs, and Pippa, sitting beside Vicki and dangling her bare legs in the clear green water of the pool while the children splashed about, heard Ken announce, "I've made up my mind to accept the managership at Noorima, Skye, despite your advice."

Pippa looked up quickly and caught a glimpse of Skye's face. His dark brows were drawn and he looked far from pleased, but before he could comment Adrian said cooly, "Well, I don't want to push anybody out, but that will suit me fine. I'm ready to go back home and take my family with me." He shot a dark look at Skye, who had strolled with Angela to the small table under the trellis to fetch a drink.

"Is this because I have Jeff back?"

Adrian shrugged unsmiling. "I've been away long enough."

Angela turned gracefully and sent him her bright, actressy smile. "I wouldn't blame you for wanting to go back, darling—not in the least. Cedar Creek's such a lovely old place."

Skye handed her a frosty glass that had the sparkle of ice and mint in it. He said, "It's entirely up to you, of course, Adrian. But Ken, we'll discuss Noorima again later." His eyes went briefly to Pippa, but she didn't think he really saw her.

Her heart was aching. For her it was obviously the beginning of the end, and she had to force herself not to think about it. She turned her attention quickly to Vicki, who was very quiet and immersed in her own thoughts: thoughts of the baby, or of this return to Jeff's family, Pippa did not know which.

"How are things working out, Vicki?" she asked quietly.

Vicki gave a noncommittal shrug. "So far so good. We're on trial. But as a matter of fact, Skye has promised that if we behave ourselves—or maybe if *I* behave myself—he'll let us build a house of our own. I'm going to take a ride around tomorrow and decide where I want my house to be."

"You mean to stay, then?"

"Yes, I do. This time Skye has been very fair. Maybe he always was, but I used not to think so." She was silent and they both watched the children while the voices of the others murmured around them. Pippa was amused at the sight of Annabel, dog-paddling ferociously and determinedly in pursuit of the big rubber ball. She thought with a little feeling of accomplishment, *I've helped her to achieve that self-confidence in the water.* She asked Vicki idly, "What happened when you were here before?"

Vicki flicked at her red curls and said wryly, "See this hair of mine? I have a temper that goes with it. I just was never cut out to be humble. I used to fight Skye like a vixen because he gave all the orders and I reckoned Jeff had a degree and didn't need to be bossed around. I wanted a house of my own, too, not just the little flat. It was my fault Jeff and I decided to go it on our own. I've learned sense since then. Jeff and I made more mistakes than I'd ever admit to Skye on that sheep station in Queensland. Jeff would have come back long ago but for me. However, I'm not a complete nitwit. Maybe the thought of having a child to bring up has made me see things differently. Jounima is Jeff's home, and I guess Skye can help him learn to be a good sheep farmer better than anyone else, if I shut up. As a matter of fact," she added confidentially with a rueful smile, "I'm even beginning to think I might grow to like Skye. What do you think, Pippa?"

"I suppose you might."

"Do you like Skye?"

Pippa said evasively, "I'm only the nanny here."

"A funny sort of a nanny! I'd guess you were an English girl in search of adventure."

"I've had my share of *that*," said Pippa. "Meanwhile, I'd better give my charges some attention." As she jumped to her feet she admitted to herself that she had misjudged Skye. He had not thrown Jeff and Vicki out; he had not tried to break up their marriage. And now he was offering to build them a house of their own on Jounima. He was, as Vicki had said, very fair.

And to Bruce, too?

That night, after she and Adrian had seen the children to bed, Pippa asked him casually, "When are you going, Adrian?"

"As soon as possible, I think. I'd like Ken to be out of the way first—we haven't all that much space at Cedar Creek with three children and a governess to accommodate. As a matter of fact, I thought you might have more idea than I have when it's likely to happen."

"Me?" said Pippa blankly.

"Yes. If Ken goes to North Star instead of to Noorima it could be any time now. And of course that's what Skye wants, and—" he paused imperceptibly "—Skye usually gets his way."

But Ken had decided on Noorima, surely, Pippa persisted.

"Skye was going to discuss it with him. Since that unpleasant business out at the black plain paddocks, the angle's shifted somewhat. I thought Bruce might have been persuaded that the time had come to throw in his hand. Aunt Elizabeth was pretty angry about that affair."

Pippa's heart had begun to thud. She and Adrian stood in the upstairs hallway talking in hushed, almost conspiratorial voices.

She said tensely, "Why? It wasn't anybody's fault, was it?"

"My dear girl, don't be so naïve. Skye had told Bruce to clear the sheep out of those paddocks long ago. He didn't do it. It's as simple as that."

Pippa, sickened, could say nothing.

"Your boyfriend's no asset as a sheep farmer, I'm afraid," Adrian said baldly. "He'd be kicked off any property but this one. I'd have tossed him out in no time if I'd had my say. Skye lets him get away with too much simply because his mother owns the place, but now... well, we shall see."

Pippa watched him go down the stairs but didn't join him. She was certainly getting a new slant on things today! Once she had been on Bruce's side, had thought he should stay at North Star, be allowed to run it his own way. Now, she was not so sure. She was sure, though, that he would hang on. He was determined to win his battle against Skye. Unlike Vicki, he had not yet learned sense.

Well, her own time on Jounima was nearly at an end. She had known all along that she could not expect to spend the rest of her life here in Skye's company, and yet now it seemed so unexpected a blow that she was mentally reeling. The prospect of moving to Cedar Creek did not appeal to her at all. It would mean that she would see Skye occasionally, but that was no longer enough. She wished now that Eve had never gone. Then for Pippa it would all have been over long ago. She would have left Jounima herself and she would not have fallen so deeply, so irrevocably into the sea of love.

She went slowly to her room to lick her wounds and shed her futile tears in private. She kicked off her shoes and loosened the long hair she had tied back and stared at herself blankly and unseeingly in the mirror. She ran her fingers with a kind of distraction through the shining golden brown strands of hair thinking dementedly of what Skye had once said about her Pocahontas hairdo, thinking how empty her life was suddenly to become, when there was a knock at the door and, as the handle was turned, Skye's voice said peremptorily, "May I come in?"

Pippa spun around. She felt the blood rush to her cheeks and ebb away.

"What do you want?" The unwelcoming words came out of her mouth of their own accord.

He had flung the door wide and stood framed, hands on hips. His dark hair was rumpled, the sleeves of his cream shirt were rolled up, and his chest showed dark where the three top buttons were undone. It was a hot airless night and Pippa felt her pulses throbbing.

"I want to come in," he said. He thrust the door shut and came toward her, and instinctively she moved back a pace, her mouth open on a silent exclamation.

He gave her a crooked smile and his eyes glinted darkly. "Relax, Pippa. I'm not going to seduce you. You surely know better than that. I merely want to talk to you privately." He stood too close, looking down at her searchingly. The light from the wall lamp shone mutedly on his face and Pippa thanked heaven her own face was in shadow. There was too much to be read in it. Her heart was beating indecently wildly and for no reason at all. She waited still, silent and wary, until he spoke.

"What arrangements have you made with Adrian?"

Pippa blinked. "Why, I'm going to Cedar Creek, I suppose."

He said flatly, "No."

"What do you mean?" Her voice wavered. "Adrian wants to take the children home. I—"

"You're not going," said Skye. "You'll tell Adrian that definitely tomorrow."

"But...but I must go!" cried Pippa; then, suddenly

realizing that he had no right to tell her what she must or must not do, she pulled herself together and stood straighter. "You're not my boss, Skye. I like my job, and the children need someone to look after them."

"There's a good motherly housekeeper at Cedar Creek. She'll keep an eye on them. If necessary, I can spare Nora or Lizzie from the staff here."

"But why?" Pippa was not about to give in to Skye, let him order her about, certainly not without knowing his motive. It could not possibly be that he wanted her to stay at Jounima—she had no illusions about that. It was more likely that he wanted, with a minimum of bother, to get her out of the Bannerman family's hair once and for all. With no job, she'd have no legitimate reason for staying—perhaps he even thought she had designs on Adrian. There was just no knowing what he might suspect her of—the girl Bruce Lightfoot had picked up at an amusement park and given a casual invitation to a party that never eventuated. And now, weeks later, here she still was, even though Bruce had quite obviously lost interest in her. The flow of Pippa's thoughts stopped abruptly. That she was still on Jounima was surely due to Skye Bannerman himself. He had been the one who suggested she take over from Eve. And now he wanted her to step down, did he? Well, Pippa decided quite definitely that she was not going to do so. She insisted aggressively, "Why shouldn't I go?"

He said after a moment, "I think if you're not there, Adrian will ask Eve to come back."

Pippa was astounded. "You say that when you told her to go? Because you didn't think a governess was good enough for a Bannerman?"

"Rubbish," he said curtly. "That has nothing to do with it. I'm prepared to make a bet with you, Pippa, that Adrian will last a month at the most before he's begging Eve to come back."

"She probably has another job," said Pippa. "And in any case, she wouldn't come. It wouldn't be fair to expect her to. She's made the break, she knows it's hopeless—"

"She'll also know that Adrian's infatuation with Angela is over."

"Infatuation?" questioned Pippa, thinking he took other people's love affairs rather lightly.

"That's what I said."

"If I were Eve, I wouldn't come," said Pippa after a moment, disconcerted by the steadiness of his gaze.

"Wouldn't you?" His lips twisted mockingly. "Not if you loved someone as Eve loves Adrian? Well, perhaps you wouldn't understand such things, Pippa. You're nineteen—you don't know what love is all about."

But Pippa thought she knew only too well. And if she were honest, she must admit to herself that if she were in Eve's position and if the man were Skye, then she would come.

"So," said Skye, watching the thoughts chase each other across her shadowed face, "you see I'm asking you to do this not for me, but for Eve."

Now it was impossible to take a stand and to say no. He might be right about both Adrian and Eve, and she would never forgive herself if she stood in the way of Eve's possible happiness. So once again Schuyler Bannerman was to have his own way.

"Very well," she said, her voice low. "I'll tell Adrian I want to be released. I shall go to Sydney and find something else."

"We'll see when the time comes," he said.

Softening the blow.

TWO NIGHTS LATER Bruce called at Jounima with the surprising news that Bron was arriving on the train. He wanted to know if Pippa would like to come with him to

Jounima Siding, and soon she was sitting beside him in the car and they were speeding between the tall trees that lined the drive.

"Want to come and stay on North Star now, Pippa?" he asked—so casually that Pippa didn't think he cared terribly much whether she wanted to come or not.

"It would be nice," she said politely, "but I can't, thank you. I have to mind the children."

She saw him grimace. "You're well and truly tied up with this job of yours, aren't you? How long are you going to hang onto it? If I were you, I'd shoot off to the city. Much more fun. Do you plan to go to Cedar Creek with Adrian?"

"How did you know Adrian was going back?" she asked in surprise.

"Well, it follows, doesn't it?" said Bruce as they drove on through the darkness. It was a journey that reminded Pippa vividly of the time she had covered the same ground with Skye. How different she herself had been then! "I'm leaving, Pippa. Didn't you know? Skye will be able to juggle and rearrange his pawns any way he likes. Great for him!"

Pippa tried to take it in. "You're leaving? I had no idea."

"Hadn't you? Well, I am, and pretty soon. Bron's coming to help me pack up. I thought someone would have told you. Skye must be jubilant, thinking his tactics have routed me." He uttered a brief laugh. "It is partly that—I don't appreciate being pushed around. And my mother's attitude wasn't helping. She insisted that Skye was free to direct or order as he chose, but I guess he put her up to that. However, it's mainly my own decision. It would have given me a lot of satisfaction to have beaten Skye, but to stay would have been cutting off my nose to spite my face. I just don't like the life here in long stretches. As a kid, I used to listen to my mother's stories about it—to dream about it, to idealize it—the wonderful, fabulous, exciting outback. But I'm a social type and that's half my trouble. It might have been different if Skye had thrown that party and you and Bron had stayed on North Star."

He paused, and Pippa, feeling he was indirectly at least putting a little of the blame on her, said inadequately, "I'm sorry, Bruce."

"You needn't be. I don't have any regrets. Except about you."

"About me?"

"I lost you to Jounima, didn't I? You've fallen in love with the whole of the Bannerman family, except me. Adrian as well as Skye now. Isn't that it? You and Angela Glas between you, dividing the spoils. Who's going to have whom?"

"If you're going to talk like that I'll begin to wish I hadn't come with you," said Pippa, annoyed.

"I was surprised you did," said Bruce.

Pippa bit back any further retort. There was no point in having an argument with Bruce.

Bronwen was casual with Pippa, too.

"Fancy your still being here! It's a funny old world, isn't it? I could have kicked myself, losing your phone number. Still, I hear you've been having a great time and that you've landed yourself a job, so I suppose everyone's happy." Although she sat in the back of the car, she leaned forward continually to talk. "I nearly fell over when I heard Jeff and Vicki had come back. Is Vicki pregnant, or does Jeff just like punishment?"

"I haven't a clue," said Bruce. He asked Pippa, "Is Vicki pregnant?"

"You'll have to ask Vicki that," said Pippa lightly.

There was a little pause. Then, "Well, Jeff's welcome to call Skye boss. I've learned my lesson. I certainly won't be coming back for more."

"You really don't mind leaving, then?" asked his sister.

"Don't mind! My dear girl, I can't get out fast enough."

"Thank goodness for that. I thought there was a great blow up about some sheep getting stuck in a dam. Mother was in a terrible flap about it."

"Don't blame that on me," said Bruce shortly. "I've been running around shifting sheep here, there and everywhere for days on end, with no one to help me except a crazy old character called Alf who hardly ever utters a word. Spends all his time chewing grass, must think he's a sheep himself. It just turned out I didn't get that particular lot moved soon enough."

Bronwen was giggling over his remarks about Alf, but Pippa couldn't help thinking that he didn't really take his responsibilities very seriously. She felt suddenly very tired and disillusioned, and she was thankful when they reached the Jounima homestead and let her out of the car.

"It's too late for social calls," said Bron. "I'll come and say hello maybe tomorrow when I've recovered from that ghastly train trip."

CHAPTER TEN

BUT BRON DIDN'T COME to Jounima the next day. During the night it began to rain, a rain that fell in torrents for the whole of the two next days. Pippa had never seen such a downpour. Then on the third day the sun shone, the sky was clear and it was as hot and bright as ever.

The children, who had been restless and inclined to become quarrelsome, were jubilant, all eagerness to be out of doors to use up some of their pent-up energy. Adrian told them, "Tomorrow we'll go back home to Cedar Creek. How will you like that?"

They liked the idea well enough, but Pippa was dismayed. Quite suddenly, it was their last day on Jounima, and quite suddenly it was the last day of Pippa's job. No one had discussed with her what was to happen to her next. Adrian had accepted what he called her "decision" not to carry on in his employ.

"It's been wonderful of you to fill in for us," he had said philosophically. "I should have done something about getting the agency in Sydney to find me another girl, but for one reason or another I've kept putting it off. This at least will force me into action." But whether or not he had contacted the agency Pippa did not know, and though Skye had said, "We'll see when the time comes," he had said nothing more to Pippa, and she thought he had forgotten all about her case.

That morning, when the skies were clear again, he told her warningly, "Don't go to Redrock Gorge with the children, Pippa. There's going to be a flood down that gorge and when it gets there it'll be a wall of water. Keep away from the river altogether, will you?"

Pippa agreed and took the children riding across the paddocks on horses that were docile and quiet and obedient and did not include the willful Louie.

It was an unremarkable last day in every way, and it ended tranquilly with a swim and a ball game in the Jounima homestead pool. Pippa played in the water with the children for half an hour, and then, as they were quite happy on their own, she came out and stood watching them while her hair dried. She was thinking that Annabel was going to miss her young companions, and that for herself everything was rushing dizzily toward an end, an end she could not bring herself to look at—parting from Skye. She hoped he would prove to be right about Adrian sending for Eve, but doubted whether she would ever hear the end of that particular love story. Nor would she know the end of Angela Glas's story.

That was the point she had reached in her reflections when Angela herself appeared, and for once she spoke directly to Pippa, whom as a rule she almost totally ignored.

"What a long face!" she commented. She stood in the shade—which was more flattering to her face than the harsh sunlight—lighting a cigarette and standing dramatically posed against a backdrop of brilliant bougainvillea. "Well, let's face it, all good things come to an end, and you've managed to wangle a lovely free holiday for yourself, haven't you?"

Pippa gave her a pleasant smile. "So have you!"

Anger burned in the other woman's eyes. "You're forgetting something. I was invited. And for me," she continued, looking thoughtfully at the tip of her cigarette and then down at the painted toenails that showed below the hem of her white caftan, "there need be no ending. Skye wants me to marry him." She said it simply and

Pippa felt her heart miss a beat and then begin to thud. She raised her arms and began to wind her towel around her head, pretending to be absorbed, praying that Angela would not look at her and see the havoc in her face. She need not have worried, for Angela was completely self-absorbed. "So, it looks as though I'll have to make a sacrifice one way or the other, to choose between two loves—two great loves." She began to pace slowly along the flagstones, head bowed, attitude thoughtful, pondering the problem of her sacrifice. Pippa, watching, could see the trained actress in the slow grace of her movements, in the hesitation as the cigarette was poised two inches from her lips. She was beautiful, fascinating, and Pippa disliked her intensely. Skye could not possibly marry her. Her whole being revolted against the thought now that it looked like it would become an actuality. But of course he could, and of course he wanted to—she had seen him making love to Angela Glas in various ways ever since she first came to Jounima. And now that Adrian had been refused, now that Skye had stood aside and let Adrian have first option, as it were, there was nothing to stop him from going ahead himself. As he apparently had. Pippa had bitten her lip so hard that it bled.

Angela's pacing brought her back to Pippa, and she raised her head and smiled a sad, thoughtful smile. "I've the offer of such a wonderful television role—a role that would lead me straight to Hollywood. Wolfgang—he's a phenomenally distinguished producer—put it that way himself, and without being immodest, I know that it's true. So it's a temptation. An enormous temptation. But I think I'm going to resist it. Wouldn't you if you were me, and Skye wanted you to marry him? She stood quite still and looked fixedly at Pippa, or at least in Pippa's direction; but she was seeing, thought Pippa, not her but Skye. Then with an effort, the older woman seemed to pull herself out of her tender, glowing reflections. "Ah well.... And so now you're out of work Pippa. I suppose you'll go back to Sydney with your friends from North Star tomorrow. Personally, I shall be glad to dispense with your services. Annabel has become quite unrecognizable since you've been meddling with her psychology—nightmares every night and unreasonable demands. Nevertheless, if you feel I owe you any money, please say so and of course you shall have it." Her eyes were half-closed, her head tilted back as she exhaled smoke.

Pippa didn't answer. Angela had said a cruel and unjust thing and the tears had come to Pippa's eyes despite herself. She turned her head away blindly, moved toward the children to intervene in a little dispute that had arisen among them. When she had composed herself again and looked around, Angela Glas had gone.

Pippa thought bleakly, *I'm not wanted here. Well, at least she's offered me a solution. It's an idea I might well take up.*

She rang through to North Star quickly, guiltily, before Skye returned to the homestead. Bronwen answered the call, and Pippa told her hurriedly what she wanted.

"My job finishes today and I'd like to get back to Sydney. The train journey is so frightful I thought I'd be an opportunist and ask if I might come with you tomorrow."

There were no problems. Bron was casually agreeable and it was all arranged. They would be leaving late in the afternoon and driving through the night to avoid the unpleasantness of traveling in the heat of the day. With a fast-beating heart, Pippa put the telephone down. She decided not to say a word to anyone till the last minute. It was cowardly, perhaps even bad-mannered, but she couldn't face saying goodbye to Skye. They should be gone before he came back to the homestead tomorrow evening, and she would simply leave him a letter of thanks.

In her heart, she said goodbye to him that night, searingly, despairingly, while he was bland and casual and unaware. They sat in the courtyard after dinner and he and Adrian talked, while Angela sat abstracted and dreamy, pondering, no doubt, her great sacrifice. Occasionally Skye flicked Pippa a smoldering enigmatic glance, but he continued to talk to Adrian, and for Pippa it was like a too prolonged goodbye. Crazy to sit there feeding her mind memories that were visual only and completely devoid of any shared emotion. "If it were done when 'tis done, then 'twere well it were done quickly...." She stood up, moved too suddenly and accidentally knocked over a liqueur glass. She heard its crystal tinkle as it flew into fragments on the ground, and chagrined, stooped to gather up the pieces. But Skye had moved, also, and stood over her saying sharply, "Leave it. No need to lacerate your fingers."

Her hand drew back, and she straightened and looked at him, her eyes wide and dark. When your heart is lacerated, what do your fingers matter?

His eyes narrowed. "Are you feeling faint? You're as white as death."

"I'm tired. I'm going up to bed," she said huskily.

"I'll see you to the stairs."

What would Angela think, she wondered. She heard someone move behind them, but to her relief no one followed them into the house. Skye's arm went lightly about her waist and it was an exquisite pleasure and an exquisite pain to be near him. Pippa thought, *At least I'll have this to remember.* A farewell that was not a farewell....They walked slowly and silently up the stairs. Pippa could feel her heart beating and fluttering like a caged bird, and she dared not look up at the man at her side no matter how much she longed to do so. When they reached her room, he pushed the door wide but did not switch on the light. With an imperceptible movement he turned her toward him and held her briefly against him, and she felt his lips on her forehead.

"Good night, Pippa."

"Good night, Skye," she murmured. She closed her eyes and leaned against him lightly, aware in every tingling nerve of her body of his lips, his hands, of the hard, living warmth of his chest.

Good night and goodbye. Her tears fell when he had gone and she was alone.

THE THINGS ANGELA HAD SAID to Pippa about her handling of Annabel hurt badly, but Pippa wasn't going to take her misery out on the child. The next day, after the other children had gone and Lizzie with them, Annabel was lonely and despondent and Pippa played with her all morning, in the pool, and later in the sand heap. She supposed that when Skye and Angela were married, Annabel would be sent off to boarding school or relegated to the care of Nora and Lizzie. Still, later there would be Vicki's baby....

Vicki usually took a siesta in the afternoon, for her pregnancy made her sleepy. Pippa would say goodbye to her later in the afternoon, but she was not going to tell Angela Glas that she was leaving. Angela would not want to say goodbye and would only rejoice at her departure.

Yet by a strange chance, it was Angela who finally and inadvertently wrecked all Pippa's plans.

Toward midafternoon Pippa went upstairs to finish her packing, leaving Annabel sitting on the ground in the courtyard drawing on a huge sheet of paper that Pippa had found for her, while Angela sat reading nearby. Pippa completed her packing, thinking inevitably and nostalgically of the night she had arrived at Jounima

Siding with her enormous suitcase. For sentimental and no doubt silly reasons, she put on her white jeans, though the gay little exclamation on the knee—Have a Nice Day!—almost made her weep. She made two narrow plaits in her hair and bound them across her forehead—her Pocahontas hairdo—and in all, she behaved very foolishly.

When at last she was packed and dressed, she had a strong inclination to throw herself on the bed and have a good weep, but madness lay that way. Or perhaps, she told her sad-eyed reflection wryly, that was going a little too far. Not madness, but weakness, for she had already begun to tell herself that she should have told Skye that she was going, that she should have said goodbye and thanked him with dignity for giving her such a wonderful taste of outback life. Skye might even have kissed her goodbye—and not just on the forehead either—in the belief that he was sending a guest away with one more happy memory.

But before she could weaken or burst into tears or even unpack, Pippa ran down the stairs. She would take Annabel for a walk. She had told her earlier on that they might look for lizards' eggs under stones in the vegetable garden.

But Annabel was no longer drawing on her large sheet of paper in the courtyard. Her drawing had blown into the pool, and Angela sat with her glasses on reading a script and gently rocking the swing seat.

Pippa said sharply, "Where's Annabel?"

Angela looked up in annoyance. Her glasses were perched halfway down her nose, ruining entirely the picture of a beautiful television star. This was the woman, intent, businesslike, hard. She said shortly, "She's gone for a ride. On Louie." And she returned to her script.

Pippa felt shock strike her like a lightning bolt. Crazy images chased each other through her mind—Louie racing for Redrock Gorge, the helpless child on his back, the flood waters roaring down, that great jutting rock crashing. Annabel....

Pippa began to run, gasping, "I'm going to Redrock Gorge. Annabel will be there!"

Later, she wondered why she hadn't stopped to use her sense, why she hadn't questioned Angela Glas further, but at the time she was filled with a sense of urgency. She knew there was a bicycle in the garage. It had belonged to Caroline in days gone by, and it still worked. She would use that. She ran outside and around the house to the garage, and soon she had wheeled the bicycle out, swung into the seat and was pedaling in a rather wobbly fashion across the yard, through a side gate and over the paddock, bumping and lurching in the direction of the river she would follow to Redrock Gorge.

She couldn't see a sign of a pony with a little girl on its back, and she wished she had asked Angela how long it had been since Annabel had left. If Angela knew. And who had saddled Louie? Had it been Angela? She was the only person who would not know that Louie was the last pony to trust with so small and inexperienced a rider as Annabel.

So thought Pippa as she pedaled rapidly along. But she did not dare to allow herself to think what might have happened to a little girl on a pony that would not be controlled, a pony that always headed instinctively for Redrock Gorge.

She could hear the rushing sound of the river, and soon beyond the trees, she could see it flowing—a fast brown frothing torrent, rising close to the top of the banks. This was on the flat. What it must be like in the gorge, she could not imagine. Whether the great, overhanging rock had crashed she had yet to discover.

She reached the gorge after what seemed an age. Her leg muscles were aching, she was impatient with the bicycle, which was so slow. *I might have found someone who could get me here faster than this*, she thought despairingly. All in all she had acted foolishly—in fact, she had more or less panicked. And she had still caught no sign of Annabel. She was in sight of the gorge now, and she saw sheep on the plain far away; she saw a flock of galahs flying to water and heard them screeching. She saw a black cockatoo with brilliant red underwings and remembered the games the children had played that day they picnicked at Redrock Gorge and Bruce had come to join them. How long ago it all seemed now!

Pippa arrived in the shelter of a group of tall river gums that overlooked the gorge, and she jumped off the bicycle, letting it fall to the ground. She hurried forward to look fearfully and intently down from the steep banks. She gasped to see that the great red rock itself had indeed collapsed, and that great slabs of it were now forming obstructions in the water, surging and foaming below. She could see that it had at some time risen to not far below where she now stood. And there, surely, in some debris that lay stranded on the bank, a tangle of long grasses, a mass of uprooted bushes, there was something caught—something red. A strip torn from a child's clothing?

Pippa's heart was in her mouth. She began to clamber down the steep, slippery bank as fast as she could. The sound of the roaring torrent grew louder in her ears. It was swirling dizzyingly, surging against the great chunks of the red rock that had toppled from its kingly position, to form a mad whirlpool before it broke through and poured down the gorge. Pippa heard her own voice floating eerily above the surging, echoing flood waters as she slipped and slid and clutched her way down into the gorge.

"Annabel! Annabel!"

There was no answer at all except a weird ghostly

sound like a horse neighing. Was it Louie? Or was it merely the ghost of Louie's mother who had disappeared long ago and now haunted the river banks?

Pippa's eyes were wide as she searched frantically, but beyond the shred of red stuff, she saw no indication of either child or horse. And when she reached that red, it was not a piece of clothing at all. It was a brilliant red feather, and Pippa sobbed with relief.

The next minute she had slipped and lost her footing, and she was tumbling down and down, sliding, lurching, until the brown water closed over her head, the strong current snatched at her and began to sweep her along.

She surfaced and fought desperately, gasping for breath, spitting out water as her mouth filled, praying that this had not happened to Annabel. She struggled to keep her head above the water, to prevent herself from being swept into that whirlpool she had seen from above. But suddenly it was all too much for her, and she quite simply gave in to the river. It might do as it liked with her, might carry her where it pleased.

As it happened, it was the best thing she could have done. The powerful current carried her toward the bank, let her gently down into the lower part of the gorge and from there almost directly to Skye, who had seen her and had waded chest-deep into the water....

"ANNABEL," CROAKED PIPPA. Her nostrils were pinched and she was still shivering badly from her ordeal in the river. She had coughed most of the water out of her lungs and now her mind was clearing, but Skye's arms held her firmly despite her struggle to be free and to continue the search.

"Annabel's safe and sound at Jounima, honey. She didn't get even as far as the stables in her little scheme for a jaunt on Louie. And *that* you'd have discovered if you'd waited to make a few inquiries instead of careering off like some female, bicyclized version of Don Quixote."

"Oh," Pippa drew a shuddering breath of relief, and her body went slack against the hardness of Skye's. Tears of thankfulness coursed unheeded down her cheeks. "Oh, thank heavens! Are you sure, Skye? Are you quite sure?"

"Well, when I saw her she was turning up stones in the kitchen garden, looking for lizards' eggs or some such nonsense. So I came out to look for you," he concluded dryly. "I think I was just in time and that it was just as well I came in to say goodbye to Bruce and Bronwen."

"Yes," said Pippa somberly. "I'm very grateful. And I'm sorry I've been such a bother." She looked up and found those inky blue eyes of his looking down at her quizzically.

He drew a finger down her cheek, slowly, almost caressingly. "No more tears, Pippa. You're wet enough already and I haven't even a dry handkerchief to offer you. I think I'd better get you up to the car before we talk any more." His look traveled down her slender length as she lay half-leaning against him, the thin shirt clinging to her breast, her jeans bedraggled. "Those jeans of yours are never going to be white again," he said ruefully. "It's a brave little slogan. Have you had many nice days on Jounima, I wonder, Pippa?"

He rose as he spoke and gathered her up in his arms to begin the climb from the narrow ledge, grassy, but sodden, where they had been resting. Held to him like this, Pippa felt herself relaxing, melting into a false heaven. "Many nice days, Skye," she murmured. She knew she should protest his carrying her like this, but she also knew that her own legs were still far too weak and wobbly to manage this steep and slippery climb. So she foolishly savored these few minutes of being held in his arms, close against the hardness of his chest, so close she could feel the slow, strong beating of his heart.

"I'm glad," he said. "I wanted it to be so. I hoped it would be so—despite everything."

Pippa suddenly stiffened, recalled to reality. Nice days on Jounima. The polite host. Her thoughts flew to Bruce, no doubt at this minute waiting for her at the homestead. If they didn't hurry, he might go without her and she would be stranded here, less wanted than ever, virtually alone at the homestead with Angela and Skye, an intruder....

She said desperately, "Please, we must hurry. Bruce will be waiting."

"Is that still on?" His voice had hardened and his breath came harshly, and when she glanced up at him she was frightened by his expression. He climbed on steadily, up and up, through the tumble of rocks, the piles of debris and uprooted scrub and the torn-off branches of trees. "I'll admit I'm disappointed in you, Pippa—planning to disappear like that, no goodbye, no thank you, nothing...."

He paused and Pippa said guiltily, miserably, "I was going to write you a letter from Sydney."

"Very considerate of you. But why the disappearing act when I'd more or less told you to wait? Just tell me that?"

"Because I'd made up my mind to get away," she said wildly. They had reached the top of the bank, and though he set her on her feet, he still kept a grip on her. And now his dark brows descended thunderously over the night blue of his eyes.

"To get away," he repeated. "Were you going with Bruce?"

"And Bron," she said weakly.

"*With Bruce?*" he repeated, his eyes boring into her compellingly.

Pippa shook her head, looking helplessly into that glittering stare. "All alone," she whispered.

The tautness of his expression relaxed, and Pippa thought despairingly, *Now he knows, and now he's laughing at me.*

"Well, that's fortunate," he said, and in a minute he helped her into the front seat of the car, handing her a towel to rub her hair dry before he climbed in beside her and started up the engine. Already she found her tightly clinging shirt and jeans were drying out in the intense heat of the late-afternoon sun, and her shivering had completely subsided.

"Why is it fortunate?" she dared to ask, as they came clear of the trees.

"Because Bruce has already gone."

She stared at him. "But he can't have gone! It was all arranged—"

"I'm afraid he *has* gone," interrupted Skye. "I told him not to wait."

"Told him? Or ordered him?" flashed Pippa.

His eyebrows tilted. "You're making a rapid recovery for a nearly drowned girl, Pippa. That's what it is to be young, I guess. But you're right this time. I ordered him."

"Then I shall take the train in the morning," she asserted.

"What is it you're so eager to escape from? Is it Jounima and the outback? Or is it me?"

"All of it," said Pippa.

"I see." He drove on in silence for a few minutes, and the homestead on its low rise came in sight. It was not until he had braked in front of the house that he said casually, "Why take the train? I'll tell you something, Pippa. I'm driving Angela to catch the plane in the afternoon. She's leaving Jounima."

She caught her breath and looked at him searchingly,

her eyes troubled. So Angela had decided to sacrifice love for her career! How did Skye like that? He didn't look in the least heartbroken; in fact, he was smiling faintly. He had no heart, she thought. Nothing touched him. And she reflected despairingly that she, too, would be taken to the plane. Well, so be it.

She opened the door and slipped quickly from the car, to find herself reeling as an attack of dizziness assailed her. She grabbed out blindly for the veranda rail, but Skye caught her before she fell, and once more she was swept up in his arms. He carried her swiftly indoors and up the stairs to her room, and there he deposited her gently on the bed. Pippa sat up, rigid and determined. "I'm not sick, Skye. I want to get out of this gear." To her dismay, her eyes filled and she turned her head away from him.

"Go ahead," he said laconically. "I'll wait."

"I'd rather you didn't," she quailed. "I'll take a hot bath and...and I'll have my dinner up here if someone will please bring it. Nora," she added hastily, in case he suggested he might come himself.

"Dinner in bed? And you've just said you're not sick? You want it both ways, don't you, Pippa? All right, go ahead and take your bath. I can wait."

"But I don't want you to wait," said Pippa tearfully. She could hardly tell him to go down to Angela now, but she was painfully aware that any more of his company would only make her own parting from him more agonizing. She had thought she had got over all that last night.

"I'm sorry," he said kindly, "but unless you're really sick I think it's best for us to have this out now. Are you going to pretend you don't know what I'm talking about?"

Pippa lay back on her piled pillows, her lovely hair in disorder, and shook her head mutely. "I don't know."

"You have no idea of my feelings?"

She bit her lip. She had thought him without heart. Perhaps it was not so after all. Perhaps he was deeply upset about Angela. Though what his emotions had to do with herself, she could not imagine. She said stiffly, "I am sorry about Angela—that she's chosen her career instead of Jounima."

He was looking at her in amazement. "For God's sake, what's all this about? Angela never had the chance to choose Jounima! Cedar Creek maybe, but Jounima never. Don't tell me, Pippa, that you're such a little innocent you've been taking all that fooling about, all those titillating love scenes, seriously?"

Of course she had, and she looked back at him in bewilderment. He had made love to Angela—in many ways. Why would he have done that if he were not in love with her? Because she was a guest? Because it was what she wanted? Pippa could not make head nor tail of it. "I...I don't understand," she stammered. And the words were barely out of her lips before she was caught up passionately in his arms.

His lips against her hair, he breathed, "There's only one thing you have to understand, Pippa, though why you haven't caught on to it before this I don't know. I love you, my precious little innocent. I don't intend letting you go—ever."

Her lips parted in a gasp of utter incredulity, and then Skye was proving to her forcibly what his feelings for her were.

When at last she was released from his embrace, she murmured, "But, Skye, I thought...I was sure it was Angela. You didn't want me here. You thought I was so young and silly...." She was silenced by the expression in his eyes as he looked down at her tenderly, quizzically.

"So you must have explanations, must you, my darling? I can see you've been shocked by my tactics with

Angela, but I'm afraid there's nothing to be done about that. I acted as I did, and that's that. But before I begin...." He stopped speaking and his glance went to her lips.

Some instinct told Pippa what he wanted of her, and she said in a low steady voice, "I love you, Skye." And to that, despite herself, she added obstinately, "But you *didn't* want me when I came here."

He smiled a little and settled her into the crook of his arm, with her head against his shoulder.

"I didn't know you then, my darling girl. Isn't that excuse enough? I already had trouble enough on my hands when you appeared on the scene. I had virtually two properties to manage, and a near-drought on one of them. I'd only a week before I returned from North Star to find Adrian up to his ears in a love affair that could only bring him disaster. And Bruce... Bruce had taken in about fifty percent of the talks he'd gone to attend in Sydney, and God only knew how he'd spent the rest of his time. It was later I discovered he'd spent part of it at an amusement park," he added with a rueful smile. "He'd apparently fallen in love with some silly young girl and wanted me to spring a party to make an occasion for inviting her to stay. Meanwhile, he was hellbent on disobeying or disregarding all my orders, all my advice. And then you turned up with that cheery little Have a Nice Day patch, jeans that looked as if they could do with a good wash, and the most enormous suitcase I ever saw so small a girl carrying."

He was smiling down at her now and Pippa laughed aloud. "And I talked about getting a job at Jounima Siding! As for my dirty jeans—though they're far dirtier now—I was landed with a small boy on the train."

"I figured that out for myself not very much later," admitted Skye. "In fact, in no time at all, my little enchantress, you'd surprised me thoroughly. You were so refreshingly honest and straight and you had such a delightful way with children. It even occurred to me you might be just the girl to persuade Bruce to grow up, might even make a sheep farmer of him. The trouble was, I was more and more attracted to you myself. I got to thinking I'd be damned if he was going to be allowed to monopolize this girl he scarcely knew. And I did a little monopolizing myself."

"In between playing out love scenes with Angela," Pippa reminded him, unable to keep a tinge of jealousy out of her voice.

"As you say. Well, that had to be. Adrian's too fine a man to have his life ruined by a disastrous marriage. It was in the cards that Angela would have accepted him had there been no one else to take her fancy, so I stepped in. It served to show Adrian pretty plainly what sort of a woman she was. She's far too like his first wife ever to bring him happiness; and therein, of course, lies her attraction. Some men are drawn despite themselves to the same type over and over again, but I think his eyes have been opened now. Angela is one of those women who like to play one man off against the other. She's vain and shallow with no concept of loyalty. She is also a very talented woman," he added—fairly, Pippa thought. "And a very determined one."

"Why didn't you send her away?"

"Do you think I'm as high-handed as all that? Or that it would have helped Adrian? But let's forget her, Pippa. I'm not a tyrant, and I have no desire to be one, except perhaps where you're concerned," he finished laughingly.

The last shadow of doubt flew from Pippa's mind, and her glance was caught momentarily by the bright patch on her knee. Have a Nice Day! Held closely in Skye's arms, with his lips against hers, she thought blissfully that from then on every day was going to be nice!

GARDEN OF THE SUN

CRAIG

Garden of the Sun

Janice Gray

Joby Lester could hardly believe her luck when her glamorous cousin, José, invited her to Peru.

Peru—the mysterious land of the Incas and Conquistadores—had always fascinated Joby. Ancient history had been her father's lifework and it was the subject she chose to teach.

But Joby's visions of ancient ruins and pagan festivals faded when she learned what lay behind her cousin's invitation.

Convinced by a broken romance that her father's money was her only attraction, Jose insisted on their switching identities temporarily. It was unfortunate that Joby met Ross Henderson then, the first man she felt she could love. Ross made it quite plain that he had an aversion to spoiled, rich girls.

CHAPTER ONE

LOOKING BACK on that blazing hot July—the hottest July for more than thirty years, so the met office informed us—it is only now that I realize that I was probably the only member of the staff of St. Olave's School for Girls who wasn't absolutely dying for the long, sultry term to end and the holidays to begin. At the time I never gave the August-September break more than a passing thought. It wasn't until I sat in the staff room on the last day of term, listening to my colleagues' animated voices as they discussed the respective merits of France and Spain and Greece and Portugal, that I suddenly felt horribly out of it all. I wasn't going anywhere—not even to a seaside resort in England.

Earlier in the year we had planned to go to Scotland—mother, the twins and I—but James Burford, a bluff, genial American, had put an end to all that. Early in April he'd come over to England to visit his sister, who had lived next door to us in Sevenoaks, and by the end of May he and mother and the twins were on their way to his ranch in Texas. The speed with which it had all happened had left me gasping. It simply hadn't occurred to me that after nine years of widowhood mother would ever feel like marrying again, though I had to admit that my new stepfather was a darling. I'd liked him from the first, otherwise I might have found it hard to forgive him for kidnapping my entire family.

"Come with us," James had urged, but I'd known better than to accept. Twelve-year-old stepsons are one thing: a twenty-two-year-old stepdaughter quite another!

I was thinking about mother and wondering how she was making out among the longhorns and the stetsons when the door of the staff room burst open and in marched Jean Mackenzie with an armful of books. She dropped them onto a table, dusted her hands and sank down into the chair next to mine with a sigh of relief.

"Thank goodness this is the last day of term! Isn't it *heaven* to think that for the next six weeks it's their mothers who'll have to cope with my homeroom class, and not us?" She fished for a cushion as she spoke and the chair's sagging springs groaned protestingly under her weight.

There was a chorus of agreement. Jean's homeroom students were reputed to be the worst in the school, though I rather liked them. They *were* inclined to be noisy, but that, I thought, was chiefly due to high spirits. Provided they were interested in what they were doing they could produce some really good work.

Perhaps Jean guessed what I was thinking, for she looked at me with a twinkle in the nice brown eyes that were her one really attractive feature.

"It's all right for you, my dear! You don't have to teach the little horrors mathematics! They seem to like your subject! Haven't you been doing the Incas with them this term? I sat next to Delphine Morris and Annabel Taylor at lunch the other day and was treated to a complete biography of one Atahuallpa! The gory details quite put me off my sausages!"

"Atahuallpa? Who on earth is he when he's at home?" Betty Ryder, assistant gym mistress, pretty and friendly, looked up from stuffing tennis shoes into an already bulging bag.

I laughed. "Just an Incan emperor! Jean's class found him fascinating, but I'm sorry you had him inflicted on you, Jean!"

"Oh, I asked for it! Like Betty just now, I made the mistake of inquiring who Atahuallpa was!" Jean leaned back in her chair and eyed me speculatively. I was much the youngest and newest member of the staff and as yet nobody had come to know me very well.

"Where are you off to for your holidays? Anywhere exciting?"

I shook my head. "'Fraid not. Still, if the weather holds I'm looking forward to some nice lazy days in the sun."

I made some excuse and got up and crossed over to the window before I could be questioned further. I'm not normally uncommunicative, but I didn't want anyone to suspect how dismayed I suddenly felt at the prospect of the next six weeks. I hadn't been in London long enough to make many friends and without the daily routine of school I realized that I was almost certain to feel appallingly lonely.

Later that day I walked out of the school gates wondering what on earth I was going to do with myself all through the long vacation. Read, go to the theater, sunbathe in the park, write to everyone to whom I owed a letter, catch up on my mending... it wasn't a very exciting programme.

On impulse I stopped at a travel agency which was conveniently situated near my bus stop and collected a pile of glossy brochures advertising sun-soaked holidays in all parts of the globe. Goodness only knew I couldn't afford any of them—I'd blown all my savings on a madly expensive wedding present for mother and James—but I thought I might enjoy the panegyric descriptions. Travel agents, like estate agents, know how to wrap up their products to the best advantage!

"Left it a bit late, haven't you, miss?" a pimply youth behind the counter said chattily. "You'll find everywhere booked up by now. January's the time to think about holidays, not July."

I bit back the withering retort which trembled on my lips. After all, he was right. Mother and I had planned our Scottish holiday sitting around a blazing fire with snowflakes drifting past the misty window. If only... but it was no use thinking along those lines.

After the family had left for America I'd been lucky enough to find a roomy bed-sitter in a big, old-fashioned house which smelt of wax polish and potpourri, an odd but rather charming combination. I made myself a cup of tea as soon as I got in, and was sitting leafing through the travel brochures—just to see what I'd missed—when there was a knock on my door.

My landlady, Mrs. Strong, was out: she always went to play whist on Wednesday afternoons. Even without this knowledge I could never have mistaken the brisk, even imperative quality of this knock for Mrs. Strong's gentle rapping. I'd heard footsteps on the stairs, but as there were two other bed-sitters besides mine, and I wasn't expecting visitors, I hadn't taken any notice.

I jumped up, scattering the brochures onto the floor in my haste, and went to the door. It opened before I got there and in the doorway stood a tall, slender girl with a gracefully poised head and the kind of clothes that announced discreetly that she'd been to Paris, and recently at that.

"José!" I must have sounded as stunned as I felt, for my visitor arched her delicate brows.

"Joby dear, you look as though you've seen a ghost! What's the matter? Aren't you pleased to see me?" She spoke reproachfully, but her dancing eyes told me that she was already sure of her welcome.

I pulled myself together and went forward with my hands outstretched. "Idiot! Oh, idiot, of course I am! It's just that—well, you're the last person I expected to see! I thought you were still in Paris and wouldn't be back in London for simply ages! Besides, I forgot to send you my address. How did you know where to find me?"

"I rang up Aunt Elisabeth." My cousin Josephine carefully shut the door and looked around her judiciously. I found myself hoping that even if she was unimpressed by the shabby furniture and the threadbare carpet, she'd find the overall effect bright and cheerful. I'd made gaily patterned curtains for the casement window and a matching divan cover, there were gold-petaled flowers on the table and bookcase, and my own treasured pictures hung on the walls.

"Mmm. Not bad," my cousin affirmed. "I must say that when I heard you'd joined the bed-sitter tribe I had my doubts, dearest! Quite slummy, some of these places!"

"As if *you'd* know!" I scoffed, pulling forward a chair. I was suddenly glowing with relief and delight, depression and loneliness things of the long-distant past. "Oh, José, I am glad you've come! Sit down and tell me all your news. Since you've only written to me once since Christmas, there must be plenty to tell!"

I was intent on getting the reproach in before it was hurled at my own head. José, however, had no intention of letting me get away with it.

"Goodness, you've no room to talk! One postcard in the last eight months is all I've had from you, Josephine Lester!"

At this point I'd better explain that Josephine is my real name. It is also my cousin's, because we were both named after our paternal grandmother. As our fathers were twins and José is only four months older than I am it might have been somewhat confusing for us to have shared the same name, but in actual fact it hadn't mattered at all. For two reasons.

To start with, my cousin has always insisted on being

called José, whereas I am stuck with the pet name, "Joby," which might have suited me when I was a nice, round, fat chuckling baby but seems singularly inappropriate now. José, incidentally, is tall and fair and elegant, I am small and dark and, according to mother, always look in dire need of a good square meal. "All spirit and no substance, that's you, my girl!" she used to say darkly.

The other reason why it hadn't mattered that we'd both been christened Josephine is that our lives have always been poles apart. We're fond of each other, and understand each other pretty well, but our meetings have been nothing if not few and far between. You see, Donald Lester—José's father—has been what I suppose people would call a terrific success. Commercially, I mean. Though he and my father were twins they weren't a scrap alike: dad was a quiet, gentle sort of person with a passion for archaeology—he taught classics at a boys' public school—and Uncle Donald was go-ahead and ambitious and an absolute wow as an engineer. By the time he was twenty-five he had formed his own company, and ten years later he was not only a very rich man, but his firm was building roads and bridges and dams all over the world.

From childhood José had been surrounded by every conceivable luxury. She had been educated at the best schools, "finished" in Switzerland, and had traveled extensively. Oddly enough, although at times I was green with envy of her pony, her grand piano, her pretty clothes and her marvelous holidays, I don't think I ever felt as though I'd have liked to have changed places with her. I adored my family and I couldn't imagine anything worse than growing up without a mother—José's had died when she was born—and in the shadow of a father who spent his life pursuing power and money.

At least, I reflected, rushing to refill the teapot, José

wasn't unbearably spoilt, even if she did like getting her own way a little too much. She was basically a much, much nicer person than her father, whom my mother once described as "a cold fish, and about as ruthless as they come!" In appearance and manner he's pleasant enough, but I've never cared for him and I've always been profoundly thankful that he wasn't my father.

However, for José's sake I'd have put up with a hundred Uncle Donalds. I poured her out a cup of tea—no milk, a dash of lemon—and we settled down to have a long, cozy chat. José described her adventures in Paris, where she'd been staying with friends, and I told her all about St. Olave's and, of course, about mother's whirlwind courtship and the wedding that had removed her to the far ends of the earth. Or practically.

I could see that José, who's been hopping on and off jet planes all her life, didn't really understand that I felt as though the few thousand miles that separated us were as good—or do I mean as bad—as several million. She thought that it was marvelous that "Aunt Melanie" had found happiness again, agreed that James Burford sounded a dear, and said how much she wished that she and her father had been invited to the wedding.

I looked at her in dismay. "Oh, José! We did think of you, honestly, but you were away and... and everything happened so quickly! They were married by special license, you know, and it was a terribly quiet affair, just me and the twins and James's sister as guests. Mother looked lovely, of course, and about ten years younger! She and James are very happy, I'm sure of that."

"Lucky them! I'm glad that somebody's love story has had the right ending!" José said, and her lips twisted. The unexpected bitterness in her voice shocked me into sudden awareness. All at once I noticed that there were dark shadows beneath my cousin's eyes, as though she hadn't been sleeping properly, and that her face looked thinner and paler than I remembered it. I hesitated, uncertain how to proceed. José noticed my hesitation and smiled, a queer, mirthless little smile.

"I suppose I may as well tell you that I've come an awful cropper, Joby. That's why I've come back to London. I...I fell in love with somebody and he—well, I had good reason to believe that he loved me. Unfortunately, I was wrong. He didn't care about me as a person at all. The only thing that was important to him was my money. Oh, and the fact that I'm Donald Lester's only daughter. He worked for daddy, you see. That's how I met him."

She spoke with a hard control that I found more moving than tears. "Oh, José! I *am* sorry!" I put my hand over hers, wondering helplessly what I could say that would banish that bleak expression from her wide, dark-shadowed eyes.

"It's an old, old story. I've only myself to blame, really. Daddy did his best to warn me, but I wouldn't listen. Mike...oh, Joby, I loved him so! I thought he was such a marvelous person. It...it's so humiliating to know that he just played me for a sucker...that every single thing he said to me was a lie from start to finish!"

"Don't think about it!" I said fiercely. "Remember that you were lucky to have found him out before it was too late. There...there'll be other men who won't care anything about your money, José. It isn't the end of the world, even if it seems rather like that at the moment."

"I'll never ever be sure of anyone again!" José said bitterly. "I'd have staked my last penny that Mike was true-blue." She gave a rueful little laugh. "One certainly lives and learns."

"That was his name—Mike?" I thought that it might do José good to talk. She had probably kept her feelings bottled up for far too long.

"Yes. Michael Frenton. He's one of daddy's Bright

Young Men—or he was. I found out last week that daddy had given him his marching orders, so he's lost out all along the line. I—I oughtn't to care, but you know, Joby, I do. I... I keep wondering how he's making out." She brushed her hand across her eyes. "Isn't that silly of me? I guess Daddy's right and I do need my head examined!"

I gave her hand a gentle squeeze. "Darling, you're much too good for the Michael Frentons of this world! Just wait, you'll be laughing at the whole thing in three months' time!"

José achieved a wan smile. "I only hope you're right. Oh, you *are* a comfort, Joby! One thing, you'll never need to worry about men falling in love with you for quite the wrong reasons!"

I pretended to be indignant. "If you're insinuating that I'm not a good catch financially, I'll have you know that I earn quite a respectable salary! I am a fully fledged B.A., you know!"

"Are you really? Darling, that's wonderful!" José said in honest admiration. "But don't you see—that's exactly what I mean! You're clever and much, much prettier than I am and you've a divine figure and—what are you laughing at, idiot?"

"You're the idiot!" I retorted. "If I'm that wonderful, what am I doing in a bed-sitter in Bayswater?"

"At the moment you're providing me with a very efficient shoulder to weep on!" José, investigating the remaining contents of the teapot, spoke with a spice of her usual self. "Have you ever been in love with anyone, Joby?"

I shook my head. "Never."

José raised her brows disbelievingly. "Heart-whole and fancy-free all the way through college?"

I had the grace to blush. "Well, perhaps not quite heart-whole. But I've never been head over heels in love, if that's what you mean." I paused, then added thoughtfully, "Thank goodness."

My cousin looked at me as if she was about to say something and then thought better of it. Instead she picked up one of the travel brochures which I'd scattered on the floor. "What are these? Are you planning to go abroad?"

I laughed. "No. Window-shopping, that's all. I'm having a stay-at-home holiday this year. What about you? How long do you mean to stay in London?"

José hesitated. "I haven't decided. Daddy's in Peru, you know."

"Oh?" I was no more than politely interested. Uncle Donald always seemed to be in some out-of-the-way spot. Never where his daughter needed him.

José extended a sandaled foot, and regarded it. "He's supposed to be on holiday in Barbados, actually. He's got friends out there, but his firm is making new roads or something out in the wilds of Peru and there's been trouble, so daddy rushed to investigate. Typical, of course! Mike used to say—" She stopped abruptly and her lips pinched.

I spoke quickly. "Your father certainly gets around!"

"He does, doesn't he? I haven't even seen him since the Mike business blew up in my face. He cabled me the other day and suggested that I might like to join him in Peru, but though I appreciate his motives I'm not too keen. Apart from anything else it's the wrong time of year: their winter, you know."

I gasped and sat up. That was just a bit too much, even from José! Perhaps if she had been talking about Spain or Greece or Italy there would have been some excuse for her sounding so blasé and bored. She'd been to those countries so many times. But... Peru! Land of the Sun, inhabited by the children of the skies whose emblem was a rainbow... beautiful, fascinating Peru with its strongly marked contrasts and its pagan, colonial and modern worlds, existing side by side! Even if it was the wrong time of year, how could José say she was "not too keen"?

I said explosively, "Now it's my turn to think your head needs examining! Have you ever been to South America? No? Well then, I think you're mad if you pass up a chance like that! Peru must be fabulous, one of the most interesting countries in the world!" I leaned forward, clasping my hands around my knees as I warmed to my subject. "I know you're not particularly keen on antiquities, but it's got the most romantic past! Land of the Incas and conquistadores... why, even today you can see the remains of Inca villages, ruins and monuments all over Peru. Nearly everywhere you go is like following the paths of history!"

I stopped, flushing under my cousin's quizzical look. Good lord, in a moment I'd start spouting about Atahuallpa!

There was a moment's silence. Then José stretched her long shapely legs in front of her and reached for a cigarette. She lit it and blew a little cloud of smoke into the air. It drifted toward me as she said, "Well, since you're so enthusiastic will you go with me?"

I honestly believed she was joking. "Oh yes! I could just about afford a trip like that!" I said, laughing. "Provided, of course, I lived on bread and water and clad myself in sackcloth and ashes for the rest of the year!"

"Don't be daft! Of course daddy will pay your expenses!" José said impatiently. "I wouldn't ask you otherwise."

She wasn't joking. The smile vanished from my face and I said blankly, "Wh-what?"

"You heard me quite well. Now for goodness' sake don't start being all prickly and independent, Joby! Daddy badly wants me to join him in Peru, but I shall tell him that it's absolutely no go unless you can come to keep me company. I mean it, old thing. I should be bored to tears on my own. I'm afraid I don't share your extraordinary passion for antiquities and I should just sit around and moon after Mike and make myself thoroughly miserable. Please say you'll come, Joby! After all, you'll be doing me the favor, not the other way around!"

I drew a deep breath, resisting the temptation to pinch myself to see if I was dreaming. "José, I...I simply don't know what to say! It's the chance of a lifetime and I'd love it, or at least I would love it if—"

"If my father didn't have to foot the bill?" José smiled a little ruefully. "I think I know how you and your family feel about money you haven't earned for yourselves! Daddy's told me several times that he's offered help to your mother and it's been refused. Perhaps you're right, but... well, don't you think that pride can sometimes be taken to quite unnecessary lengths?"

I was silent, my gaze bent out of the window down the dingy London street. It was true that my family had always valued its independence, and the thought of being beholden to Uncle Donald for anything at all did rather stick in my throat. On the other hand....

I said slowly, "José, I can't possibly give you an answer now! I need time to think about it."

"Rubbish! There's nothing to think about! Let me ring daddy up and see what he says. Please, Joby!"

It was the pleading note in José's voice that decided me. That, and the remembrance of the despair I'd glimpsed earlier. I said, "All right. But you're to promise me that if he quibbles—" I stopped. I knew he wouldn't. Whatever José wanted, she could have. It had always been like that.

José obviously had no qualms. "Of course he won't quibble! He'll be thrilled to bits," she said confidently.

"Leave it all to me, Joby. There's nothing to worry about! I can draw on daddy's bank in London for the money for our air fares and Daddy will fix us up with somewhere to stay in Lima. He's sure to know the best hotels."

José made it all sound so easy, I thought wryly. Well, perhaps it was if you were a rich man's daughter. Suddenly I found myself remembering what José had once said when I'd asked her what she was going to do when she left school.

"Nothing in the way of a job, that's for sure! With all daddy's money mine for the asking it seems a bit daft to do anything but enjoy it!"

I picked up the travel brochures and threw them into the wastepaper basket. How could the thought of sardine-packed beaches in Spain or Italy excite me now?

José said, "We'll need visas. You have got a passport, I suppose, Joby?"

I nodded. "Mother and the boys and I went to Holland last summer." I added that it was the first time I'd ever been abroad, except for school trips, and José looked horrified.

"How awful! Poor you!" Then, quickly, "No, I didn't mean that. I've always rather envied you, you know, Joby."

My eyes widened. "Envied *me*? But why?"

"You've got such a super family," José said simply. "I've got daddy, I know, but... well, he's never really had an awful lot of time for me. And, anyway, I'm fast coming to the conclusion that being his daughter is a distinct liability!"

"Liability?" I raised my brows and looked pointedly at José's dashing and expensive clothes, which must, I thought, make my own homemade cotton dress look positively dowdy in comparison. No one looking at the two of us could fail to realize who was the heiress and who the hard-up schoolteacher, yet oddly enough I was far more like Donald Lester to look at than was his own daughter. He and my father had been identical twins and I had inherited their dark hair and eyes. José, blonde and blue eyed, was like her mother.

Now she moved restlessly in her chair. "Oh, I've loved it up to now... being able to buy whatever I want and not having to worry about the bills! I like luxury and I don't mind admitting it. But—oh, I don't know! Perhaps it sounds silly to you, but Mike has shaken my confidence. I... I can't help wondering how many people I know really like me for myself and... and not just because I'm Donald Lester's only daughter."

"José! You noodle!" I said indignantly. "Of course people like you for yourself! Why on earth shouldn't they?"

"Well, you do. I know that. But—oh, forget it!" and José suddenly laughed. "One day I'll keep quiet about my distinguished parent, and then perhaps I'll find out if I really do have any identity except as his daughter!"

I bit my lips, uncomfortably aware that despite my denial there might be a grain of truth in what José had said. I must have hesitated too long before answering, for she shot me a glance that was suddenly pure mischief.

"Don't look so worried! I'm not really down in the mouth. In fact, I think perhaps Peru may be rather fun after all. I'm going to forget all about Mike... write him down to experience. That's what daddy told me to do."

I eyed her thoughtfully, wondering for the first time what she had meant when she'd said that her father had done his best to warn her. Warn her about what? Shrewd and worldly-wise, had he realized from the outset that Michael Frenton was merely a fortune hunter? Some day, I decided, I must ask José how she herself had come to discover that painful fact. But not now—not while her hurt was still so raw!

José was rummaging in her handbag for another cigarette. It was just like her, I thought ruefully, to ignore the dangers attached to smoking. She said casually, "By the way, I don't suppose that as daddy has problems he'll be able to lay much on for us in the way of entertainment, Joby. We'll probably be left pretty well to our own devices. You won't mind that, will you?"

Mind! I suppressed a grin. Then, feeling that I ought to make at least a show of interest, I asked, "What sort of problems is uncle having to cope with?"

"I don't know exactly. I just gathered that everything that possibly could go wrong has gone wrong. There was some kind of a ghastly accident to begin with, I think, and that's why daddy cut his holiday short, to find out what happened and why. He's very jealous of the firm's reputation, you know, and accidents don't exactly help it."

Memory stirred. I said, "Wasn't there a landslide... some people injured? There was a paragraph about it in *The Times.*"

José looked at me in awe. "My dear, you don't actually read *The Times*? No wonder you're a B.A.!" Then, as I threw a cushion at her, "Yes, that sounds rather like it. It must have been an awful business."

I wrinkled my brow thoughtfully. "It can't be easy making new roads anywhere, and it must be doubly difficult in a country like Peru. Isn't the river still the main highway in some parts? I'm sure I read somewhere that there are immense areas of forest and jungle where roads are almost nonexistent."

"Mphm."

Rightly or wrongly, I assumed from that noncommittal rejoinder that my cousin was entirely vague about the geography of Peru. I leaned back in my chair, for the first time giving way to my rising tide of excitement. All my life I'd been fascinated by the history of Latin America and Peru, with its traces of a civilization four thousand years old, was the country I'd most longed to visit. I could scarcely believe, even now, that the chance lay within my grasp.

I said dreamily, "Do you know, José, that there's a fantastic mountain retreat, surrounded by mists, that was the last retreat of the Incas? It was never discovered by the Spaniards nor by anyone else, for that matter, until 1911. It was an explorer called Hiram Bingham who stumbled by chance upon its ruins—"

I stopped. It was patently obvious that José wasn't listening to a word I said. She was staring unseeingly at a blank wall, her face set in an expression I was to come to know well. Wherever her thoughts were they certainly weren't in Peru.

I frowned to myself. José simply had to forget about the man who had treated her so shabbily, and the easiest way she could do that was to fall in love with someone else...someone who wasn't a fortune hunter! I got up to clear away the teacups. Perhaps a handsome Peruvian, descendant of some lordly black-haired conquistador, would fit the bill!

CHAPTER TWO

LESS THAN A FORTNIGHT LATER, my Bayswater bed-sitter was thousands of miles behind me. Leaning out of a hotel window, I saw the lights of Lima, Peru's capital city, spread out below me like a million tiny jewels set in blue velvet. Those in the far distance were tremulous, like stars.

A queer feeling seized me. This was Peru. Really Peru. The Peru of the geography and history books... the land I had always dreamed about. Romantic, beautiful, vibrant, cruel. The tiger astride the Andes.

I shivered, partly from cold, partly from excitement. Stepping back, I pulled the heavy velvet curtains across the window, shutting out the old and the new that had, in Lima, achieved such a memorable truce. Tomorrow, I told myself, José and I would start to explore the city. We had only four days to do it in, for at the end of the week we were due to join José's father in Cuzco, the first capital of Spanish Peru.

José and I had been given adjoining bedrooms, both thickly carpeted and charmingly decorated, and we were sharing a luxurious bathroom. It sounded rather as though José had appropriated it already. At any rate I could hear the taps running.

I sat down on my bed and tried to unscramble my confused impressions of the day's events. What did I remember most vividly? My first glimpse of the blue Caribbean? The moment when we'd been told that we were now flying over South America and I'd looked down from the big jet aircraft to see rivers that looked like twisting ribbons of silver, jade-flecked forests and snowcapped montains that had seemed to fill the sky with icebergs? The surprised expression worn by the immigration officer at Lima's handsome, modern airport when he'd examined our passports and discovered that he was dealing with two Josephine Lesters? I smiled to myself. He'd been charming. But then so had everybody. Charming and friendly.

The door of the bathroom opened and José walked into my room, decoratively if inadequately wrapped in a fleecy white towel.

"I'm going to have a bath," she announced unnecessarily. "The water's heavenly...piping hot! If daddy rings up while I'm still submerged you'll speak to him, won't you, Joby? Tell him we've had a super flight and the hotel's marvelous and we adore everything!"

I laughed. In the last few days José had recovered quite a lot of her usual sparkle. I hoped that it was a sign that her unhappy memories were fast receding.

"Will do, but don't be too long!"

A few moments later I heard the sound of uninhibited splashing and my cousin's voice raised in loud, uproarious song. At least she could sing in tune. That was something!

I knelt down on the floor and began unpacking two rather shabby suitcases which had seen me through college and were still going strong. José, of course, had elegant luggage in cream-colored hide, all stamped with her initials in gold. I was shaking the creases out of my favorite dress—a dreamy creation in green and silver—when the telephone beside my bed rang shrilly.

I didn't doubt that it was Uncle Donald. He'd told José that he wouldn't be able to meet us in Lima, but that he would contact her immediately after we arrived. Apparently he'd made his own headquarters in Cuzco, since the road that was giving so much trouble was being constructed through the rugged mountainous region surrounding the one-time capital of the Incan Empire. Out of sheer curiosity I'd studied a map of the area, and I may as well say here and now that I didn't envy the Lester International Construction Company one teeny-weeny bit. There had to be easier ways of making money than by hewing a road through that improbable landscape!

I could still hear the sound of splashing, so I gathered that José was still in the bath and that although she must have heard the telephone she had no intention of answering it. The insistent ringing couldn't be ignored much longer, however, so I picked up the receiver and said, "Hello? Josephine Lester speaking."

I knew, of course, that Uncle Donald would immediately realize that from his point of view I was the wrong Josephine. Apart from the fact that his daughter never used her full name, my voice had a Scottish lilt imparted to it by my mother, whose origins were unmistakable even after years of living among the Sassenachs. I wasn't altogether surprised, therefore, by the momentary silence at the other end of the line. Then, distant in my ear, a deep, pleasant-sounding voice which certainly didn't belong to Uncle Donald said crisply, "Ross Henderson here, speaking from Cuzco. I'm sorry, but I'm afraid I have some bad news for you, Miss Lester."

Ross Henderson? I'd never heard of him, but I wasn't worried about that. Then. It was what he'd said about bad news that made me go cold with apprehension and grip the receiver more tightly so that my knuckles showed white.

"B-bad news?" My voice quavered as the paragraph I'd read in *The Times* about the disastrous landslide flashed into my mind. Dear God, there hadn't been another? Uncle Donald hadn't...wasn't...?

"Your father's had an accident." Ross Henderson's next words confirmed my worst fears, then a split second later I drew a deep sigh of relief as he went on, "He's hurt, but not as seriously as he might have been. A few broken ribs, a broken ankle, slight concussion and a hell of a lot of bruises. Enough to put him out of action for the next couple of months, but not enough for anyone to start manning panic stations. He's going to be all right."

He sounded brusque, but oddly enough it was the very fact of his brusqueness that I found so reassuring. Obviously he wasn't the sort of man to waste sympathy where it wasn't really needed! I could be sure that what he'd said was nothing more nor less than the absolute truth.

I drew a deep breath. I don't know why I didn't tell him, there and then, that I wasn't Donald Lester's daughter, merely his niece. It was just that it seemed, at that moment, to be completely unimportant. Instead I said, "Wh-what happened?" because I knew that when I broke the news to José she'd expect me to be able to tell every single relevant detail.

"It was a car accident. The brakes failed." Ross Henderson sounded grim. "He was lucky. He'd descended sixteen thousand feet of hairpin bends before it happened. He went off the road at the only point where he had any chance at all of escaping with his life."

I shut my eyes, as if by so doing I could blot out the nightmare picture that his words had conjured up. I said huskily, "We'll come at once. He's in hosital in Cuzco, I suppose?"

"No. To the best of my knowledge he arrived in Barbados an hour ago." Then, as I gave an incredulous exclamation, "I was fortunate enough to be able to arrange a special flight for him. He was fit enough to travel, and I thought that from every point of view Barbados was probably the best place for him. Not only will he receive first-class medical treatment, he'll be among friends. They'll look after him when he comes out of hospital. He's got a long convalescence in front of him and he'll need plenty of distractions."

There was a pause. Then, bewildered, I said, "But he knew we were coming! Did he *want* to go to Barbados? Surely—"

Ross Henderson interrupted me. "He really had very little choice in the matter," he said flatly. "He was under sedation."

It took a moment or two for the penny to drop. "You mean...you took it on yourself to...look, who are you?" I demanded indignantly. For once in my life my sympathies were entirely with Uncle Donald. Ross Henderson's calm air of self-assurance, which at first I'd found comforting, was now making my hackles rise. He had spoken of sending Uncle Donald to Barbados in much the same way that he might have spoken of dispatching a brown-paper parcel, and it annoyed me intensely. Surely, oh, surely, he couldn't be one of the firm's employees? From what José had told me they all went in fear and trembling of their redoubtable chairman!

"I told you. My name is Ross Henderson."

"That isn't what I meant, and you damn well know it!" I snapped. "I want to know—"

Again I was interrupted. Whatever else he was, Ross Henderson was obviously no gentleman. "Miss Lester, I've made allowances for the fact that you are worried and upset about your father, but the fact remains that I'm a very busy man. I've told you everything I can, and I've done everything in my power to help. The rest, I'm afraid, isn't up to me. If there's anything else you want to know, I suggest you get in touch with Barbados."

There was no doubt about it. This time Ross Henderson's voice was ragged with impatience. And—unless I was greatly mistaken—cold with dislike. I opened my mouth, then shut it again. I was still wondering whether I was hearing right when he fired what turned out to be his parting shot.

"In the circumstances I very much doubt whether you'll find it worth your while to prolong your stay, Miss Lester. Why not join your father in Barbados? Peru's a fascinating country, but as far as I know it hasn't yet acquired the reputation of being a playground for popsies!"

I was hearing all right. There was a moment's silence, than a sharp little click which told me that the receiver at the other end of the line had just been cradled. I was still staring dazedly at my own receiver when José, pink-cheeked and fragrant and wearing a negligée that smacked of Hollywood in its heyday, chose to emerge from the bathroom.

"Oh, lord, has he rung off? What was the hurry, for goodness' sake?" she began, and then catching sight of my face, "Joby! What's the matter?"

I told her. I didn't break the news to her as abruptly as it had been broken to me, which was perhaps why she took it far more calmly. She was sorry, of course, I could see that, but she obviously had no intention of getting into a tizz just because her parent was suffering from a few broken bones and a bump on his head!

"I suppose that means we'll have to go to Cuzco tomorrow instead of waiting until the end of the week," she said, absentmindedly borrowing my hairbrush. "Bother! Oh well, I suppose it can't be helped!"

I looked at her in sheer disbelief, then remembered just in time that there are some things that can't be bought. Uncle Donald really didn't deserve much more from his daughter than the lukewarm affection she was displaying now.

I said grimly, "Think again, dear coz. Your father's

not even in Peru, let alone Cuzco! He's in Barbados!"

"*Barbados*?" José's voice was almost, if not quite, a squeak.

I repeated, practically word for word, what Ross Henderson had said to me. When I'd finished José's wide blue eyes had opened to their fullest extent.

"You mean he's got rid of daddy? Just like that?"

She might have expressed herself more elegantly, but she certainly had the right idea.

"Just like that." I took a long breath. "Who," I asked carefully, "is Ross Henderson, apart from being the most rude, arrogant, conceited, callous and bloody-minded man I've ever had the misfortune to talk to?"

José stared at me, apparently fascinated. "*Joby!* You mean you found all that out in five minutes' conversation?"

"Less."

My cousin giggled. "You sound positively *trenchant!* Is that how you quell your recalcitrant pupils?"

I eyed her sourly. "Your vocabulary's improving. Congratulations. I repeat, who is Ross Henderson?"

José puckered her brow. "My dear, I simply haven't a clue! I've never heard of him before. He must be something to do with daddy's company, but I don't know what." She paused, then added ingenuously, "Why are you so upset? On the whole I think it was really rather a good idea to send daddy back to Barbados. Isabel will visit him in hospital and take him grapes and make a great fuss over him."

"Isabel?" I said blankly.

"A beautiful widow. She's been terribly fond of daddy ever since I can remember. She's the reason he takes a vacation in Barbados year after year, but he doesn't seem to want to get married to her. Being in hospital might change all that," José said hopefully.

I got up from the floor. Over my shoulder I said,

"That's as may be. However, I received the distinct impression that your father hadn't been packed off to Barbados for his own good, or for Isabel's, but for Ross Henderson's. And though I'll admit that normally he's more than capable of taking care of himself—"

"Don't worry. I wouldn't mind betting he still is. It would take more than a few broken bones to subdue daddy!" José's voice was soothing. Really, I thought, struggling between amusement and exasperation, anyone would think that it was my father and not hers! I suppose I must still have looked unconvinced, for her face suddenly brightened.

"I know! After we've had dinner I'll ring up Isabel! She's sure to know what's what and how daddy is feeling and whether he'll want us to stay put or go rushing off to join him in Barbados!"

I felt a hollow sensation in the pit of my stomach. Leave Peru before we'd even had a chance to visit Machu Picchu, the Lost City of the Incas? Or Sacsuhuaman and Arequipa? I crushed down my dismay, wondering guiltily whether some of my annoyance with Ross Henderson stemmed from the fact that it was quite on the cards that our plans might have to undergo a drastic change. I didn't want to go to Barbados. At least, not yet!

José's talk with Isabel occupied the best part of half an hour and must have cost a small fortune. However, that wasn't my concern. I lay on my bed while it was going on, rereading, for the umpteenth time, William H. Prescott's *Conquest of Peru.* The walls of my twentieth-century hotel bedroom blurred, wavered and finally dissolved as I became lost to the everyday world. I was back in the days of the Incan Empire of Táhuantinsuyu, the Place of the Four Directions, and tingling anew to the story of Atahuallpa. Atahuallpa, the brave, ambitious prince who usurped his brother's throne, was captured by the conquistadores and then made the fatal mistake of trying to buy his life with a house filled with gold, twenty feet high and eighteen broad....

"Joby!" said my cousin's voice, and I knew from her tone that it was not for the first time. She was standing beside my bed and her hair, in the lamplight, was a mass of burnished gold.

With an effort I dragged my thoughts back from the past. Just for a little while I'd been a split personality, one part of me accepting the voluptuous comfort of a silk-covered divan, the other identifying in a strange sort of way with the triumphs and tragedies of those long-ago Peruvians. Perhaps I looked bemused and stupid, for José laughed and passed her hand in front of my eyes.

"Wake up, old dear, I've things to tell you!" she said gaily. "It's quite all right and you needn't have worried, Daddy's in a *marvelous* nursing home in Bridgetown and Isabel's own doctor is looking after him. Isabel says that at first he was simply furious with Ross for taking the law into his own hands but that he sees now that he acted for the best and—"

I interrupted her breathless flow. One name had riveted my attention. "Ross? Then you *have* found out who he is?"

José's eyes were wide and innocent. "Oh yes! He's Isabel's cousin, not one of daddy's Bright Young Men at all, at least not yet. But he is an engineer and absolutely brilliant, Isabel says. He flew out with daddy after the landslide and more or less took charge then and there. Well, somebody had to!" as I raised my brows. "The man who'd been responsible before was badly hurt, and apart from daddy, Ross Henderson was the only person available with the right know-how and experience. It was lucky he was there!"

"I'm sure," I said dryly. José hadn't talked to Ross Henderson. I had. And I couldn't forget his rudeness... or the dislike he hadn't even bothered to try to conceal. But why? Why should he dislike a girl he hadn't even met?

Then I forgot about Ross Henderson, at least for the time being. Because José was saying "...And Isabel thinks it's best for us to stay put, Joby, and do exactly as we'd planned. As she says, it's not as though daddy needs me or anything like that, he's got lots of friends in Barbados and they'll look after him. Beautifully." She paused, then added mischievously, "I'm not going to say that Isabel is glad about the car smash, but I don't think she's exactly sorry. If she doesn't manage to squeeze a proposal out of daddy during the course of the next few weeks I'm certain sure it won't be for the want of trying!"

I looked at her curiously, a little puzzled by her apparent flippancy. "Would you mind? Having Isabel for a stepmother, I mean?"

"Heavens, no! I like her. I always have. Daddy could do a lot, lot worse." José, obviously disinclined to discuss the subject further, glanced at her watch. "Come on! I'm dying for a drink. Let's go downstairs and get acquainted with our fellow guests."

On our way down to the hotel lounge we were waylaid by the manager, a dark, dapper little man who had already greeted us on arrival. He had, it seemed, just learned of Donald Lester's accident—we were later to discover that the evening newspapers carried a full report—and he was full of regret and genuine solicitude.

"Mr. Lester stayed here when he first arrived in Peru. A charming gentleman. We were delighted to learn that we were also to have the honor of entertaining his beautiful daughter," he said, smiling expansively at me. And then, inclining his head graciously towards José, "and his niece, of course."

It was a natural mistake. As I've already said, I do bear a marked resemblance to Uncle Donald, and José, slim and fair in her white sheath dress, looked nothing like him. She wasn't even wearing any of the expensive jewelry he had given her, just a slender gold bracelet on one sun-browned wrist.

I opened my mouth to explain, and felt José's hand gripping my arm. Warningly. Before I could say a word she said quickly, "Thank you, *señor.* We are very happy to be here."

More effusions, and then the little man departed, leaving me staring at my cousin in complete mystification. I knew from experience what that sparkle in her blue eyes portended. "She's up to something," my young brothers would have said.

"Why did you let him think that I was you? He's bound to discover the truth sooner or later!" I protested. "Besides, what's the point? I don't see that it matters!"

"But it does!" My cousin gave an excited little laugh. "It's just come to me—a bright idea, I mean. For the next three weeks you can be me, and I'll be you! It's the chance I wanted, to find out what it's like *not* being Donald Lester's daughter!"

I stared at her dazedly. "But—but people know you...."

"Who? Nobody in Peru, that's for sure!" José seized my wrist. "We can't discuss it here, too many people coming and going. We'll find a corner to ourselves in the lounge."

I followed her downstairs, my thoughts whirling. I couldn't believe that she was really serious and yet she was. I found that out within the space of the next few minutes. And José being José, she wouldn't listen to a word I said in protest.

"I've told you, nobody in Peru has ever seen either of us," she said calmly, wriggling her slender body deeper into her velvet-cushioned armchair. "We couldn't change over if daddy was here, of course, but as he's safely in Barbados there's absolutely no problem. You can be the heiress, and I'll be the schoolteacher. I want to see what happens!"

I stared helplessly around the crowded room, almost as though I hoped I'd be able to point to someone and exclaim, "Look! He knows who we really are!" But of course they were all strangers, though the collection seemed varied enough. Without really trying I could spot at least half a dozen different nationalities.

José sat watching me, an amused smile hovering around her lips. She knew I thought she'd temporarily taken leave of her senses and it didn't worry her in the least.

I said feebly, "But I don't even look like an heiress! I look—"

"Sufficiently like my father for people to jump to entirely the wrong conclusion! Provided I remember to be meek and self-effacing, which I admit may be a little difficult, I can't see any reason why we shouldn't switch over quite successfully!" José said cheerfully. Then, as I still looked dubious, "Oh, Joby, don't be awkward! After all—" She broke off, flushing a little, her mouth drooping sulkily at the corners. I knew what she'd been going to say. After all, it was thanks to her that I was having the holiday of a lifetime. The least I could do was to cooperate!

I now realized why my mother had always stressed the importance of being independent. Feeling as though I'd been driven into a corner, I stared down at my hands and said slowly, "If it's really what you want I...I suppose there isn't any harm in it."

There wasn't. I knew that. It was just that I wasn't much good at playacting. And I hated the idea of masquerading under false colors.

José's face was all smiles again. "Angel! You mean you agree?"

"Yes. But honestly, José, I don't think we'll be able to keep it up! I feel sure we shall give ourselves away sooner or later!"

"I don't see why. You've only got to remember to say 'my father' instead of 'Uncle Donald' and it's the other way around for me. There won't be any complications!"

I looked past her. "Maybe you're right. Unless, perhaps, one is approaching now?"

José's eyes followed mine. A stately lady with keen gray eyes and carefully coiffured purple hair was bearing down upon us from the right. There was no mistaking her purpose. José and I exchanged alarmed glances and braced ourselves for whatever lay in store.

"Miss Lester?" The rather loud voice was English, yet I thought it possible that the owner had lived for some time in the States. At any rate she possessed the unshakable self-confidence of the average American matron, for without waiting for a reply she pulled forward the chair nearest to mine and proceeded to introduce herself in a brisk, businesslike sort of way.

"I'm Millie Stevenson. You don't know me, of course, but I met your poor father in Cuzco last week and he told me he was expecting his daughter to join him. I guessed who you must be directly I laid eyes on you. 'Millie,' I said to myself, 'that's Donald Lester's girl.' You're very like him, aren't you? But I did look in the hotel register to make sure."

Her remarks were quite unmistakably addressed to me. I felt José's foot nudge mine under the table and gave her a quick look. There was a gleam of triumph in her blue eyes. She'd been right. Everyone who'd ever met Donald Lester was going to take it for granted that I, and not José, was his daughter.

I said "Er... yes. H-how do you do, Mrs. Stevenson." And then, seeing the sharp gray eyes fasten on José I added, "This is my cousin José."

José smiled sweetly but said nothing. Doubtless she was practicing self-effacement, I thought bitterly. Mrs. Stevenson probably thought that she was shy, for she immediately switched her attention back to me.

"So you two young people are visiting Peru together. How nice. At least...." She hesitated, then dropped her voice and smoothed her face into an expression of commiseration. "You must be feeling that your father's accident has been a bad start. I'm so sorry about it, my dear. The news quite upset me. I do hope that what it says in the paper is right and he's not too badly hurt? As I said to Bobby—that's my husband, dear, he's in textiles, but his hobby is archaeology, that's why we're here—no one should be surprised at *anything* happening in those parts. The roads are a disgrace, I've always said so. It's time there were some new ones, and the sooner the better. A public benefactor, that's what your father is, Miss Lester!"

I'd heard Uncle Donald called many things, but never that. I daren't look at José. Praying I wouldn't betray my inner amusement—I knew the good lady would be horrified by the merest flicker of a smile! I said, "Have...have you been in Peru long, Mrs. Stevenson?"

"The last six weeks. In the *sierra*, mostly. You'll be going to Cuzco when you've finished with Lima, I suppose? Remember me to your father and to Mr. Henderson."

I stiffened. I couldn't help it. "Oh, you know Mr. Henderson?"

"Your father introduced me to him. Good-looking young man, but rather taciturn, I thought. Still, I suppose he's got his hands full one way and another. You know, of course, there's been a lot of trouble over that new road they're constructing?"

"Yes. Yes, I did."

"First there was that landslide, then a strike. Labour's hard to come by, your father said. Of course, there's a lot of local opposition to the whole scheme. Stupid, I call it. What does it matter if the road does cut through some old valley the Indians are crazy about? This is the twentieth century and we've got to progress. Don't you agree, Miss Lester?"

I was spared the necessity of finding an appropriate answer. Mrs. Stevenson had suddenly spotted someone at the far end of the lounge and was waving vigorously in that direction.

"I must go and have a word with Mrs. Baker. Her husband's in textiles, too, isn't that a funny coincidence? But his passion is painting, not archaeology. I don't kow which is worse." She smiled kindly at us both. "I expect I shall see you again before you go. Let me know if there's any way I can help, won't you? You'll like Lima, plenty to do, good shops. Don't let them cheat you, though! Make sure you drive a hard bargain!"

And she was off, billowing across the lounge like a ship in full sail. I caught José's eye and found that she was grinning.

"Well? What could have been easier than that, coz?"

"It was easy because she doesn't really know your father. Or anything about you and me." I hesitated. "What happens when we arrive in Cuzco?"

José raised her brows. "Well, what does?"

"Supposing we bump into Ross Henderson? It's more than likely."

My cousin tilted her head and sent me a long look. Her blue eyes held a hint of mockery. "I hope it is! Isabel says he's a perfect dish. I know you received an entirely different impression, dearest, but—"

I interrupted her, suddenly angry. "I talked to him,

you didn't! He's nobody's fool, José. It won't be so easy to pull the wool over *his* eyes!"

José rang for a drink. "Where's your spirit of adventure?"

"Where's your common sense?"

José's face was suddenly bleak. "I lost it. Didn't you know? Along with my head, three months ago."

I bit my lip, finally silenced. José was doing her best to salvage her pride, to rebuild the confidence that Michael Frenton had to cruelly shattered. Did I, who had never suffered from either a bruised ego or a broken heart, have the right to question how she did it?

CHAPTER THREE

JOSÉ LIKED IT because it was gay and fun-loving, but in some ways I found Lima oddly disappointing. The twentieth century had encroached too freely upon what had once been a beautiful colonial city: the past had been too ruthlessly crowded out by the present.

"I don't know what you're grumbling about. I feel far more at home with neon signs and skyscrapers than with those old palaces and baroque churches you keep dragging me to see!" José said, laughing.

A breeze lifted her shining hair and I thought how gay she looked, and how pretty. She was wearing a soft, brightly colored poncho that she had bought only that morning and her arms were full of souvenirs. When it came to spending money, José was apt to forget that she was supposed to be an impecunious schoolteacher!

I smiled and turned my head. Gracefully bowing trees lined the wide boulevard that stretched out in front of us. The center parkways were ablaze with colorful plants and flowers and huge buildings all around us reached for the sky. Shop windows glittered with every conceivable commodity that the mind of the tourist could imagine. This was central Lima. Colorful, noisy, cosmopolitan.

As Mrs. Stevenson had said, one had to progress. Only in the colonial section of Lima did a few baroque churches, some splendid palaces and an occasional eighteenth-century mansion with fancifully carved stonework and screened balconies bring to mind the Spanish nobles who had once lived in a semi-feudal splendor of gilded coaches and golden tableware. If I tried I could sometimes see, in my mind's eye, the proud Spanish viceroy surrounded by his footguard and followed by files of lancers, their gaily colored pennants twirling and curling in the breeze. Only the illusion never lasted long, because José was always there to tug at my arm. History bored my cousin. In that respect she was like her father.

"Don't forget you're supposed to be me!" I reminded her when she groaned at my tentative suggestion that we should drive to the Holy City of Pachamacamac to see the ruins of pre-Inca temples and palaces. "For a history graduate—"

"Darling, why couldn't you have been an actress or a model or something *civilized*? I can't, positively can't, work up any enthusiasm for dirty old ruins!" my cousin said plaintively, wrinkling her pretty nose. "This is our last day in Lima, and I want to find that little shop Mrs. Stevenson told us about—the one that's supposed to sell the most gorgeous Indian skirts and blouses." She looked appraisingly at me. "I ought to buy something of the sort for you. You'd look sensational as an Indian maiden, especially if you plaited that lovely dark hair of yours and wore a silver band across your forehead! I'm too fair, I'd just look silly."

"Thanks, but I don't think I'll bother!" I said, laughing. Perhaps it was a good thing that José didn't seem to know that there *was* Indian blood in our family, a long way back. I suddenly caught sight of my reflection in a big plate-glass window. Black eyes, a black fall of hair, arms and legs burned to a deep tan... why, I thought incredulously, I could almost pass as a Peruvian myself!

Of course, we didn't go to Pachamacamac. We spent the whole afternoon exploring the Jiron de la Union, said to be the most exciting shopping street in South America and surely, I thought, the noisiest! Vendors hawking their wares...screaming men and women selling lottery tickets...bands playing with relentless gaiety...more music blaring from store interiors...tired children crying...no wonder, perhaps, that José returned to the hotel with a thumping headache!

She certainly did look pale. I wasn't surprised when she decided that she'd like to have dinner sent up to her instead of eating in the hotel dining room and I hastily said I'd join her. I didn't want to sit at our table alone, feeling myself to be the cynosure of all eyes. Perhaps I wouldn't have been, really, but the word had got around that I was Josephine Lester, the only daughter of Donald Lester, multi-millionaire, and as a result I'd been paid a lot of attention. It had made me feel acutely uncomfortable. I was beginning to understand why José, hurt and bewildered by Mike's betrayal, had begun to suspect that people were only nice to her for a reason, that nobody ever wanted to be friends with her for her own sake.

The meal sent up to us was delicious. Our hotel was renowned for its *criollo* cooking...spiced but usually not too *picante* Peruvian dishes resulting from a blend of Indian and Spanish recipes...but José ate only a very little. I eyed her anxiously. Tomorrow we were due to fly to Cuzco, eleven thousand feet above sea level, and we'd need to feel fit to cope with the unaccustomed altitude.

"Oh, I'll be all right if I take things quietly," José said when I questioned her. "I'm as tough as old boots, really I am." Then, as I still looked dissatisfied, "Pass me my handbag, will you, please, Joby? I thought that you might like to read Isabel's letter."

We'd both had letters brought to us with our early morning fruit juice. Mine had been a long, newsy epistle from mother, crowded and crossed with items of interest and containing impassioned appeals from the twins for Peruvian stamps. José's had been from Isabel.

I don't know why, but I felt a certain amount of curiosity about the woman whom my cousin seemed to think stood a good chance of becoming the second Mrs. Donald Lester. I didn't really expect her letter to tell me very much about her personality, but oddly enough it did. I thought she sounded kind, sympathetic and genuinely fond of José as well as devoted to Uncle Donald. The latter, I decided, was in better hands than he deserved. Then I hastily reproached myself for ingratitude. He had never been anything but kind to me and it wasn't his fault if certain of his other qualities had always somewhat repelled me.

At any rate, according to Isabel he seemed to be making a good recovery from his injuries—thanks, she thought, to an iron constitution as well as to excellent nursing. Apparently he sent his love to José and myself, hoped we'd enjoy ourselves and suggested that instead of José returning to England at the end of our four weeks she should join him in Barbados.

"Will you?" I asked, looking up from the letter.

"I might. I like Barbados." José flung herself on her bed and watched me as I turned over the page. Curled up on the silken cover, she reminded me of a pretty cat.

It was the end of Isabel's letter that interested me.

> When you go to Cuzco you'll be staying at the same hotel as Ross, who is now in complete charge of the road building. I wonder what you will make of him and whether you will succeed where I've failed? To make friends with him, I mean. Until he came to Barbados last month I hadn't seen him for years, not since he was quite a small boy, so that really he was a complete stranger—rather a baffling stranger, too. I won't go into details, but he hasn't had an easy life and as a result he seems to have built some pretty severe barriers around himself. I think he finds it difficult to let

them down—at any rate he certainly kept me at arm's length!

I think I ought to warn you, darling, that he didn't really want to go with your father to Peru: it was I who persuaded him. Perhaps it was a mistake. Right from the start there was friction between them—I suppose you might almost have called it a clash of two very domineering personalities! I gather that the situation became highly explosive and that only Donald's accident prevented one goddam almighty row which would, I suppose, have ended only one way, in an open breach. I'm only telling you this so that you don't expect V.I.P. treatment simply because you're the boss's daughter! You won't get it, but be nice to him all the same, honey. He's all the family I've got!

Well, I thought, laying the letter down, that explained a lot! Why Ross Henderson had been in such an almighty hurry to send Uncle Donald back to Barbados...why he had sounded so brusque and unfriendly the night he had phoned from Cuzco. And yet....

José's voice broke into my thoughts. "I might just do that, you know."

"Sorry. I don't quite—?"

"Be nice to Isabel's Ross. The possibilities intrigue me."

I looked at her, startled. There was quite a lot I could have said, but I contented myself with just one flat statement. "I don't suppose we'll see much of him. After all, he's got a job to do, and a pretty exacting one at that, from all accounts."

"I've told you before that you lack a spirit of adventure. I see him as a challenge." José's face suddenly wore an expression I'd never seen before. Hard, almost calculating. It made me uneasy.

"José—" I began, and then I stopped and shrugged.

A proverb that my mother had been fond of quoting came suddenly into my mind. "Never trouble trouble until trouble troubles you." It was good advice... and I meant to follow it.

LUCKILY JOSÉ'S HEADACHE had disappeared by morning. We drove to the airport in a gray drizzle which, as we alighted from the taxi and walked to the airport building, settled on our faces and pearled our clothes.

The flight was fully booked. When we were finally allowed to take our seats José and I found ourselves sitting behind a slender, dark-haired girl with a sweet, demure face and a curly-headed little boy of about six who appeared to be her brother. We had noticed them before, not only because the girl was sitrikingly attractive but because she was obviously having difficulty in controlling the child. A lively, mischievous-looking little monkey with impudent black eyes and a lopsided grin, he had swarmed all over the airport building and now that he was actually seated in the plane he still wriggled about like a little eel.

"Marcos! Be still!" the girl scolded him, and I smiled ruefully. The twins had been a headache on long journeys, just like Marcos, and it had always been my job to keep them amused. This pretty girl... Marcos called her Consuelo... seemed to prefer to read a book. She must, I thought, have considerable powers of concentration, for even after we were airborne Marcos continued to bob up and down in his seat like a jack-in-the-box.

From the map, open on my lap, I realized that we were flying the shortest way to Cuzco, straight over the mountains. Shortly after takeoff we had sighted a range of brown-red peaks and off on the horizon the snowcapped Andes. Soon they were all around us, filling the sky with huge, forbidding peaks, and a steward came around to instruct us in the use of sterilized oxygen masks.

I don't think I have ever seen anything as beautiful as those soaring mountains. They were one vast solitude and yet, far down below, a few villages nestled in emerald green valleys, small lakes gleamed like aquamarines. Even José, judging by her expression, was awed and impressed.

We flew into a cloud and for a few moments the icebergs all around us were enveloped in swirling mist. I dragged my eyes from the window to look down at my map and as I did so I realized that Marcos was hanging over the back of his seat giving both me and my map the benefit of his earnest attention. Our eyes met. He smiled...a cautious, somewhat experimental little smile...and I smiled back.

Greatly encouraged, Marcos twinkled, leaned over still farther and prodded the map with one small brown finger. "That is where *I* live," he announced triumphantly. And, of course, in Spanish. Luckily, though my knowledge of the language wasn't all that extensive, I understood him.

"That is a good place to live," I said gravely, in slow, careful Spanish.

"Marcos!" the girl exclaimed, looking up from her book and promptly hauling him down from the back of the seat.

She then turned and addressed herself to me, speaking so fast and so volubly that I couldn't understand more than one word out of five.

I spread my hands helplessly and laughed. "Sorry. I'm English. Please, could you speak more slowly?"

"English?" The dark eyes opened wide, the lovely little face broke into a delighted smile. She was, I realized, much younger than I had at first thought, probably not more than fifteen or sixteen.

"I would not have guessed." Her eyes went from me to José, whose fairness seemed accentuated by the white woolly jacket she was wearing. "Your friend is English, too, yes?"

It was really more of a statement than a question, but José laughed and nodded. Like me, I think, she was charmed by Consuelo's shy friendliness.

By the time we reached Cuzco the four of us were talking as if we had known each other all our lives. I won Marcos's heart—and incidentally kept him still for an astonishing length of time—by showing him how to make paper boats, and Consuelo, speaking very good English, told us about her family and her home, a large *hacienda* in the mountains.

"Marcos and I have been staying with my grandparents in Lima," she explained in her soft, pretty voice. "Marcos's nurse came with us, but she was taken ill two days ago and she has not yet recovered sufficiently to make the journey back to Cuzco. We decided to return on our own partly because Marcos was homesick and partly because it is my elder brother's *fiesta* tomorrow and we did not want to miss it."

Consuelo's father, we learned, was dead, and the *hacienda* now belonged to the eldest son, Ramon de Noveli. "I would like you to meet him, and also my mother," she said wistfully. "Perhaps it would be possible for you to visit us? We would enjoy that very much, would we not, Marcos?"

José and I exchanged delighted glances and assured her with enthusiasm that we would enjoy it, too. Then Marcos, pressing his button nose against the window, announced importantly that we were coming in to land and we saw, spread out below us, a lush green valley of neatly squared fields against bare, red hills rising sharply to high mountains. From the air the cluster of red-tiled roofs and domed churches looked beautiful, rather like a fairy-tale village.

"Probably you will find breathing a little difficult at

first, because of the altitude, you know," Consuelo warned us. "Most visitors go straight to their hotel and spend their first several hours in bed!"

It was the last thing she said to us before we landed. In the inevitable crush we lost sight of her and of Marcos, but after we'd collected our luggage we had one last glimpse of them being whirled away from the airport in a huge black car. I thought I saw Marcos waving frantically in our direction from the back seat, but I couldn't be sure.

"Nice kids," José said casually. "I hope we meet up with them again."

I hoped so, too. Not only did I like them but Consuelo had informed us that the de Noveli family was very, very old. That being so, I was sure that they must be in possession of some fascinating links with the past!

Outside the handsome, modern airport it was like another world, part Indian, part Spanish, part yesterday, part today. Not that we were able to gain more than a quick impression, for our taxi whisked us through the narrow cobbled streets at a horrifying speed and deposited us at our hotel almost before we'd time to collect our thoughts. To my confusion we were received by the manager and what appeared to be his entire staff, all intent on giving us what amounted to a royal welcome.

"You ought to be used to it by now," José murmured wickedly in my ear as at last I managed to extricate myself from the reception committee. "Try and look slightly bored, as though you're only receiving your just dues!"

"Shut up!" I hissed. "If you don't I shall tell them that I'm the wrong Josephine."

"They wouldn't believe you. Not now," José said smugly, and I reflected wryly that that was probably true. For the first time in my life I rather regretted my black hair and eyes. Why couldn't I have looked more like my red-haired, green-eyed mother? Perhaps if I had borne less resemblance to her father, José wouldn't have had the crazy notion of pretending to be me!

Our rooms were full of flowers, gorgeous, exotic blooms that filled the air with a heavy, soporific fragrance. As José and I both felt exhausted, the first thing we did was to lie down on our beds and go to sleep. After all, hadn't Consuelo told us that that was what nearly all visitors did? In our case I didn't think we'd find it particularly difficult to adjust to living at an altitude of eleven thousand feet, but it seemed silly to take chances.

I had no more than a catnap, a doze of half an hour or so, but I awoke feeling refreshed and invigorated. Much to my relief I found that I was able to breathe quite easily. I looked at my watch and stretched lazily. Plenty of time to unpack and change before dinner. Afterwards, perhaps, we could stroll around the town.

It was then that I made the annoying discovery that one of my suitcases was missing. I knew that it had been brought into the hotel and I was sure, too, that it hadn't been taken into José's room by mistake. I stretched out my hand to press the bell by my bed, and then withdrew it. The habit of doing things for myself was too strong to be easily shaken off. José wouldn't have thought twice about summoning the entire staff to her room—but I wasn't José.

I ran a comb through my hair and splashed some cold water on to my face. Then I went downstairs to the hotel lobby. It was empty, save for three people behind the reception desk and a tall, broad-shouldered man leaning over it with his back toward me. As I approached he straightened and turned to look at me. If I hadn't been worried about my case I might have registered more than the simple fact that he was dark-haired and bronze-skinned, though at the same time unmistakably English-looking.

I smiled at one of the girls behind the reception desk, explained about my missing suitcase and received a prompt assurance that it would be traced and brought to my room immediately.

"Muchas gracias." I turned to go back upstairs, but found my path barred by the tall Englishman. He was, now I came to notice him properly, formidably large and formidably good-looking in a tough, rugged sort of way... blazing blue eyes in a lean brown face, straight black brows, a hard mouth and the indefinable air of a man who matters.

He said, not aggressively but not politely, "I thought I recognized your voice. I don't know where you acquired that Scottish lilt, Miss Lester, but it's as unmistakable as your resemblance to your father." His eyes regarded me slowly and appraisingly. "So you decided to come to Cuzco after all, did you? I must say I'm surprised."

I had stiffened with shock. I had recognized his voice, too—though I'd only heard it once before, at the end of a telephone line. I said stupidly, "You... must be Ross Henderson!" and could have kicked myself because I felt the color rushing into my cheeks. Of course, I thought bitterly, I might have known he'd look like this. Tough, arrogant and about as warm and lovable as the Rock of Gibraltar!

"Correct." His gaze still raked over me and though his face expressed nothing I suddenly felt as nervous and embarrassed as any schoolgirl. Then pride stiffened my spine. *Damn the man!* I thought furiously. *What the hell gives him the right to look at me like that, as if I was some kind of troublesome insect?*

I lifted my head and glared. In the tone of voice I had hitherto reserved for my pupils at their very worst I said, "When you've stopped staring at me, Mr. Henderson, perhaps you'll be good enough to stand aside and let me pass. I happen to want to go to my room!"

There was a flicker of—what? Mockery?...in the very blue eyes. "Spoken in the true Lester manner," he said sardonically, making not the slightest effort to move. "Why the hurry? Surely you're going to allow me the opportunity of asking after your father's health?"

He's not my father! I longed to fling the words at him, if only for the pleasure of seeing his reaction to being proved wrong. Somehow or other I choked them back. Conscious that everyone behind the reception desk had stopped work in order to listen to our exchange, I said shortly, "He's better."

"I felt sure he must be. Otherwise, of course, you'd hardly be here, would you?"

This time the sarcasm was apparent. I was still trying to think of a suitable retort when he added, with an abrupt change of tone and expression, "It might have been better if you'd gone to Barbados anyway. In fact, after what I've just found out I wish to God you had."

I stared at him openmouthed, uncertain for a moment what he meant. After reading Isabel's letter I hadn't expected to be welcomed with open arms, but there were limits!

"*You wish*—? Look, Mr. Henderson—"

He interrupted me. "I can see from your outraged expression that that could have been better phrased. Perhaps I ought to explain, but this is scarcely the ideal place. Will you and...your cousin, isn't it—have dinner with me?" Perhaps he anticipated my refusal, for he added quickly, "Don't worry, even though we *are* staying in the same hotel I won't make a habit of inflicting my presence on you! It's just that for my own peace of mind there are one or two things that I'd better make clear. Straightaway."

He spoke with his former brusqueness, but with something else underlying it. I didn't know what it was, until looking at him I suddenly noticed the strain lines from nostrils to mouth and the shadow around his eyes. The gray look of worry.

I restrained what was surely a perfectly natural impulse to ask him what was the matter. As he'd pointed out, the hotel lobby was hardly an ideal place in which to hold a conversation. Three pairs of ears were obviously straining to catch every word we said, three pairs of eyes were unashamedly watching our every movement.

I heard myself saying, albeit reluctantly, "All right," and Ross Henderson looked at his watch. It was nothing like the beautiful gold watch with the woven gold band that Uncle Donald always wore, but expensive or not I wouldn't have minded betting that it kept perfect time. Belonging to whom it did, it would have to.

"I'll meet you in—let's see, twenty minutes' time—in the cocktail lounge. All right?"

Quite obviously it was merely a rhetorical question. The very last thing I was expected to do was to argue or disagree. Ross Henderson, I thought grimly, was used to giving orders and to having those orders obeyed. No wonder he and Uncle Donald—who also expected people to start jumping whenever he felt like cracking a whip—had fallen out!

I drew a deep breath, conscious that I was being eyed quizzically. I said coolly, "Well, we'll try to make it by then. But though perhaps you're scarcely aware of the difference, we *are* women, and not navvies. That being so, it does take us just a little longer to get ready!"

I swept past him toward the staircase as I spoke. I really thought it was quite a dignified exit, but halfway up the stairs I risked spoiling it by stopping and looking back. Subconsciously I suppose I hoped that Ross Henderson would be staring blankly after me, but no such thing. He had already returned to the reception desk, so that all I saw was his unyielding back. I had the distinct feeling that I had already been forgotten.

The fact that the knowledge annoyed me so much that I slammed my bedroom door with quite unnecessary violence should have warned me. It didn't. I merely said something rude about Ross Henderson under my breath, noted with satisfaction that my missing suitcase had miraculously reappeared and charged into José's bedroom to tell her that she'd got exactly twenty minutes to get bathed, changed and beautified.

And why.

CHAPTER FOUR

IN THE END it was a lot more than twenty minutes later when we joined Ross Henderson in the cocktail lounge, but that was as much José's fault as mine. She reacted to the news that we were dining with him with so much enthusiasm that I was obliged to repeat practically every single word that had passed between us.

"And there I was sleeping while you were chatting up the one man I've heard of who sounds remotely interesting! Honestly, Joby, you have all the luck!" she mourned.

"I'd hardly call it luck," I said crisply. "Quite frankly, the only reason I agreed to accept his invitation was because I was curious. He really did look worried. And though it sounds crazy I have a feeling that it's... well, something to do with us. Being here, I mean."

José stared. "Oh, but how could it be? Don't be a dope, Joby!"

"I said it sounded crazy. But... oh, I don't know! Anyway, he's said he'll explain."

José began brushing her long golden hair. "What's he like? Dark? Fair? Good-looking? Isabel said he was, but she's probably prejudiced."

Ross Henderson's dark, mocking face swam, unbidden, into my mind. I said reluctantly, "Definitely good-looking, though I can't say that he's the type that appeals to me."

"Type?"

I opened my suitcase and pulled out an armful of

dresses. What should I wear tonight? Something sleek and simple to lend me an air of pseudosophistication? It was probably what Ross Henderson would expect.

Aloud I said, "Rough... tough... he-man, or whatever you like to call it. The sort who'd look marvelous in a bearskin, swinging a club."

José gave a sudden gurgle of laughter. "Darling, you are funny! Evidently your taste in men hasn't altered much. Do you remember when you were about ten and you had that fearful crush on Rupert Brooke? You had his photograph beside your bed and his poems hidden beneath your pillow!"

"That was a long time ago, but I still prefer brains to brawn. In the present instance it's probably just as well. Maybe it's only because he thinks I'm your father's daughter, but I have a feeling that Mr. Ross Henderson doesn't care for me at all!"

"In other words, the field is clear for me?"

"It is, but unless you want to start off on the wrong foot I advise you to hurry up. Believe me, the gentleman won't take at all kindly to being kept waiting!"

José giggled, "If we're late I'll blame it on to you."

"Do." I pulled a gold-colored dress over my head and was struggling with the zipper when I happened to catch sight of José's face.

"José! What's the matter?"

"I... I was thinking of Mike. I always kept him waiting, or nearly always, but he never seemed to mind, he used to make a joke of it." She paused, then said almost desperately, "Joby, I *am* trying, I'm trying as hard as I possibly can, but do you think I'll *ever* be able to forget him?"

I went to her swiftly. "Oh, José, of course you will! It's just a matter of time!"

"That's what I keep telling myself. But I'm sure the only way I'll forget him is to fall in love with somebody else, and up to now I've been too frightened to think of doing that, in case I happened to pick another fortune hunter!" José said dismally.

I looked at her. "Well, presumably the whole idea of the little charade that you and I are indulging in is to convince the world in general, and attractive specimens of the opposite sex in particular, that all you have to commend you is your beauty and charm! So far, you seem to have done quite well—at any rate, I haven't noticed anyone exactly cold-shouldering you!"

José gave a reluctant little laugh. "No. Everyone's been terribly nice and kind."

"Well, with that thought to console you, come and practice your wiles on Ross Henderson! Not, mind you, that I think it will do you much good. I should imagine he's a hard nut to crack—"

"No, but I can try. That's what I made up my mind to do, back in Lima," José told me.

"I rather thought you had." I drew a long breath. "Well, I wish you luck, honey. Personally I'd as soon try to attract a bear or a gorilla, but—"

"I like he-men. Mike was tough and chunky, too." José made an obvious effort to speak lightly, then looked at me and smiled. "We must find someone for you. A long-haired intellectual."

"Thanks, but I didn't come to Peru with the intention of looking for romance—at least, not the kind of romance *you* mean! José, *do* hurry up! It's not that I'm worried about keeping Ross Henderson waiting, but I'm absolutely starving!"

I think she did hurry then—or as much as José is ever capable of hurrying—but as I've already said, it took us a lot longer that twenty minutes to join Ross Henderson. I thought he'd be champing at the bit, but if he was annoyed he certainly didn't show it.

Sitting alone in a corner, the light of a subdued wall

lamp falling upon him from behind, he saw us immediately we came through the big swing doors and strode forward to meet us. Beside me, I heard José catch her breath.

"Darling, how could you?" she murmured reproachfully. "It would have to be a Savile Row bearskin *at least*!"

I knew just what she meant. When I'd met him before he'd been wearing faded khaki slacks and a chunky sweater. He'd looked good in those, but in a faultlessly cut suit and an immaculate cream silk shirt he was devastating. The odd thing was that he seemed genuinely unaware of the fact. It was rather a pity, I thought, that I couldn't add "narcissism" to the formidable list of character defects I'd already stacked up against him!

I realized that José was looking at me expectantly. I pulled myself together and made the necessary introductions. Ross Henderson shook hands politely, assured us that we hadn't kept him waiting and then asked us what we would like to drink.

"Pisco sour, please." José and I spoke in unison. We had both developed a liking for the national grape brandy, white in color, which as a sour, comes iced with beaten egg white and lemon.

Ross Henderson gave the order and I watched the barman rush to fulfil it. Then I looked at José. As far as I was concerned the next move was up to her.

"You know, I'm afraid we *are* a bit late. I'm sorry." She smiled at him over the rim of her glass and, surprisingly, his lips twitched.

"Don't worry. I didn't expect you to be here any earlier. I estimated the time I thought it would take you to get ready, then halved it. I hoped it might act as an incentive, and obviously it has."

He must have intercepted my venomous glance, for he added with a touch of mockery, "For your information, Miss Lester, I *am* aware of the difference between women and navvies. I am also appreciative of it—sometimes."

As he spoke I thought his eyes lingered admiringly on José, who was wearing a low-cut, haze-blue dress which revealed quite a lot of her shapely figure. Whatever his opinion of petite brunettes, I thought sourly, it was perfectly obvious that he had something of a *penchant* for blue-eyed blondes!

José spoke quickly. "You know, we're both Miss Lester! We were both christened Josephine, too. It's awfully confusing. Couldn't we be Joby and José?"

"Of course, I think you already know my Christian name." He smiled at her. "I knew you were cousins, but I didn't realize that you were both called Josephine. You must be Joby, I suppose?"

There was a fractional pause. The very first hurdle, I thought grimly. Ten to one Ross had heard the name "José" mentioned a hundred times, either by his cousin or by Donald Lester.

"No. I'm José."

Ross looked slightly taken aback, as well he might. "Oh? But I thought—"

"We both like to be called José." My cousin's face was the picture of innocence. "We tossed for it, and I won. So she—" nodding in my direction "—had to be content with the nearest thing—Joby."

I made a mental note to ask José where she had learned to tell fibs so convincingly. It was a talent I had never hitherto suspected.

Ross's face cleared. "Oh, I see." He looked from her to me. "You're totally unalike. I suppose in view of the name business that's just as well."

He raised his glass to his lips and José shot me a swift look. *Don't leave it all to me!* her eyes said.

This is your pigeon, I signaled back. In actual fact I was feeling distinctly dismayed. How much had Ross heard about the real José? Would we really be able to get through the evening without his tumbling to the truth? Only, I thought, if we both pretended, involved ourselves in a tissue of lies....

"Would you like another drink or shall we go in to dinner?" Ross put his glass down and looked at us questioningly.

We both plumped for dinner. Ross led the way into a dining room which was very much larger and grander than I had expected and a bowing, smiling waiter escorted us to a table set in an alcove, lit softly by wall lights. I had a quick impression of white damask and cut glass and gleaming silver and a huge spray of crimson flowers, then I was comfortably settled in a velvet-upholstered chair and the waiter was there.

I don't remember much about the food we ate that evening, except that it was beautifully cooked and attractively served. I was hungry, but I didn't really enjoy it. The trouble was that I felt I had to be on my guard all the time. It would be so desperately easy to slip up... to reveal my real identity by a casual reference to someone or something. Like mother, or St. Olave's.

Ross, I quickly discovered, knew only a little about me—or rather, the girl I was supposed to be. It seemed to be enough to make him regard me with a jaundiced eye. Somehow or another he managed to convey the impression that he had absolutely no use for social butterflies who were content to let their fathers subsidize their pleasures and featherbed their lives. I could tell, just by his general attitude, that he thought I was a pretty useless specimen.

To José, however, he was charming and I'm sure she probably made a terrific impression. If I was having difficulty in adopting her identity, she was certainly having none at all in adopting mine. With a mischievous glance in my direction, which Ross luckily didn't see, she calmly appropriated *my* B.A., recounted some of *my* experiences at college, and claimed that she was holding down *my* job!

"It makes a pleasant change to find a girl who is as intelligent as she is beautiful." Ross smiled at her across the table, his eyes crinkling at the corners. "So you teach history, do you? No wonder you wanted to come with Joby to Peru!"

José's long, gold-tipped lashes fluttered. "Oh yes! Machu Picchu... Atahuallpa...."

I choked on a morsel of bread. Careful, dear coz, I thought. You conjured those names out of thin air and you obviously don't know that Atahuallpa is a person and not a place!

Ross refilled our glasses with sparkling, claret-colored wine. "Did you visit Pachamacamac while you were in Lima?" he asked, and I almost choked again.

"I'm afraid not." José looked and sounded wistful. "Joby doesn't much care for old ruins, do you, Joby? We went shopping instead."

"I see." That was all that Ross said, but his tone spoke volumes.

It was time, I thought grimly, for my cousin José to reap just a little of what she had been so busily sowing. I leaned across the table.

"Oh, but we're both absolutely *dying* to visit Machu Picchu! It sounds fascinating! José's told me all about it."

I met José's eyes. They held an appreciative gleam as I added, "We'll have to go there pretty soon, won't we, darling?"

Ross's lower lip curled sarcastically. "I should think about that rather carefully if I were you. It's a pretty tough trip and the hotel's a bit low on creature comforts. Not the sort of thing I'm sure you're used to."

It wasn't so much what he said as the way he said it, and the look he gave me, that really nettled me. Up until that moment I had been an unwilling partner in José's game of pretense, fulfilling my role with a reluctance that almost amounted to distaste. But not anymore. I suddenly decided that since Ross obviously thought of me as a spoilt little rich girl who preferred luxury to anything else I'd jolly well play the part to the best of my ability. And blow the consequences!

I was abominable—I admit that. I hadn't realized how easy it would be to give the impression that I was a pampered little doll who cared for nothing save her own pleasure. I saw José staring at me in wide-eyed consternation, but it wasn't her reaction that I was worried about. It was Ross's. And the more disapproving he looked, the more reckless I became!

On the whole he behaved extremely well. He must have longed to slap me down, but he didn't. It wasn't until we had almost reached the end of our meal that he very effectively put a stop to my posturing. Leaning back in his chair he said very quietly, "Do you mind if we talk seriously for a moment? I told you, Joby, that I had a reason for asking you and José to have dinner with me tonight. I'd like, now, to explain what I meant."

His face, suddenly shadowed, looked somber and purposeful. Gone was the charming host: in his place was the man in command.

"I annoyed you, Joby, by telling you that I wished you hadn't come to Cuzco. I meant nothing personal. I still wish you hadn't." He drew a short breath. "To put it bluntly, after what I learned this afternoon I... well, I'm not too sure that I can guarantee your safety."

The wine in our glasses glowed ruby red, spilling puddles of ruddy light on to the white tablecloth. In the silence that followed Ross's words José looked at me and I looked at her. I don't think either of us was entirely sure that we'd heard properly. Ross waited. After a moment or two I said uncertainly, "I... I don't think I know what you mean. What did you find out this afternoon? And how on earth does it affect our safety?"

Ross was staring down at the tablecloth, making patterns on it with the handle of his knife. He said somberly, "I realize it sounds absurd... melodramatic. I'm sorry. Believe me, if I could laugh it off I'd be only too glad to do so." He lit a cigarette and over the flame his eyes were heavy with worry and fatigue. "You both know what we're trying to do here in Peru, don't you? Your father must have told you, Joby, about the road that's being constructed. It's to connect Cuzco with a new copper mine that's been discovered in the *sierra* and it's to lead over some pretty rough terrain."

I nodded. "Yes, I know about that."

"Well, to cut quite a long story short, ever since work started on the road there's been vociferous opposition to the route that we're planning to take. The Indians claim that it will mean the desecration of a valley that they're particularly keen about. It's one of the most desolate spots on God's earth, but for some reason or other they've always regarded it as a sacred place. It's called the Valley of Skulls."

Memory stirred. I said, "A valley... didn't Mrs. Stevenson mention a valley, José?"

José nodded and Ross's face showed his surprise. "Mrs. Stevenson?"

"Someone we met in Lima. She... she said she knew you. And my father."

"Oh, I remember. A very garrulous lady." Ross stubbed out his cigarette. "Well, the long and the short of it all is that the Indians feel strongly enough about the matter to do a lot more than merely make representations to the company. They've also thought up some ingenious ways of sticking a spanner in the works. Including, I'm sorry to say, attempted murder. And now blackmail."

All around us other diners were laughing and talking. There was the chink of silver and glass, the sound of background music. Into the gay, relaxed atmosphere Ross's word fell like a heavy stone.

"*Murder?* Blackmail?" José's eyes were wide and disbelieving.

"There was a landslide, early on, which was meant to look like an accident but almost certainly wasn't. Fourteen men were injured, some very badly. It was a miracle that no one was killed." Ross paused and looked at me. "And then there was your father's accident the other day, only that wasn't an accident either. There is no doubt whatsoever about that. I sent the car he was driving to be examined by an expert and I received his report only this afternoon. The brakes had been tampered with. That's why they failed."

"You...you mean someone wanted to...to *kill* my...uncle?" Even at that moment, in the midst of her shock and disbelief, José remembered her role.

"I'm afraid so."

I brushed my hand across my eyes. Attempted murder. It was the kind of thing, I thought desperately, that in England one read about in the daily newspapers. There was never any chance of its intruding into one's own personal life. Only this wasn't England. This was Peru, the land where the blood of the formidable Huancas still flowed in the veins of modern peasants and the speech of the Incas still lingered on their lips!

I said, trying hard to sound calm and dispassionate, "Obviously you have good grounds for believing that an attempt was made on my father's life. But...but what did you mean when you said that you weren't sure that you could guarantee our safety? What have we got to do with it? Why should anyone want to harm us?"

Ross's lips twisted. He put his hand into his breast pocket and pulled out a piece of very grubby paper, which he unfolded and laid on the table. The words scrawled upon it were written with a dark pencil and the letters were straggling and ill-formed.

"Do you understand Spanish?"

I shook my head. "Only a word here and there."

"Then I'll translate. 'Señor Lester was lucky. He escaped with a few broken bones. The next one might not be so lucky. You, Señor Henderson? or perhaps one of the young English ladies. You have been warned. Leave the Valley of Skulls alone.'"

There was a moment's silence after Ross had finished speaking.

Then I said incredulously, "Who wrote that? And where did you find it?"

"It was delivered to me this afternoon. I haven't the faintest idea who wrote it. I had thought that the vast majority of the Indians were completely illiterate. They haven't much chance of a formal education, poor devils."

"You've notified the police, of course?"

Ross gave me a withering look. José said slowly, "But...but I don't understand! That note is...is a definite threat. How are you supposed to react?"

Ross sighed. "I would have thought that that was obvious. The main objective of whoever is behind all this is to get the road rerouted, missing out the Valley of Skulls. Since representations have failed, they've resorted to more...drastic measures." He paused, and his brows drew together in a heavy frown. "There have been other incidents, besides the landslide and your father's alleged accident. Morale among the men isn't good. In fact, it's as much as I can do to keep it from disintegrating altogether. As far as they're concerned, what happened to Donald Lester was very nearly the last straw. What do you think would be the result if they learned of a similar 'accident' to his daugher or his niece?"

"Is it... well, generally known that we've arrived in Cuzco?" I asked.

"Of course. Hence this latest threat."

I saw José run her tongue around her lips. "You... you don't really think we're in any sort of danger, do you?"

"I don't know what to think, but in view of what has already happened I'd much rather not take chances," Ross answered her brusquely. "As I've already said, it's a thousand pities that you're here at all. If I had my way, I'd put you both on the first plane back to Lima. I suppose—?" He looked at us interrogatively.

We both knew what he meant. I waited to take my cue from José. Whatever deception we were practicing, she was still the one who had the right to call the tune.

"No!" she said firmly. "We're staying!"

I echoed her words and Ross frowned. At me, not at José. Then he shrugged. "I knew, really, that you'd say that."

I was silent. I was glad that José had answered as she had. Whether or not any danger existed, I simply couldn't bear the thought of leaving Cuzco without seeing the lonely grandeur of Machu Picchu... the palaces of the Incas... the ancient fortress of Sacsuhuaman!

And José? Her reasons for wanting to stay, I thought wryly, were possibly more complex. Her blue eyes were sparkling with—what? Excitement? Anticipation? I couldn't tell. She probably thought the whole thing was rather a thrill, something with which to regale her friends.

She said gaily, "Oh, we're not afraid! We can look after ourselves, can't we, Joby?"

"Famous last words." Ross spoke dryly and stubbed

out his cigarette. "Well, if you're staying there are two things I'm afraid I must absolutely insist on. One, I don't want either of you to come anywhere near the road-works. Two, I want you to keep me informed of all your movements—in advance. Oh, don't worry..." as I made an instinctive gesture of protest "...I'm not going to act as a sort of policeman, or even a nursemaid, how-ever much you may need one. My hands are quite full enough already. It's simply that it will make things just that bit easier if I know where you are, and what you're doing."

"It's a deal." José smiled at him across the table and the stern lines of his face momentarily relaxed.

"Thanks." He didn't even look in my direction. Not for the first time that evening I felt as though he had deliberately shut me out.

Even though he did think I was the spoiled and pampered daughter of a man he didn't much care about I didn't see why I should go on standing for that sort of treatment. Besides, I had something I badly wanted to say. I leaned across the table, practically forcing him to give me his reluctant attention.

"Is it absolutely impossible to do what the Indians want? I mean... *can't* you re-route the road, since the wretched valley obviously means so much to them?"

I thought I detected a flicker, certainly no more than that, of surprise in his expression.

"It isn't impossible, no. Originally, in fact, the road wasn't planned to go anywhere near the valley. It was only later that the route was changed to save the expense of buying good arable land. Nothing at all grows in the Valley of Skulls, so it was bought comparatively cheap-ly."

"But surely—"

Ross's eyes were coldly steady. "You can't give in to murderers and blackmailers, however much you may secretly sympathize with their cause. You ought to know that. In point of fact, your father was pressed very hard to reconsider the alternative route long before the real trouble started. Naturally, however, he held firm."

"Naturally?"

His broad shoulders lifted in the slightest of contemptuous shrugs. "Your father is a good businessman. He considers costs before everything else. What are the outraged feelings of a few thousand illiterate Indians compared with the unnecessary expenditure of a few thousand pounds?"

José put her hand to her mouth and stifled a small gasp. We both looked at her and she said hurriedly, "I...I've forgotten my handkerchief. Please excuse me for a moment!"

She jumped up and I saw Ross's eyes follow her across the room. I daren't return to the subject of Uncle Donald. Instead I said abruptly, "You say you're worried about what might happen to us, but surely you're in much worse danger? After all, you're the person in sole charge of the road works now that...now that my father is in Barbados."

"Leave me to worry about my own skin, will you?" Ross paused, then added sardonically, "I really wouldn't have thought that that advice was necessary."

I flushed and bit my lip. "I'm naturally concerned—"

Ross's lips had thinned. "You are? Then in that case why don't you make sure that your cousin leaves Cuzco before any harm can possibly befall her? Obviously she can't leave if you want to stay—"

I gasped, "That isn't true!" I saw Ross's brows lift quizzically and added lamely, "We...we both want to stay. José said she did."

"Yes, but I'm afraid that poor relations have a habit of saying and doing what they think their benefactors want them to say and do. I'm quite sure you don't really need me to remind you of that." Ross leaned back in his chair, his eyes hard and unsmiling. "You know, I can't help admiring your cousin. She's quite a girl. The odds are stacked against her, but she still refuses to be completely overshadowed by you. That, I imagine, takes some doing."

In the circumstances that was so funny that despite my indignation I couldn't help smiling. José was amused, too, when later in the privacy of my bedroom I repeated the gist of Ross's remarks.

"Well, I'm glad I seem to have made a favorable impression!" she said, laughing. "I hoped I had."

I raised my brows. "Even though you've made it under false pretenses?"

José dived at me. "Darling, don't go all priggish and schoolteacherish on me! It's only a bit of fun!"

"Fun for you, perhaps, but not for me," I retorted. "I'm not sure that I like being so heartily disapproved of. It... it's deflating!"

"Look on it as a new and interesting experience! And honestly, Joby, you *were* awful! If I thought you'd really been trying to act like me I'd commit suicide! All that piffle you talked—"

I grinned a trifle shamefacedly. "I know. But he made me so mad! He'd obviously made up his mind what I—you—were like, and—José, what did you think of him?"

"As Isabel said, he's a dish." José turned away. Over her shoulder she added flippantly, "At any rate I'm not averse to a little mild flirtation!"

"As long as it doesn't turn into the real thing—"

"Don't worry, I'm not ready to go through all that again. Not yet."

Jose's expression had become suddenly bleak and I hastily changed the subject. "José, you really *do* want to stay, don't you? In spite of everything?"

José laughed. "My dear, the possibility of being assassinated has added a definite spice to my life! Not, on reflection, that I'm inclined to take that grubby little piece of paper very seriously. I think it's probably just a bluff and Ross is flapping unnecessarily. I'm not in the least worried. Are you?"

I hesitated. I had an uncomfortable conviction that men like Ross Henderson weren't prone to flapping unnecessarily. And Uncle Donald's car *had* been tampered with...there was definite proof of that. I said slowly, "No. No, I'm not exactly worried. But I think perhaps we'd better watch our step a bit, José. Stick together. that sort of thing."

"Okay. Night-night, grandma." José disappeared into her own room. It wasn't until a few moments later that I remembered what I'd meant to give her.

I stuck my head around her door. "Here! Catch!"

I sent a book spinning through the air and José caught it protestingly. "I've already got something to read! What is it?"

"Prescott's *Conquest of Peru.* I thought you'd better read it before Ross Henderson has a chance to discover that for a history teacher there are some appalling gaps in your knowledge!" I said unkindly.

I heard José laughing as I closed the door behind me. Tomorrow, I thought, I must remember to tell her about Atahuallpa. But not in front of Ross Henderson!

CHAPTER FIVE

I DON'T KNOW whether José found it as difficult to fall asleep as I did. She said, when I asked her the next day, that she'd had no trouble at all, but I'm not sure she was speaking the truth.

I myself tossed and turned until after two in the morning watching the moon, silver and solitary, outside the open curtains. In the distance, very faintly, I could hear the sound of late-night revelers. At last I dozed fitfully, but I was wide awake at six and I'd washed and slipped into slacks and a thick, turtleneck sweater by ten past. I wrote a long letter to mother and then peeped into José's bedroom to see if she was awake. All I could see was a web of golden hair on her pillow, so I went downstairs by myself.

It was a cold, crisp morning and I was glad of my warm clothes. I smiled and said *"Buenos dias"* to a couple of people I met on the stairs, tried not to think how welcome a cup of hot coffee would be, and wandered through the hotel lobby into a small, cobbled courtyard I had noticed the previous evening. It was empty, save for a large tortoiseshell cat which was sitting on a step and washing its face with immaculate white paws. I like cats, so I sat down beside it and tickled its ears. It looked at me with big, yellow eyes, then rubbed its head on my sleeve.

I must have been there several minutes, stroking the cat's soft fur and crooning to it in cat language, when a shadow fell across me. I looked up and saw Ross standing a few feet away. He must have approached very quietly because I hadn't heard a thing. "Good morning," Ross said coolly, and stretched out his own hand to the cat. It got up, yawned, turned its back on us both and stalked away.

"Your familiar, I suppose?" Ross asked with mock gravity.

"My...what?" I must have been less wide awake than I thought, for I stared blankly.

"Your demon in disguise. I thought last night that you looked rather like an enchantress from some medieval romance. Melusine, perhaps, or the witch, Vivien." Ross stuck his hands in his pockets and I saw the mockery at the back of his eyes as I flushed. "Even in slacks and a jersey you have a somewhat...fey look."

I was well aware of the fact that his remarks were not intended to be complimentary. That didn't worry me. What *did* surprise me was that a man like him should be able to refer so casually not only to the enchantress of the Arthurian romances but also to one of the most famous of the French *fees*!

He didn't give me a chance to answer, which was probably just as well since I couldn't think of any really devastating riposte. Glancing at his watch he said, with an abrupt change of subject, "You're up early. Couldn't you sleep?"

"Not very well."

"Bad luck. What does a millionaire's daughter do when she can't sleep? Count moneybags instead of sheep?"

The blood tingled in my cheeks. I said furiously, "You really are—"

"The absolute end?" Ross studied me with a queer sort of detached amusement, tinged by mockery. "I'm sorry. My question really was prompted by genuine curiosity."

He asked for it. Again. I smiled brilliantly. "You must

forgive me if I don't attempt to satisfy it. I'm really not accustomed to discussing my personal habits with my father's employees!"

He gave a short laugh. "Strictly speaking, I'm not one of your father's employees. Nothing would ever induce me to take a permanent job with the Lester International Construction Company. I prefer to be able to call my soul my own."

His attitude had made me so angry that I forgot that in normal circumstances I'd have applauded every word he said. "What don't you like about my father?" I flung at him. "Apart, of course, from the fact that he's been a darn sight more successful than you're ever likely to be?"

It was a cheap little gibe and I wasn't surprised that Ross gave me a chilled look. "I don't like his methods, his philosophy or his personality. Come to that, I don't much like his daughter. You really have been spoiled rotten, haven't you? I'd been told that you had but—"

"*Told?* Who told you that?"

He didn't answer that. A dark, compact little man with a swarthy complexion and Mongolian features had come hurrying up to us and proceeded to address Ross in a flow of rapid Spanish. Ross listened, nodded, then turned to me.

"I have to go," he said curtly. "First of all, though, you'd better tell me what you're planning to do today. Explore the town?"

Over the stone wall surrounding the courtyard I glimpsed the soaring church towers of Cuzco, like unlighted torches in a pale saffron sky. I said, flicking back my hair, "Correct. What do we look out for—booby traps, land mines, masked criminals or highwaymen?"

I wouldn't have spoken with such bitter sarcasm if I hadn't been absolutely seething. That remark of his about being "spoiled rotten" had really flicked me on the raw. It made no difference that I wasn't José. In bed the previous night I'd tried to tell myself that it wasn't actually me he disliked, just the pampered little rich girl he thought me to be, but now I wasn't so sure. The way we struck sparks off each other whenever we came into contact the chances were that we'd be at loggerheads even if he knew my real identity. We were—what was the time-honored word? Incompatible.

I saw his lips tighten. "You haven't taken what I told you last night very seriously, have you?"

Dear sweet heaven! Hadn't I? Hadn't I lain awake last night thinking over every single thing he'd said? I met his eyes defiantly.

"Why should I? I don't see why a vague threat of danger—and on your own admission it's no more than that—should ruin our entire holiday! We've come to Peru to enjoy ourselves, and that, I assure you, is precisely what we're going to do!"

I heard my own voice with a kind of disbelieving horror. Ross did something to me that I couldn't understand. He made me act completely out of character, not like me but like the person he seemed to believe I was.

There was a moment's silence. A tiny whirlwind twisted a column of dust into a spiral up and down the cobbles. A *mestiza* woman wearing a brilliantly colored skirt and a peculiar white hat passed us carrying a pile of laundry. Then Ross shrugged and turned away. He followed the little Peruvian into the hotel, walking lightly for such a big man.

I set my teeth and made up the tail of the procession. My one thought was to wake José and tell her what Ross had said, but I thought better of it long before I reached her room.

"You really have been spoiled rotten... I'd been told that you had...." That was what Ross had said yet how could I repeat those telltale words to José? Obviously somebody had painted an unflattering portrait of Donald Lester's only daugher...and the obvious culprit, it seemed to me, was Ross's cousin, Isabel, whom José liked and trusted. I clenched my hands. She didn't deserve another letdown! Not after what Michael Frenton had done to her!

I tapped at her bedroom door, but there was no answer. I turned the handle very softly and went in. José was still asleep, her long lashes fanning her June-rose cheeks. As I bent over her, I caught sight of my reflection in a mirror. Gipsy dark, my eyes enormous in a face that was a glimmer of ivory. The witch, Vivien....

Hastily I averted my eyes and stared down at my sleeping cousin. If Ross knew the truth about us, would he still think that José had been "spoiled rotten"? I doubted it. As far as he was concerned, she was the gold, I was the dross. Well, I didn't care, did I? What did it matter what he thought?

I sighed and bent to pick up José's blue dress from the floor. I was hanging it in her wardrobe when she stirred and blinked sleepily.

"Hello! What are you doing dressed? Is it time to get up already?"

"More than time. I've been awake for ages."

Jose sat up in bed. "Wretch! You haven't been exploring without me, have you?" Her voice was indignant.

I decided, at that moment, to say nothing at all about my encounter with Ross. "Of course not. Hurry up and get showered! What are you going to wear—this red pantsuit? You'll need something fairly warm."

"What? Oh yes, I suppose that will do." José slid out of bed, rubbing her knuckles childishly in her eyes. With her tousled hair and in her yellow pajamas she looked younger and more vulnerable than she usually did.

"You don't think it will startle the natives too much, do you? It *is* a bit bright."

I thought of the viridian greens, turquoise blues, shocking pinks and electric scarlets I had glimpsed briefly on our way from the railway station to our hotel and laughed and shook my head. "When in Rome...." I quoted, and laughed again at José's puzzled expression.

She realized what I meant as soon as we left the hotel. Mingling with Cuzco's colorful mixture of people—barefooted Indians in brilliant ponchos and peculiar hats and well-dressed Peruvians—we merely became part of a rainbow scene, vibrant and stirring. I forgot the grayness of the sky and the fine cloudy mist which blanketed the whole city. I even forgot—at least for a little while—how much I disliked Ross Henderson and how angry he had made me.

Many of the houses we saw were nearly as colorful as the people—a gay motley of blue and coral and yellow and green, with wooden balconies of every known size and description. Fascinated, José and I wandered through a maze of narrow, cobbled streets that rose and fell, twisted and turned and led us to Spanish churches and dusty curio shops full of brooches and bracelets of quaint design and fans of old lace and painted parchment.

Though Spanish architecture predominated, everywhere we saw evidence of the engineering skills of the long-dead Incas. Something caught painfully at my throat as I laid my hand on a huge black Inca stone which was part of the foundation of a seventeenth-century house with elegant miradors and airy Moorish arches. It was rough and cold against my fingers and I shivered involuntarily. It was easy, here in Cuzco, to resurrect the past...to people the streets with ghosts from a bygone age. Every shadow, every doorway, seemed to hold a hint of mystery, as though something of the fierce and tragic history of "the Lords of the Sun" still inhered in the megalithic foundations upon which the Spanish conquerors had built.

I don't know when it was that I became convinced that as we wove our way through the narrow streets we were being followed. At first I dismissed the idea as a ridiculous fancy, the inevitable result of Ross's warnings coupled with Cuzco's strange atmosphere but I couldn't shake off a feeling of disquiet. I found myself listening for the sound of footsteps behind us... stopping to look surreptitiously over my shoulder. I never saw anyone who was acting in the least suspiciously, but my uneasiness persised and grew. I looked at José, wondering if by any chance she shared my apprehension, but her expression was untroubled. I must have an over-active imagination, I told myself ruefully, and tried adjuring myself to use my common sense.

I wasn't particularly successful, but at least José noticed nothing amiss. I was rather amused to discover that for once she seemed genuinely interested in the kind of thing that in Lima had bored her stiff. She seemed as eager as I was to catch a glimpse of the awesome ruins of Sacsuhuaman, lying on the northern outskirts of the city, and it was she, not I, who suggested a visit to Cuzco's Archaeological Museum. Of course, I thought wryly, following her though a big stone doorway, it was probably all part of the act. Next time she saw Ross Henderson she'd be able to enthuse about what she had seen!

José was gazing at some beautiful pre-Inca embroidered tapestries in golds, greens, silvers and pinks against deep blue and I was admiring a collection of wooden Inca ceremonial vases, the figures painted in Chinese red and yellow against black, when I suddenly became quite sure that I was being watched. It was like an extra sense... the consciousness of imminent danger.

I *couldn't* be wrong. Not this time! I turned like a flash. For a moment or two I stood rigid, my eyes sweeping round the hall, then slowly I relaxed. José and I were alone, save for two men who were bending over a case containing some antique wooden scepters banded with engraved silver.

I was frightened...and I didn't know why. Suddenly I found myself longing for the densely populated Plaza de Armas, where we would see new cars and modern buses and be surrounded by pigtailed, apple-checked children eager to sell us attractive, homemade things like alpaca rugs, llama slippers, funny-face ski masks and brightly colored bags. I'd had enough, for one day, of shadows and ghosts and distorted imaginings: I wanted something ordinary and homely and reassuring, like an Elizabeth Arden salon or a Wimpy snack bar.

I walked over to José and touched her arm. "Let's go now, shall we?"

She looked surprised, then laughed. "What's up? I didn't think I'd be able even to *drag* you away from all this! Aren't these tapestries gorgeous? I just can't believe that they're *centuries* old!"

"Beautiful," I said briefly, barely glancing in their direction. My spine was tingling. There was someone lurking in the shadows at the back of the hall...someone who had moved when I did. Out of the corner of my eye I had glimpsed a flash of white.

Paradoxically, now that I was sure that I hadn't been imagining things I was no longer frightened. I waited until we were outside the building, then turned quickly to José.

"Bother, I think I've dropped my handkerchief. I'll just go and see. Wait for me, I won't be a sec."

Before she could answer I darted back. My hunch was right. Someone was just coming out of the museum...someone small and dark and compact.

Someone I'd seen before. With a shock of utter disbelief I recognized the man who had approached Ross Henderson in the hotel courtyard only that morning.

Our eyes met. If I had had any doubts that he was the man who had been following us they were resolved there and then. Just for one telltale moment his swarthy face betrayed confusion, then it again became masklike. He would have passed me hurriedly and without a word if I hadn't grabbed hold of his arm.

"Look," I said furiously, "I don't know what game you think you're playing at and I don't particularly care, but unless you stop following us around I'm going straight to the police! You've been dogging our footsteps all morning—and don't say you haven't, because I know jolly well that you have! And I'm fed up with it!" I paused for breath. The man's face was blank. *"Comprende usted?"*

I don't think he understood my words, but I suppose he must have gathered from my tone that I was blazingly angry. At any rate, he didn't stop to argue. With a quick movement he jerked himself free, muttered something unintelligible under his breath and disappeared into the crowded street. I watched him go, my thoughts whirling. Who was he? What was his connection with Ross Henderson? And for heaven's sake why had he been following us?

People streamed past me, but I saw them only vaguely. It wasn't until I was accidentally jostled that I stepped back and tried to force myself to think rationally. Obviously, however much I disliked the idea of approaching Ross Henderson with such an extraordinary story he would have to be told what had happened. Through him I could perhaps learn the identity of the man whose lurking shadow had ruined my day. My first, long-looked-forward-to day in Cuzco.

I began to walk slowly. Should I tell José? I thought

not. Ignorance was bliss...sometimes. There was no need for her to be as worried and perplexed as I was. I squared my shoulders and drew a deep breath, making a conscious effort to compose myself. I was still as jumpy as a cat: the result, I suppose, of prolonged nervous tension. I could only hope that José wouldn't notice.

She was waiting for me a few yards from where I'd left her, peering into the window of a little gift shop. A white alpaca beret had taken her fancy and I accompanied her into the shop to buy it. I looked behind me, but there was no sign of the man who had been following us. On our way to the Plaza de Armas, after José had made her purchase, I felt reasonably sure that I had frightened him off for good and all. Yet why had he been following us in the first place? Why, why, why?

I didn't know the answer to that question until much later. When José and I returned to our hotel I stopped at the reception desk and had a quick word with one of the girls. She was a little older than me and plumpish, with merry black eyes and a nice smile. As a result of our conversation the telephone rang in my room just as I was about to start getting ready for dinner.

"Miss Lester? Mr. Henderson has just come in. He's gone straight to his room—number fifty-three, on the second floor."

I thanked the receptionist and put the receiver down. For a moment I hesitated, then I made up my mind. José was in the bath. I could speak to Ross and be back in my own room again before ever she missed me.

I knocked at the door of number fifty-three and Ross's voice shouted "Come in." I drew a long breath, then obeyed.

He was lying sprawled upon his bed, smoking a cigarette, his arms behind his head. His shirt was open at the neck and his sleeves rolled up, revealing tanned, muscular forearms. My first thought was that I'd never seen anyone looking so deathly tired, my second that I'd been a fool to come. I should have waited and tried to see him alone downstairs.

"Joby!" He said the name slowly, his surprise apparent. He swung himself to his feet, stubbed out his cigarette and reached for the tie and lightweight jacket which were slung carelessly over the back of a small cane chair.

"I'm sorry to receive you like this," he said coolly, knotting his tie. "I wasn't expecting... visitors."

I felt myself go scarlet. "No, of course not. It... it's I who should apologize. I wouldn't have dreamed of disturbing you except... except that there's something I think you ought to know. It... it might be important."

I stopped, instinctively bracing myself for some kind of wisecrack, but none came. Ross's expression had changed.

"What's the matter?" he asked sharply. "Has anything happened?" And then, before I could answer, "Your cousin... she's all right, isn't she?"

"Yes. Oh, yes." I paused, then added a little unsteadily, "Something *has* happened, though. Something rather... disturbing. A man has been following us around Cuzco, practically all day."

There was a moment's silence. To my relief Ross didn't scoff. He merely said, "How do you know?"

I told him, as briefly as I could. He listened to me in silence, his eyes never leaving my face. I couldn't tell from his expression what he was thinking. I wished I could.

"... So I thought I ought to tell you at once, since you seem to know the man," I concluded. "Who is he? Do you know him well? And have you any idea why he was following us?"

Ross pulled out his cigarettes and lit a match. Over the flame his eyes met mine and they held a disconcerting gleam. "Perhaps because he was merely obeying my instructions," he said mildly.

I couldn't believe he was serious. I stared at him incredulously, but his brown face was impassive. "You...you don't mean—"

"I mean that I told Esteban to follow you. I had no idea, of course, that you'd find out." He bowed to me a little ironically. "My congratulations, Miss Lester. You're very much more astute than I thought."

I stood rigid, flaming with anger and resentment. We'd been followed on Ross Henderson's instructions. There'd been no danger, no need for my lovely day to have been spoilt. I could have rejoiced in a gourmet's feast of antiquities without being conscious, all the time, of a chilling tinge of apprehension.

I said furiously, "How *dare* you do such a thing? It...it's monstrous! You've no idea how awful I felt! You'd told us that there might be danger and...and I didn't know what was going to happen or—"

He interrupted me, his voice brusque. "I told you last night that I wasn't at all happy about your being in Cuzco. All I asked Esteban to do was to keep an eye on you both and see that you didn't run into any kind of trouble or do anything rash or stupid. That seemed only too likely, judging from your uncooperative attitude this morning—"

"That was your fault!" I almost flung the words at him. "You provoked me! Did you expect me to take the things you said to me lying down?" I averted my face, conscious of the fact that my eyes were brimming over wth angry tears.

I'm not a weepy sort of person usually; I can only think that I was tired and badly overwrought. "Well, I hope you're happy now! You—you've ruined my day, and I was looking forward to it so much! I...I didn't enjoy anything and I couldn't tell José—"

Ross moved sharply. "*What* couldn't you tell José?"

"That I was afraid we were being followed. I...I didn't want to worry her unnecessarily. At first I wasn't sure, and then when I was—"

There was a queer expression on Ross's face. I couldn't analyze it. "You'd better sit down," he said abruptly, and pushed forward a chair.

I took it thankfully. Ross sat down on the edge of his bed and regarded me frowningly, rather as though I was a piece of mechanism that had suddenly veered off at an unexpected tangent.

"Perhaps I do owe you an apology," he said surprisingly. "I'm sorry. I realize that you must have had a rather unpleasant experience."

It was the first time that he had ever addressed me with anything approaching friendliness and I was instantly disarmed. Forgetting that only a few moments ago I could cheerfully have wrung his neck, I drew a long breath. "It was *hellish*!" I said with feeling. "I didn't know whether we were going to be stabbed with poisoned darts or pushed under the wheels of a bus or—" I stopped at something I saw in his face. Then I said slowly, "Nothing like that could happen. Could it?"

"I sincerely hope not," Ross answered me soberly. "But this is Peru, remember, and not England. Scratch the veneer of civilization and what lies beneath? Crazy superstitions...wild primitive passions." He paused, then added almost reluctantly, "There's been more trouble today. We almost lost a truckload of valuable equipment. If we had, work would have been held up for days, perhaps even weeks."

Ignoring my shocked exclamation, he ran his fingers through his thick dark hair. "If only I could find the ringleaders...."

I looked at him, remembering the way he had lain sprawled upon his bed, that awful look of exhaustion on his face. It had gone now. He just looked tired and strained. I said tentatively, "What happened?"

"What? Oh, I suppose you mean the truck. It had been parked too near the edge of a precipice and the brakes weren't on properly. It started to roll. Luckily I saw what was happening just in time."

I caught my breath. "It...it was meant to go over the precipice?"

"I'm sure of it."

"Wh-what did you do?"

"The only thing possible. Jumped into the driving seat and steered away from the edge." Ross spoke rather shortly, as though impatient of my insistence, and I guessed that that was all he was prepared to say about that particular incident. The risk, though, must have been enormous. It would take a man with nerves of steel to do what he had done. A runaway truck...a precipice...I shivered, and he looked at me quickly.

I said the very first thing that came into my head. "Have you built roads in Peru before?"

"Not in Peru, but in other parts of South America where the conditions are not dissimilar."

"There must be appalling hazards? Natural ones, I mean."

Ross shrugged. "There are easier ways of earning a living, I suppose. We have to cope with things like landslides, floods and changing temperatures which crack or peel or tumble new road. New jungle plants pop up about as fast as they can be cut down. Skilled workmen are hard to come by."

I said impulsively, "That makes the Incas' achievements even more remarkable, doesn't it? I mean, they built some nine thousand miles of roads, didn't they, with no machinery or modern equipment to help them. Nothing stopped them. They crossed mountains and swamps and ravines and rivers."

A smile of pure amusement relaxed the hard lines of Ross's face, making him look ten years younger and about twice as attractive. "Hey! Are you trying to tell me that we don't compare too well with the ancient Incas?" he asked, laughing. "Obviously you've been borrowing your cousin's history books!"

Momentarily I had forgotten about José. She'd be furious if she knew where I was. I got quickly to my feet.

"I must go. I...I'm sorry I disturbed your rest."

"And I'm sorry I spoiled your day." The laughter died out of Ross's face and his dark blue eyes held mine. "However, there'll be others."

"Yes." I hesitated. "You know, there's no need to provide a chaperon for us in future. We'll be very careful not to add to your problems. I promise."

"I appreciate that," Ross said quietly. He held the door open for me and as I was about to pass through he added, "I don't suppose I shall see you again tonight. I'm having a meal sent up to my room."

"Oh?" José would be disappointed, I thought.

"I have to write the latest reports for Don—your father." In some subtle way Ross's whole attitude changed completely with those words. Somehow or another I had the feeling that for a short time he had forgotten who I was, but that he'd suddenly remembered. And the remembrance was like a cold breeze, chilling eyes and voice and face in a manner which dismayed me. He still didn't like Joby Lester. I was sure of it.

I went quickly back to my own room. I'd already showered; all I had to do was to change my dress. I chose one in lightweight wool, a lovely lotus pink, and was pulling it over my head when José burst in. She was wearing a blue floral dress and had obviously taken special pains with her hair and makeup. Her eyelids shimmered with silvery blue shadow and her lipstick was a subtle blush rose. She wouldn't be too happy, I thought wryly, when she discovered that Ross wasn't going to make an appearance tonight.

However, for the moment it didn't seem to be Ross who was on her mind. She looked extremely pleased with herself, rather like a pretty, purring kitten.

"Guess who's just rung up?"

"The President of Peru?" My flippancy hid relief that José hadn't missed me.

"Idiot! Guess again. Someone we both know."

I thought for a moment, then shook my head. "Tell me."

"The girl we met on the plane—Consuelo de Noveli." José's tone was triumphant. "You know she said she'd like to see us again and I told her where we were staying? Well, she phoned a few minutes ago to ask if we'd like to spend the day with her at her brother's *hacienda* tomorrow. I knew you'd be keen, so of course I said yes—"

"I should hope you did!"

"—and a car is coming to pick us up at eleven o'clock tomorrow morning. It will be fun, won't it? Just what we hoped for!"

I agreed enthusiastically that it was. Like José, I'd been strongly attracted by the friendly Consuelo, and the opportunity to visit her home and meet the rest of her family was much too good to miss.

As I zipped up my dress I remembered the promise I'd made to Ross. I'd leave a note for him at the reception desk, I decided, telling him of our invitation to the de Noveli *hacienda*. He'd receive it first thing in the morning, before he left the hotel to drive to the roadworks, and he'd know that for one day, at least, he need entertain no misgivings as to our safety!

CHAPTER SIX

WE KNEW, of course, that one had to have strong nerves to travel anywhere in Peru by car, but I don't think that either José or myself had any idea that the journey to the de Noveli *hacienda*, high in the mountains, would be anything like as spine-chillingly hazardous as it proved to be.

"Good grief! This country can certainly do with some new roads!" José exclaimed, clinging onto her seat as the car that had been sent for us lurched and bumped along a narrow dirt track—barely wide enough for a single vehicle—which climbed the steep wall of an emerald valley in a series of mind-boggling hairpin bends.

I agreed fervently. I had had all too many intimate roadside glimpses of two-thousand-foot drop-offs, and yet there had been compensations. We'd seen lovely little lakes with marvelous reflections of the clouds in them, herds of llamas and donkeys with their Indian drivers, clumps of eucalyptus with a hazy blue overtone hanging over them like the suggestion of smoke, and fields that were golden yellow with the end of harvest.

My feelings were so mixed that I didn't know whether to be glad or sorry when we finally arrived at the *hacienda.* The large, old, Spanish-designed house was built around a central courtyard and had a wonderful arabesque doorway, two stories high, and to each side of that, huge, boxed-in wooden balconies.

Consuelo, as gay and pretty as the bougainvillea vines that splashed the white walls of the *hacienda*, came running out to greet us as soon as the car stopped. She led us into a large square hall where llama skins and alpaca rugs were scattered on a mosaic-tiled floor and introduced us to her mother, dark haired and youthful looking in an almond green dress.

"Welcome," she said, smiling, and I thought that I had never heard that simple word spoken with more obvious sincerity.

Marcos was playing with some toy cars in the spacious sitting room, which was carpeted in Tiber blue and exquisitely furnished. Four or five beautifully colored rugs hung upon the walls and I noticed a wonderful gilded Cuzqueñan mirror and a magnificent crystal chandelier before Marcos rushed to show me what was evidently the pride and joy of *his* heart—a scale model of a Rolls-Royce!

"Marcos has talked of nothing but the beautiful English lady who showed him how to make paper boats," Señora de Noveli said laughingly to me. Her English, like her daughter's, was excellent. "You have made a conquest. You are fond of children, perhaps?"

The image of the twins' cheeky, freckled faces flashed into my mind. "I have two small brothers of my own," I told her, and then stopped, dismayed, as José shot me a warning look. I still found it hard to remember that I mustn't talk about my real family and background, that I had to claim as my own the sheltered, pampered upbringing that Donald Lester had insisted on for José.

"Really? You must tell us about them," Señora de Noveli exclaimed. "I have another son myself—Ramon, as doubtless Consuelo will have told you. I hope he will be able to join us for lunch."

I made a polite rejoinder and hoped that my hostess wouldn't attribute my heightened color to the wrong reason. We spent a few minutes talking about the journey. "I am sorry if it was an ordeal. Pablo, our chauffeur, is an experienced driver, but I have to admit that even I sometimes feel that his luck cannot last forever!" Señora de Noveli said wryly, and then Consuelo carried us off to see the house. It was full—as I'd hoped—of marvelous treasures that had been lovingly collected by the de Noveli family over the centuries. All were examples of first-class craftmanship, glowing with the patina of time and assiduous care.

Lunch was served in a beautiful white-walled room, full of atmosphere. There was a long, dark oak table that could have seated at least a dozen people, but a smaller, white painted table of wrought iron with a glass top had been set for lunch. Under the glass were trays filled with scarlet and yellow hibiscus, roses and sprays of bougainvillea, which glowed through the glass to give guests an impression of dining on a bed of flowers.

We were exclaiming over this when someone else came into the room. Tall and dark and moving with a kind of springy, rapier grace, he was so like Consuelo and Marcos that I guessed at once that this must be their older brother—Ramon de Noveli, owner of the *hacienda.*

His mother introduced José and me and he smiled, showing perfect, white teeth. I sat next to him during lunch and I thought he was charming, if perhaps a little too conscious of the fact. At the end of the meal he turned to me and and said, "I have met your father, Miss Lester. I have had—how shall I say?—business dealings with his company."

I must have shown my surprise, for he went on to explain, "The road your father's company is building—it cuts through part of my land."

I stared. "But surely the new road runs nowhere near here?"

Ramon de Noveli laughed. "Come outside for a moment." He led me through a French window into a lovely tropical garden. "Look at this valley. Then turn and look up at the snow peaks behind the house. All the land you can see belongs to me, and a great deal more besides. The new road will cut through the northern perimeter."

"But there's a village farther down in the valley!" I protested. "That can't be yours!"

Ramon shrugged. "But yes. This land was granted to my family by the king of Spain many hundreds of years ago. There are many villages on my land, and many hundreds of Indian *peones* and their families live in them. They belong to my *hacienda*, too," he added with a flash of his white teeth.

"Belong?"

"Each family must give me three days' work each week. The rest of the time the men may work in their own small fields and the children may herd their flocks. Those three days a week, however, belong to me. They must work in my fields, harvest my crops and tend my flocks."

His voice was perfectly matter-of-fact. I said incredulously, "But that's feudal! It's a system that was abolished in England centuries ago!"

Ramon looked amused. "You do not approve? But that is how the *haciendas* have always been worked."

I bit my lip. I couldn't argue with my host. Instead I said a little coldly, "You must have many responsibilities."

"Very many," he agreed. "Your father and I have much in common. He has the responsibilities of a huge international company, I—my *hacienda*."

I stared at the distant snow peaks. "I suppose despite all the acres you own it isn't all good farmland?"

Ramon laughed. "No. Although naturally I held out for a good price I was secretly quite glad to get rid of the land that was wanted for the road. Nothing has ever grown in the Valley of Skulls: it is quite bleak and barren."

"The Valley of Skulls?" I echoed his words. "Did that...belong to you?"

"Yes." He caught sight of my face. "Why? What is the matter?"

"Nothing. It's just that I seem to have heard that name mentioned so often. The Indians...isn't it rather a special valley as far as they're concerned? Somebody said..." my voice trailed away as Ramon laughed.

"Who cares about the Indians, *señorita*? They did not want me to sell the valley, that is true, but naturally I paid no attention to what they said."

There was an uncomfortable little silence. To break it I said, "Why is it called the Valley of Skulls? It seems such a queer name!"

Ramon spread out his hands and I surprised myself by thinking how different they were from Ross Henderson's. Long and slender, whereas Ross's were square and strong and capable.

"There are two rocks at the entrance to the valley, shaped like skulls."

"Oh!" I was silent for a moment, my eyes fixed unseeingly on arbors bright with tropical flowers. We were standing beside a trellis which was a mass of scarlet hibiscus and unthinkingly I plucked a spray and twisted it between my fingers.

"Allow me." Ramon spoke quickly. Before I had realized his intention he had taken the spray from me and pinned it in my hair.

"Perfect!" he said, smiling. "Have you any idea, *señorita*, how well you fit into these surroundings? You are not like your cousin, an insipid English rose...you are very beautiful. My sister was quite right."

I am not sure how I would have answered if I hadn't heard the sound of footsteps. I turned quickly and saw

José standing behind us. I thought she looked at me a little strangely and I couldn't help wondering how much she had overheard.

Ramon greeted her politely but without any noticeable enthusiasm. I can't accuse him of deliberately trying to make her feel *de trop*, his manners were too good for that, but I have to admit that later when he and Consuelo showed us over the *hacienda*, he went to considerable pains to ensure that José paired off with Consuelo, I with him. I didn't much care for his maneuvers, but there wasn't a great deal I could do, short of being downright rude.

Ramon's attentions apart, I enjoyed the day tremendously. I already knew, of course, of the Latin Americans' almost unsurpassed reputation for friendliness and hospitality, but even so the kindness of the de Noveli family was almost overwhelming. Nothing seemed to be too much trouble for them, and I felt sure that I should remember their thoughtful courtesy long after other impressions of my visit to Peru had perhaps dimmed or faded.

After a delicious evening meal of *anticuchos* (an appetizer of spitted beef heart with a garlic sauce) and *aji de pollo* (chicken cooked with onions) we all sat around a blazing fire and Señora de Noveli told us some of the stories and legends that are part of any very old family's indisputable heritage. Marcos, who had begged to be allowed to sit up a little later than usual, curled himself up on a big alpaca rug with his curly head against my knee. After a time I noticed his long lashes drooping onto his cheeks and I smiled at his mother.

"Marcos is very nearly asleep, I think."

"Yes. It is long past his bedtime. I will ring for Luisa," Señora de Noveli said, and rose to her feet.

Marcos's eyes flew open at the mention of his nurse's name. "But I am not tired! Please, I want to stay!"

"It is late, little one," his mother told him, ruffling his hair. "Soon, I am afraid, we must send our visitors back to their hotel."

"But you will come again, won't you?" Marcos looked pleadingly at José and myself.

It was Ramon who answered him. "We all very much hope so." He looked at us, smiling. "You will, won't you?"

"We have enjoyed your visit so much," Consuelo put in. "PLease come again soon!"

"Thank you. We'd love to!" José and I spoke in unison and I drew a breath of relief. She wasn't, then, upset by Ramon's obvious preference for my company. I was half afraid she might be.

Back in our hotel she even tried to make a joke of it. "Well, you certainly made a conquest today! Ramon de Noveli could scarcely keep his eyes off you!" she said teasingly.

I laughed and answered her in the same vein. "Perhaps he's a fortune hunter!"

"I hardly think so. The family doesn't strike me as being exactly short of cash!" José retorted dryly. "He thinks you're beautiful. I heard him say so." She stood in front of a mirror, and stared dismally at her own reflection. "He's right, of course. I do look insipid, compared with you."

Oh, lord, I thought. Aloud I said quickly, "Tell that to Ross Henderson! Don't forget, one man's meat is another man's poison! And vice versa, of course."

The strained look left José's face. "Yes, I do think that Ross prefers blondes to brunettes," she agreed, smiling a little. And then, "I wonder if we shall see him tonight?"

I glanced at my watch. "He'll have had dinner by now. He may be in the lounge, if you're really interested."

"I think I am. I need a little male admiration to restore

my morale!" José said, picking up her handbag. "Let's go and see if we can find him, shall we?"

I followed her reluctantly. As I'd thought, Ross was sitting in the lounge, reading a newspaper. He put it down when he saw us and rose to his feet. "Good evening. May I order you a drink?" he asked politely.

"Thanks. Sure we're not disturbing your peace?" José smiled at him mischievously as she sank into the chair he held out for her. It was next to his. I found my own, a little way apart.

He laughed. "It's nice to have company. At least, if it's the right kind!"

He looked, I thought, rather less tired than he had the previous evening, but the worry lines were still etched deeply around his mouth. He caught me studying him and I saw a sudden gleam in his blue eyes before I flushed and hastily turned my head away.

"Thank you for your note," he said coolly. "I trust you had a pleasant day?"

"Marvelous," I said with a coolness to match his.

José plunged into an animated account of the day's events. Looking at her sparkling face, I wondered wryly how Ramon de Noveli could possibly justify his use of the word "insipid." When Ross was around my cousin was a different person. The sort of person that any man could quite easily fall in love with. Even a man like Ross....

"...And there's this heavenly *hacienda,* more like a palace than anything else, and it all belongs to Ramon de Noveli because his father was killed in an accident a couple of years ago," I heard her say. "It's a gorgeous place, isn't it, Joby?"

"Yes," I agreed colorlessly.

"Ramon de Noveli thinks that Joby's gorgeous, too." José looked laughingly at Ross. "She made a terrific hit. Didn't you, darling?"

There was nothing malicious about her remark, but I felt my cheeks burn. I was glad that the waiter chose that moment to bring our drinks, but Ross returned to the subject as soon as the man had gone. Leaning back in his chair, he said, "I've never actually met de Noveli, but I've heard of him, of course. He's one of the biggest *hacienda* owners in Peru." He looked at me, I thought mockingly. "So you made a good impression, did you? I'm sure it must have been mutual."

I stiffened. "Oh? Why?"

"Like calling to like," Ross said blandly.

I gripped the stem of my glass a little more tightly, my temper rising. I knew quite well what he meant—that Ramon and I had both been born with silver spoons in our mouths!

I said angrily, "Yes, he did make a favourable impression! He was kind and courteous. I don't suppose those are qualities you particularly admire, but—"

Ross interrupted me, his mouth hard. "Kind? How can you call any man 'kind' who exploits the peasants the way he does? The poor devils on *haciendas* like his lead one hell of a life, they're scarcely better than slaves!"

He stubbed out his cigarette and I was almost shocked by the suppressed violence of the gesture. "Until the Spanish conquest, the land was roughly owned by those who tilled it. They retained one third of their production for themselves and contributed one-third each to the Inca Church and the State. The profit system was unheard-of. Do you know that today eighty-two percent of Peruvian land is held by point eight of the total number of landowners—people like your friend de Noveli—and a million peasants are landless? Do you know that Peru is one of only three countries in the western hemisphere where serfdom still persists?" He paused and then added, his voice low but charged with intense feeling, "Do you know—and do you care? Like hell you do! A *hacienda* owner pays you a few pretty compliments and so you call him *kind*!"

I was speechless. I agreed with every single word that Ross had said, but my tongue seemed stuck to the roof of my mouth.

It was José who broke the silence.

She said gently, "Ross, you're making Joby feel awfully bad, I'm sure. She liked the de Novelis so much and so did I. They really were kind to us. The system may be bad, but not the *people*! Not *all* of them!"

Ross looked at her and I saw the blaze die out of his eyes. "I'm sorry. The plight of the Peruvian peasant is something I happen to feel pretty strongly about, but this is neither the time nor the place to air my views. Let's change the subject, shall we?"

With an effort I spoke. Even to my own ears my voice sounded husky. "Before we do...Ross, I suppose you know that Ramon de Noveli was the original owner of the Valley of Skulls? He...he told me that the Indians begged him not to sell it."

"Yes, I know."

Ross's words were bluntly uncompromising. I stared down at my glass, my throat aching with suppressed emotion. If only I didn't have to pretend to be a frivolous little socialite! There was so much that I wanted to say, but I couldn't say it. Not now. Perhaps not ever.

After a moment or two Ross spoke again. Casually, this time. "By the way, José, someone asked me today what, if any, were the basic similarities between the Aztecs and the Incas. I'm afraid I hadn't a clue, but I suppose you know?"

The silence stretched. In a moment, I thought despairingly, even Ross would realize that José's blank face meant that she was completely at a loss. Why didn't she improvize...play for time...do *anything* except just sit there waiting for Ross to tumble to the fact that she simply didn't know what he was talking about!

There was only one thing to do, and I did it. The glass that I knocked over was almost full and the contents literally poured into my lap. I jumped up, exclaiming over my clumsiness. My annoyance wasn't altogether feigned, either. I liked the dress I was wearing, it was practically new and I had a horrible feeling that it was completely ruined!

"Oh, darling! What a mess!" José produced her handkerchief and mopped the spreading stain vigorously but ineffectually. "*Angel! Thank you!*" said her grateful look.

"I'll have to go and change," I said hurriedly, afraid to look in Ross's direction. "Oh, gosh, it is a mess...I'm sorry, terribly stupid of me! Please excuse me!" and I fled.

Upstairs in my room I took off the dress and soaked the stain in cold water. It didn't seem to make much difference. I stared gloomily at the ruin of fifteen pounds. I wouldn't go downstairs again, I decided. I'd leave José to have a tête-à-tête with Ross. I was sure they'd both enjoy it. If she played her cards right, he'd stop worrying about the basic similarities between the Incas and the Aztecs. At least, most men would, and I didn't see why Ross Henderson should be any exception!

It was nearly midnight when José came into my room. She knew I wasn't asleep because I had the light on, reading.

"Darling, why didn't you come down again when you'd changed your dress?" José sat down on the edge of my bed and looked at me with eyes that were more brilliant than usual. "We thought you were going to!"

"I decided not to bother." I laid down my book. "You're not going to tell me that you missed me?"

She ignored that. "What about your dress? Is it all right? Honestly, Joby, you saved my life! I couldn't think what to say or do! Who are the Aztecs, anyway? I've never *heard* of them!"

"That was patently obvious—at least, it was to me," I said dryly. "I hope Ross didn't repeat his question at a moment when a mug like me wasn't handy."

José giggled. "Don't be like that! He didn't, actually. We had, er, more interesting things to talk about!" She clasped her hands behind her head and looked at me with dancing eyes. "We had a marvelous stroll around Cuzco by moonlight. Frightfully romantic! Ross was sweet. He really was."

I could imagine. Only I didn't want to. I said hurriedly, "Spare me the details! You're cured, then?"

"Cured?" José raised her brows.

"Of Mike."

"Oh, Mike." José got up and went over to my washbasin, in which my dress was still soaking. "He belongs to a past aeon. Ross is *now*."

She poked at the folds of my dress. "Oh, lord, the stain hasn't come out... I'll buy you a new dress, darling. You deserve it!"

"Don't bother. Next time, though, I might think twice about saving you!"

José giggled again. "I'll try to make sure there isn't a next time! You'd better tell me about the Aztecs and the Incas, though—just in case."

"Not now. Tomorrow." I reached out my hand to switch off my bedside lamp. "God night, coz! Sweet dreams!"

"Same to you." José took the hint and disappeared into her own bedroom. I switched off the light and lay staring into the darkness. I tried to think about the de Novelis and the wonderful welcome they had given us... about Ramon, about the Valley of Skulls... but always and always the same images insisted on crowding into my mind. Ross and José walking along the quiet moonlit streets of Cuzco, José's hair a silvery splendor and Ross's arm around her shoulders... Ross and José saying good night... *Good grief,* I thought desperately, *was I actually jealous?*

I couldn't be, I told myself sternly. Why, I didn't even like Ross Henderson. He simply wasn't my type at all. And even if he was, I certainly wasn't his! I shut my eyes and burrowed down into my bed.

"Wouldn't you think," I said, addressing my pillow, "that a girl with a B.A. would have more sense?"

It wasn't, I admit, a very coherent question, but pillows, unlike people, don't ask for long and wordy explanations. They don't answer back, either. Which, in certain circumstances, is just as well!

THE NEXT FEW days were lovely. And uneventful. By that I mean nothing frightful happened: José and I just spent long lazy days sightseeing and shopping and falling more and more in love with Peru and its people.

We visited Sacsuhuaman, the Kenko amphitheater with its subterranean tunnels and caves where sacrifices were made; the ritual baths of the Incas at Tampumachay, and the ruins of a strategic *pucra* (fortress) dominating two valleys, with tunnels supposedly running to Sacsuhuaman and Cuzco. We spent another day with the de Noveli family at their *hacienda* and on Sunday morning Ramon and Consuelo insisted on taking us to Pisac, a colorful little Indian village with an incredible market selling everything from fur rugs and hats to slippers and beautifully dressed dolls. This particular journey took us along mountain crests and precipices, with snowcapped peaks, canyons and terraced slopes on all sides—scenery which even José said afterward was among the most beautiful she had ever seen.

Ramon seemed to enjoy being our chauffeur and guide and he certainly made a very charming companion. I saw very little of the other man in my life—Ross—as whenever he, José and I dined *à trois* I made a point of making myself scarce at the first opportunity. José protested at first, but only halfheartedly. Ross never said anything very much at all. We argued less than we used to, but the silent cold war that existed between us was even more of a strain. I now regretted the fact that I'd behaved so badly that I had indeed convinced him that I was "spoiled rotten," but it was too late for regrets. Far, far too late!

Perhaps because on all sides we were treated with such wonderful kindness, José and I had almost forgotten the threatening letter that Ross had shown us on the first night of our arrival in Cuzco. There had been no more trouble and though we knew that Ross was still trying to find the ringleaders of the plot to sabotage the road scheme, it really seemed as though all danger was past. At any rate I hoped so.

Letters came from Barbados telling us of the steady improvement in Uncle Donald's health. Much to my relief Ross rarely mentioned him—or his cousin Isabel. Of course, she'd said in her letter that they didn't know each other very well. I wondered, sometimes, about his family and background and the kind of life he had led as a boy, but he never seemed to volunteer any information about himself, even to José. I'd never met anyone with quite so much reserve. I could see why Isabel had felt that she'd been kept at arm's length, though I had to admit he seemed to have no difficulty in finding things to say to José!

It was at the end of our first week in Cuzco that I noticed that José's newfound enthusiasm for sightseeing seemed to be flagging. She complained once or twice of feeling unwell and when we returned to the hotel—much earlier than usual—she flung herself down upon her bed without even bothering to take off her shoes. I looked at her anxiously, noting her flushed cheeks and over-bright eyes. She looked to me to be slightly feverish, but I optimistically agreed with her that an aspirin, a hot drink and an early night would probably put things right, just as they had in Lima.

We were both wrong. In the morning she looked definitely worse and she complained, too, of some swelling and tenderness in the glands of her neck.

"You don't think I've caught some strange Peruvian virus, do you? Sleeping sickness or something like that?" she asked plaintively.

Despite my anxiety I managed to laugh. "Most unlikely, but I think you'd better have the doctor, all the same."

José moved her head restlessly on her pillow. "If only my neck didn't hurt so! Tell Ross, Joby. He may be able to recommend a decent doctor."

I looked at my watch. Luckily it was still very early. I might be able to contact Ross before he left the hotel for the roadworks.

He was, in fact, on the point of leaving when I tapped on his door.

"Yes? What is it?" he asked peremptorily when he saw me. We were always on the defensive with each other: José had once said that we reminded her of a couple of prizefighters at the start of a round!

"It's José. She—she's not too well." I looked at him anxiously. "I'm terribly afraid she's picked up some beastly virus. She's got a temperature and she says her neck hurts. It looks swollen to me."

"I'll have a look at her." Ross shrugged himself into his jacket. "I've been kicking around South America long enough to know what most of the more common tropical viral infections look like!"

José was sitting up in bed when I took Ross into her room. He took one look at her and I saw his face register shock. Then, incredibly, relief.

"My dear girl," he said, laughing, "I'm no medico, but I *do* know what's wrong with you! You've got mumps!"

CHAPTER SEVEN

JOSÉ AND I spoke together. "*Mumps!*" My voice was a squeak; José's a wail.

"I'm afraid so. But never mind, just be thankful that it isn't something worse," Ross said consolingly. "You'll have to stay in bed for a few days, of course, but after that you should feel as right as rain again!"

Poor José stared at him and I saw two big tears gather in her blue eyes and roll down her pale cheeks. I was mentally kicking myself for not having thought of mumps, but the thing was that I'd never had the disease myself and I had only the vaguest idea of the symptoms.

José gulped. "M-mumps? Oh, Ross, are you sure?" Her mouth quivered. "I...I shall be all swollen and ugly...you'll all laugh at me—"

Ross sat down on the edge of her bed and took her hand in his. In a gentler voice than I had ever heard him use he said, "Don't be a silly girl. How could anyone possibly think you were ugly? Even with mumps, measles and chicken pox rolled into one I'd still back you to win the Miss World beauty contest!"

José smiled through her tears. Ross pulled a clean handkerchief from his pocket and gently wiped her face, just as if he was comforting an unhappy child. The tenderness of the gesture, from an iron man like him, made me catch my breath. I saw his dark head close to hers, heard him say, "I've had mumps, so you needn't worry about me," and then I turned quickly away and went and stood by the window. I was staring out over a sea of rooftops when Ross came and stood next to me.

"I'm sure it's mumps, but the doctor had better see her," he said curtly. And then, as an obvious afterthought, "You've had mumps yourself, of course?"

"N-no. No, I haven't. Only measles and chicken pox."

Ross stared at me incredulously for a moment, and then he groaned. "Good lord, in that case you shouldn't be anywhere near José! It's only moderately contagious, I believe, but—"

"Even if it was the bubonic plague it would make no difference!" I retorted. "How, may I ask, do you think we're going to manage if I *don't* go anywhere near José? Who's going to look after her?"

Ross stuck his hands into his pockets, his jaw a little squarer than usual and his gaze inimical. "We'll have to find someone. Someone who won't be at risk."

"Risk!" I echoed the word scornfully. "Good heavens, mumps is nothing to worry about! I don't care if I catch it or not. Besides, I'm sure that José would much rather have me looking after her than a complete stranger!"

I met his eyes defiantly and saw his mouth go down at one corner. "Quite the self-sacrificing little heroine, aren't you?" he said sardonically. "I know mumps is only a mild disease, but if you catch it it will only mean that once she's better José will have to turn around and start looking after you! Rather a pointless exercise, don't you think?"

I bristled. "Mumps is probably communicable long before the swellings appear! I might be hatching it already, for all you know!"

"You might. On the other hand, you might not." Ross spoke with an exaggerated patience which made me long to hit him.

"Ross is right, Joby." Quite unexpectedly José,

who'd been listening, took his part. "Go away! I don't want you anywhere near me! It's bad enough having mumps myself without having to feel guilty in case I've given the beastly thing to you!"

"Don't be silly—"

"I'm not being silly. Am I, Ross?"

"No. Eminently sensible." Ross looked dourly at me. "I'll give you the name of a reliable doctor and you'll probably find that he'll be able to recommend some nice woman who'll be only too glad to look after José until she's better." He paused as if struck by a sudden thought. "What were you going to do today? Anything special?"

It was futile to argue. I knew that. He'd made up his mind and José was backing him. I said, "Yes. We were going to spend the day with the de Novelis. I... whatever else I do or don't do, I shall have to get in touch with them to tell them that we can't come."

"Of course." Ross glanced at his watch. "I think perhaps I'll get on to the doctor while you're doing just that."

He had taken charge completely, almost as though he considered he had the right. I minded, but José didn't seem to. Perhaps, ill as she was, she found his cool assurance comforting.

It was Señora de Noveli herself who answered the telephone. I apologized for the early call and then explained what had happened. Her exclamation of dismay cut me short.

"You poor children! I am so sorry! Poor little José, how unhappy she must be feeling! To be ill on holiday, and in an hotel in a foreign country—oh, it is too bad!" And then, after a pause so brief as to be almost imperceptible, "Could she not come here, to us?"

I couldn't believe my ears. "To you? But, *señora*—"

"We have all had mumps and second attacks are extremely rare, I believe. We would be only too happy to look after her," Señora de Noveli said warmly. "Is she well enough to travel? We could send the car for her this morning."

"I think she's well enough, yes. But, *señora—*"

"No 'buts'! They are quite unnecessary, my child. We shall look forward to welcoming you both."

"Both?"

"You are naturally included in my invitation. Unless—oh! perhaps you have not had mumps?"

Reluctantly I admitted that mumps was something that up until now I'd managed to avoid.

"Then I really feel that it would be better if you stayed in Cuzco." Señora de Noveli's voice was regretful but firm. "With any luck you may escape infection. Your cousin will be well looked after, and you can rely on Ramon and Consuelo to see that she does not become too bored and lonely."

"I'm sure I can." My throat felt suddenly tight. "*Señora*, I simply don't know how to thank you. It's the kindest thing I ever heard! To offer to take a comparative stranger into your home and nurse her—"

"Oh, but you and José are not comparative strangers! You are our friends!"

I repeated this remark to José when telling her, a few minutes later, of Señora de Noveli's invitation. I wasn't surprised to see my cousin's eyes fill with tears.

"Oh, Joby, isn't she kind! It's the first time in my life that someone's wanted to do something for *me*, and not for Donald Lester's daughter!"

"You do intend to accept, then?" I had wondered, on reflection, whether José would miss Ross too much. As he had already had mumps, there was no reason why he should keep away from her. Except, of course, that she probably wouldn't want him to see her with a balloon-like face. I'd forgotten that.

"Yes, of course. But what will you do?" José looked doubtfully at me. "Won't it be rather awful for you, being on your own?"

"I shall be all right. For heaven's sake don't worry about me.... José!"

"Yes?"

"You've just said that it's the first time in your life that someone's done something that you know is for you and has nothing whatsoever to do with your father. Haven't you proved, now, that people *do* like you for yourself? Don't you think it's time we told the truth? About us, I mean."

José stared at me incredulously. "You must be joking! Why now?"

"For several reasons. The chief one being that it...it seems so awful to go on deceiving people who are being so kind to us. José, I'm sure it wouldn't make any difference! Honestly, it wouldn't!"

"I don't want to tell. Not yet. Joby, you won't say anything to Ross, will you? Promise?"

I looked at her. "José—"

"Joby! Promise me!"

I bit my lip. The urgency in José's voice, the sudden fear in her eyes, confirmed what I had already come uneasily to suspect. José was falling in love with Ross. But how could she hope to keep the truth from him? He'd have to know eventually that we'd swapped identities. Perhaps she hoped that by then he'd be so much in love with her that it wouldn't matter. I wasn't so sure. Somehow I had a feeling that Ross wasn't the sort of man to take kindly to the knowledge that he'd been tricked and lied to.

However, I told myself, that was José's problem and not mine. All I could do, for now, was to give her the assurance she obviously wanted.

"All right, José, I promise. I won't tell him."

"Tell him what? Or shouldn't I ask?" I'd forgotten to close the door and Ross had appeared in the open doorway.

I felt the color creep up under my skin. It was José who answered.

"We were talking about Ramon," she said hurriedly. "I don't want Joby to tell him that she can't see him any more until I'm better."

I decided once again that José must have had a lot more practice than I'd had at wriggling out of awkward situations. I'd never found it easy to tell fibs, and even though José was responsible for this one I had a hard job to choke back an instinctive protest.

Ross looked at me, his eyes unfriendly. "Surely this is hardly the moment for a discussion of your love life?" And then, turning to José, "The doctor will be here in a moment, my dear. I think you'll like him, and he's promised to see what he can do about finding a nurse."

"That won't be necessary." Still smarting from the crack about my love life—nonexistent, anyway—I couldn't help my voice being tinged with a kind of bitter satisfaction. "She's going to stay with the de Novelis. A car is coming to fetch her later this morning."

Ross stared at José. "Is this true?"

"Yes. They... they really want me, Ross, and I'd like to go. It will be much easier, all around, than staying here."

"I can see that. What about Joby?"

"I was invited, too, but when Señora de Noveli heard that I hadn't had mumps she decided that perhaps I'd better stay here. Like you, she seems to think that I ought to try to steer clear of infection."

Ross didn't answer for a moment, but I saw his brows draw together in a slight frown.

I said quickly, "It doesn't really make much difference to me whether José stays here or goes to the *hacienda.*

Either way, it seems, I'm to be left to my own devices."

"Yes. Well, we can talk about that later. I can't stop now, I'm afraid I'm already very late." Ross sounded curt, but his face, when he looked toward José, had softened miraculously. I didn't wait to hear him say goodbye. I went into my own room and stayed there until footsteps in the corridor outside told me that Ross had left.

José refused to let me do her packing for her. Instead, she gave a few *sols* to a pretty, curly-haired little chambermaid who assured us solemnly, in passably good English, that she had already had mumps. "My face, she was like a watermelon! Much, much worse than the señorita's!"

José groaned. "I suppose that's meant to be comforting! Joby dear, do go away. There isn't a thing you can do and the longer you hover around the more risk there is of your ending up with a face like a watermelon too."

"Don't be ridiculous!" I exploded. "I'm at least ten feet away from you and standing by an open window. I can't for the life of me see why there has to be so much fuss!"

"Anybody would think you wanted to catch the beastly thing!" José seemed a lot happier since learning that she was not to be incarcerated in a hotel bedroom with a strange nurse in attendance. "We won't be separated for long, Joby. I'm only a menace to you until the swelling of the glands has disappeared."

"How long is that?"

"About a week, or even less, the doctor says."

A week. Seven days. It seemed a very long time.

Waving goodbye to José as, later that morning, the big de Noveli car sped into the mist-shrouded distance, I realized somewhat gloomily that I was going to miss my cousin badly. Our tastes were different, but nonetheless José was fun to be with. Sightseeing on my own would lose some of its flavor now that José was no longer there to amuse me with her pungent remarks.

I did make another visit to Sacsuhuaman, which fifty-thousand men had taken fifty years to build and with which José had become thoroughly bored after the first fifteen minutes, but I returned to the hotel in the middle of the afternoon and wrote another long letter to mother. I didn't quite know what I should do about writing to Uncle Donald. He really ought to be told that José had contracted mumps and that she was staying with good friends who were looking after her, but I didn't dare do anything like that without first asking José's permission. In a day or two, of course, she'd probably feel well enough to write to him herself.

I had just finished scribbling a few lines to the twins when there was a tap at the door and a small page boy with a face rather like a wizened monkey handed me a note. It was from Ross, asking me to join him for a drink in the cocktail bar and to have dinner with him afterward.

My first impulse was to refuse. The whole thing would be far too much of a strain without José there to divert his attention and to act as peacemaker whenever it looked as though we might be going to get involved in an argument. Besides, the way the note was couched it was a royal command rather than a pleasant invitation!

I said, "Please tell Señor Henderson that Señorita Lester is very sorry, but she has a bad headache."

The little page boy was back again within five minutes, his black eyes dancing with unholy glee. "Señor Henderson, he say he is very sorry, too. He forgot to say 'please.'"

In spite of myself I couldn't help smiling. Oh, but I could like Ross! If only things were different, I could like him enormously. If. What was it they said? "If wishes were horses, then beggars would ride...."

Feeling ridiculously nervous, I changed into a flame-colored dress, swept up my hair on top of my head and fastened it in place with a tiny silver comb. When I went down to join Ross for a drink something flickered across his face that I couldn't quite analyze.

He said, "You look very nice," but so unenthusiastically that I knew at once that he was only saying what he thought I expected him to say. I'd made up my mind that I wouldn't let him provoke me, but I unmade it again in about two seconds flat.

"Meaning that tonight I look rather less like Melusine, or more?" Then, as his lips twitched, "You needn't bother with compliments. I know perfectly well you haven't invited me to join you merely for the pleasure of my company!"

"Really? Then why have I invited you?"

"I haven't the least idea. Unless you want to talk about José."

He regarded me enigmatically. "That isn't a bad idea. Do you think she'll be happy with the de Novelis?"

"I'm sure she will. You needn't worry about that."

"No. Oddly enough, the person I'm worried about is you."

I stared at him. "Me? But why?"

"Because you're now on your own. On thinking it over, I'm not so sure that it wouldn't have been better to let you run the risk of catching mumps from José." He paused, then said soberly, "I had another of those anonymous letters today. I can't show it to you: the police have it. But it mentioned you and José again. This time by name."

I drew a deep breath. "So?"

"So I don't think that while José is indisposed you ought to go around on your own. You're much too vulnerable."

I was sitting opposite a big gilded mirror. As if in a

dream I watched the play of emotion on the face of a dark-haired girl whose dress was a shimmer of red and gold. She looked not exactly frightened, but bewildered. It was several seconds before I realized that I was staring at myself.

"But I thought...everything seemed to have quietened down....I thought all the hoo-ha was over!"

"The saboteurs...I suppose that's what one can call them...have been playing a waiting game. They've been hanging on, I think, to see if their previous threats would have any effect. We are now within half a mile of the Valley of Skulls. Hence, I imagine, this latest development. It remains to be seen whether they really mean business."

My throat felt dry. "Well, José is safe enough! That's something to be thankful for! But what on earth do you expect me to do? I can't shut myself up in my bedroom all day and every day—"

"Of course not. You have, I think, a couple of alternatives. You can join José at the *hacienda*, or—" he paused, and I sensed his reluctance to continue.

"Or?"

"Or you can come and work for me. Just as a sort of safety measure, and only for a few days. Once we've started blasting our way through the valley the Indians will know they've lost and that there's no point in carrying out their threats."

There was a long silence. Then I said carefully, "Work for you?"

He shrugged. "If it's any consolation you'd be working for your father as well. That might help to make it bearable."

I let that pass. "But...but what could I do? I mean, I can't type or anything...."

"You'd be surprised how useful you could be." Ross's voice was slightly rueful. "I'm not much good at paperwork, I'm afraid, and there've been so many complications since work on the road started that a lot of stuff has accumulated. At any rate the office looks a bit chaotic!"

"Office?"

"I do have one on the site—a converted camper. I'm not going to pretend that it's as comfortable as the de Noveli *hacienda*, but there're a couple of chairs and a table, even a stove. Not," he added, grinning, "that I'd expect you to use that."

I flushed. Staring down at my glass I said slowly, "You once said that you didn't want José or me anywhere near the roadworks. Why have you changed your mind?"

"One, there's now a strict security system in operation. Two, if you're working for me you'll at least be where I can keep an eye on you. All in the line of duty, of course!" he added hastily. And, as far as I was concerned, quite unnecessarily.

I stiffened. "Duty?"

"It's up to me to protect your father's interests. I'm sure, aren't you, that those include his only daughter?"

"No! There's no earthly need for you to feel responsible for me—"

"The fact remains that I do." Ross's tone brooked no argument. He leaned back in his chair, watching my face. "Well, Joby, what is it to be? The luxurious *hacienda* plus the slight risk of catching mumps, or the roadworks with the undoubted drawbacks of noise, dust, a modicum of discomfort—and me?"

I was silent. I wasn't really bothered about catching mumps. I never had been. It was everyone else who had fussed such a lot. No, the only thing that worried me about staying at the *hacienda* was that I was beginning to feel a little uneasy about Ramon. He liked me very much... too much. I'm not unduly conceited—at least, I hope I'm not—but I'd have to be a complete nitwit not to have realized that. I was pretty sure that given half a chance—or even less—he'd try to embroil me in a passionate affair for which I had no inclination.

The thought of rushing around for an entire week avoiding moments of unsought-for passion appalled me. At least if I was working for Ross all I'd have to worry about was keeping my temper. I certainly wouldn't have to fight off any amorous advances! The thought made me smile. Ruefully. I looked up, and surprised a strange expression on Ross's face. Afterward I wasn't even sure that I'd seen it at all.

"Well?" He sounded almost angry. Perhaps he thought that I'd taken too long to make up my mind.

I said quietly, "I'll come and work for you."

"You're sure?"

"Yes." I paused, summoning up every ounce of courage that I possessed. My lips had gone suddenly dry, and I moistened them with the tip of my tongue. "Before I do...Ross, why had you made up your mind, before ever we met, that you weren't going to like me? Was it just because you don't care for my father and everything he stands for, or was there another reason as well?"

I think he was taken aback. For a moment he looked almost nonplussed and I saw something flicker at the back of his eyes.

"You do favor the direct approach, don't you?" he said slowly. "I've noticed it before. It's funny...I wouldn't have expected it. Your father is one of the most devious characters I've ever met—"

"Thanks!"

"And I'd heard that you...well, never mind." He reached into his pocket and pulled out his cigarettes.

I said sharply, "That's the second time you've insinuated that you've heard something detrimental about me! Who's your informant? Isabel?"

"Isabel?" Ross stared at me bleakly, and then he gave a short laugh. "Good God, no! You don't think I'd pay any attention to anything she said, do you? Besides, she likes you."

"Then who?"

Ross lit his cigarette. Over the glowing tip his eyes met mine. "Mike Frenton," he said quietly.

I don't know what I'd expected him to say. Almost anything but that. For a long moment I said nothing. My brain felt bemused, almost numb.

"M-Mike?"

"Don't say you've forgotten him already." Ross's voice held something that might have been quiet anger. "Even though you did play him such a scurvy trick—"

A page boy was hovering. "There is a telephone call for the *señorita.*" He bent over my chair. "It is Senor de Noveli, *señorita.*"

I jumped to my feet, immeasurably relieved at the interruption. It could have been my worst enemy wanting to speak to me, I'd still have shown the same eagerness to get to the phone. Metaphorically speaking, Ross's angry accusation had almost winded me: I needed a few minutes to recover my breath.

"Joby?" Ramon's voice was a velvety caress, his charm formidable. It wasn't his fault that it left me cold. Or that once I'd satisfied myself that José was all right I had the hardest job in the world to concentrate on what he was saying. Ross's last sentence kept hammering at my brains. "Even though you did play him such a scurvy trick...."

José had played *Mike* a scurvy trick? But that simply wasn't true! It was the other way around! José had loved Mike. I was certain of that. And in return he'd hurt her so badly that he'd shattered her self-confidence, destroyed every illusion she'd ever had. Oh no, Ross Henderson wasn't going to get away with that!

I had replaced the receiver and was halfway back to the cocktail bar before I suddenly realized, with a chilling sense of shock, that I couldn't possibly argue with him. I simply didn't know what had happened between José and Mike. I hadn't liked to question her and she had never volunteered any information beyond the mere fact that she had discovered that Mike was a fortune hunter.

Ross was still sitting where I'd left him, head bent, watching the brandy swirl in the bottom of his glass. He looked up as I approached and the light fell on his frowning brows, the hard, exciting line of his cheeks, his firmly molded mouth.

"Surprise, surprise. I didn't expect you back so soon."

"Then you overestimated my interest in Ramon," I said coolly.

Ross's brows rose skeptically, but he didn't pursue the subject. Instead he said, "How's José?"

I thought, as I answered him, that his concern indicated how very fond of her he'd become. It wasn't surprising. She'd been at pains to charm him. But how would he react when he learned the truth?

I knew that somehow or another I would have to try to bring the conversation back to Mike Frenton, but the opportunity didn't present itself during dinner. In fact, we hardly talked at all. I thought Ross seemed nearly as ill at ease as I was myself, though undoubtedly for different reasons!

It wasn't until I was saying good night that I plucked up the courage to ask what I simply had to know if ever I was to get wink of sleep.

"Ross, what scurvy trick do you think I played on Mike?"

He looked at me incredulously. "You really want me to tell you? Why?"

"I...I'd like to know if the version you've heard is...is anything like mine."

"You would? Well, I'm afraid I don't know the whole story." This time his voice held no emotion, not the slightest trace of interest. "Mike merely told me that you and he were very much in love, that you promised to marry him and that your father threatened to disinherit you if you did. It didn't matter to Mike. However, he has nothing but his salary, as you know, so that when you were called upon to choose between him and a large fortune...." He left his sentence unfinished and gave a tiny contemptuous shrug of his shoulders.

I dug my fingernails into the palms of my hands. Breathlessly I said, "But...but that simply isn't true! I never—"

Ross interrupted me. His face was still unreadable but his eyes were bleak. "Joby, before you attempt to whitewash yourself I think you should know that I went to school with Mike. He's one of my best friends. Never, in the years I have known him, have I ever heard him tell a lie."

I stared at him and then turned sharply away, bewildered and feeling a little sick. If Ross was right, that meant—what? That José had lied to me?

CHAPTER EIGHT

WHATEVER ROSS SAID about Mike Frenton's integrity, José hadn't told me anything except the truth. After tossing and turning half the night, I came to this conclusion around about three in the morning. I was convinced that she had loved Mike passionately, enough even to have given up her inheritance for him if that had been necessary. But she had never even hinted that her father had threatened her with disinheritance!

I frowned to myself in the darkness. There had been so much that she hadn't explained about her unhappy love affair, and that in itself was proof how badly she'd been hurt. I tried to remember what she had told me the day she had called at my bed-sitter in Bayswater. Hadn't she said something about her father trying to warn her that Mike was merely a fortune hunter?

I felt myself go tense as a startling idea suddenly occurred to me. Could Donald Lester have had anything to do with the breakup of the romance between his only daughter and his young employee? Goodness knows he was ruthless enough. He had always been ambitious for José and over anxious—or so mother had said—for her to make a good marriage. Good, of course, from a worldly point of view. Ross had made it pretty plain last night that Mike Frenton hadn't possessed the wealthy background of many of José's previous boyfriends. Wasn't it just possible that Donald Lester had decided that he'd make a thoroughly unsuitable son-in-law and that with a complete disregard for his daughter's happiness he had taken drastic steps to end the whole affair?

It was an interesting theory but only a theory. I knew that. I might be quite wrong. But *someone* was to blame for what had happened and if Ross was sure that it wasn't Mike and I was equally sure that it wasn't José who did that leave but Donald Lester? I thumped my pillow resolutely. The first chance that came my way I intended to ask José exactly what had happened between her and Mike. She probably wouldn't mind talking about it now, since she'd obviously found consolation in the shape of Ross.

I rolled over to face the wall. It was about as blank as my own future. One day, I thought, José was going to have to tell Ross who she really was. If he really loved her—and I was pretty sure he did—he wouldn't mind too much that she was the daughter of a man he thoroughly disliked. But, unless I was greatly mistaken, he wouldn't easily forgive her for the way he thought she had treated his friend. For both their sakes, that wretched business simply *had* to be cleared up—and as quickly as possible.

My last conscious thoughts, before I finally drifted off to sleep, were centered around Ross. I wondered whether Donald Lester would approve of Ross as a husband for José. Probably not, but it wouldn't matter too much. If Ross really wanted to marry José then I'd back him to do it, Donald Lester or no Donald Lester. Come to that, I'd back Ross to do anything at all that he'd set his heart on. The man was granite. Cold, cold granite....

The granite look was well in evidence when we met in the hotel foyer early next morning. I fancied he glanced disapprovingly at my dark slacks and bright yellow sweater as he said, "Good morning," and immediately I prepared to do battle.

"What's the matter? Aren't I suitably dressed or something?"

His lips twitched. "Indeed you are. I'm pleasantly surprised. I thought I might have to ask you to leave your diamonds behind."

I grinned reluctantly. "Actually I haven't any."

"I'm glad."

"Glad?"

"Yes. They're not your stone." Ross led the way outside. "Too hard and glittering... too banal."

"Then what is my stone?"

He regarded me enigmatically as he opened the door of a rather shabby Land Rover. "I'm afraid I'm not an authority on precious stones. Rubies, perhaps."

"Oh yes! I love them!" I slid into the front seat of the Land Rover as I spoke and Ross got in beside me. His expression seemed suddenly to close up.

"Well, let's hope your husband-to-be is rich enough to be able to buy you as many as you want." Then, as I stiffened, "I apologize for this mode of transport, by the way. I realize you're used to something far more streamlined, but as far as I'm concerned it's the only vehicle that's really practical."

I said coldly, "I don't mind in the least. What's good enough for you is quite good enough for me!"

He laughed. "Do you know, I really believe you're speaking the truth? You're an odd mixture, Joby Lester. One minute you're a haughty heiress, the next you're quite...." He paused, then added, "likable."

I felt angry tears sting the backs of my eyes. "I haven't asked you to like me!"

Ross let in the clutch and the Rover moved off. "You certainly haven't. In fact, if anything you've deliberately gone out of your way to annoy me. Why, I wonder?"

I sought refuge in flippancy. "Perhaps because most women feel that it's rather better to be annoying than to be ignored!"

"But you're not most women." Ross was frowning at the road ahead, his face unreadable.

I wasn't quite sure how to answer that, so I said nothing. The car nosed its way through the narrow streets of Cuzco, already teeming with activity although it was still so early. Ross put his hand in his pocket and drew out two envelopes.

"I've just remembered. There were a couple of letters for you." He tossed both envelopes into my lap.

One was for José. Not only was it addressed to her, it bore a Barbados stamp. My letter, addressed simply to Miss J. Lester, was from mother. I recognized her handwriting immediately. I was about to slide my finger eagerly beneath the flap when I suddenly checked myself. I realized that Ross would probably think it odd if I didn't open it, but I simply didn't dare. Mother invariably started her letters to me with "My darling daughter." If Ross happened to glance in my direction he might not be able to help noticing. And then the fat really would be in the fire!

As if reading my thoughts Ross shot me a mocking glance. "I promise I'm not interested in peeking at your private correspondence!"

I felt the color creep into my cheeks. "I... I thought I'd save it until later. It... it will be something to look forward to. It's from—" I stopped and added lamely, "a very old friend."

Ross's brows were two mocking crescents, but he said nothing for a moment or two. Then quite casually he remarked, "Aren't you even going to open Isabel's? I thought you'd be only too anxious to know how your father is progressing."

"But it's—" I stopped, biting my lip in confusion. I'd been going to say, "It's José's letter." Instead I said, "How do you know it's from Isabel?"

He shrugged. "Because I had one myself. I should open it if I were you. You'll probably find that it contains some interesting news."

There was no help for it. I'd have to explain to José later. I tore open the envelope and withdrew two closely written sheets. Ross concentrated on his driving. The road was very rough, a series of ruts and potholes, and I felt as though at any minute I might be shaken out onto the dusty surface.

I read the letter twice. Very carefully. Then slowly I said, "I can see what you meant by the interesting news."

"Do you mind?" Ross's voice sounded oddly abrupt.

"That I'm going to have Isabel for a stepmother? Of course not. I'm...I'm very pleased." Thank goodness, I thought, that knowing the real José's views on the subject of her father's possible remarriage I could speak with absolute sincerity. I knew José would be overjoyed.

Ross shot me a quick look. "You really mean that, don't you?"

"Yes. I'm very fond of Isabel. I always hoped this would happen."

"Even though it may mean that your nose is put out of joint a little?"

"I don't see why it should. But anyway I want my father and Isabel to be happy, and I think they will be."

Ross gave something which sounded suspiciously like a snort of exasperation. "Why are you always so damned unpredictable?"

I raised my brows. "Am I?"

"You know damn well you are! I never know which way you're going to jump!"

I laughed. He sounded more amused than annoyed. "What did Isabel say in her letter to you? Didn't she think I'd be pleased?"

"She hoped you would be. She said that she thought you knew that she'd been in love with your father for a long time. Apparently she'd almost given up hope of his ever asking her to marry him, though."

"What is it they say? Something about its being an ill wind that blows no one any good?"

"I presume you're referring to your father's accident. In case you're wondering, I didn't exactly envisage this particular development when I took steps to have your father sent back to Barbados!"

The wind, blowing through the open car window, whipped my hair witchlike all around me.

A long strand of it touched Ross's cheek and I saw him flinch sharply.

I closed the window. Smoothing back my hair with hands that shook a little, I said nastily, "You sound rather as though you mind! Can't you bear the thought of being related to the detestable Lesters, father and daughter, even if it's only by marriage?"

Ross gave a short laugh. "My dear good girl, I don't mind at all! I can't say that I admire Isabel's taste, but that's neither here nor there. It's her life, not mine."

I might never have such a good opportunity again. "She...she said a little while ago that you were all the family she'd got. Isn't there...haven't you got somebody else, beside her?"

For a moment I thought he wasn't going to answer. Then he said very quietly, "My parents were both killed in an air crash when I was ten. My sister and I were left in the care of a very beautiful and glamorous aunt who couldn't bear children and who invariably made that fact exceedingly plain."

I caught my breath. "Oh, what rotten luck! For you—and for your sister! Where is she now? Have you left her in England?"

Ross turned his head and looked at me and I almost cried out at the bleakness in his eyes. "She was a lot younger than I was. She died, seven years ago, on her eighteenth birthday. A runaway bus crushed her against a wall."

I knew, at that moment, that I would never again make the mistake of thinking Ross Henderson a cold man. He still cared deeply for his young sister, still raged at the circumstances of her tragic death. I knew now the reason for the barriers of which Isabel had spoken. I knew, and I sympathized, and yet I couldn't find a single thing to say.

I opened my handbag to put the two letters away. Just as I did so Ross swerved sharply to avoid a deep pothole and, caught off balance, I was thrown against him. He braked and instinctively, I suppose, flung one arm around me to break my fall. It was like a steel band. Through the thick wool of his navy blue sweater I was conscious of the warmth of his body and the strong beating of his heart. I felt his muscles tense, heard him suck in his breath, and then almost roughly he pushed me away from him.

"Are you all right?"

"Yes. Sorry about that." I spoke through my teeth. It was the second time within a very few minutes that Ross had made it abundantly clear that he disliked me so much that any physical contact with me had almost a stingray effect!

"It wasn't your fault. This damned road is full of potholes." He spoke brusquely. "We shall be hitting the new road a couple of miles farther on and then the going will be a bit easier."

"Will it? I'm so glad."

I felt, rather than saw, his glance of surprise and averted my head. "Don't you think that perhaps it would be better if we didn't talk? I'm sure you need all your attention for the road."

There was a moment's silence. Then Ross said evenly, "Good idea." He must have accelerated a little, for I saw the dust spurting out from beneath the wheels of the truck.

We didn't exchange another word for the rest of the journey. Ross concentrated on his driving, I stared stonily out of the window. Not that I was interested in the scenery, unforgettably beautiful though it was. I was wishing with all my heart that I'd plumped for the *hacienda*, plus Ramon, plus mumps. I wouldn't be able to stand Ross Henderson in large doses for an entire week. What on earth had ever made me think I could?

I had to admit—though only to myself—that the new road, though rocky and winding, was very much better than any other road I had traveled on in Peru. The engineering skill that had gone into its constrution made my mind boggle, but I pretended to be completely unimpressed.

We rounded a bend, and I saw the roadworks ahead, a slaggy confusion of stones and rocks and rubble, dotted with brown-skinned figures. Ross brought the Land Rover to a halt, and as I climbed out my ears were assailed by a cacophony of shrill and deafening noises from the various machines in use. The air was thick with dust which made me cough and splutter and my eyes water.

Beside me, Ross laughed.

"The office is over there. I'm afraid that just at first you'll be bothered by the noise, but you'll soon get used to it."

"*And* the dust?"

"I did warn you." Ross sounded suddenly grim. "I agree it isn't exactly the Garden of Eden, but—"

I interrupted him, shading my eyes with the back of my hand. "Is that the Valley of Skulls, down there?"

"Yes, that's it."

I had thought of it as wild and desolate, a barren valley where nothing grew. I hadn't expected it to be beautiful, but it was. It was full of purple shadows and the gigantic peaks above it had snowy caps that were tinged with ethereal pink by the strengthening sun.

"Come on." I thought Ross sounded impatient, so reluctantly I turned and followed him to a sparsely grassed site where there was an encampment of tents with several jeeps and Land Rovers parked beside it.

I was conscious of the fact that most of the men had stopped work and were watching us. It suddenly occurred to me that I was the only woman for—what? How many miles? Ross should never have suggested my coming here, I thought angrily. Why, if he was so concerned about my safety, hadn't he thought of something else?

"Here we are." Ross unlocked the door of the office and stood aside to let me precede him up the steps.

Inside it was very untidy and very dusty. There were papers scattered all over the desk and an ashtray and a wastepaper basket were filled to overflowing. There seemed to be a thick layer of dust over everything in sight, including the chairs. I stared around me, my nose crinkling in distaste, and Ross spoke from behind me.

"I'm sorry," he said ruefully. "It's a far cry from the sort of office your father has in London and New York, isn't it? All thick carpets and the very latest in office equipment. Also I hadn't reallized until now, I'm afraid, that it was quite so dirty. Go and sit in the Land Rover and I'll see if I can clean things up a bit."

I drew a deep breath and turned to face him. "I know you think I'm practically useless, Ross Henderson, and that I'm only here because you can't think what else to do with me, but I assure you that I do know that dirt can quite easily be removed with a bucket of soapy water! If you can get someone to provide me with that I'm quite capable of doing the job myself!"

Ross stared at me incredulously. It was the first time I had ever seen him looking completely nonplussed. "You mean...you're quite prepared to roll up your sleeves and get down to, er, charring?"

I returned his stare. Belligerently. "Provided you lay off the dirty cracks, yes, I am."

There was a moment's silence. Then: "Well, well," Ross said softly. "As I said earlier, you're full of surprises, Joby Lester."

I took off my coat. "Do I get that soapy water, or don't I?"

I got it. And used it. At the end of an hour and a half I was reasonably well satisfied with my efforts. I was filthy, but the office was clean. Almost shining.

Ross came back just as I was finishing. He took one look at my disheveled hair and dirt-streaked face, and burst out laughing.

"If only your father could see you now!"

I eyed him coldly. "I stipulated no dirty cracks, remember?"

He sobered instantly. "I remember. I apologize." He looked around him. "It's a pity you're an heiress. You do this sort of thing so well!"

He spoke lightly, but his blue eyes were warm with approval. And something else which I didn't recognize but which made me feel oddly breathless. I said, stammering a little, "I'm... I'm glad you think it's an improvement."

"It certainly is that. I think you've more than earned five minutes' rest and a cup of coffee." Ross's smile made me forget my aching arms and dust-filled lungs. Thoughts of the de Noveli *hacienda* began to recede further and further from my mind. Working for Ross might not be so bad after all. In fact, I began to think I might even enjoy it!

At the end of the day, when Ross drove me back to our hotel, I was glowing with the satisfaction of knowing that even if I couldn't persuade myself that I'd been completely indispensable, at least I *had* been moderately useful! I'd sorted through piles of correspondence that

Ross said he'd been too busy to deal with and I'd even done a bit of typing, using, of course, the two-finger method. There seemed no reason at all why I shouldn't help to prepare the daily progress reports which Ross found such a chore, but when I offered he looked at me curiously.

"Look, you've already done a hell of a lot. Quite frankly, I didn't really expect—"

"That I'd be any use at all? I know you didn't," I agreed. "It just shows that life does hold its little surprises, doesn't it?"

He smiled a little wryly. We were sitting in the office after lunch, which had been another of the "little surprises" I'd just mentioned. It had been a native stew called *sancochado*, rich in peppers, and my helping had been so enormous that I'd been devoutly thankful for my high-mountain appetite! Ross had eaten with me, thought he normally sat with the men at long trestle tables set out in the open air near the cook-house.

"I rather thought that one day out here would be more than enough and that you'd be diving off to join José at the first opportunity!" he said, stirring his coffee.

I shook my head and laughed. "Do you know, I've rather enjoyed it? I've even got used to the noise, though I must admit that what I'm looking forward to more than anything else is a nice hot shower! I don't feel as though I'll ever be clean again!"

He grinned. "Now that you've washed your face you look quite presentable, though you've still got a powdering of dust all over your hair." He put out his hand as he spoke as if to brush the dust off, then quickly withdrew it. When he next spoke his voice had changed, become curt and businesslike. In fact, his attitude was strictly impersonal for the rest of the day and I reflected somewhat bitterly that it was obvious that he still mistrusted me. It seemed as if one minute he was wanting to know me better, the next he was trying to push me aside.

When we arrived back in Cuzco he announced somewhat brusquely that he wouldn't be seeing me again that evening as he'd been invited to dinner with friends. On the whole I was relieved. Too much of Ross Henderson's company would be extremely bad for my peace of mind. I was convinced of that. Anyway, I had letters to write. And I wanted to see if José felt well enough to talk to me over the phone. She had a right to know at once about Isabel and her father: it would be a piece of good news to brighten her illness.

In the event it was Ramon who answered the phone.

"Joby! Where have you been all day? I have been trying to contact you! When I rang the hotel they told me that you had left very early this morning with Señor Henderson."

"Yes. I'm working for him," I said with would-be airiness. Somehow or another I didn't think Ramon would be in favor of the idea and I was right. He wasn't.

"*Working*? For Señor Henderson? You? But where?"

"At the site. Oh, I'm not doing very much, just sorting through correspondence and doing a bit of typing. That sort of thing," I explained.

"But surely...are you not the only woman?" Ramon's voice absolutely oozed shocked disapproval. "It is most unsuitable! I would not have thought that Señor Henderson would have allowed you to expose yourself to such a situation!"

Well aware of the code governing the relations between the sexes in Latin America, I decided not to become involved in an argument which could only lead us nowhere. Anyway, it was really none of Ramon's business to question what I did.

I said crisply, "Well, he does have his reasons, but I

can't possibly go into them now, Ramon. It would take too long. I'd like to speak to José, please, if she's well enough."

"I have been told that she is feeling much better today. You can speak to her in a moment." Ramon sounded very much like the descendant of an arrogant *conquistador.* "First, though, I want—"

I interrupted him. "Ramon, not now, *please*! There's something I badly want to tell José. It...it's about her family, and it's frightfully important."

There was a moment's silence. Then Ramon said in a stiff, slightly offended voice, "Very well. Will you hold the line a moment, please?"

I felt a momentary pang of compunction. Most girls, I felt sure, would have found Ramon's combination of wealth, good looks and sophisticated charm almost irresistible. I liked him, I was grateful for what he and his family were doing for José—but the stark fact was that he didn't make my wayward heart miss even a single beat!

"Hello? Joby?" José's voice at the other end of the line lacked its customary sparkle, but the squeal she gave when I told her about Isabel and her father proved that she really was feeling a lot better.

"Joby! How marvelous! Oh, I *am* glad! It's exactly what I hoped would happen."

"I knew you'd be pleased. I...I don't think Ross was, though."

"Ross?"

I explained, then, where I had spent my day and why. I had wondered a little uneasily whether she, too, might object to my working for Ross, but her reaction was perfectly cheerful and matter-of-fact.

"Poor you! What a way to spend a holiday. I think I'd almost rather have mumps! The noise must be ghastly!"

"You get used to that. It's the dust I hate."

"Dust as well? My dear! I repeat—what a holiday!" Then, curiously, "What did Ross find you to do?"

I told her, but I got the impression that she wasn't listening very hard. "Darling, what do you think I should say when I write to congratulate daddy and Isabel? Shall I tell them I've got mumps?"

I hesitated. "I don't know. What do you think?"

"Might be better to keep quiet. Is Ross still worrried about me? He was sweet, wasn't he? Do you know he kissed me goodbye even though I must have looked a perfect fright?"

I didn't realize, until I looked down and saw my knuckles showing white, how hard I was gripping the receiver.

"He's very fond of you. You...you like him a lot, too, don't you, José?"

"Like him? I *adore* him!"

I frowned. I'd heard José say, with much the same enthusiasm, that she "adored" dark chocolate, gray kittens and Tchaikovsky's "Pathétique." However....

José interrupted my thoughts. "You haven't told him? About us, I mean."

I said a little drearily, "No," and went on to talk about something else. I really wanted to tell her what Ross had said about Mike but though it was important I thought that this was scarcely the right moment. She'd begun to sound tired. Come to that, I was tired myself—and oddly dispirited. Lack of sleep, I told myself. One good night and I'd be on top of the world again.

I took a couple of aspirins before I went to bed, something I very rarely do. As a result I *did* sleep, but far too heavily, and I got up in the morning feeling muzzy and—I must admit—distinctly irritable. I think that perhaps Ross must have sensed my mood, for he said very little on the way to the roadworks. I couldn't help thinking that he looked as though he hadn't been sleeping too well himself. The first part of the morning was uneventful. In fact, after about eleven o'clock time began to drag a little. Ross kept well away from the office, but occasionally I caught a glimpse in the distance of his familiar figure, so much taller and broader shouldered than anyone else's.

I stared moodily at the pile of papers in front of me. I recognized Ross's handwriting on the top sheet. Bold, black, distinctive, revealing strength and character.

There was a tap on the door. I called "Come in" without looking round. I thought it was probably Sandy Mackenzie, a pleasant, ginger-haired young man whom I had met the previous day and who appeared to be Ross's second-in-command.

It wasn't. It was Ramon de Noveli. He stood in the doorway, handsome and smiling and self-confident.

He was the very last person I had expected to see. I said stupidly, "Ramon! What... whatever are you doing here?"

"I came to find you. Since you refused to talk to me over the telephone yesterday evening—"

I stared at him in dismay. I didn't quite know what had happened to the security check designed to prevent unauthorized people from wandering onto the site, but I did know that Ramon's presence would probably be frowned upon.

"Look, you shouldn't have come! I told you I was working—"

Ramon raised his brows. "You don't look particularly busy as of this moment. You can spare me five minutes of your valuable time, surely?"

His smile had vanished and he looked—and sounded—rather sulky. It occurred to me that up to now Ramon de Noveli might well have enjoyed some easy conquests.

Obviously I wouldn't be able to get rid of him without

an argument, so I sighed and said, "All right. Five minutes."

"I've come to ask you if you'd like to visit Machu Picchu tomorrow. I know you want to see it and even though José won't be able to accompany us we can perhaps arrange another visit when she is better."

Macchu Picchu! The one place in Peru I was dying to see! I drew a deep breath. "Oh, Ramon, I... I'd love to, and it's awfully kind of you to think of it, but—but I can't. Not this week."

"You mean—you prefer Señor Henderson's company to mine?" There was no mistaking the sulkiness now.

"Of course not! I didn't say... it's just that I think it would be better to wait for José!"

"But I want you to myself."

I wasn't prepared for what happened next. I suddenly found myself in Ramon's arms and he was trying to kiss me.

For a moment I was too surprised to resist. Then I put my hands on his chest and tried—I must admit not very successfully—to push him away.

"*Don't*, Ramon. You mustn't—"

"I'm sorry to interrupt you, Joby, but I'm afraid I must ask your—friend—to leave." That was Ross's voice, colder than I had ever heard it before. Because of the noise of the pneumatic drills, a constant throb in the background, I hadn't heard him coming, but when I whirled around it was to find him standing looking at us with bleak, unsmiling eyes.

He addressed Ramon, who looked flushed and angry. "Unauthorized persons are not allowed on the site. I believe you have already been told that, Señor de Noveli, but apparently you chose to assume that the embargo did not apply to you. Unfortunately, your assumption was incorrect."

Ramon drew himself up to his full height, though even then Ross topped him by two inches. "This is my land—"

"Pardon me. It *was* your land. You sold it. You have, therefore, no right at all to be here. Will you please conclude your—business—with Miss Lester and leave her to get on with her work?" Ross's eyes flicked over me as he spoke and they were cold with anger.

I saw Ramon step forward, his fists clenched, his eyes blazing, and dreading a scene, I spoke hurriedly.

"Señor de Noveli was just leaving anyway, Ross. He...he only came to ask me if I'd like to visit Machu Picchu."

Ramon still looked belligerent and for a moment I held my breath, but perhaps he saw the pleading in my eyes, for he suddenly gave an angry little shrug. He said something in Spanish which I didn't understand, then swiveled on his heel and walked, not without dignity, toward the door. I heard him going down the wooden steps and relief mingled for an instant with my dismay.

"I think I'd better see him off the site." Ross spoke grimly. "In future, Joby, I'd be very grateful if you could persuade your admirers to restrain their quite natural ardor until you're in a position to give them your full attention!"

A hot ache closed my throat. I muttered "You...you make me feel cheap! It wasn't my fault—" but I don't think he even heard me. I watched him follow quickly after Ramon and catch him up, then I turned blindly away.

Ross didn't return to the office. He didn't even have lunch with me. As a result I only managed to swallow two mouthfuls of the meal that was brought in to me, though it tasted delicious. The noise of the drills jabbed at my head, the sides of the caravan seemed to be closing in on me. By two I was almost desperate, engulfed in a horrifying mixture of depression and loneliness and acute claustrophobia.

There was only one thing I felt that I could do to save my sanity. I went for a walk. The insidious beauty of the Valley of Skulls had fascinated me from the first and its wild solitude was just what I needed. I had no intention, at first, of going very far, but once I had left the road-works behind me the valley, dark like jasper in the shadow of the towering peaks which enclosed it, proved to be even more alluring than I'd realized.

It wasn't until I heard an angry voice hailing me that I realized just how long I'd been wandering in my rocky wilderness. I knew, even before I turned, who had followed me, and I felt my heart plummet in dismay.

"You little fool!" Ross, as he caught me up, sounded out of breath and I thought I'd never seen his face look so grim. "My God, are you determined to make a thorough nuisance of yourself today? What the hell made you wander off like that? Don't you realize the danger? When I found you were missing I... if one of the men hadn't seen you walking in this direction—" He stopped and then said roughly, "After all I've told you about the need to be careful! You deserve to be beaten!"

I'd had just about enough. I said furiously, "Will you please stop lecturing me! I'm sorry I wandered off without telling anyone, I guess I just didn't think, but... but there's no need to keep on!"

I made as if to brush past him but, blinded by angry tears, I stumbled and almost fell. Ross put his hand to steady me, but I knocked it away.

"I shouldn't touch me if I were you! You never know, I... I might put a spell on you! Turn you into a snake or a toad or something like that!"

It was childish and I knew it. I expected a scathing retort, but Ross's face was suddenly dark and tense. In the voice of a man goaded to the limit of his endurance he said in a mutter I could scarcely catch, "It's not that sort of spell I'm afraid of!"

For the second time that day I found myself in a man's arms. Ross's arms. He took hold of my hair and pulled my head back, not gently, and for a moment I had a dizzy glimpse of his face as it swam before me. Then his mouth was on mine, bruising my lips in a kiss which seemed to last for a long, long time. I wouldn't have minded if it had lasted forever.

When he released me we stood staring at each other in a queer, shaken silence. Then Ross said huskily, "I think you had that coming to you... Melusine!"

I didn't answer. I don't think he expected me to. We walked side by side back to the roadworks, but though it seemed as though we were only a few inches apart I knew that a chasm stretched between us.

CHAPTER NINE

I TELEPHONED JOSÉ that same evening to find out what had really gone wrong between her and Mike. I'd meant to wait another day or two, but now I didn't dare to put it off. After what had happened in the Valley of Skulls I was afraid that I might just be selfish enough to grudge Ross to José...even to hope that when he found out who she really was he might turn to me.

It wasn't that I thought Ross was in any danger of falling in love with me. I knew how he felt about José, had noticed how tender, even protective, he was toward her. But I also knew that there was something between us, some pull of attraction which might on his part be purely physical but which for me went a good deal deeper. Perhaps, if the circumstances had been different, if he hadn't believed from the very first that I was the girl who'd ditched his friend....I sighed, and picked up the receiver resolutely.

It was José herself who nearly defeated my good intentions. She clammed up as soon as I mentioned Mike's name and it was quite obvious that she didn't want to talk about him.

"Joby, do we have to rake up the past? I...I want to forget about it! I told you—"

"Yes, I know, but José, listen! Ross knows Mike and...and he...well, he thinks that what happened was entirely your fault. Not Mike's!"

I heard José catch her breath. *"Mine?"*

I told her, then, exactly what Ross had said, and

waited anxiously for her reaction. "Joby! I never...I never said I wouldn't marry him! I said that even if daddy disowned me it didn't make any difference, that I didn't care about the money as long as we could be together. It was true! I loved him so!"

I said slowly, "Then Uncle Donald did threaten to disinherit you? Ross was right about that?"

"Yes, but daddy didn't mean it, Joby! It was a test, he said, just to see if Mike really loved me. He was sure from the very beginning that he was just a fortune hunter. And he was right, because directly Mike knew that there wouldn't be any money he sheered off! I never saw or heard from him again!"

José sounded agitated. I couldn't doubt that she was speaking the truth.

I said, "Look, I know it's a painful subject, but can I just get things straight? What exactly did Mike say to you after you'd told him that your father was going to disinherit you?"

There was a small silence. Then José said, "Well, it wasn't I who actually told him. It was daddy. He...he said it would sound better coming from him, that Mike might not believe me."

I caught my breath. "But you saw him afterward, surely?"

"No. I was in Paris, you see, and Mike had been sent to New York. I wrote, twice, but he never answered my letters. At last I had to believe that daddy was quite right, that he didn't want me without my money. The rest you know."

I said incredulously, "But I don't understand! Why didn't you try to see him? Or phone him?"

"I...I felt so awful about the whole thing. I wished I'd never agreed to go along with daddy. It seemed easier to write. Then, when he never answered—"

"He might not have received your letters!"

"In that case, why weren't they sent back to me? He must have received them, Joby! Oh, I suppose one letter might just possibly have gone astray, but not two! That would be too much of a coincidence!"

"Where did you send them?"

"To his hotel in New York. Daddy's secretary gave me the address without daddy knowing. She even told me his room number! She was terribly sweet and helpful. I was a bit surprised, actually, because she's normally a bit of a gorgon, but—"

"But you thought she was on your side?"

"Well... yes." José sounded defensive.

I thought for a few minutes, then I drew a deep breath. "José, maybe I've got a beastly, low, suspicious mind, but I wouldn't mind betting that between them, your father and his secretary pulled a fast one on you! And that Mike didn't receive your letters. It's the only possible explanation!"

There was a little gasp at the other end of the line. Then José said angrily, "Are you mad? You must have got a pretty poor opinion of my father, Joby Lester!"

"He... he might truly and honestly have thought he was doing the right thing! He—"

"*Shut up!* I don't want to talk about it any more!" José had never spoken to me in that tone before. In fact, she sounded perilously close to tears.

I said despairingly, "José, please! I'm only trying to help! At the moment Ross is convinced that José Lester played his best friend a rotten trick. You must be able to convince him otherwise, or—"

I was going to say, "Or you'll lose your second chance of happiness, too," but José interrupted me.

"I can handle Ross Henderson! Don't try to interfere, please, Joby, or... or I'll hate you!" Then, almost in the same breath, "No, I won't! Of course I won't, whatever you do! Oh, Joby, please forgive me! I didn't mean to say that! It's just that... I've got a splitting headache and I feel so rotten, anyway...."

"Yes, of course. Don't worry about it, José. I understand. It's just that I wanted..." my voice trailed away.

"To help? It's sweet of you, Joby, but I don't need help. Honestly."

Well, maybe she didn't, I thought as a few minutes later I replaced the phone. Maybe she felt sure enough of Ross's love to be reasonably confident that she could persuade him to believe her story, and not Mike's. I wished that I could share her confidence, and yet wasn't trust an essential ingredient of love? Perhaps it would be all right after all. At any rate for José....

EXCEPT FOR THE JOURNEY to and from the roadworks, I didn't see much of Ross during the next two days. His manner toward me was pleasant, but remote. I guessed that he probably bitterly regretted that brief encounter in the Valley of Skulls, when he had momentarily been shaken off balance by a mixture of anxiety and exasperation, and that his chilliness was meant to serve as a warning to me not to read too much into a solitary kiss. Well, I was certainly in no danger of doing that. I only knew that as long as I lived I'd remember the steely strength of Ross's arms, the feel of his lips on mine, the way the valley, briefly, had enfolded us. Funny, I hadn't expected that sort of memory as a legacy of my holiday in Peru. Was I richer or poorer for it? I didn't know.

José was making an excellent recovery from mumps and was already making eager plans to return to Cuzco. I knew I would be more than glad to see her, especially as her return would mean that Ross would no longer feel any dire obligation to keep me under close surveillance. There wasn't going to be any more trouble with the Indians, anyway. Even he seemed thankfully to have reached that conclusion. No doubt despite their continued threats they had realized that in any battle with a large and powerful international company they were bound to find themselves on the losing side. I didn't approve of what they'd done—how could I?—but I did share their regret that the solitude of their supposedly sacred valley was soon to be brutally invaded.

Friday was payday for the men. "What are we going to do about Miss Lester?" Sandy Mackenzie asked, grinning at Ross. "Not working just for love, is she?"

Of course he was only joking, but I felt a flush burn into my cheeks. I don't know whether Ross noticed my embarrassment, but all he said was, "I don't think she's exactly expecting a pay packet from us, Sandy."

"Maybe not, but she ought to have some sort of reward. A big box of chocolates, perhaps, or a bottle of Chanel." Sandy looked at me, his gray eyes twinkling. "What's it to be, Miss Lester?"

Ross answered for me. "I don't think there's any reward we could offer that would interest Miss Lester, Sandy."

The way he said it annoyed me. I lifted my chin. "No? What makes you so sure of that? I'd love a reward. But not chocolates, or Chanel. I don't like either."

"Oh? Then what?" Ross asked with a cold smile.

I felt suddenly reckless. I didn't care whether I annoyed him or not. "Will you take me to Machu Picchu? On Sunday?"

"Machu Picchu?" I had the satisfaction of seeing him look thoroughly startled, then he quickly recovered. "I thought you said de Noveli was taking you there?"

"He invited me, but I didn't accept." I smiled as provocatively as I knew how. "Of course, it was you who warned me that it wasn't a very comfortable trip, wasn't it? And I believe someone told me that there are even poisonous snakes. If you'd really rather not...."

I saw his lips tighten, saw the gleam of anger in his

eyes and felt a spurt of malicious pleasure. Then, unexpectedly, he smiled. "Yes, I'll take you."

"You will?" Now it was my turn to look startled. I realized with dismay that my malice had boomeranged. All I wanted to do was to put him in a spot in front of Sandy, to get my own back. I'd been so sure that he'd try to find some good excuse not to take me!

"Yes." He was obviously enjoying my discomfiture. "I think it's a good idea." He turned to Sandy. "What about you and that pretty girl you've been dating recently? Would you care to join us...make up a foursome?"

I held my breath, then expelled it in a tiny sigh of relief as Sandy said enthusiastically, "I'll have to check with Maria, but that sounds just great. I've heard a lot about Machu Picchu from folk who've been there...some of 'em reckon there's nothing to touch it in the whole wide world!"

"Good. Then that's settled." Ross turned back to me. *That'll teach you to play games with me, my girl,* his look said, and my heart did a disconcerting somersault. Hoist with my own petard, I thought ruefully. Oh, hell, hell, hell....

"You don't want to, er, back out?" Ross's smile was definitely unpleasant. He knew quite well what I'd tried to do, and that was why he had turned the tables on me so neatly. "I'm sure that both Sandy and I realize that you suggested the trip entirely on the spur of the moment. If on second thoughts...?"

I lifted my chin, accepting his mocking challenge. "Certainly I don't want to back out! You can't think how I'm looking forward to it!"

In a way it was perfectly true. I did want to see fabulous Machu Picchu, more than anything else in the world. More, even, than I wanted to see the Parthenon in Greece, the Colosseum in Rome. Only...not with

Ross Henderson. How could I bear the slow, sad ache of beauty if every nerve in my body was already aching for him? Besides, how could I explain to José? Come to that, how could he?

As if he could read my thoughts he said casually, "It's a pity that José won't be able to be with us, but never mind, I can arrange to take her another time. She'll probably enjoy it better on her own, anyway. Her interest is likely to be rather more academic than yours or Sandy's, I imagine."

In spite of myself I almost laughed. If José wasn't careful she might find that she was another one hoist with her own petard. During our first week in Cuzco she'd very firmly resisted all my attempts to persuade hr to visit Machu Picchu, but unless she revealed her real identity fairly soon I thought it quite likely that she'd find herself there, with Ross, the very first time he was free.

We took an *autocarril*—a bus with flanged wheels run on regular railroad tracks—to Machu Picchu; Ross, myself, Sandy and a pretty Peruvian girl who looked very gay and charming in a scarlet skirt and a matching shawl threaded with gold. She was introduced to me as Maria de Lorcha and Ross told me that she was the daughter of the manager of a large *hacienda.*

"How did Sandy get to know her?" I asked, shivering a little in the early morning darkness as we waited for the *autocarril* to arrive. Listening to Sandy and Maria as they kept up a constant line of chatter, half teasing, half amorous, I couldn't help wishing that the relationship between Ross and myself was not so strained and unnatural.

Ross shrugged. "The company has had dealings with Señor d'Alvarez, Maria's father's *patrón.* Originally he hoped they'd buy a great deal of his land, but he asked such a stiff price that they were forced to work out an alternative route. I think I told you about that."

I glanced at him. "Yes, you did. So that's how the Indians came to lose their sacred valley?"

"Correct. D'Alvarez wasn't too pleased, he rather thought he had the company over a barrel. Still, he's been quite helpful since."

The wind was bitter. I drew my duffel coat closer around me, glad that I'd thought of including it in my luggage. It wasn't smart, it wasn't new, but on this chilly morning I was more than grateful for its comfortable warmth.

I saw Ross looking at me. "Are you cold?" Then, as I shook my head, "That coat looks warm. And serviceable."

I laughed. "In my experience, 'serviceable' is a euphemism for dowdy!"

"You couldn't possibly look dowdy, whatever you wore." Ross's eyes were reflective, even puzzled as he added, "Nevertheless, a duffel coat isn't a garment I'd expect Miss Joby Lester to have in her wardrobe. What's happened to your mink?"

"I left it at home, along with those diamonds we were talking about a few days ago."

I spoke a little too quickly, and with a tinge of defiance which made Ross's fine dark eyebrows rise quizzically. Luckily, just at that moment the *autocarril* arrived and we all clambered inside. Almost inevitably I found myself sitting next to Ross, with Sandy and Maria, as gay as two children on a Sunday-school outing, sitting opposite. Their hands were linked. I tried hard not to envy them, but I didn't quite succeed.

Ross shifted his position slightly to make more room for the rather plump woman sitting on his other side and I felt the pressure of his arm against mine. I was suddenly afraid that he would realize how strongly his nearness affected me. I had the window seat, so I leaned as far away from him as I could and pressed my nose against the glass.

At any rate the scenery was well worth looking at. After four switchbacks to clear the cup of steep hills surrounding Cuzco, we plunged down into a wide and fertile valley beyond which glacier-clad peaks thrust upward to the sky. Then came more rugged country, the railway following the banks and awesome canyon of the swirling, turbulent river Urumbamba, which swept, green and lucid, over white stones that the water had sculptured into beautiful curved shapes.

"From now on the scenery will become more and more tropical." Ross's quiet voice spoke in my ear as we passed the mighty stronghold of Ollontaytambo. "Jungle, in fact."

I nodded. "Hiram Bingham practically had to hack down a forest to reach Machu Picchu, didn't he? It must have been a marvelous moment for him when he realized what a fantastic city he'd found."

"Yes. I've been reading the book he wrote about it." He hesitated. "Perhaps you'd like to borrow it some time. If you're interested, that is."

"Rather!" I exclaimed. "I tried to borrow it from the library when I knew we were coming to Peru, but it was already out. I managed to get hold of Prescott's *History of Peru*, though: have you read that? It—"

I stopped abruptly, flushing scarlet under his sudden intent gaze. Stupid, stupid creature that I was, I'd entirely forgotten that Joby Lester was supposed to be bored stiff by anything remotely connected with history!

Ross's eyes seemed to be boring out my secret. I bent my head, hiding my flushed, guilty face under the shelter of my black hair. I heard him say very deliberately, "What a strange girl you are! Almost a Jekyll and Hyde personality. Just as I think I've about got you taped—"

"Machu Picchu!" The stentorian cry saved me. We had arrived at our destination, though our journey was by no means over. We all had to pile into the minibus which was to take us up the next two thousand feet by five miles of steep, zigzag road and hairpin curves on the side of the mountain. Maria's head was on Sandy's shoulder, her black hair flying in the wind. She was pretending to be scared, but it was obvious that she was enjoying herself thoroughly.

"She'd probably be just as happy if she was on the switchback at Battersea Fun Fair!" I thought, and was horrified to realize that I had nearly spoken the thought aloud. What was the matter with me? I wasn't usually so sour and cynical!

The minibus was transporting us into a fairy-tale land of steep sugar-loaf peaks, covered to their summits in green. I waited breathlessly for my first glimpse of Machu Picchu, but it wasn't until we had rounded the last bend of the zigzag that it came into sight... a labyrinth of soft gray walls in a saddle between two mighty peaks. It was drizzling slightly, and gossamer mists wreathed the mountains like the veils of some cosmic Salome. It wasn't real, I thought dazedly. Nothing so beautiful could possibly be real!

"Incredible, isn't it?" Ross's eyes, like mine, were full of wonderment. I wondered if, again like me, he was drunk with the rapture of a dream.

I didn't answer. I didn't need to. At that moment there was something almost telepathic between us. It didn't last, of course. Sandy shattered it with some teasing remark about snakes. Maria gave a little scream and though I didn't really believe that we'd see any I felt glad that I was wearing tough brogues.

The minibus disgorged us outside the little government tourist hotel where, later, we intended to have lunch. It was a pleasant, white-walled and dark-wooded building nestling unobtrusively into the hillside. From here we set off on foot, threading our way in single file through a gate in the ramparts of the lost city, and then clambering up over the terraces and along the steep llama roads between the ruined houses on the higher levels.

Although I had read so much about Machu Picchu, I don't think I'd realized that the buildings would be quite so well preserved. It was a complete city—temples, palaces, terraces, staircases, towers, roofless stone houses, fountains and even a huge sundial still recording the hours. As the four of us wandered through the maze of buildings and clambered up and down the narrow stepped streets I could almost feel the presence of the people who had lived in Machu Picchu ten centuries ago. I had the strange, fey impression that the city was only momentarily deserted...that the population might come surging back at any moment and drive out the brash intruders from the twentieth century.

Maria was complaining of feeling tired by the time we had reached the highest point of the city, where the sacred dial stone called the Hitching Post of the Sun cast its sharp noon shadow among the roofless temples. From a special watch platform we looked down over the gray contours of the city and into the vast canyon below. Huge cloud shadows lay in indigo masses, heavy with storm and menace. I couldn't help thinking, with a little shiver, about how many lives must have been expended in the building of this huge and ancient fortress, and even in its maintenance.

"Come back to the world," Ross said to me softly, and I stared at him blankly, almost uncomprehendingly.

"I have the vertigo." Maria, at least, had seen enough. Probably she wanted her lunch. Her scarlet skirt was a red light flashing through the gray stones...a warning. Sandy and Ross followed her, arguing about the method that the Incas, who were minus lifting tackle or tools or iron and steel, must have adopted to maneuver granite blocks weighing fifteen tons or more into place. Purposely I lingered behind. Only by myself would I be able to capture the real "feel" of this place.

It was surprisingly easy. One minute I could hear the rise and fall of Ross's and Sandy's voices, Maria's rather high-pitched giggle. The next I was quite alone... alone in a gray city of sleeping ghosts. The mist swirled around me as I walked slowly up a deserted street. Where was the building that was said to have been an Inca mausoleum where mummies of the dead rulers were kept, covered up or wrapped in gold?

I stopped and examined my guidebook. As I did so I was suddenly attacked by the feeling that someone was watching me. It was exactly the same sensation I had experienced that awful day in the Archaeological Museum in Cuzco. As on that occasion, I tried desperately to persuade myself that my imagination was playing tricks. But, when I began quickly to walk back the way I had come, as eager now for company as I had previously been for solitude, the sound of footsteps, quiet, stealthy, followed me.

Somewhere in my brain a warning bell was shrilling insistently. What a fool I'd been to let myself get parted from the others! I stopped, and the footsteps stopped, too. I began to walk on, taking lone rapid strides, and the pace of my pursuer quickened as well.

Sheer blind panic swept over me and I began to run. If only I could find the others! They surely couldn't be far away! I didn't dare to look back, but I knew that whoever was behind me was running too. And gaining on me... dear God, *he was gaining on me!* My breath was coming in short, painful gasps as the altitude began to take its inevitable toll. I couldn't run much longer—I simply couldn't.

It was desperation that made me stop and turn. Not courage. Dark and lithe and silent, with high cheekbones and black eyes with a Mongolian slant, my pursuer was only two or three paces behind me. There was something in his hand...something long and shining. A knife...?

I opened my mouth to scream, but as in a nightmare no scream came. I was hypnotized by terror. Then, suddenly, I heard someone—a man—calling my name.

"Joby! Joby, where are you?"

Ross! it was Ross! As I recognized his voice I felt a flood of relief sweep over me from top to toe, banishing fear and weakness. I saw the man stop, hesitate, saw the expression of uneasy doubt which spread over his swarthy features. It was his momentary irresolution which galvanized me into action. I screamed "Ross!" at the top of my voice and began running again, and this time it seemed to me my feet had wings.

I don't know how much distance I'd covered when I saw Ross. I only know that as I saw him he held out his arms, and that sobbing with fear and reaction I flung myself into them. It took me a few seconds to realize that we were alone, quite alone, in a pagan setting of great grandeur and beauty. The man with the black slanting eyes...the man with a knife...had melted away into the mist, as if he had never been.

I clutched Ross with frenzied hands. "Ross! Oh, Ross! A man...he was following me...he had a knife...I'm almost *sure* he had a knife...."

"Hush, darling, hush! You're safe!" Ross held me tightly. My body was pressed to his, melted into his strength. It was just like that other time in the Valley of Skulls and yet at the same time it was quite different, for now Ross's lips, though hard, were tender, and he whispered my name even as he kissed me.

It seems strange that at that moment, the summit of my tenderest dreams, I should have remembered José, yet I did. He must have felt me try to break away, for his arms fell immediately to his sides and I saw his expression change.

I don't know what he would have said to me, for just at that moment we were joined by Maria and Sandy. I discovered later that they and Ross had split up in order to search for me.

I left the explanations to Ross. Not that he said much, only that I'd had a nasty fright and needed a little while to get over it. Maria was suitably sympathetic, Sandy kind and concerned. There was a brief exchange between him and Ross that I didn't hear, but I saw Sandy's lips tighten and knew that he, like Ross, had no intention of putting my story down to an over-active imagination.

In the little tourist hotel, while Maria and Sandy were ordering drinks, Ross questioned me carefully.

"The man who was following you... you'd never seen him before?" Then, as I shook my head, "If you met him again do you think you'd recognize him?" I shivered. "Yes! Oh yes! That face will haunt my dreams till the day I die!"

"Don't be silly!" Ross sounded brusque. Had I only imagined his tenderness, a short while ago?

In a low voice I asked, "Ross, do you think that that man... do you think he knew who I was?"

Ross's face was a cold mask behind which his thoughts and feelings were hidden from me.

"What you really want to know, Joby, is whether I think the fright you had has any connection with those blackmailing notes. The answer is that I'm not sure. Whatever I said I could be completely wrong."

"Nobody knew I was coming here—"

He looked at me quickly. "Nobody? You're sure of that?"

"Well, I mentioned it to José. That's all."

Involuntarily I shivered, remembering her gay "Have a good time, darling. Don't disturb too many ghosts while you're prowling around your lost city!"

"She was the only one I mentioned the trip to, as well."

I said nothing, just stared down at my hands. I already knew how frequently he'd been in touch with José. He'd sent her fruit and flowers and chocolates. She'd told me. So why did I feel such a bitter pang of jealousy? Because I'd flung myself into his arms and he'd reacted as most normal, red-blooded males would have reacted in such a situation?

"That leaves Sandy. And Maria." Ross's voice was quiet, reflective. He repeated the last name slowly. "Maria."

I said sharply, "You don't think—"

"I don't think anything. Here comes Maria and Sandy now, with our drinks." Ross rose to his feet and stood looking down at me, his face somber. "Just before they get here... that kiss, Joby. I hope you didn't attach too much, er, importance to it. I was... well, offering some kind of comfort, I suppose, but—"

My face flamed. Maria and Sandy were not yet within earshot when I said in a voice so hard that I scarcely recognized it as my own, "You really don't have to explain, Ross, I have been kissed before, you know, and that rather clumsy embrace of yours definitely didn't come in the 'great lover' category! It had 'amateur opportunist' stamped all over it!"

He didn't say anything. He hadn't time. I took my drink from Sandy and smiled my thanks. The fiery liquid burnt my throat as I raised my glass, but though it warmed my chilled body it did nothing to disperse the cold despair that had settled around my heart.

I wished, at that moment, that I had never come to Peru. I would, I thought bitterly, have been better off in Bayswater. At least I wouldn't have hated myself, the way I did now.

CHAPTER TEN

SEÑORA DE NOVELI, satisfied that José was no longer a source of possible infection, rang me up on my return from Machu Picchu to ask me if I would like to spend the last two or three days of José's convalescence at the *hacienda*.

This time I accepted the invitation eagerly, for several reasons. One, I was more shaken by what had happened at Machu Picchu than I would have cared to admit. Whether or not the man who had followed me had really meant to do me harm, the fact remained that I was nervous and jumpy and I found it difficult to refrain from constantly looking over my shoulder. I felt sure that at the *hacienda* I would find it easier to forget my nightmare experience, or at least to push it to the back of my mind.

My other two reasons for accepting Señora de Noveli's invitation with enthusiasm were just as important in their own way. Specifically, I was no longer worried that Ramon would embarrass me with what I suppose a lady novelist, fifty years ago, would have coyly described as "unwelcome advances." Since that day when Ross had practically ordered him off the site of the roadworks he had made no further attempt to contact me. I guessed, somewhat wryly, that he felt he'd lost face and that his pride would not allow him to run the risk of courting another rebuff.

Then there was Ross himself. The less I saw of him, the better for my peace of mind. For his, too, perhaps. Though afterward we'd both tried to make light of it, that kiss at Machu Picchu had packed a pretty lethal charge. There was a strong physical attraction between us, we both knew that, but equally we both knew that it had to be stamped out. I intrigued Ross, but he was in love with José. I loved her myself, and I owed her loyalty. I could never forget that, any more than Ross could forget that he despised me for being Donald Lester's daughter, the girl who had given up the man she loved rather than run the risk of losing a share of her father's fortune.

When I told Ross that I intended to spend a couple of days at the de Noveli *hacienda* I thought he looked relieved.

"Good. You'll be well taken care of there, I should think. After what happened at Machu Picchu—" He left his sentence unfinished, but his eyes were bleak.

"It was really my fault. I shouldn't have strayed away from you and Sandy and Maria. It was silly."

"It was bloody stupid!" Ross spoke with barely suppressed violence. "However, though I'm sorry you had such a nasty fright I've now realized something I hadn't realized before." He paused, then added somberly, "Thanks to that nasty little incident I now know, I think, who is really behind all the trouble we've had just lately. And it isn't the Indians. Poor devils, they're just the pawns in the game."

I stared at him, and he must have anticipated the question forming itself on my lips, for he shook his head.

"No, I don't intend to say any more. My hunch may be wrong, though I don't think so. At any rate I mean to turn detective for a while."

I hadn't meant to say it, the words just tumbled out. "Ross, you...you will be careful, won't you? You're...you're starting work in the valley later this week, Sandy told me so. If...if the saboteurs are really desperate—"

Ross looked at me. Then he said bitterly, "What are you worred about? That your father may have to pay my funeral expenses and there'll be less pocket money for little Joby to spend on useless gewgaws?"

I went white. It was by far the cruellest thing that anyone had ever said to me. *"Ross!"*

Perhaps he realized how much he had hurt me, for almost immediately he said, "I'm sorry." He passed his hand over his head, rumpling his thick black hair, and then he said almost angrily, "God Joby, what do you do to me? I know I've got the devil's own temper, but—"

I said unsteadily, "Perhaps...perhaps I'm just an abrasive influence. Never mind. You'll have José back in a couple of days."

I turned away so that I wouldn't see his expression lighten. I couldn't take much more, I told myself desperately, yet even at that moment I knew that the worst hurt of all was still to come. When José came back....

She looked surprisingly well, even robust. That was my first thought when she ran out to the car to greet me on my arrival at the *hacienda.* It wasn't until later, when I'd had a chance to observe her more closely, that I realized that in some peculiar way she had changed. I couldn't quite analyze it, but there was something almost secretive about her expression. More than once I felt that she was on the point of telling me something, but that each time she managed to choke the words back.

I couldn't help wondering if it was anything to do with Ross, but I couldn't question her. Whatever she had to tell me, she'd tell me when she was ready. In the meantime, I had my own secret to hide. Because I, too, seemed to have changed. At least, according to José.

"Darling, what on earth have you been doing to yourself this last week? I swear you're pounds thinner and your eyes look awful, as though you haven't slep a wink! Did that wretch Ross make you work too hard?"

I managed to laugh. "Of course not. I didn't do anything, really, just fiddled around. I expect I was more of a nuisance than a help, but Ross... well, Ross seemed to think that he ought to keep an eye on me. For 'daddy's' sake, of course, not my own!" I added hastily.

José looked amused. "You two are not still scrapping? Honestly, Joby, how juvenile!" she protested, laughing.

The very last person I wanted to talk about was Ross. Especially to José. I said, "Oh, you know how it is. People sometimes rub each other up the wrong way without even meaning to. He... he has a lot of good points, José. I do admit that."

"Well, I suppose that's something!" José said, laughing again. She hesitated, twisting a pretty lace handkerchief between her fingers.

It was a trick of hers when she was nervous or excited, and again I had the impression that there was something she badly wanted to tell me but that she couldn't bring herself to do it.

Determined to steer the conversation into less dangerous channels, I said brightly, "Will you be sorry to leave the *hacienda*? The de Novelis have been marvelously kind, haven't they?"

"Yes, they have. When daddy and Isabel are married I'm going to invite Consuelo to come and stay with us. Do you think she'll like that?"

"She'll be thrilled to bits, I expect. You do mean eventually, then, to tell them who you really are?"

"Yes. I suppose I'd better." She paused, and then said casually, "Ross, too. Unless... unless you'd like to tell him for me, darling? You might be able to make him understand."

I stared at her aghast. "José! No, I couldn't! Not possibly! He—I... I... you owe it to him to tell him yourself!"

She sighed. "I suppose you're right. As usual! Joby—"

"Yes?"

"Oh, nothing." My cousin, usually undemonstrative, bent suddenly and brushed her lips across my cheek. I was aware of her scent, faintly flowerlike. "You're a good sort, old thing. I think perhaps I may owe you rather a lot."

Bitterness washed over me. Bitterness and self-disgust. What would she say if she knew that I'd fallen madly, crazily in love with Ross? That he'd held me in his arms, not once but twice, and that even now I took a queer hurting pleasure in the memory of those brief but passionate embraces?

I said with a brusqueness worthy of Ross himself, "I just want to see you happy again, that's all."

"I think perhaps I'm going to be. Quite soon," José said, and she smiled at me. "Well? Aren't you going to ask me why?"

I managed to laugh. "Just so that you can have the pleasure of telling me to wait and see?"

"You know me too well!" José grumbled, and we went down to dinner.

Like José, Señora de Noveli also seemed concerned about my pale cheeks and the smudges under my eyes.

"You look much too tired, my dear. You must have a good rest while you're here," she said kindly.

"Perhaps she is sickening for mumps." Ramon spoke coldly, and, I thought, with a tinge of malice. Since my arrival he had treated me with such exquisite courtesy that I guessed that he was still seriously displeased with me.

"What a dreadful idea!" Consuelo protested, twinkling at me across the table. "Please, do not take any notice of my brother!"

I laughed and agreed that I wouldn't. In fact, by the

end of the evening Ramon had thawed out sufficiently to consent to play the guitar while his sister, who had a charming voice, sang some Peruvian folk songs. For the rest of my visit he was quite pleasant and friendly, but as there were no more intense glances or meaningful sighs I thankfully came to the conclusion that he no longer cherished any romantic ambitions where I was concerned!

All in all they were three very happy days that I spent in the *hacienda* and when finally José and I departed for Cuzco I was feeling a great deal better. I had told José about the fright I had had at Machu Picchu and though I tried not to make too much of the incident she was both shocked and alarmed.

"You poor thing! What a ghastly experience! I hope Ross won't still want to take *me* to Machu Picchu! He did say something about it a little while ago, but now I've got a perfectly good excuse for saying no! Thank goodness!"

I agreed colorlessly. Ross had telephoned José each evening I had been at the *hacienda.* On one occasion she had called me to speak to him, but I had made some excuse to remain where I was. I didn't want to have to steel myself against the foolish painful wrench that I knew would tear at my heart at the sound of his deep, slow voice.

We arrived back at the hotel in Cuzco about an hour before dinner. José's first avowed intention was to give herself a manicure and a facial and I sat down on my bed to scribble a few lines to mother.

The telephone rang before I'd covered half a page. I think I guessed, even before I picked up the receiver, that Ross would be at the other end of the line, though I couldn't think why he wanted to speak to me and not to José.

"Joby? You're wanted downstairs, in the cocktail bar."

That was all he said. No preliminaries. No anything. Even his voice sounded abrupt and strained.

I said stupidly, "*Now?* But it's still early! Who wants to see me?"

"Never mind! Hurry up!"

I heard a click at the other end of the line as the receiver was replaced and felt a rush of indignation tinged with bewilderment. For two pins I'd have stayed where I was, but curiosity got the better of me

I did wonder whether I should tell José where I was going, but I guessed that she was in the middle of applying her facial and wouldn't take too kindly to an interruption. In the end I shrugged, ran a comb through my hair, applied some fresh lipstick and went downstairs to solve the mystery without further delay.

There weren't many people in the cocktail bar and there was certainly no one I recognized. I gazed around me with a certain amount of bewilderment. No one had paid any attention to me except a tall young man sitting just inside the door. Blue-eyed and with a head of unruly wheat-colored hair, he had looked up quickly as I had entered the bar and had half risen to his feet. Then, almost immediately, he had sat down again with a look of disappointment on his good-looking face. Whoever he was expecting to see, I thought sympathetically, it certainly wasn't Joby Lester!

For a moment I hesitated. Then, as the bartender was eyeing me curiously, I sat down on a high stool and ordered a pisco sour. Perhaps whoever it was who wanted to see me had been called away and would be back in a few minutes.

At the end of quarter of an hour I was still sitting on my high stool, I had almost finished my drink and I was feeling distinctly cross. I didn't like sitting in bars by myself. And I wanted to finish my letters. Two more minutes, I told myself grimly, and I was going back to my room. I had just drained my glass when Ross came through the big swing doors. He looked, I thought, very pale, and the skin over his cheekbones was even more tightly drawn than before. I jumped to my feet, and so did the fair young man. We both converged on Ross together.

"She hasn't come." That was the fair young man.

"How much longer have I got to wait?" That was me. Then we both stopped and stared at each other.

For a moment there was a tense silence. Ross, his eyes incredulous, looked from me to the fair young man. Our bewildered expressions were probably identical. It must have been glaringly obvious that we'd never met before in the whole of our lives.

"I think," Ross said at last, in a voice like black ice, "that I'd better introduce you, though I had believed that no introductions were necessary. Miss Joby Lester—Mr. Michael Frenton."

I dropped my glass. I couldn't help it. It shattered into a thousand fragments on the polished floor, and I didn't even apologize to the barman who came rushing towards me with a dustpan and brush.

I said stupidly "Mike!" and wished that the floor would open up and swallow me. Of all the possibilities I'd envisaged, I'd never envisaged this!

Mike Frenton was still looking stupefied. "*Joby* Lester? Joby? Then where's José?"

I said wretchedly, "Upstairs." I turned to Ross, and my heart plummeted at the expression on his face. "Look, I can explain—"

"I don't think that will be necessary. I'm quite capable of putting two and two together for myself." Ross's voice was glacial. "You and José changed places, isn't that so? *She* is Donald Lester's daughter. *You* are the cousin." He paused, then added oh, so sarcastically, "*Not* the heiress, despite your valiant attempts to behave like one. Just Miss Joby Lester, B.A. Congratulations. It was a clever trick, and I'm sure it must have given you and José endless amusement!"

"Look, Ross, I don't know what the devil has been going on here, but I do know that I've been waiting nearly an hour to see José and I'm darned if I'm going to wait any longer!" Mike spoke with a pugnacity which would have done credit to Ross himself. They were very alike, those two, I thought inconsequentially. Chunky he-men... that had been José's ridiculous description!

Mike turned to me, his jaw set. "Where is José? In her room? Because if she is, I'm going right up! What number is it?"

"Number 103. But... but she doesn't want... I mean..." I stopped helplessly. I'd never felt more hopelessly in the dark.

"Doesn't want to see me? Oh yes, she does! She sent for me!" And Mike was gone, his tall figure striding purposefully in the direction of the stairs.

I looked at Ross and wondered if I had imagined the hurt and anger I'd seen in his eyes a few moments ago. His face was again a blank mask, drained of all emotion.

I said uncertainly, "I... I don't understand. Did... did José really send for him?"

"She didn't take you into her confidence? How remiss of her!" I winced at Ross's tone. "I don't think she actually asked him to come to Peru, but she did send him a cable, which I've seen. I gather she somehow discovered that her father had been responsible for the breakup of their affair, but I'm afraid I know very few details. However, doubtless José will fill up the blanks for you, at a later date." Ross glanced at his watch. "Now, if you'll excuse me...."

His voice held no emotion, barely even a flicker of interest, but I knew how badly he must be feeling. He loved José and he'd lost her. That was my fault. All mine. If I had kept quiet about Mike, let things take their natural course....

I put out my hand and touched his sleeve. The tweed was rough against my fingers. I felt him stiffen and set my teeth.

"Ross, there's so much that I want to say and I just don't know where to start. Please don't think too badly of us! Our...our deception...we honestly didn't mean any harm by it! We...it—"

"I'm really not interested. You've had your little joke at my expense and I'm sure you've enjoyed it enormously." He gave a mirthless little laugh. "I suppose I ought to have guessed what you'd cooked up between you. Looking back, I realize there were plenty of clues."

"I...I wanted to tell you...."

Ross raised his brows. "And spoil all the fun?"

"I wasn't like that! Oh, please believe me!" To my horror I heard my voice break and I couldn't go on. People were beginning to stare at us, their eyes curious, speculative. I said almost inaudibly, "I'll try and explain...later."

"You don't have to explain anything at all. I understand perfectly."

He didn't, I thought. He didn't understand anything except those José and I had lied to him and Mike had come back and he had lost the girl he'd come to love. The tears were salt on my lips as I went slowly back to my room, and the pain inside me was almost more than I could bear. He'd never thought well of me so it didn't matter too much if he branded me as a cheat and a liar. But José....

I heard voices inside her room and after a moment's hesitation I knocked on the door. I leaned against the jamb because I didn't feel as though my own legs would support me. I felt frozen, disembodied.

"Darling!" José pounced on me and drew me inside

her room. She was without makeup, not even a trace of powder or lipstick, but her mouth was soft and her eyes glowed. I have never seen her look lovelier.

Mike was standing by the window, his unruly fair hair untidier than ever. I realized for the first time that he had a merry mobile mouth and warm, blue eyes. He and Ross had both been cast in the same mold, I thought, but it looked as though life had been kinder to Mike than it had been to Ross.

Mike grinned when José introduced us. "I guess I owe you an apology, Joby. I'm afraid I was none too polite to you downstairs."

"Think nothing of it," I told him. "I realized at the time that yours was definitely a one-track mind!" José laughed.

"That's the way she talks, Mike. She's a B.A., and frightfully clever, and next to you she's my favorite person! Because if it hadn't been for her—"

"I wouldn't be here now." Mike put his arm around José's shoulders and kissed the top of her head. They were so obviously, blatantly head over heels in love with each other that I felt tears prick the back of my eyelids.

I said, "You know, I'm still very much in the dark. Would someone like to explain to me how this, er, touching reunion has come about?"

José sat down on her bed beside me but kept her hand in Mike's.

"Well, it was what you said about Mike on the phone that made me think. You seemed so sure that...that daddy had somehow pulled a fast one on me. I couldn't believe it at first, I didn't *want* to believe it, but I couldn't get it out of my mind." She drew a deep breath. "So I did what I suppose I ought to have done in the first place. I checked up. I telephoned the hotel at which Mike was supposd to have been staying and made them look through their register to see if they could find his name.

They couldn't, so of course I knew then he could never have received my letters. I don't know what happened to them, but I rather suspect that daddy's secretary instructed the hotel to send them back to daddy."

I marveled inwardly at José's matter-of-fact acceptance of a situation which filled me with bitter indignation. Perhaps, I thought, she was feeling too happy to be angry with her father. Aloud I said, "Go on. What happened next?"

José drew another deep breath. "Well, I think you knew I'd never stopped loving Mike, even though I'd tried hard. Directly I was sure he'd never had my letters I telephoned his mother, who lives in Hampshire. She gave me Mike's address. I sent him a cable telling him that there'd been a ghastly mistake and—"

"And I packed my bag and caught the first available flight to Peru." Mike was grinning. "It's as simple as that, Cousin Joby."

Was it? I looked at him. "Uncle Donald *did* tell you that he was going to disinherit José?"

"Oh yes, he told me that all right. He also said that José had begged him to ask me not to get in touch with her. I... I suppose I ought not to have taken any notice of that, but to tell you the truth I was so hurt and angry that I just couldn't think straight." He made a comical little grimace and looked at José. "We made it too easy for your father, José love. We should have thought less of our pride and put up more of a fight... both ofus."

"I know. Nothing like that will ever happen again." José squeezed his hand, then looked at me. "I can tell what you're thinking, Joby. It's written all over your face. You're thinking that I ought to be furiously angry with daddy for trying to ruin my happiness. But I'm much too happy to want to indulge in useless recriminations, and you yourself said that he probably thought he was acting in my best interests!"

"Yes. Yes, I did." Privately I thought that Mike and José were disposed to take far too lenient a view of Donald Lester's unscrupulous attempt to ruin his daughter's romance, but that was their business, not mine, and it wasn't up to me to sound a dissentient note.

"We're going to have a real celebration." Mike sounded jubilant. "You and me, José, and Joby and Ross."

My heart missed a beat. No! Oh no! They couldn't do that to Ross! I looked disbelievingly at José's radiant face as she nodded agreement. Surely she must know how Ross felt about her? She'd gone to so much trouble to charm him, deliberately encouraged him to fall in love with her. Did she now expect him to sit back and calmly drink a toast to her happiness? Hers and Mike's?

For the first time in my life I didn't like my cousin very much. Happy and excited though she was, there was surely no excuse for her thoughtlessness.

I said coolly, "I don't think that's a good idea at all. You two haven't seen each other for months and I'm sure you've got lots to talk about. Ross and I will only feel horribly *de trop.* Go away somewhere by yourselves!"

José looked wistfully at Mike. "I suppose the celebration could wait! It would be rather nice to have this evening just to ourselves, wouldn't it?"

"Rather! I just didn't want to be too selfish about it," Mike said, and I thought, *He's not like Ross... he's too ingenuous. No wonder Uncle Donald found it easy to dispose of him!*

I abandoned that line of thought to hear Mike saying to José, "Where would you like to go, darling? Anywhere in particular?"

José laughed a little ruefully. "I'm afraid the choice is strictly limited! But anywhere will do, as long as I'm with you."

Mike disappeared to change. José rushed to her wardrobe. "What shall I *wear*? I must look decent! Do you know, I'd only just removed my face pack when Mike knocked at the door? Wouldn't it have been ghastly if I'd still got it on? Poor Mike, he'd have died!"

"I doubt it. Your Mike doesn't exactly strike me as a wilting lily!"

José looked at me, her eyes luminous. "Isn't he a dear? You do like him, don't you, Joby? You do see why I simply couldn't forget him?"

"Oh yes! The wonder to me is how you ever came to mistrust him in the first place! If ever I saw anyone less like a fortune hunter—"

José went pink. "Oh, Joby, please don't rub it in! You've never been in love, so you don't know how awful it can be and how mixed-up and stupid you can get! Wait until it's your turn! Then you'll see!"

Bitterness welled up inside me and stuck in my throat. With difficulty I said, "What about Ross? Have you spared a thought for him?"

"Ross?"

"Yes. Hasn't it occurred to you that all this must be a very unpleasant shock for him?"

"I don't see why! Mike's his best friend and he seems to be quite fond of me."

I stared at her incredulously, but José didn't seem to notice my expression. She added cheerfully, "The only thing I suppose he could be a bit mad about, just at first, is the way we both deceived him! We'll have to tell him we're sorry about that."

"Don't worry! I already have."

José, about to brush her hair, flung her arms around my neck instead.

"Joby! You've got that schoolteacher look on your face again! Oh, *please* be happy for me! Are you cross because I didn't tell you that I'd got in touch with Mike?

I didn't mean to shut you out, honestly!" It was no good. I couldn't lecture her, spoil her happiness. Not tonight, anyway. I couldn't do anything tonight. I couldn't even face Ross. Not because I was ashamed, but because I knew I couldn't bear to see again the bitterness of his face, the emptiness in his eyes.

CHAPTER ELEVEN

ODDLY ENOUGH, Ross seemed to be far angrier with me than he was with José. It was a bit unfair of him, all things considered, but I supposed that he found it easier to blame me than anyone else. At any rate, when next I saw him—at dinner the next evening—he appeared to be laughing and talking quite naturally and freely with Mike and José, but the moment I put in an appearance his face froze.

José unintentionally made things worse, at least from my point of view. Looking at Ross across the table she said laughingly, "Well, now you see Joby and me in our own true colors! It's me you'll have to twit about being a pampered heiress, and Joby who'll tell you all you want to know about the difference between the Aztecs and the Incas!"

"I'll certainly bear her qualifications in mind," Ross said coolly. He did manage to look at me—just, but his eyes were hard and unfriendly.

There was an awkward little pause, then Mike rushed to fill it. Obviously, I thought, he had no idea that his friend had fallen in love with José. Ross kept his secrets well...perhaps too well.

Because I knew it was expected of me I picked up my champagne. "To you." My throat ached a little as I saw José look up at Mike with a gay softness in her eyes. I'd never seen her like this before...putting out such a glow. If it had an effect even on me, what did it do to Ross? I turned my head, but his eyes weren't fixed on

José, they were fixed on me. I felt the color rush into my cheeks and bent my head hurriedly over my plate. Just at that moment a waiter came up and, leaning over, murmured something in José's ear. Immediately she sprang to her feet.

"Isabel, ringing from Barbados. I cabled her last night."

She and Mike disappeared in the direction of the telephone room. Ross and I were left sitting at the table. In silence.

I cleared my throat nervously. This was too silly. Someone had to say something!

"Do...do you think they'll meet with much opposition from José's father? Or will he accept the inevitable?"

Ross took his time about answering. "I really don't know. Offhand, I should say he'll probably accept the inevitable, just as José and Mike seem to have accepted the fact that originally he played them a very dirty trick. They both have forgiving natures. Which is nice for them, and for Donald Lester."

I stared down at my glass. "*You* don't forgive very easily, do you?"

"I presume by that remark that you're disappointed I'm not going to congratulate you yet again on the success of your shabby little masquerade. I'm sorry. I thought I made my attitude plain last night."

"You did. And I told you that I wanted to explain."

"As far as I am concerned there's nothing to explain."

"But there is! You think we changed places for fun! We didn't. It was to help José—"

I stopped. The bleak, bitter look was back on his face. It was no good. He wouldn't listen to me. And after all, why should he? Basically, all I was trying to do was whitewash myself, and Ross wasn't interested in me. Only in José. And José was going to marry another man....

We didn't exchange another word until José and Mike eventually rejoined us. They both looked as though they were walking on air. Donald Lester, it seemed, had climbed down with a vengeance. Faced with the fact that his daughter knew how he had tried to prevent her marriage to Mike, he had first apologized and then indicated that he was perfectly willing to make amends by accepting Mike as a son-in-law without further fuss or argument.

"I must say I didn't expect him to capitulate so easily! I think Isabel must have been working on him," José said. "He's *mellowed*, somehow! I suppose that's love for you." She looked at Ross and laughed. "Your cousin is a very remarkable woman, Ross. She sent her love to you, by the way."

I remembered what Isabel had said to José in her letter. "Be nice to him, honey, he's all the family I've got...." *Somebody* cared about Ross, anyway. Somebody else besides me. Even though he didn't want either of us, we still cared.

Abruptly I pushed back my chair and rose to my feet. "I'm rather tired. If nobody minds I think I'll go to bed."

Nobody did mind. They all said good night and José added "Happy dreams." I didn't look in Ross's direction, but I felt sure that it wouldn't be long before he, too, made his excuses. He and I were the odd ones out. And we'd better get used to the fact.

Inevitably, of course, Mike's arrival in Cuzco meant that I had to play fifth wheel far more than I liked. After hearing the story of the battle to save the Valley of Skulls and, more specifically, what had happened to me at Machu Picchu, Mike could scarcely bear to let either José or myself out of his sight. His protective attitude was, I had to admit, rather endearing. In fact, as I got to know him better I liked him more and more, and I felt reasonably certain that he would make José as happy as even her father would wish.

Their plans were cut and dried. At the end of our holiday in Peru they intended to fly to Barbados for José's father's wedding and then make the necessary arrangements for their own. Donald Lester had promised Mike that he would be reinstated in the firm and he and José thought that for a year or two, at least, they would be living in Paris.

Mother in America...José in Paris. The thought made me feel lonelier than ever. I wondered if Ross, too, felt the same way. I didn't see him very often, and never alone. He had re-erected his barriers with a vengeance, I thought with a pang. It was almost impossible to equate the cool, impersonal stranger who looked at me with bleak, wintry eyes with the man who had held me close in his arms and left the feel of his lip indelibly printed upon my mind. José "confessed" her real identity to Señora de Noveli, who made very little of it. As I had always thought, it didn't matter to her who we were or whether we were rich or poor. She had liked us for our own sakes. I think, though, that José was probably her favorite, and she welcomed the news of her engagement to Mike with almost as much pleasure as if she had been her real daughter. José promised to invite the whole family to her wedding, and I thought it very likely that they would accept.

At any rate they all came to the celebration party that Mike and José laid on at our hotel. Ross was there, too, and though I'd half expected that there'd be a certain amount of antagonism between him and Ramon, any ill-feeling that might have existed was swiftly dissipated by the festival atmosphere. It was a gay and lively party and I...well, perhaps I was the gayest of all. Outwardly, at least.

I was sitting opposite Ross and all through the meal I

was more aware of him than of anyone or anything else. Like me, he seemed anxious to give the impression that he was enjoying himself. Perhaps he really was, I thought. Perhaps the disappointment of losing José was already less acute. Then I stole a glance at him when he thought he was unobserved, and I saw that his dark blue eyes held a strange hunger, were lonelier than perhaps he knew.

A small band was playing. The Andean music seemed to me to contain as much melancholy as gaiety, and I was glad when at Mike's request they switched to something livelier. I danced, first with Ramon and then with Mike, but not with Ross. Nobody seemed to notice that he hadn't asked me.

In the end he was practically forced to, simply because all the others were dancing and we were left alone at the table. His obvious reluctance hurt me, and I sought refuge in sarcasm.

"I don't bite, you know. And the dances aren't long."

His face was chilly as he led me out onto the floor. "I'm afraid that dancing really isn't much in my line."

"No? You seemed to be enjoying yourself a few minutes ago, when you had Consuelo as your partner!" I retorted, and could then have bitten out my tongue. I didn't want him to have any idea how closely I'd been watching him.

Something flickered behind his eyes, but he said nothing. He held me firmly and we danced well together, but all the time I was conscious that there was a void between us. My heart felt as heavy as lead when the dance finished and we went back to our table, and recklessly I allowed Mike to pour me some more pisco. At first the wonderful carefree sense that spread through me was marvelous, but after a time the effect wore off and I was left with a throbbing headache none the more bearable for being richly deserved.

I longed for a breath of cool, fresh air and when the de Novelis reluctantly piled into their car for the long journey back to the *hacienda*, I turned impulsively to José.

"What about a stroll around the town?"

"Good idea—if the men will accompany us, that is! It's a lovely night." She looked at Mike and Ross. "Joby and I fancy a stroll. Escorts, please!"

Neither of them grumbled. As José had said, it was a lovely night, still and clear. A young moon had set, leaving a star-filled vault above. We wandered into the Plaza de Armas, where the massive stone walls of former Inca temples were palely illuminated by a few glowing streetlamps, and sat by the fountain, which played its water droplets onto the pool below. The sound was oddly soothing. Mike's arm was around José. Ross, standing just behind them, looked gaunt and dark, almost forbidding.

The plaza seemed deserted, yet from behind the shuttered windows of the tall buildings light crept and we could hear, dimly, the sound of merriment. A black cat came out of the night to rub itself against my leg and automatically I bent to stroke it. I saw Ross watching me, and wondered, with a queer tightening of my throat, whether he was remembering that first morning in Cuzco when he'd said that I reminded him of Melusine...or the witch Vivien.

I think he was just about to say something when the door of a building across the plaza opened, and a stream of brilliant light poured out. For a moment or two the figure of a man was silhouetted in the doorway, his brown face clearly visible to us all.

The shock that passed through me was the twenty-thousand-volt variety. *I had seen that face before!* Only once in reality, but many, many times in imagination. I knew I couldn't be mistaken.

I clutched hold of Ross's arm and said hoarsely, "*Ross!* That man—over there! He's the one who followed me at Machu Picchu!"

I felt his muscles tense, heard him suck in his breath as he followed the direction of my gaze. "*Him?* Are you sure?"

I shuddered. Even now the sight of those high cheekbones and slanting eyes made me feel sick with remembered fear. "I'm sure!"

The door closed. The figure moved away, began to melt into the shadows. I saw Mike start forward. "For God's sake, man! We'll lose him!"

Incredible as at that moment it seemed, Ross did not move. He said quietly, "No matter. I know who he is. And where I can find him, at any time."

"You know? But...but—"

Ross looked at me. "I've seen him before. His name is Grimaldo Carrera and he works for Señor Florez d'Alvarez!"

What he said, and the import of his words, froze our little group. Ross moved forward. His face was harder than I had ever seen it and he bit off the words crisply as he said, "Thank you, Joby! By identifying Carrera you've provided me with the final proof I needed!"

"Proof?" José, Mike and I all spoke together.

Ross jammed his fists into his pockets. "Yes. Proof that Señor Florez d'Alvarez has been behind the Indians in their attempts to sabotage the road scheme! I've suspected it for some time, and ought to have suspected it from the first. He was absolutely furious when the company refused to pay the price he wanted for his land and decided, instead, to plan an alternative route via the Valley of Skulls. It's my guess that he meant to try and force us to revert to the original plan and so he incited the Indians to revolt by playing on their ancient superstitions regarding the Valley."

A streetlamp suddenly went out and the cat mewed, the sound so loud in the chill night air that we all jumped. I said with a catch in my breath, "Maria...?"

Ross knew what quick fear had suddenly leapt into my mind. "Innocent, I'm sure, of any deliberate harm. But because of her friendship with Sandy she must have been useful to d'Alvarez. She was able to tell him our plans. And she knew, of course, Joby, that you would be at Machu Picchu. That's why Carrera—" He stopped as I shivered and touched my hands lightly. It was only a gesture of reassurance, I knew that, but it warmed the whole of my chilled body. I hadn't expected even the crumbs of kindness from this man. Not now, not ever.

José's eyes were wide. "Do...do you think he really meant to kill Joby?"

Ross shook his head. "No. No, I don't. But I do think he meant to give her a very bad fright." He paused, then added grimly, "I intend to see that he suffers for that."

"What are you planning to do?" That was Mike.

"First of all, force a confession from Carrera. Then have a showdown with d'Alvarez. Unfortunately, much as I should like to see him behind bars I don't for one moment think that that will come about. I've got enough evidence to satisfy myself that he's the main troublemaker, but I doubt very much whether that same evidence would carry much weight in a court of law."

"Then...then what—"

Ross's eyes were very cold. "I intent to put the fear of the Lord into him. When I've finished with Señor Florez d'Alvarez, I guarantee that there will be no more monkey business. Of any kind."

I believed him. And I didn't envy Señor d'Alvarez one little tiny bit.

José drew a long breath. "Well, it will be nice to know that it's all over! I did so want our last week here to be a happy one!"

Her words went into my ears and down into my heart, where they lay cold and heavy. It wouldn't be a happy week for me.

In fact, I'd sometimes thought, these last few days, that I'd never be really happy again.

TWO DAYS LATER Mike, José and myself paid a visit to the roadworks, at Ross's invitation. The men had already started bulldozing their way through the Valley of Skulls, but it was not, as yet, changed out of all recognition. What had changed was the atmosphere, no longer one of fear and uneasy suspicion but of cheerful optimism.

Ross's interview with Señor d'Alvarez had been far more successful than he had dared to hope. At first the *hacienda* owner had hotly denied responsibility for the plot to sabotage the road scheme, but when he was told that Grimaldo Carrera had already confessed not only to frightening me at Machu Picchu but also to tampering with the brakes on Uncle Donald's car he had broken down completely. Realizing for the first time that the man was quite unbalanced, Ross had sent for the police and the matter was now in their hands.

Without d'Alvarez to play upon their credultiy and to incite them to rebellion, the Indians were no longer an ever-present threat. Ross claimed that in time they would even benefit by the existence of the new road, since once the copper mine was a going concern there would be jobs for many of them, and consequently a better standard of living. I hoped he was right. If they had to lose their sacred valley, then they were surely entitled to something in the form of compensation!

I was glad for Ross's sake that the road could now be driven through the valley without let or hindrance, but I tried my hardest not to accompany Mike and José on their visit to the roadworks. Unfortunately, they wouldn't hear of my being left behind in Cuzco, and I could hardly tell them I wanted to avoid Ross as much as I possibly could. I'd long ago given up all hope of bridging the gulf between us, and since I wasn't a masochist I saw no point in continually rubbing salt into an open wound.

Ross was in the office when we arrived at the site. He greeted Mike and José warmly, then turned to me with a smile on his lips which did not reach his eyes.

"I'm afraid the dust has accumulated again. Better be careful where you sit."

I was tense and ill at ease and trying desperately not to show it. "Oh well, I won't ask you for a pail of soapy water this time."

"A pail of soapy water?" José raised her brows.

I bit my lip. What on earth possessed me to bring that up? Ross said smoothly, "Your cousin has many talents, José. 'Charring' appears to be one of them. Hasn't she told you?" He looked at me mockingly. "I suppose I should have known then that there was no such thing as a domesticated heiress!"

"Hey! Do you mind?" José said indignantly. "I have been known to make my own bed. And I'm going to do the cooking when Mike and I are married!"

"After I've taught her to cook!" Mike murmured *sotto voce.*

Even Ross laughed. Then he and Mike became absorbed in technicalities—after all, they were both engineers—and I looked at José.

"It's terribly stuffy in here. What about a walk? I know the scenery looks a bit rugged, but it's actually rather beautiful."

José hesitated, then pulled a slight face. "Oh, Joby, I don't think it looks very inviting! Besides, my shoes aren't right for walking. You go, if you like. I'll hang around here and wait for Mike."

I nodded. I'd rather be alone, anyway. I knew what I

wanted to do—walk as far as the point where Ross had taken me into his arms and kissed me, that first time. Foolish? Sentimental? Yes. But it was my way of saying goodbye, and it seemed at least as good as any other.

If Ross saw me go he didn't try to stop me. He probably didn't care what I did, I thought bitterly, scrambling over jagged rocks that were soon to be displaced by a modern highway. Unlike José, I had taken the precaution of wearing my toughest shoes, which rather proved that I'd had this sentimental journey in mind even before we started.

Last time I had explored the valley I have been struck by its grave and desolate beauty. This time the stillness, the dense, fuzzy shadows of the overhanging cliffs and the monotony of color somehow combined to create a somewhat ominous atmosphere. I stopped still and listened. I couldn't hear anything, not even the sound of machinery. Utter silence reigned—a silence that had almost a consistency and a weight.

The peculiar rock formation on my right seemed familiar. Wasn't it about here that Ross had pulled me into his arms and kissed me? I closed my eyes, remembering, and the strange stillness I had noticed before seemed even more accentuated.

Perhaps, if I had lived for long in Peru, that stillness would have warned me. As it was, when the earth gave a slight shudder I was completely unprepared. Alarmed, I opened my eyes, and as I did so a soft rumble grew from nothing and vibrated in the heavy air. The shudder gathered in strength until the ground shook violently, and all the while there came a howling, thundering roar that seemed to echo from the very bowels of the earth.

Earthquake! Even as the horrified realization flashed into my mind the ground was shaking in convulsive spasms under my feet. I think I screamed. I know I staggered and fell, clawing convulsively at the air for support. I felt my head hit a rock, and then the blackness of oblivion engulfed me.

I WAS AWARE, dimly, of someone speaking my name. There was pain... a dull ache in my head. I was lying on something hard and stony. The ground. Everywhere around me was red. I tried to raise my head.

"Lie still," said a voice. Ross's voice.

But I couldn't lie still. The earth was still shaking and I was falling, falling. There was nothing under me but space and I pulled my eyes open. "Ross! Hold me!"

"It's all right, darling. It's all right." Ross was kneeling beside me. He was in his shirt sleeves and after a moment I realized that my head was pillowed on something soft and warm. His sweater.

I put out my hand and touched the ground beside me. Wonderingly. It felt cold and firm. I said weakly, "There was an earthquake... I thought I was going to be swallowed up...."

"It wasn't a quake. Just a tremor." Ross's voice was calm and matter-of-fact. He added, with the ghost of a smile, "But very frightening for all that. You should have stayed in the office. Then you'd have been all right."

I thought for a moment, then said indignantly, "Why didn't you?"

"Stay in the office?"

I nodded. "Because I wanted to be with you," Ross said simply.

I stared up at his face. It looked pale and tense, and though he was smiling his eyes were hard and anxious.

I frowned. What he'd just said didn't make sense. Perhaps I was suffering from concussion. Delusions, even. Because he *couldn't* have said, "I wanted to be with you." Could he?

"You hate me."

Ross laughed. "I love you." I *was* suffering from concussion, and it was the most wonderful thing that had ever happened to me.

I decided to make the most of it. "You'll have to convince me of that."

He seemed to think I needed an awful lot of convincing. When finally he raised his head I scrambled into a sitting position, put a hand to my aching head and said shakily, "I don't believe I have got concussion, have I? That was for real!"

"That was for real." Ross kissed me again, just to make sure I'd got the message. "I love you, love you, love you!"

Hearing him say that was a dream come true. It was Machu Picchu and the Parthenon and the Colosseum rolled into one. I said breathlessly, "And I love *you.* But I don't understand. You were so horrid to me and I thought...you and José...."

His hands tightened painfully on my arms. "She reminded me of my sister. Her coloring is exactly the same and she's just like Grace used to be, pretty and gay and vivacious. I...I wanted to pet and spoil her, the way I used to pet and spoil Grace." He paused, then said in a very different tone, "I did *not* want to make love to her, you little idiot!"

I forced a laugh to cover the tears in my voice. "All right, I believe you!"

"You'd better. Because there's been no one for me except you, Melusine, from the very first moment I met you." Ross pulled me closer. "Not, mind you, that I was prepared to admit it, even to myself. I thought I had much too much sense to fall in love with a spoilt and pampered rich girl who'd thrown over my best friend because she preferred money and luxury to everything else—"

"I can understand your not wanting to do that! What I *don't* understand is why you were so angry when you discovered the real truth! I thought it was because you were so upset at losing José to Mike that you had to take your frustration out on someone, and that someone happened to be me! But—"

Ross groaned. "Joby! Darling, use your imagination! I'd been struggling like hell against the idea of loving you, even the idea of *liking* you, and it had been a losing battle from the very word go! Every time I saw you I wanted to make love to you—"

"Beat me, you mean!"

"Only when you were more infuriating than usual! You can't blame me for that, darling. You did your best to keep that pampered heiress act going convincingly!" He kissed the tip of my nose. "Then, when I realized that in spite of everything I had fallen head over ears in love with you and that it was absolutely no good because I had nothing more to offer you than Mike had had, I suddenly found out that you weren't José after all. I was hurt and angry because I thought you'd deliberately made a fool of me—oh yes, Joby, I did!" as I protested. He paused, then added soberly, "Pride is one of the seven deadly sins, you know, and hurt pride is particularly destructive."

"What made you decide I wasn't such a villainess after all?" I enquired provocatively.

"My own heart, darling. It was a wilderness without you. I couldn't bear it any longer."

His lips brushed my temple as I said dreamily, "I wonder what José and Mike will say?"

"Probably that it's taken an earthquake to bring us to our senses!" Ross said, laughing as he helped me to scramble to my feet. Then his arms tightened around me. "You do know that I'll have to stay here, in Peru, until the road is finished?"

"Yes. And I'll have to go back to school," I said, smiling. I didn't mind. It would only be for one term and then Ross and I would be together, forever and always.

"You'll be able to tell them a lot more about Attahuallpa!" Ross said teasingly, and I grinned.

"Oh no! I'll tell them all about Ross Henderson instead! Knowing my students, I bet they'll find him even more interesting than Atahuallpa!"

Ross didn't believe me, but I was right. They did!